BLOOD ORBIT

BLOOD ORBIT

A Gattis File Novel

K. R. RICHARDSON

an imprint of Prometheus Books
Amherst, NY

Published 2018 by Pyr®, an imprint of Prometheus Books

This is a work of fiction. Characters, organizations, products, locales, and events portrayed in this novel are either products of the author's imagination or used fictitiously.

Cover illustration © Maurizio Manzieri
Cover design by Jacqueline Nasso Cooke
Cover design © Prometheus Books

Inquiries should be addressed to
Pyr
59 John Glenn Drive
Amherst, New York 14228
VOICE: 716–691–0133
FAX: 716–691–0137
WWW.PYRSF.COM

22 21 20 19 18   5 4 3 2 1

Library of Congress Cataloging-in-Publication Data

Names: Richardson, K. R., 1964- author.
Title: Blood orbit : a Gattis file novel / by K. R. Richardson.
Description: Amherst, NY : Pyr, an imprint of Prometheus Books, 2018. |
    Identifiers: LCCN 2017050513 (print) | LCCN 2017060906 (ebook) |
    ISBN 9781633884403 (ebook) | ISBN 9781633884397 (paperback)
Subjects: LCSH: Police—Fiction. | Cyborgs—Fiction. | BISAC: FICTION / Science
    Fiction / High Tech. | FICTION / Mystery & Detective / Police Procedural. |
    GSAFD: Science fiction.
Classification: LCC PS3618.I344694 (ebook) | LCC PS3618.I344694 B56 2018
    (print) | DDC 813/.6—dc23
LC record available at https://lccn.loc.gov/2017050513

Printed in the United States of America

CHAPTER ONE

Day 1: Wednesday,
Dreihleat Angra Dastrelas—0221

"Matheson! Get here now!" Santos, his training officer, sounded panicked.

Matheson snatched the mobile data device out of its two horizontal loops on his shirt. "Where are you?"

"At the—At Paz. Y'know, the jasso on the alley. Fuck . . . somethin's wrong. Door's locked. The door should be open—it's always open!"

Matheson turned back the way he'd come and started running for the alley. He *knew* they shouldn't have split, not even to finish rounds on time. He raced through wisps of rising fog, the multi-colored glow from OLED vines woven to form pictographic signs above every shopfront scattering copies of his tall, thin shadow along the walls. His boot steps were loud in the twisty, filthy streets, and the tropical humidity made his breath rasp in his throat and his hair cling around his face in straight, black strands.

Everything legal in the ethnic ghetto was closed now, and most of the tourists had gone back to their clean, safe hotels near the quay. If there was anyone else around aside from drunks dozing in alleys between the squat low-rise buildings of carved blue stone, they slipped out of sight as Matheson approached. Only a handful of jassos—illegal gambling clubs, fight pits, and the more genteel variety of drug dens—were still operating at this hour. They were inescapable features of the city's tourist-based economy, and not the priority of rookie patch-pounders like Matheson—so Santos had told him.

Santos whipped around as Matheson rushed into the narrow passage. The older, shorter ofiçe was halfway across the alley as if he'd been pacing and his sudden turn made his injured knee wobble. He caught his balance by grabbing at the club's massive entryway pillars. A discreet lamp barely illuminated the door within the deep shadow cast by an overhanging second story. No other light shone from around the doorframe.

Santos pointed toward the door with a shaking hand. "Check it."

Matheson hesitated. Santos was trembling more than his weakened knee should have caused and his brown eyes showed too much white. "Didn't you do that already?"

"Yeah. But—This door ain't never locked before 0500 on a festival night and if there's somethin' wrong, I don't want nobody sayin' we didn't do this right. You check it."

Warily, Matheson pulled the Sun Spot off his belt—*why wasn't Santos using his?*—and shined it on the door as he edged up to it. He stayed well clear of a dark shadow on the ground as he reached to try the handle. "It's locked. As you said. Did you try your override?"

"Not that kinda lock, kid. That's a bolt-and-key—old school."

"But there's a lock pad—"

"Don't you tell me what there is and isn't, Fishbait. Override won't do shit—you try it."

Matheson ran his ID badge through the lock and entered his access code, pressing his shoulder to the door so it would spring free.

The door lurched a little under his weight, but remained closed.

Santos moved up beside him and drew his baton from his belt as Matheson tried again.

Nothing changed.

Matheson pounded on the door. "GISA ofiçe! Open up!"

Silence. Then a metallic slide and rattle as Santos flicked his baton out to full extension. "Break it," the older man said. "Break it down." His voice was rough and Matheson could smell him sweating.

"Why? Maybe they closed up early."

"It's an after-hours club for the locals! They should be open by now on a festival night and Loni or someone should be in there, but they're not sayin' nothin'. Break the fuckin' door!"

Santos's nerves convinced him. Matheson stowed his light and badge, and used his own baton to break the handle. Then he stepped back and drove his heel hard against the latch plate.

The door groaned and splintered around the lock. Matheson's second kick popped it open and he reached for his Sun Spot again as Santos lurched into the darkened room beyond.

The stink hit at the same time the light cast harsh illumination inside. The thin green and white carpet and gold-trimmed walls were splashed crimson around four human figures that lay like broken dolls on the bar room floor. *Merry fucking hell.* Matheson gagged and turned his head and the light to the right, but there was no relief there. More bodies lay in a loose arc across the floor of the gaming room. His spot-light's beam gleamed white on an eye that had been blown from its socket, and sparked a rainbow glitter from a woman's jeweled shoe and stocking. The smell of bloody death clotted in his nose and, for an instant, it seemed like there were a hundred corpses—a thousand brown-and-yellow bodies—sinking into darkness that swelled from the unlit corners.

Santos let out a choking sound as Matheson wrenched away from the scene.

Santos's leg folded under as he twisted away, and he fell forward, slamming his head and shoulder into the pillar. He collapsed against the wall and down to the ground as Matheson bolted past him and vomited in the alley.

When the heaves stopped, the shivers started. Matheson put all his weight against the nearest wall and keyed his mobile. But he couldn't remember the codes or what to say. He managed to give his identification but the rest was still out of his grasp. "We need assistance. My partner—my TO—is down. He's injured . . . And we have a murder. No. Ten . . . at least ten bodies here . . ."

"I'll get the Investigation Officer of the Day for you and dispatch assistance to your location."

How can she be so calm? Matheson thought.

"Stay put and keep your comms open."

He gulped and nodded before he remembered to speak. "O-okay."

Santos didn't move as Matheson slid down the wall to sit shivering and tasting the bile in his mouth as he waited.

CHAPTER TWO

Day 1: Hospital—Pre-dawn

M erry hell, what a nightmare. Matheson had escorted Santos to Public Health, but he wasn't allowed to leave, yet, because it took three Gattis Corporation regional directors arguing for hours to decide if a mass murder in an ethnic ghetto was worth investigating, how it would be paid for, and who would get stuck with it.

Sit tight, they'd ordered, and then accompany the CIFO to the site. Without his TO to whisper in his ear, the Assistant Regional Director had had to remind Matheson: "Chief Investigating Forensic Ofiçe—not 'Officer.' You're employees of Gattis Corporation, not officers of the law." It wasn't what he'd learned at the academy, but if they didn't want a real policeman, he didn't know why he'd been sent to Gattis. He felt he was barely treading water in the sea of everything he didn't know.

Callista said I wouldn't last three days as a cop. She was wrong, but . . . did I really know what I was getting into? Or was I just being contrary? He was five months and six days out of the academy, galaxies removed from Central System, and so horrified and tired he could barely stand.

Matheson had lost track of how many hours he had been awake and his eyes itched from lack of sleep, but he kept them open as he rested his forehead against the window, watching the changing illumination of the city below. The hospital had been gouged into the cliff at the beginning of the terraform, so long ago now that no one noticed it had a view billionaires would vie for. The upper half of the Angra Dastrelas—the Cove of Stars for which the city was named—was framed in the waning night sky by the Pillars of Archon. The two megaliths guarded a hole in the stone scarp that circled the crater and pinched the throat of the shallow inlet forming the actual cove. The nighttime water reflected and multiplied innumerable stars, while the landscape and a quirk of the tropical atmosphere made it look like they swirled from the bay and flooded upward into space. Beautiful. But now dawn crept in, and Gattis's planetary capital seemed to ooze from the bottom of the cove and across the floor of Trant's Crater like a stain.

Behind him the endless news feed and its chatter about upcoming festival schedules, politics, unrest in the agricamps, and which impossibly pretty celebrity was visiting town for Spring Moon poured through Matheson's ears as an irritant. That and the cool, dry air of the building on the back of his neck were all that kept him from falling asleep on the spot. He fought the urge by recalling his first view from the jumpway: Gattis, its single thin ring and solitary moon above a slowly spinning ball of vibrant deep-water blue with two vast continents—Ariel and Agria—and the jeweled scatter of the Verdan Archipelago between them. Then the long flight down from jumpway to orbital, and the planetward fall until Ariel filled every view and the planetary capital seemed to rise out of the tropical jungle cut clean by the crater's edge. Now he concentrated on trying to pick the Angra Dastrelas spaceport out of the riot of city lights and emerging shapes. He spotted the tidy squares of the pad lights at last, far across the crater floor, remembered the instantly sticky heat, and the stink of fish and fuel that had wrapped him as he'd stepped out of Worker Intake—

"Ofiçe!"

Startled, he turned toward the shout. The lab-coated woman

glaring at him was a hard, compact package of restrained fury under a shock of brush-cut, light-colored hair that was going gray. Early fifties, a little under average height, her complexion would have been a bland shade of Central System light brown if she hadn't been slightly ruddy with anger. Her face was far from beautiful and her expression was sharp enough to cut ice.

"Just what sort of rear-echelon idiocy is this?" she demanded, brandishing the digital data pad she was holding. "I have an order to release my patient to you. He's supposed to have six weeks recovery and evaluation after surgery and he's only had two. This is a delicate experiment and the system isn't fully integrated yet."

Matheson blinked and frowned at her, shaking his head. "I'm sorry, Doctor. It's not up to me. I was just told to fetch him."

"I don't care what you were told to do. If you take him and anything goes wrong he could die, and I won't be set back to square one on this project because Director Pritchet can't hold his water."

Matheson glared back. "This is not my doing. And I have no other orders but to wait for his release. If you expect me to do anything other than stand here until you give way or I get redirected, you're going to be very disappointed."

She glowered at him a moment longer. "You always do what you're told?"

I am too tired for this. "No, but in this case, I don't have a choice."

She growled as she thought about it, and then her mouth set into a sour quirk. "You break him and I'll hold you responsible."

"It's not my—"

"Hah! Oh, yes it is. He's not ready to go into the field. The surgery breached the blood/brain barrier and if the site gets infected, things will go very wrong very fast. So until he's back in my hands for re-evaluation, you are not to let him wander around unattended. The instant—and I do mean the *instant* he seems to be in distress, you will return him to me. Got it?"

Probably hunt me down and flay me alive if I don't. He didn't relish being a nanny, but it beat explaining to Regional Director Pritchet why he hadn't done as ordered. "Fine," he snapped.

"Right answer." She slapped the digital pad flat against his chest. "Sign this—and what the hell's your name, anyway?"

"Matheson," he replied, laying his ID on the pad and verifying it with his official hashmark. "Who are you?"

She took the pad back. "Doctor Andreus. The Forensic Integration Project is *my* baby, which makes Inspector Dillal my special concern." She gave him a shrewd look. "Here's what you need to know, in a nutshell: The system I've installed is part on-the-fly forensic sampling and analysis, and part communication and data integration, which makes him the link between Forensic Tech and Investigation. Theoretically, he can sample and analyze a simple crime scene on the spot, but I haven't been able to test him. He's functionally and physiologically unique. He's also a pigheaded pain in the ass." She paused and studied Matheson again. "You'll be two of a kind."

Matheson might have taken exception if he'd had the energy, but he only cared about getting it over with.

"Against my better judgment, I'm letting you take him." Dr. Andreus turned and pointed deeper into the facility. "It's the room at the end of the green slideway." She turned back and gave him a hard look. "Don't fuck me over."

Matheson let his eyes close a moment. "Thank you." His eyelids were so gritty and heavy that they seemed to scratch his eyeballs raw. He tugged at his wrinkled uniform and headed for the slideway, happy to leave the doctor behind.

His head was spinning with fatigue by the time he reached the room at the end of the sliding walkway. The door stood open, so he entered. The room was gloomy and it had an odd smell, like industrial solvent and copper. *Better than the jasso . . .*

A small, bright light snapped on over the bed and he took a step back, dazzled for a moment. A soft rustling sound, then nothing. He peered toward the glare.

"Dillal?" He stumbled over the pronunciation a little and moved deeper into the room. "I'm SO Eric Matheson. I'm looking for Inspector J. P. Dillal."

The figure in the bed moved, and the room lights came up.

Even after what he had already seen that day, Matheson flinched away from the half-human visage that stared up into his own face. *What did Andreus do?* The left side of the patient's skull had been shaved from the temple down all the way to the back. Cinnamon-red hair hadn't grown out enough yet to hide the inorganic shape of something inserted beneath the flesh and bone. The orbit of the left eye had been redefined by an unnatural, hard edge and a livid incision, patched all around forehead and cheek with brown and olive spray skin that didn't match the patient's muddy amber complexion. The eye itself was too large and open to match the one on the right, and the iris was not the same brown, but a transparent gold color through which light reflected red.

Matheson tried to catalog the person lying in the bed. *Male, thirty to thirty-five, under average height . . .* but there he stumbled. The man was too distinctly colored for most of Central System, yet didn't fit any of the planet's ethnic groups, either. Too short for Dreihle, too slight for Ohba, and he certainly wasn't Gattian, with their skin and hair tinged the same vivid blue as the planet's pervasive sand. Judging by the size of his remaining pupil and the way he clenched his jaw, the patient was in some pain, but if he was drugged, it wasn't much. That jarred Matheson back to his duty.

He swallowed and asked, "Are you Inspector Dillal? Did I say that right?"

The man in the bed shrugged one shoulder and tilted his head. Only the brown eye blinked. "Close enough." His voice was soft and tired.

Matheson dropped his gaze. "Sir, you're being recalled to active duty. The Regional Director pushed the paper through and Dr. Andreus released you to me. I know you've only had surgery recently, but this case—Well, Pritchet opened full cooperation and funding for a week, through half-moon." He glanced back up, half expecting to be told off.

Dillal eased up to sitting. Then he narrowed his eyes and peered at Matheson. Something clicked as the lid around the strange golden eye tightened. "The case . . . is what sort of crime?" The inspector rolled his Rs slightly and his slow voice had an odd, round intonation.

Matheson's empty stomach churned. "It's a—a massacre, sir. Maybe a gang execution. In a jasso."

Dillal rubbed his face gently with both hands and pushed his fingers through his hair and stubble. Then he swung his feet out of the tall hospital bed. They didn't quite reach the floor. Matheson started forward to help him, but Dillal waved him off and pointed at the closet. "My clothes. Please."

Matheson retrieved a flat, vacuum-sealed package and laid it on the bed. Then he turned his back, grateful not to look at the inspector for a moment—nothing Pritchet or Andreus had said had prepared him for that unsettling face, and only the horror he had recently seen kept sick fascination at bay.

He could hear Dillal drawing the clothes on and hissing at sudden pains. The bed squeaked and then there was silence. Matheson edged back around. Discarded vacuum wrap lay at the end of the bed beside a scuffed MDD and a closed ID folder. The inspector, now fully dressed in a loose charcoal suit, was turned half away from Matheson and had braced his hands against the mattress. His head hung between his stiff arms and he'd clenched his eyes shut while he took impossibly deep, slow breaths.

"Are you all right, sir?" Matheson's voice scraped his throat like a handful of tacks.

Dillal gave a low grunt as he straightened and turned his head to regard Matheson over his shoulder. "You have a report?" he asked, taking a few things from the bedside table, then tucking his mobile and ID into his jacket pockets.

"We don't have one, yet, sir. Senior Detive Neme is waiting on-scene to hand off to you."

The inspector turned all the way around, then put his hand over his strange eye for a moment. "Yes. All right." He took another long breath, dropped his hand, then started out the door at a steady pace. "Which jasso? Which district?"

"The Paz da Sorte in the Dreihleat."

Dillal stopped. "Paz?" He looked startled. Or that's what half his face looked. The left side didn't move above the merest downturn of his mouth.

"What?" Matheson asked.

Dillal shook off his concern, his whole mismatched face going blank. "Irony—Paz means 'peace.' There's no preliminary whatsoever?"

Preliminary peace? Oh. "Only my own recording, which isn't much."

"You were on-scene?"

"It was on our patch—my TO's and mine. I can send what I have to your mobile . . ."

"If you would," the inspector said, taking the battered device from his jacket pocket and holding it out as they walked on.

Odd. He expected Matheson to transfer the file directly by contact link. It was a more secure protocol than sending it though the data system, but harder to track and not much used. Dillal's strangeness lay in more than his face.

The inspector's mobile was strictly as-issued and displayed nothing personal; it bore only the Gattis Investigation and Security Administration's orange logo of an eight-pointed star with the horizontal arms extending into a stripe across the top of the screen and the acronym just below. Matheson's own Peerless MDD—even at three years old—looked like a thoroughbred trying to mate with a broken down pony. *Ugh, there's an image to forget.* He handed the device back as soon as the confirmation pinged.

Matheson glanced at the message—it didn't give the inspector's rank or regional, only his name. *Huh.* He slipped the Peerless back into its loops on his shirt front.

The humidity clung the moment they were outside and Matheson was quick to open the passenger door of the GISA-issued skimmer, hoping the inspector would get in before the interior of the vehicle caught too much thick air. He hurried to his own door and ducked in, flipping the environmental controls even as he slid into the seat, sighing in the first whiff of drier air. Everyone said it wasn't too bad yet, but even this early in the morning, the moist air felt like wool in his throat. It smelled of earth and fish and industrial waste near the health center—not much improvement on the Dreihleat, and summer would be worse.

Matheson dove the skimmer into Angra Dastrelas traffic, concentrating on that, not on the inspector beside him, and *not* on the scene that awaited ahead. He jinked it through the anarchy of vehicles rushing across and around the crater, with no airway markers or apparent rules but those the pilots made up on the spot. It still scared the shit out of him, even though he'd yet to be hit by another skimmer. He understood why most tourists stuck to cabs and the slideways, rightly terrified to go aloft in anything less than a continent-class transport.

"What do you know about this jasso?" Dillal asked as they plunged into the maelstrom of traffic. He spoke as if he measured out every word from a limited ration.

"Almost nothing—some kind of local business owners' after-hours place that doubled-up in legal drinking and illegal gambling. I barely knew it was there. I've only been on Gattis for a month and I was assigned to this patch in the Dreihleat with my TO two weeks ago. First posting after graduating Fresnel."

Dillal nodded without turning to look at him. "Gattis's corporate-ruled security and investigation protocols differ from Central System law enforcement you learned at the academy."

"Yes, sir."

"Are you falling in?"

Matheson hesitated, and twitched the skimmer into a momentarily empty stretch of air. "I'm . . . coming to terms."

As the skimmer shrieked on its way, Dillal said nothing and turned his attention to his mobile. After a minute or so, he pressed his head back against the seat and covered his golden eye with one hand. By the time Matheson set the skimmer down on the street near the Paz da Sorte, Dillal had closed both eyes and set the MDD down on his leg. Matheson thought the inspector was asleep, but his eyes opened—the left eye emitting another quiet mechanical click—just as the skimmer leveled to land. The inspector was out of the little vehicle before Matheson had flipped the engine switch down.

CHAPTER THREE

Day 1: Early morning

Matheson fell in behind the inspector's brisk stride down the street, surprised by the man's resilience and apparent cool, and sure his own singlet and uniform shirt were clinging to the small of his back by the time he'd gone four steps.

A handful of early-morning loiterers, mostly Dreihleen and a few hard-luck out-system immigrants, stared toward the alley that was now choked with GISA personnel and official vehicles. Most winced and stepped aside with averted eyes when they saw the inspector; one Dreihle looked at Dillal as if he were a thing that had crept up from a sewer full of nightmares. The man backed away before turning and hurrying off.

Beyond the gawkers, SOs and a few Investigation Ofiçes blocked the way while a scattering of technicians in white coveralls moved purposefully in the alley behind them. Matheson saw no sign of issued firearms; plainly the situation didn't merit breaking that part of the administration's "don't scare the tourists" policy. Dillal stopped beside the Security Ofiçes forming the cordon at the edge of the crime scene. The nearest of them, a muscular woman with shoulders that would do a transport cargo master proud, glanced down at the inspector as if to shoo him away, then stiffened and gaped at his patchwork face.

Dillal ignored her expression and put his left hand out palm up, showing the shiny black-and-red checkerboard of a high-level ID array incised in the skin just above his wrist. "I'm the Chief Investigating Forensic Ofiçe." His voice remained soft, measured, and cool.

The SO swiped her mobile's screen in a pro forma wave over the ID crystals, still appalled. If the inspector unnerved her, she hadn't seen the inside of the nightclub.

"Detive Neme is in the transport down the alley," the ofiçe mumbled and added, "In-inspector."

Dillal nodded and stepped past her, motioning Matheson to follow. The ofiçe muttered as they passed, "Mother of fucking stars. Couldn't pay *me* enough to do that, promotion or not." The inspector gave no sign that he'd heard, but he couldn't have missed it.

Dillal paused inside the cordon and looked around, his gaze moving slowly over the exterior of the buildings, then down to the ground. He squinted a little and rubbed at his shaved temple with his fingertips.

"Matheson. I need a light, here," he said, pointing to the ground in front of the jasso's broken door.

A broadening arc of stares followed as Matheson walked over, pulled his Sun Spot from his belt, and turned the bright white light where the inspector indicated.

The spotlight illuminated a curving red-brown line on the old ash-clay tiles. Two rippled blotches of the same color lay within the bracket-shaped line. *Was there something here earlier?* He couldn't recall.

Dillal crouched down and peered at the marks, his golden eye gleaming. He squinted and a series of quiet clicks sounded as he touched his temple. Then he humphed to himself and closed his eyes, leaning forward a little while breathing deeply through his nose and mouth. Finally he rocked back and rested on his heels with his forearms on his knees. He frowned as he opened his eyes.

"What is it?" Matheson asked.

Dillal seemed to have forgotten him. "Hm? It's a sole impression. In blood." He indicated the curved line. "That's the outside edge of someone's right shoe." He pointed at the enclosed blotches. "Those are part of the traction pattern at the ball and heel. I'm not getting a clear idea of the blood constituent or origin. It's dried, but that shouldn't cause such a problem." He stood up, still scowling, and tapped the shaved side of his skull. "The equipment is still strange to me. The calibration—there's so much noise . . ." he muttered.

He shifted his disconcerting stare to Matheson's face and studied him with the same intensity he'd turned on the bloody footprint.

Does he know I lost it earlier? He can't. Matheson drew himself up and stared back. An approving smile flickered across half the inspector's face before he turned his gaze back down.

Dillal pointed to the bloodstain. "ForTech will take a reference still, if they haven't already, but take an additional one now, please, and join me inside." Then he stepped over the footprint with care and eased through the open doorway, tucking his hands into his jacket pockets.

Matheson took the picture with his mobile and tagged it. He was just a pace behind Dillal when he heard him gag. A reek of blood, human waste, and burned flesh still hung on the air inside. The room was growing stuffy as well, now that the sun was rising, intensifying the stench that attracted flies and scavenger centipedes.

The ventilation system was off and racks of lamps had been set up in the corners. Hard white light fell on the crusting pools of blood that surrounded the bodies and stuck everything to the floor in gruesome tableaux. In the harsh illumination, it all looked worse than before. Most of the victims had black zip tape sealed across their mouths. More swathes of the stuff bound their arms at the wrists and their legs above the knees. Most lay on their sides or face down in the gore and fluids that had poured out of them. There were small ragged holes—

some charred around the edges—in their heads and necks. Twelve dead in the gaming room, lying amid the scatter of brightly colored chips, white dice, and cocktail glasses rimed red, game tiles, and cards going rust brown as they dried. Directly before them, four bodies in the bar room had fallen randomly at the foot of the bar. A small table had been overturned, spilling cups of tea and a plate of food, now writhing with insects, across the white-clad belly of a Dreihle youth, his expression of shock punctuated with a small bullet hole in his forehead.

Matheson forced down the acid creeping up his throat.

Dillal had covered his eyes and mouth, then slowly drew his hands away again. He swept the rooms with his strange gaze, and took a short breath through his mouth. He coughed and gagged a little, shaking his head like a wet dog. He tasted the air again, then he shuddered and switched to sniffing, the right side of his mouth curling in disgust. "This will take a while. Fetch Detive Neme, please." Dillal skirted the walls with his hands once again in his pockets as he stepped deeper into the room.

I should stay with the inspector. But even the threat of Dr. Andreus's ire if something went wrong didn't stop Matheson leaving. It was a relief to retreat from the slaughter house scene and leave Dillal alone for a moment. The carnage was repellant—even the worst virtuals his instructors had thrown at him hadn't hardened him against what-ever had played out inside the club. It should have been better in the light, where his imagination couldn't fill in horrors, but it wasn't, and remaining detached and observant was a struggle.

Outside, he tapped the nearest ofiçe on the shoulder—a guy he didn't recognize, wearing Investigation Ofiçe insignia on his uniform. "Go in and assist the CIFO until I get back."

The IO bristled and shook his head. "No fucking way. I have seen some gruesome shit—race riots, some drug dealer dismembered by his gang for going grass . . . Bad enough to get hauled in on my off shift to cover something that makes those scenes look cheery, but on top of that, you think I should work up close and personal with that *bong met*? You're out of your blighted mind, junior."

Met he'd heard before—an insult that meant "mixed," though some embraced it as a badge of identity. Matheson didn't know this new slur, but it carried a lash of corrosive loathing. He gaped at the IO—who certainly couldn't claim to be pure anything, unless it was asshole. "What? You won't even give the man your spray seal and stand by the door? Why? You think his color will rub off on you?"

The IO glared. "You don't get it, do you? That's J. P. Di-frigging-llal. He just disappeared about a year and a half ago and we all figured somebody'd finally whacked the half-yellow bastard. Now we got a bunch of dreck clan boys killing another bunch, and *he's* in charge? That's some messed up shit."

Fury tightened Matheson's fists.

A bored voice came from close behind Matheson before he could lose his horror-frayed temper. "Shut it, Vicenne."

Matheson spun, expecting more trouble, and found a mild-faced man whose cheap tan suit clashed with his smoky, dark brown complexion. He had to be from Investigation and was clearly a step up from IO Vicenne. *Not a Detive. An IAD?*

The stranger offered an apologetic smile and stepped around him to address Vicenne. "Your gutter mouth could be why you're still an IO."

The IO spat on the ground. "Go jump, Istvalk."

The man in the suit sighed. "Still wouldn't boot you up if I did. Give me your kit and *I'll* take it in."

Vicenne glowered, but he took the compact scene kit from his pocket and handed it over. "Kiss ass," he muttered.

Istvalk rolled his eyes and waved the other man away. Then he started for the jasso door without another word.

Matheson frowned after him. "Thanks," he called, but the other just shrugged and walked on. Matheson took a deep breath and started down the narrow alley.

The operations transport was set down in the crossing alley like a gargantuan cat that had chased a rat into a too-narrow hole. He shook his head. *They'll have to vertical the damned thing out when they're done here. Not sure how they got it in to begin with.*

When Matheson stepped inside, Aleztra Neme was pacing the width of the transport and talking to someone out of view. She was in her mid-thirties, slim to average build, a little over average height for a Gattian woman, and could trace her family back to before First Settlement—as they all could. She didn't have the typical deathly, cyanic pallor—her skin was dusty gray and the distinctive Gattian blue tinge seemed to float over it like the sheen on the surface of a pearl. She dressed in casually expensive simplicity that only the wealthy could afford, and she might have been beautiful if she hadn't had the personality of a rogue crocodile.

". . . Not like courts martial investigations—" she was saying. She cut herself off and turned her glare on Matheson. "Well?" Neme snapped. Her curling indigo hair seemed to spark with the static electricity of her annoyance.

He'd met Senior Detive Neme only twice before, but had come to dislike her the first time. "Inspector Dillal would like to speak with you in the jasso."

"Inspector! All that cut-rate surgery comes with a nice promotion. How's he doing?"

Matheson shrugged, as non-committal and bland as possible. *Don't give her an opening.* "Fine, sir."

"I'll bet." Neme glanced at the other GISA investigator who sat farther back in the transport. "Well, we now know that the price of ambition is one eye and a chunk of your brain," she said.

The older detive sprawled in his seat, drinking something that steamed from a black mug between his grit-spangled hands. *Investigation Officer of the Day . . . what's his name?* They'd met earlier, but Matheson hadn't been tracking well at the time. The man offered Neme a thin smile. "It's less than a soul."

"Maybe, but you wouldn't catch me handing *that* over to the lowest bidder, either. Not just to vault GISA's ladder, anyway."

"Not your damn problem, though, is it, Neme?" the man said. "Privilege of birth."

"*Rank*." Neme sniffed and turned back to Matheson. "Okay, let's go. Orris, you're coming, too."

Orris sighed and followed them out of the transport. He looked about fifty and his Central-tan skin had acquired an indoor pallor. He was on the tall side of average, but stooped a little and carried extra weight around his middle that exaggerated his bad posture. His graying blond hair was thinning on top and brushed straight back, and he clearly gave no sort of a damn for elegance—over his street clothes he wore an ancient uniform jacket so stained and worn it looked pale blue rather than the buff-and-khaki Matheson wore. Neme's barbs didn't bother him either.

They crossed the few meters of alley in silence and entered the building. Matheson stayed at the rear, rubbing the back of his sweaty neck as fine needles of tamped panic stabbed into his empty gut.

Neme coughed in revulsion and Matheson looked past her, searching for Inspector Dillal. He saw Istvalk lurking near the inner security door and taking shallow breaths through his mouth. He continued his visual search for the inspector, not sure what to do next.

Dillal was crouching beside one of the bodies in the gaming room and, aside from the stirring and breathing of the people beside Matheson, all was silence.

"GISA graces us with its new Forensic Ofiçe," Neme observed aloud, shattering the momentary calm. She began to walk across the bar room floor. "Quite a jump—IAD to Inspector in a year. I didn't think Pritchet would send his precious new toy out for a gang war."

Without turning, Dillal pointed a warning finger at Neme. "Don't contaminate my scene."

"The hell—?" Neme snorted and stared at him in affront.

Dillal turned without rising and gave her a baleful stare. The artificial eye cast a red gleam toward the Gattian and Neme stiffened, recoiling from her first view of Dillal's face before she stopped herself and let a flicker of disgust curl her lip.

The inspector did not break his cold expression with an answering reaction. "The blood in the carpeting is still fluid," he said. "If you step onto the floor here, you'll track DNA into these samples. I've already found several patches of cross-contamination. I'd prefer not to have more." His tone could have chilled nitrogen liquid from the air.

Surprise rippled over Neme's face before her usual sneer slid back into place. "Really? What about your own feet, you officious little rag?"

Dillal, entirely composed, rose and pointed to a bit of clear sheeting nearby. "IAD Istvalk provided me spray seal and sheath—per procedure." He looked at the IAD. "You can go now."

Istvalk's gaze flickered to Neme, who narrowed her eyes and twitched her head at him in dismissal. As the IAD left, Dillal stepped over the body and onto the sheath material, making his way back along the edges of the room to the bar.

Neme glowered, but stepped back onto the ash-clay tiles near the vestibule, waiting in the less-sensitive zone away from the blood-soaked carpets. Self-important ass, but not stupid. And it appeared that the inspector had decided to own her insult rather than take umbrage. Orris stood slightly behind Neme with his arms crossed over his chest, hands tucked into his armpits so a band of scruffy wrist was all that showed.

Dillal joined them, glancing at Matheson as he stepped onto the tiles. He rubbed his fingertips together and the spray seal peeled here and there, rolling into tiny gray grains that clung to his skin. Orris reached in front of Neme and handed the inspector a packet of clean up wipes from his own pocket. Matheson caught himself frowning at the gesture, too tired to wonder why.

"Thank you." Dillal wiped the translucent coating off his hands and wrists. He didn't move to clean the spray off his shoes, though Matheson could see the film on their surfaces.

"So," Neme began. "I assume your magical analysis has already solved the case and it's just a matter of rounding the bastards up. Right?"

Dillal shot her a dismissive frown. "There are sixteen bodies here and a great deal of other material to be sorted out. The forensic system does not run any faster in my skull than it does in the lab, Detive, though it does run more discreetly." He finished wiping down his hands and looked up at Neme, who was practicing her superior smile. "However, it should allow me to proceed with a thorough investigation much faster than you would." He looked at Orris.

The older man just shrugged, his hands tucked away again. "If Pritchet says it's yours, I got no argument."

Neme bridled and her expression went cold. *"For the record,* what does the evidence say, right now?" She was following protocol on handing it off, though normally she'd be the one reciting sit rep, not the incoming investigator. *She doesn't like handing off, or is it just handing off to* him?

Dillal tilted his head and studied her for a long moment. He quirked the right corner of his mouth into an ironic smile and turned back to regard the scene. "The victims are all Dreihleen adults—six female and ten male, from fifteen to seventy-two years of age. All local and all recorded in the database as required—do you want the names?"

Neme scowled and shook her head. "Get on with it."

Dillal nodded. "They died about four hours ago—between oh-one-thirty and oh-two-thirty, most likely. Causes of death are variously trauma or blood loss from wounds to the head and neck. These wounds were inflicted with two types of weapons—short-plasma projectors, and small-caliber firearms. As yet, no casings or bullets have been recovered, so I can't say if all the shots were from the same weapon or from several—"

Neme smirked. "You're not sure?"

Dillal cast his red-sparked stare back at her. "The bullets will have to be removed from the bodies for comparison before I can make absolute statements. We're not set up for an autopsy here—much less sixteen of them." He returned his gaze to the bodies. "The plasma burns are most likely from pen torches, but, even if we find them, the weapons wouldn't be much evidentiary use in court without DNA and prints to tie them to suspects."

Neme clenched her teeth. Orris stood and watched the byplay with a sarcastic smile of long familiarity and Matheson had an inkling of what had induced Dillal to submit to such ghastly surgery.

The inspector continued, "By the evidence, the victims were robbed, bound, and gagged, and placed on the floor, but not all at once. They were collected over an hour or more while the killers robbed the premises and lay in wait for more victims. Two of the victims weren't tied when they died." He paused to point to two bodies that lay the farthest back in the room, away from the rest. "They appear to be the only ones with defensive wounds—but all were killed within a few minutes of each other. Then the killers left. Possibly one of them—or one of our own men—tracked blood onto the tiles in the vestibule and alley, leaving partial sole impressions. Either before or after the robbery, the door lock was broken."

Neme had glowered through the whole recitation, now she interrupted again. "Santos and Matheson were first on the scene. The rookie says they broke the lock to gain access."

Dillal turned to Matheson, inquiring with a look. "Santos—my TO—ordered me to break it when I arrived," Matheson said, scowling. *All of this was in my report.* "We'd split the block because of the alley and his knee was slowing him down—he'd twisted it earlier while we were in pursuit of a pickpocket. I was about halfway around, rousting a dealer from a doorway, when he called me. When I got here, Santos was just outside the door. He thought the situation was suspicious, so I checked the door myself and broke the lock. We stepped inside and saw the scene, then I called it in."

"Why did Santos call you?"

"He was concerned that the jasso was locked up when it should have been open for after-hours business. He's been on this patch for a long time and I guess—"

"Don't guess. Where is Santos?"

Matheson shifted his eyes away from Dillal's gaze. "He . . . was injured, sir."

"He went jumpwise," Orris answered, "and knocked his brain loose. He was just sittin' up again when I got here. The rook—" he added, jerking his thumb at Matheson, "blew lunch, but he stuck on until I arrived. Sent Santos to Public Health, and Admin held Matheson there to spring you while they argued with the docs. The rest of us have been standin' around like the Pillars and readin' the graffiti until you got here."

Matheson was sure he could see something moving in Dillal's head. *What sort of machine did Andreus shove in there?*

"Do you surmise that the killers locked the door as they left?" Dillal asked.

"Must have," Matheson replied, feeling a little queasy.

"Was the ventilation off when you arrived on the scene?"

Matheson had to think before he could answer. "No. It was on."

"Who turned it off?"

Orris answered for him. "ForTech. To put collection filters in the vents."

Dillal's right eyebrow descended into half a scowl. "Humidity and insects degrade evidence and the filters will catch nothing if there's no draft."

Orris nodded, but didn't move.

"What about the shoe?" Neme asked.

"Shoe?" Dillal seemed thrown by the question.

"The one that made the bloody print by the door. Can't you tell whose it is?" she sneered.

"It's an indeterminate print. I need to make comparisons and eliminate all the GISA personnel on scene. It may be Santos's or Matheson's as easily as one of the killers'."

"You seem pretty sure there's more than one perp."

"Yes. The holding and binding of the victims would require two, but it was probably more."

"The more gang members there are, the more likely one'll grass," Neme said. "You know the fucking drecks and humps always brag their kills—they've been slaughtering each other over clan rights since before First Settlement."

"This wasn't clan against clan or Ohba against Dreihleen," Dillal stated in his dry, measured tone. "The Paz da Sorte is neutral territory in the Dreihleat, and there aren't any society marks in evidence, either Ohba or Dreihleen."

Neme peered down her nose at the inspector. "And you should know."

Dillal cocked an eyebrow at her. "As well as you should." Then he changed the subject. "Have the ofiçes learned anything from witnesses, yet? It's not likely anyone heard the shooting with such small caliber projectiles and plasmas, but perhaps something—"

"Something is nothing," Neme snapped back. "So far, no one saw or heard anything. Which is why it's got to be a clan thing. It's not system-hoppers, and if it was humps or mets, the drecks would be crushing each other in their rush to point fingers. These insular duck-fuckers are tighter than a mouse's ass when it's their own people for the chop."

Dillal didn't seem to hear Neme's slurs. "Then we'll continue asking. Coordinate the canvass in the Dreihleat before you go, and turn the reports over to me later. Matheson and I will continue with the scene. Detive Orris, are you still on shift as IOD?"

"About four hours into overtime, just like the kid, here. Half the guys assigned to this patch were up too late the night before, too—you know this fuckin' festival schedule."

Matheson had had his baptism by fire: his first week on the street was the second week of Spring Moon—a month-long mutation of some agricultural fertility festival Angra Dastrelas clung to like a greedy monkey that couldn't stand to pull its fist empty out of a nut jar. With engineered agribusiness, the festival's timing was moot these days, but the tourism and its revenue stream remained—which was all the planetary corporation cared about. The showier events were staged in more glamorous or family-friendly venues near Cove Quay, run by and for people higher on the social scale, but the hardcore traditionalists and culture mavens could still find the real thing in the Dreihleat—if they didn't mind the pickpockets and drug dealers.

Dillal nodded at Orris. "No reason for you to stay. Tell someone to turn the ventilation back on as you go, and send your report to my office before your next shift. I'll check on Santos."

Orris flipped a sardonic salute to the inspector and wasted no time leaving the building. Dillal, Neme, and Matheson followed him outside and toward the transport.

Matheson sucked in purging lungfuls of thick air scented with boozy urine and the odors of early breakfasts cooking. The keyhole glimpses of sky over the alley showed pink. He looked at his mobile: 0537. He'd thought it was later.

The comparatively clean air was no substitute for sleep. He was abraded by exhaustion and the rough grit of his reined and unsorted emotions—he was too tired to be horrified, now—he only felt chilled, and so detached from his own brain that he moved in slow motion.

"You going to toss it again, rook?" Neme asked.

Matheson squeezed his eyes and ground his teeth against a surge of fury that was pleasantly warm. *Probably thinks overtime's beneath her.* He caught a breath through his nose and cut a look at the senior detive. "No, sir."

"Detive," Dillal said.

Neme turned her superior smirk toward Inspector Dillal. *Rank or not, she thinks he's beneath her, too.*

Neither spoke for a moment.

"As Santos is not available," Dillal said, "I'll require SO Matheson's presence here a while longer, and I'd like to second him to my office for the duration of the investigation. As you are handing off, do you have an objection?"

Neme frowned and flipped a hand dismissively. "Oh, now you're by the book are you?"

"Have you ever known me not to be? I could go to Belcourso, or Pritchet, if you prefer . . ."

She snorted—it almost seemed as if she spat. "No. Why should I object? What good is he on this patch if he falls apart over a bit of blood? He'll be your millstone, now."

Matheson scowled after her as she walked away into the alley, patting her pockets.

CHAPTER FOUR

Day 1: Morning

*W*hat does he want with me? Matheson was nearly too tired to care. The smells of cooking teased his nose, but his stomach gurgled whenever memory of the jasso's interior raised its head, and he thought the only cure would be to spend the next twenty hours in the embrace of a mattress and cool, dry air. Not that he'd get that.

". . . Matheson?"

He jumped, realizing that Dillal had spoken his name several times already. "Sorry, sir. Yes, sir. What can I do?"

Dillal blinked at him a few times, his eyelids unsettlingly out of sync and his expression an unreadable, swift montage that faded to blankness. He shook his head. "Get some coffee—or whatever will keep you awake a few hours longer. I'd send you home too, but now I'm here, I can't leave so soon and I wouldn't like to risk Andreus's ire by working alone," he added in a dry tone.

"The doctor—"

Dillal stopped him with a raised hand. "I can imagine what she said. This," he added, touching the shaved left side of his head, "is experimental and not to be left unobserved in the field. Yes?"

Nanny duty . . . Matheson cast his gaze down and nodded as a shameful heat rose in his face again. He tried to change the subject. "There may be coffee in the transport."

Dillal gave the barest smile and shook his head. "Orris will have drunk it all, if it was drinkable. There used to be a café on Rua dos Peixes, facing the park."

"There's still one there." Not salvation, but at least a temporary respite from his foggy state. "How do you take your coffee, sir?"

"If there's a man at the counter, tell him I sent you. Otherwise, plain."

Matheson started to turn, then frowned and turned back. "Sir," he said, turning back, "didn't we just agree you're not to be alone?"

This time he got a real smile out of the inspector—it was one-sided and didn't show any teeth, but it tugged the raw skin around the prosthesis and brightened his remaining human eye for a flickering second. *Was that a test?*

Dillal motioned to one of the ofiçes at the cordon—Charley Tyreda, olive-skinned, baggy-eyed, and stuck with the extra shift like the rest of them. "Tyreda, assist me for a moment."

"Ah, fuck, Dillal . . . Why me?" Tyreda muttered, but he went along like a lamb—a skittish lamb in the company of what could be a small, but dangerous wolf.

Dillal knelt by the door in the glare of Tyreda's Sun Spot and examined the lock. It yielded no useful information. He scowled and went back into the jasso, pausing to reapply the spray seal to his shoes and hands. The slowly stirring air inside smelled of aerosol solvents more than it did of blood and excrement and the beginnings of tropical rot for a moment before the humidity and stink fell back onto them.

Tyreda followed the inspector's example before trudging after him, disgust and horror vying for control of his expression. "Why are you bothering with all this crap?" he asked.

Dillal paused on the sheath beside the bar room wall and turned slowly back to face the SO. He narrowed his eyes, the left responding a beat slower than the right. "Bothering? With the investigation of murder?"

Tyreda dragged his gaze away from Dillal's face and shuddered. "No. With all this." He flapped his hands as if dismissing a cloud of smoke between them. "This on-site forensic cat shit. There's no fuckin' way that cybernetic freak show is actually functional."

"You think not?" Dillal's voice was cool.

Tyreda swallowed hard and glared back. "Yeah, I 'think not.' I mean . . . I gotta credit you with some hefty balls for goin' through with it—I knew you were crazy, Dillal, knew you were ambitious— but this stuff . . . How does it even work? Takes a database the size of a desk and a room full of techs with machines and microscopes to manage scene analysis any other time, but here's you, what . . . sixty-eight, seventy kilos and a head half-full of hardware and you can do it right here, right now? It's gotta be a con. You agree to the show, they promote you—for whatever reason Pritchet's got, which I don't know and don't want to," he added, holding up his hands to ward the information away, "—and you finally get out from under that blue-assed bitch, get a promotion you shoulda had years ago. That's a good deal. But the rest . . . ?"

"It works."

"Cat shit."

Dillal cocked his head and waited.

Tyreda couldn't hold out more than a minute before dropping his gaze. "That's cold, that silent thing you do. It's even creepier with your face like that and I've known you . . . what? Six years?"

"Seven."

Tyreda shrugged. "Whatever, but since before you booted up to IAD and left this patch to me."

"Have you ever known me to lie about my abilities before?"

Tyreda paused and frowned, thinking before he answered, "No. You're the best street investigator I ever saw—even when the guys you're trying to help would rather see you dead than say thanks. But you're kind of an asshole—you're arrogant and you don't know your place—"

"My place . . ." Dillal gave a bitter chuckle. "How is my parentage or the color of my skin an indication of my worth, my willingness, or my intelligence?"

"We've done this before," Tyreda said, shaking his head. "You're the wrong guy every time, but you just keep going till you hit the wall. And then you force your way through it anyhow. I admire your guts, but you're nobody's kid—not Dreihleen enough, not Ohba enough, and not somethin' else, either. You're too smart, too pushy, and too colored for your own good, no matter who's measuring."

Dillal sounded irritated, but less than Tyreda's words might merit. "I'm no *more* colored than you—just an inconvenient shade. The Dreihleen and Ohba have been here longer than any so-called First Settlement family and will be until whenever the corporation finds an excuse to wipe them out."

Tyreda rolled his eyes. "That again . . . I'd think you'd be too busy keeping your own skin intact to worry about the future of folks who keep trying to kill you—Neme included. I don't suppose you give a razor cat's howl what happens to her sort, though I never thought you'd go this far to get past the color bar."

Dillal gave the SO a sideways look, tilting his head slightly as if measuring Tyreda in his red-glinting eye. "I'll go as far as I have to."

Tyreda stared back at him, then he turned his head a little and closed his eyes, muttering, "Fuck me . . ."

The inspector neither moved nor spoke. Tyreda didn't look at him, but after a minute of silence, he said, "So . . . this hopper-headed shit works?"

Now Dillal smiled with only the right side of his face—the left blank and unresponsive. "Help me collect the bullets and I'll show you."

I should feel belittled, maybe, being sent off for coffee, but, damn, anything to get away for a while. Matheson knew he was missing things—hints about the inspector, things about the crime that just weren't coming together in his head—but his brain felt like a loose bag of mud in his skull and incapable of connecting anything more complex than "put one foot in front of the other." And even that wasn't so easy. His legs were rubbery and he dropped into a walk as he rounded the corner onto Rua dos Peixes and headed toward Yshteppa Park, and the canal beside it that marked the north and west edges of the ghetto. Just like the night before, chasing the pickpocket.

The district was busier here on the wider street, but not quite as it should have been. Under the green and gold Spring Moon banners that crossed from building to building over the road, the universally tall, slim Dreihleen weren't rushing to work or festival pleasures. They didn't pause to listen to the street corner political speakers or park bench revolutionaries whose numbers seemed to multiply daily in the Dreihleat, but walked with nervous steps and anxious glances. The dawn light gilded their skin brighter gold, flax yellow, and amber, but it didn't lighten their mood. A crew of workers in orange Criminal Detention coveralls skimmed the trash from the green water of Southern Star Canal in preparation for the canoe races, but they didn't speak, glared over by a single well-armed supervisor in a GISA uniform with a rugged-looking dog pacing at his side. Shop keepers swept up last night's trash or roused the last of the homeless and addled who'd been sleeping in their doorways and sent them away with whispered admonishments. Even the children who picked through the festival trash for dropped treasures worked without chatter.

Gazes brushed over Matheson, and then away, and whispers sounded behind him like the brushing and ticking of bare branches against windows late at night. The unsettled feeling he hadn't had in days crawled up his neck and across his scalp like a spider. *They already know. But how could they miss two-dozen GISA personnel crowded into one alley?*

He turned in at the café's door. The strong scent of fresh coffee and hot baked goods shocked his numbed senses. For a moment he just stood still in the doorway and breathed it in. It left him dumb and weak after the grim reek of the crime scene and the hospital, and too many hours without sleep.

"Heh," the counterman muttered—his features seemed undecided, but his voice was low enough that Matheson decided to stick with "male," for now. "What I can do for you?" The distinctive rolling R and the Dreihleen clicking of the man's tongue against his closed teeth brought Matheson back to himself.

"Coffee. Two. Very large."

The lanky man had drawn his dark brown hair into a short spray of tiny braids at his nape. Matheson hadn't yet got the knack of consistently reading a Dreihle's age with a look and had to guess at something between thirty and forty-five. The counterman issued an interrogative sort of snort. "How you're want them?" The hard consonants were clipped, the vowels throaty behind habitually clenched teeth that turned "them" into "zem."

"Umm . . . Inspector Dillal sent me to get them. Plain is fine."

"Huh. Is Inspector now, is't?" the other replied, turning toward his steam pipes and samovars.

Matheson only nodded and watched the man juggling hot liquids like soft toys. *How to answer that?* He didn't say anything.

"He working that thing over Paz? What'zat?"

Matheson shook his head. "I couldn't say."

The counterman squeezed lids onto the cups, pressing them tight and shooting a sideways glance at Matheson. "Murder." It came out "mare't. dair." "Is bad. Is what I hear." The word "is" buzzed into a long Z.

Matheson frowned. "Really . . . I can't say. Not yet."

The man nodded and put the sealed cups into a gossamer-thin box, his whole body bobbing in thoughtful agreement; he waved Matheson's payment away.

"No," Matheson insisted. "It wouldn't be right, otherwise."

The counterman gave him a cockeyed smile. "Right man, heh?" He chuckled to himself and swiped Matheson's mobile with the payment wand, but he didn't hand the drinks over at once. He dropped two small pastries in and folded down the top of the box. Then he handed the package over the counter. "Keep you well, Ofiçe. And keep you right."

Weird turn of phrase. Puzzling over it, Matheson gave an absent nod to a Dreihle woman who had stopped just inside the doorway. She ducked her head away while watching him from the corners of her eyes. He'd seen the odd glance so often, he'd begun to think of it as "Dreihle-wise," though hers was sharper than most.

It all felt strange and it wasn't due to his own anxiety and lack of sleep alone. The counterman had met his eye and spoken directly to him about what was happening at Paz. But most Dreihleen wouldn't look straight at non-Dreihleen, just like the woman in the doorway hadn't. *Yet another mystery.* Matheson couldn't quite hear the conversation in the café behind him—and wouldn't have understood the language if he had—before the door hissed shut. *Gossiping about the crime.* He shivered.

He trudged back to the crime scene, keeping his head down. He was aware of quickly averted glances. Uncomfortable thoughts dogged him. *How much information's leaked into the neighborhood by now? Is it already muddying the witness statements? Will the street-corner agitators try to spin this into a corporate conspiracy? Rumor'll be a nightmare . . . though it won't be worse than the reality.*

He crossed through the cordon, searched for Dillal, and found him back inside the club. Even with the ventilation on, the stink still crawled over Matheson like a cloud of gnats, but he barely flinched this time. It wasn't that he was used to it—*please, don't let me ever become used to it*—but he didn't have the energy left to be sickened.

The inspector and Tyreda stood at the end of the bar, examining something laid on the surface under a harsh light.

". . . Off-world," Dillal was saying. "Possibly military origin . . ."

Matheson stopped on the entry tiles and both men turned toward him. Tyreda looked unnerved. The inspector made no show of noticing, but he said, "Tyreda, find someone to stand guard outside the door while Matheson and I take these back to the transport. And see about organizing relief for the remaining SOs and IOs—we can start sending them home once the alley survey is done."

"Sure, D—sir," Tyreda stuttered, hurrying to pass Matheson and get out of the bloodstained room as quickly as possible.

Dillal took a handful of evidence bags off the bar and shut off the lamp before walking over to join Matheson on the tiles. "The woman wasn't in the shop?" he asked.

"Huh?" It took a second for Matheson figure what Dillal meant. "Oh. No. A man and a female customer. How—?"

"I can smell the pastries. She would never have given you those. He's a useful man to know." Dillal cast a look back into the room. "There's too much yet to do, but it won't spoil in a few minutes." He glanced at Matheson's mobile, secured in the parallel loops on his uniform shirt. "Fifteen minutes for coffee should be all right. These must go into the catalog, in any event," he added, holding up the bags as he walked toward the door.

Matheson peered over Dillal's shoulder at the contents of the bags. "Bullets?"

"From the walls in the bar room. Come along, before the coffee's cold."

Matheson followed, though he was beginning to feel that he spent all his time shuttling from one place to another, learning nothing, and expecting something awful to happen. It was a relief to sit down in the dry and quiet of the transport and just drink coffee. It had cooled enough to feel wonderful going down. As the internal heat and caffeine hit, he closed his eyes and let his shoulders slump. *Not as good as a bed or a bath, but better than the street, or the nauseating air of the jasso.* Coffee wouldn't carry him far, but it would keep him from collapsing just yet.

"You should swallow that," Dillal said and Matheson felt something nudge against his arm, which he'd rested against the work table, "though I can't imagine you'll enjoy it."

With an effort, he sat up and opened his eyes, mumbling, "Sir," automatically. One of the small pastries sat on a square of flimsy beside his elbow: Caked in sugar icing, it was cup-shaped, about as large as the first knuckle of his thumb, and filled with some kind of tiny seeds in brown paste. He wasn't sure what the paste was: Gattis grew some damned strange plants and many of them had *interesting* pharmaceutical qualities. He couldn't even be sure what the crust was made from, though it looked like ordinary pastry dough. He blinked at the morsel, wondering what the risk was.

"Gattian water poppy seeds are a stimulant." Dillal's measured voice sounded muffled and tired. "They'd be addictive if they didn't taste like filth."

Matheson glanced at the inspector, who'd propped his elbows on the table edge and buried his face in his hands, rubbing his fingers against his temples once again. His whole body sagged. *It's like that moment in the hospital room . . . but he's been fine since.* "Sir?"

Dillal jerked his head up as if Matheson had startled him from sleep, and clapped his palms down onto the table top. His natural eye was wide and blinking rapidly, while the other remained half-closed. "Callista Matheson."

"What?"

"Your sister. Your father's K. Parkman Matheson." Dillal's face went still and blank again. "Yes or no?"

Matheson drew back, feeling his shoulders tighten involuntarily. *It was going to come up sometime* . . . His last wretched meeting with Callista swam into his mind:

"A policeman isn't much use to the family, Eric."

"I want to do something beneficial—"

"Then start a charity!"

He shook away the memory of her icy disgust and the sharp ring of her heels on the floor as she'd left him. He gave the inspector a wary look. "Yes. Why?"

"Ah," Dillal said and shrugged it away. "Just a data point. Drink your coffee. I want to finish with this scene by 0900, if possible." He reached forward, pulled a data stylus and keyboard out of the nearest console, and began typing.

"Sir, I don't understand . . ."

The inspector didn't look at Matheson, but at the small pile of bagged bullets, entering their information in the evidence catalog. "Nor do I, yet. What do you think of our crime scene?"

Matheson's head was spinning. He couldn't keep up with the inspector's mercurial changes of mood and topic, any more than he understood the hostility and discomfort that he provoked. Matheson gave up trying to sort it. "I think it's merry fucked," he blurted. Then he bolted down half his coffee and forced his mind back to the crime scene before he said more. "It's not a crime of passion, so it didn't start and stop at the doorway. The Dreihleen have a history of conflict with the Ohba, but we didn't hear of any Ohba sighted in the Dreihleat last night and Neme thinks it's clannish—"

"I already know what Senior Detive Neme believes. What do you think?"

"I think . . . that I don't know enough."

The inspector's voice was still soft, but cut clearly. "You're avoiding my question. You were the first man on the scene—or near enough." He finished typing and put the entry equipment away, turning his disturbing gaze back to Matheson. Dillal's jaw and the corner of his right eye were tight from fatigue or pain. "You're academy-trained, which means you're not stupid, you're well-educated, and you *might* have some innate skill at this. So, before you were four hours into overtime, when you first saw this scene, what was your immediate impression?"

"*My* first impression? Was merry fucking hell, but someone's a sick bastard. Or very angry. To kill like that . . . so many people . . ." Matheson's innards twisted and the coffee burned back up his throat.

The inspector watched him. "But I agree with you that the crime is not one of passion, in spite of the violence of it. It was planned. It was careful—" he raised a finger between them—"up to a point. If this is an act of anger, it's a very cold sort," he finished, letting his hand drop.

"That doesn't comfort me."

One of his twitching, wry smiles escaped Dillal before he said, "No. It implies a disciplined mind at the heart of the matter, and that will make our job much harder."

"*Our* job? I'm just a foot patrolman, an SO. Not even a real cop, just a corporate enforcement officer at the absolute bottom of the ladder." *Yes, I'm bitter. Everyone starts at the bottom—and I wanted to—but not here, not like this.*

Dillal was silent a few seconds, thinking and peering at Matheson as if he could read something off his skin. Then he said, "You won't be for long."

"Which means?"

The inspector tilted his head but didn't answer. He just picked up his coffee and stuffed the remaining pastry into his mouth. The right side of his face pulled down in an expression of disgust and he gulped coffee until the cup was empty. Then he coughed and shivered. "Escudos taste abominable, but they'll keep you awake a while longer."

Matheson followed the inspector's lead and ate the little pastry in one bite. He almost spewed. No amount of sugar and sweet bean paste could cover the horrendous taste of the water poppy seeds: like fermented eggs spiced with strychnine. "Ugh, it's like being poisoned!"

"If it had any odor, it would be a perfect aversive." The inspector gave a faint snort that might have been a rueful laugh. "It's mostly benign except for the taste."

Matheson coughed and drained his coffee. *Please, let that terrible flavor fade quickly . . . and don't let me vomit—how much more awful will it be coming back up?* "If it's so useful as a stimulant, why don't they just put it in capsules?"

"There's always a fool or two who wants to prove how hard they are—why not accommodate them? Capsules don't taste any better." The inspector shook himself, rose, and put the evidence bags away in one of the lockers. Then he took a pair of disposable coveralls out of the supply drawer. Matheson despaired of the clammy discomfort they represented.

"Can you continue, now?" Dillal asked. The expression he offered wasn't unkind, but it wasn't warm, either, and the lack of mobility on the left side of his face didn't help.

Matheson checked himself. He did feel more alert, even if his mouth tasted like something had died in it. Actually . . . he was more than alert; an almost itchy feeling was starting just under his skin, as if his blood was filled with hyperactive spiders and his nerves were slightly raw. He rubbed his forearm and gasped at the sensation—like sandpaper on wet skin. "I think so," he said. "If I don't go crazy first."

"It's temporary."

Did he mean the itching, or the insanity?

CHAPTER FIVE

Day 1: Afternoon

Two more hours sweating inside coveralls and spray seal killed off the too-lively sensation under Matheson's skin and almost any thought aside from his desire to sleep. Even with a team of scene technicians from ForTech, the sheer volume of the work was deadening. Every body, every bullet hole, and every scrap of potential evidence had to be collected and recorded in notes, and motion or still video, and the inspector wanted to see as much of it as possible in situ. Matheson plodded through the rooms in Dillal's wake, the inspector pausing to crouch and peer at the victims' hands and faces, and give each one a name, turning them back into humans, not just stiffening, stinking corpses. Matheson's chest, throat, and eyes ached.

Dillal took particular interest in one man and one woman— Denenshe Leran and Venn Robesh—who were slightly removed from the rest of those in the gaming room. They were both dead in the same way as the others, but neither of them had been bound with tape. They lay partially across one another, the man—Leran—face down across the woman's bent legs as she lay on her side, facing him.

Matheson recorded it all and Dillal rested on his heels, studying them. "These two . . ." he muttered. "Defensive wounds, not bound, no sign of having been forced to kneel on the floor with the rest. Whoever they are, whatever they were to each other, or to the rest, this is the key."

"How are you certain?" Matheson asked.

"How are you not?" Dillal replied lifting his gaze to Matheson without raising his head. "They're the anomaly in the pattern." He returned his unsettling stare to the murdered couple and spoke gently, as if to them. "Explain the anomaly and you explain the crime." Dillal looked at them for another minute in silence. Then he rose without a word and retreated from the room. Matheson followed.

The alley was no more comfortable with the sun now heating the humid air, but it was a change of scene that was at least less grim. The OLED picto-signs had folded into their leaves, leaving only sunlight to work by. Dillal was no less thorough there. He observed or checked everything, from the removal and recording of twenty-five pictogram handbills from the alley walls—including several political posters with the ubiquitous "Relief, Redress, Revolt!" icons loaded on cheap flimsy—to a sweep of the usual ghetto trash, from the lip ends of cigarettes, food wrappers, alcohol containers, sex and drug paraphernalia, to small injector capsules from single hits of Wire.

Dillal squatted down beside something near the back of the transport and looked back over his shoulder toward the doors of Paz, his unnatural eye squinting with a whispering hint of machinery beneath his skin. "Twelve meters?" he muttered. "Matheson, do you have the visible beam pointer?"

"No, sir," Matheson replied, closing the distance between them and taking care where he put his feet.

Dillal pointed to the ground just in front of himself—one more bloody shoe print and a broken pen torch lay just past the transport, near a runoff drain. "This is the same pattern as the print by the door. I'd like the true measurement of the distance from the center of one mark to the center of the other."

Matheson fetched the beam pointer from the transport and set it up. Dillal squatted down again and squinted at the mark as Matheson adjusted the beam to his requirements.

Matheson twisted the handle a little.

"Stop there. Now tell me the distance reading."

"Twelve-point-one-one meters," Matheson read.

Dillal grunted. "Mark it, and use your MDD to record the new track, the distance measured, and the beam in place with both evidence markers visible. Please."

The beam measure could store the information in its own memo, but Matheson did as the inspector asked. The narrowness of the alley made it difficult to back off far enough to get both markers into the mobile's recording frame. When he'd finished he started to return to the inspector's side, but the smaller man called out. "No. Stop. Can you see the first mark clearly from there?"

Matheson squinted. "No. Just the marker. The tiles are a little sunken."

Dillal stood up and waved Matheson to return. "Twelve meters from one footprint to the next, but less than one meter from the last footprint to here. Copy the evidence logs when you put this in the transport, and bring them along. I'll meet you at the skimmer."

Matheson fought a yawn in the cool dimness of the transport as he put the beam measure away, and uploaded and copied the logs. *What's the inspector up to?* His mind staggered around, groping for answers as exhaustion dragged on him again.

He stepped outside and blinked in the sunshine that had begun falling into the alley like shards of broken, dirty glass as the sunlight finally reached over the walls on the east. In a few more hours, the sun would slice down on the narrow alley like a guillotine and he would be nine hours into overtime. The thought made him dizzy.

Dillal was waiting for him in the same skimmer they'd arrived in, his head bent over his mobile once more. The sun played mercilessly on the patchwork skin and the metal beneath it around his mechanical eye. He didn't say a word until the vehicle was in the air.

"There are no additional impressions between the first track and the second," the inspector murmured as Matheson guided the skimmer through thickening traffic. "Take us up higher, please."

It took a moment for Matheson to realize the two sentences weren't connected and another minute to bring the skimmer up above the normal traffic limits where only automated freight and emergency craft were allowed. *Having an inspector aboard qualifies as an emergency . . . doesn't it?* Matheson was too tired to care if it didn't. He felt safer up here where the traffic was thinner and seemed less bent on killing him.

"I checked the path between the two markers while you were in the transport," Dillal explained, glancing up and out the front window. "We did not miss more shoe prints—there are none. The second one falls within one very long stride or a short jump to the transport's door and I saw no other marks proceeding down the alley outside our cordon. There may be more under the transport, but unless ForTech finds some, those two are an interesting conundrum. Did you see any bloody footmarks in the transport?"

Matheson was concentrating on piloting the skimmer, but he said, "Mostly smears."

"What would you imagine their origin to be? Could they be from whomever left the other two marks?"

Matheson let out a tired little laugh. "You want me to *guess* now?"

"Not so much a guess, in fact, but what your instinct tells you about the tracks on the transport's floor."

"I think they were made by Neme, Orris, and the scene techs. We'll have no luck picking one particular track out of that."

The inspector grunted. "I need to find out who left them. ForTech will get elimination impressions from all the GISA personnel who entered the site before we arrived. Otherwise, evidence that the tracks were or were not left by SO Santos will be thrown into doubt."

"Santos? What? You think Santos did that . . . that?" Matheson felt sick and couldn't think of a word that fit.

"I don't. But he may have opened the door and stepped inside before he called you to the scene."

"Wouldn't he need a key?"

"Not if the door was open at the time. You have only his word it was locked. His MDD will have recorded his movement, but the detail may not be fine enough to show whether he entered the building or merely went to the door—"

"He broke his mobile's screen earlier, so it might not have been recording video or position," Matheson said.

"Broke it? How convenient . . ."

"It was an accident," Matheson objected. "He fell—"

"While chasing the pickpocket?" The inspector grunted dismissively. "Whatever the case, I'm not certain that he didn't enter the jasso earlier than you claimed."

"You think I lied?" Matheson snapped.

Dillal turned a bland expression on Matheson. "No. I think he did. Santos has been assigned to this patch for a long time. He's refused opportunities to move to other, less controversial areas."

Matheson's brain seemed to freeze around any useful thought and he scowled. "Why? If he had the chance to go somewhere better, why stay in the Dreihleat?"

"For the bribes."

Matheson stared at the inspector, feeling his stomach fall, and then whipped his gaze to the front windshield in time to slip the skimmer sideways out of the path of an automated freight transport. "What?" was all he managed to say.

Dillal had turned his head forward again, but he was clearly aware of Matheson while he spoke. "You haven't been here long, but I'm certain you haven't missed it. Bribery and corruption are an endemic part of the system here, even more than the chartered principles."

"It shouldn't be that way—one set of rules for the quay and another for the ghetto!"

Dillal shook his head with a slight, twisted smile on his lips. "*Should be* and *are* rarely share the same bed on Gattis. Everything here is artificial and shaped by human desire, from the culture to the depth of the sea. You'll have to learn to bear it."

"Bear it? How?" Matheson demanded. "I saw how you were treated today. Is that something you should *bear?*"

Dillal turned his head and studied Matheson with the same cool absorption he'd given to the dead—the glinting ocular making minute clicks. Then he looked aside again, making a speculative noise in his throat. "We should leave that topic for another time. Return your mind to the case. I started my career in Ang'Das on that patch and I know firsthand that to keep operating, the owners of jassos and other businesses pay bribes to the police—not to someone like me, of course, but to a senior SO or a District Coordinator. If Santos was the bag man—the collector of the bribes—for that end of the Dreihleat, he may have had a key to the club. It's common enough for the same patrolmen who take the bribes to work as security for the jassos on their off hours. A very close arrangement that ensures that the interests of the businesses are not neglected. Since Paz caters to local businessmen after hours, it would have been a convenient way to contact many of his clients at once. This would have been the reason he separated from you when he had not done so before."

Santos was too upset by the locked door and I didn't question splitting the block. I just went along . . . Matheson felt more ill than ever and his mind was leaping and wandering wildly. "But," he objected, "he fainted when we opened the door." *Shaking down the tourists is one thing. This . . .*

The inspector shook his head. "It may have been a sham, or he may not have seen the extent of the slaughter within until you brought your Sun Spot to the scene. You reacted strongly on seeing it a second time—why wouldn't he?"

Matheson latched onto the next thing that jarred his mind. "How do you know I used the Sun Spot?"

"It's academy protocol to illuminate a dark and suspicious area in such a situation. Didn't you do so?"

"I—" Matheson hesitated. The memory was hazier than it should have been and he had to try hard to get it. "I did."

"And what did Santos do when you shined the light on the scene within?"

"He made a noise—maybe he said something. I didn't hear it well. But he was in front of me. I followed him back out—we'd only stepped over the threshold. But his knee gave, and he ran into that pillar so hard he brained himself."

Dillal nodded to himself. "Went jumpwise. I'll ask him."

Matheson's own thoughts were a scattered mess. The city was awake and bustling now and he had to concentrate all his attention on piloting the skimmer to Public Health or they'd end up smashed on the crater floor. But he did it.

Once again Dillal was out of the skimmer and striding toward the building first. Matheson dragged behind the inspector, tripped over the health center's doorsill, and stumbled, banging his right shoulder into the nearest wall. *Just like Santos.* He shook his head to clear it and wondered why it was so dark inside. He shook his head again, resting his weight against the wall to fight the dizziness that washed over him.

"Matheson."

He couldn't get Dillal in focus. *Is that someone with the inspector? No . . . just a big shadow. Why'd they dim the lights?*

The shadow glided forward and touched Matheson on the shoulder. It stabbed his eyes with a bright light. "How long since you slept, ofiçe?" The shadow had a rumbling voice. Matheson could hear Dillal's voice, too, but he couldn't understand it.

"Don't know . . . forty-two?" Matheson replied.

The shadow rumbled a little more and started towing Matheson down the hall. Long, dark hall . . .

CHAPTER SIX

Day 1: Late Afternoon

"Water poppy reaction," the nurse affirmed, and made notes on his data pad as Matheson was removed to sleep it off. "Happens to most first-time users with that kind of sleep dep. Forty-two hours?"

"So he says," Dillal replied. "My guess is forty-six or more."

The nurse shook his head. "Cops . . ."

"There is another ofiçe—Eron Santos—I'd like to speak to him."

The nurse checked his pad and replied without looking up. "Discharged. Not much wrong with either of these guys that rest won't cure." He held out the pad. "Sign off."

Dillal entered his hashmark on the pad and turned away.

"Wait." The nurse caught his arm and stared at his face. "You're J. P. Dillal? Your surgeon wants to see you. If you have time." His tone implied that Dillal had better have time or make some.

The inspector heaved an annoyed sigh and pulled his arm free. "Very well."

"Her lab's just past—"

"I know where her lab is."

Dillal made his way through a tangle of slideways and corridors to Andreus's domain. There, he suffered through a physical exam and a raft of questions about the state of his pain, and how his interface and forensic equipment were working. She seemed unconvinced by his answers as she ran her gloved fingers over recent surgical scars among scrawls of older, rougher marks on his chest and head.

"So . . . nothing oozing or nonfunctional? Nothing that just *feels* wrong?" she asked.

"No," Dillal replied. "Uncalibrated, still integrating, and, of course, I'm not used to it, but to say it's *wrong* would be ridiculous in light of certain arguments against the whole program. Don't you agree, Doctor?"

Andreus gave him an indecipherable glance from the corner of her eye. "Yes. All right. Let me scan the system before you hare off again."

"Hare off?" Dillal repeated.

"Yes. Don't you have hares on this planet? Wild rabbits with long ears and legs?"

"No."

The doctor made a huffing sound through her nose at the conversation's crib-death.

She picked up a data cable that was connected to a medical analyzer suite and located the tiny socket behind Dillal's left ear. "There's some damned weird stuff going on in your brain, but so far it's all positive—I'm not seeing any sign of rejection or system over-reach . . ." she muttered. With her other hand, she swabbed the plug and socket with disinfectant. "Well, the socket is healing all right." She connected the cable to his head. "Good firm seat and no sign of infection. Your chimeric physiology and immune function have been boons in the flesh-and-bone end of this, in spite of insufficient convalescence. Let's just see what's going on in the cybernetic and mechanical end."

She turned away from him and put her attention on the analyzer equipment, which made some discreet whirring and clicking sounds as graphs and numbers began to fill the various displays. Dillal sat rigidly still, except for his fingers and the lid of his normal eye, which twitched in repeating cycles of two, three, one, two, three, one . . . until the doctor was satisfied. She gestured over the screens, and the small noises stopped, the graphs and numbers no longer changing.

She peered at the monitors. "Some of the connections aren't returning the sort of sensitivity or stability I'd like to see, and the antenna isn't coming online every time. Any trouble accessing the main system via remote?"

"Occasionally. But I was in the Dreihleat, where the microtransmitter density is lower."

"Shouldn't have been a problem. Analysis suite is operating at only eighty-seven percent. Well. I'll give it a few days to build over the scaffold a little more, but I'm not pleased with the response." She turned, pursing her mouth, and cast a speculating glance over him. "You've just come back from a crime scene. How did it go?"

"In terms of system performance—marginal."

Andreus growled with disgust. "In light of this . . . 'marginal' performance, what was the response of your colleagues—and Pritchet?"

"I've not seen the Regional Director yet. And I don't have any intention of telling him that the initial phase of the investigation was more dependent on my experience and ability to lie than on your system."

"Was it, indeed?" she asked, narrowing her eyes.

Dillal stared back at her. "Connectivity was problematic, but the system did give results once I'd adjusted it sufficiently."

"You adjusted it manually? Did you have to reset the ocular?"

"Yes. But it wasn't inconvenient. Better to control it manually than have it overrule my normal senses without authorization."

"Hah!" she scoffed. "That's how you see it, is it? A control issue? Well, if it were doing its job as I designed it, that wouldn't be a problem."

"It is not a problem now. I prefer to push the system rather than be pushed."

The doctor laughed cynically. "I'll bet you do."

Dillal made no reply.

Andreus studied him for a moment. "If it doesn't start to function and integrate as I'd intended, I'll have to go back in there and modify a few things—which would be very risky." She pointed at him. "*You* need to be vigilant about the possibility of infection or malfunction, because anything of that nature could be fatal and you know the protocol demands deintegration if the system fails. I don't want to have to scrap you—even though you've been a major pain in my ass. Let me know what it's doing—especially anything that doesn't meet spec or fails to respond."

"I will."

"I'll pretend I believe that." She stripped her gloves and turned back to her machines. "I'm going to adjust a couple of the sensor parameters so you don't get fades and overloads like the ones I'm seeing here on the particle intake and spectrum shift. It's firmware, so it'll take a few minutes." She made some gestures over the screens and the suite of equipment hummed again for a few moments while Dillal winced, his fingers spasming into hooks and releasing in swift repetitions.

Once the doctor shut off her machines and returned to her patient, he was sitting as still and upright as she'd left him. She looked Dillal over with narrowed eyes, then got several boxes out of a cabinet and handed them to him. "The lower edges of the ocular interface frame aren't closing with the tissue well and that tear duct may prove to be a problem. Use these wipes—and *wipe* is a misnomer here, since you need to dab gently with them—around the area three times a day. Tell the pharmakids to give you the Paracemid I'm going to set up for you—that would be a particularly bad place to get an infection, and it'll dull some of the pain."

"I'm not in pain."

"I appreciate that you don't want to be impaired on the job but I've put enough people back together in field hospitals from Marshel to Kora to know suppression when I see it. If you clench any more, you'll break a tooth. Don't be such a fragging man about it—take the darkness-blighted pills they're going to give you. If you want something else, let me know. I won't put it on your records and I'm not going to turf you to Pritchet for walking off the straight-and-narrow—not that either of us is familiar with that road. If you decide to take something . . . off-schedule, don't choose Wire. Blackness and burn, but that'll frag you up worse than jumps. Don't submit yourself to any extreme pressure changes, electric shocks, unusual physical loads, or breathe anything that isn't normal air for a while. Keep me apprised of *everything*. Ideally, the system reports back, but if it breaks down, I won't know what the problem is until you're on a table—and you had better hope it's in the OR and not the morgue. Don't fuck with this—do as I tell you and keep me in the loop."

Dillal stretched one side of his mouth upward in something not really a smile. "I promise to be a good little patient, Doctor."

"Liar. If you were the type to do as you're told, you'd never have ended up here. Just don't be stupid about it." She flapped a hand at him in dismissal. "Get the hell out of my lab and take proper care of my work. Or I'll perform the deintegration while you're still alive."

He got up from the edge of the exam table, looking a little pale even under his patchwork spray skin.

"You should get some sleep, too," the doctor added. "That goes with the 'taking care of my work' part of that directive."

"I have sixteen dead human beings to examine."

"Take my word for it, Inspector, the dead don't mind if you cop a nap first."

"But *I* will."

"Get one of the med/legal people to do the postmortems for you."

"They aren't always discreet. As you know . . ."

"Oh, the famous evidentiary procedure scandal. Yeah, I see your problem. Good luck with it." She turned away.

He started out the door with a scowl.

"I'll come by later and oversee those autopsies, if you like," the doctor added, not looking back at him.

Dillal turned around, grinding his teeth a moment before he said, "I would be very grateful if you did."

"Fine. Now get out of here before I decide I need to recalibrate your sense of humility."

He almost smiled. "Good night, Doctor."

"Good night, Inspector."

He ate and slept at home—but only for a few hours before bathing, and dressing in fresh clothes that fit no better than what he'd taken off.

The SO on duty at the GISA headquarters' front desk called out as he passed. "Hey, you! You need to check in."

Dillal wheeled around and marched back. He stared into the SO's face and watched the man blanch and shiver. With exaggerated precision, he turned back his cuff and put his hand down on the desktop, palm up so the ID crystals in his wrist gleamed under the lights.

"Chief Investigating Forensic Ofiçe, Inspector J. P. Dillal."

The SO blinked and stammered. "Umm . . . I-I didn't recognize you." Dillal quirked his right eyebrow. "Sir."

"I assume you will in future. I'm hard to forget."

"Sir," the ofiçe said, scribbling something on a piece of flimsy and handing it over. "Your office isn't quite finished . . ."

Dillal took the small sheet, barely glancing at it, and said, "I'll be in the morgue for a few hours. Let us hope my office is at least usable by then, and no longer a storage closet."

The SO continued to stare, but he nodded and sketched a distracted salute. "Sir. Yes, sir."

"Thank you." Dillal turned and continued down the hallways to the Forensic Technology wing.

The lab and morgue were still busy when he entered. A few of the med/legal techs bustled around, finishing up day schedule chores, setting up overnight analysis jobs, and clearing up their paperwork. Two of the techs looked up as he entered, and stopped what they were doing. Their stillness spread like crystal growth across a petri dish until all human activity had become nothing but silent gaping in his direction.

Dillal held his position just inside the doorway. "Good evening," he said, quietly. "Please forgive my disrupting you. Where are the Paz da Sorte victims?"

For a moment no one stirred, then one of the techs stepped forward, winding through the rest from the back of the room. He was drug-addict thin, with chestnut skin, bleached-white hair, and a resigned demeanor. His motion seemed to release each person he passed from their stupor, so they turned back to their work with a shiver or a blush, and quickly averted eyes. The tech stopped in front of Dillal, looking nervous, his eyes a little too wide and his fists thrust into his lab coat pockets deep enough to pull the material taut over his knobby knuckles. "They've been prepped for autopsy. I can show you."

"Your name?" Dillal asked.

"Jem Starna."

"Do you know who I am?"

"I do, sir. We all do. We've been . . . expecting a CIFO for almost a year." He made it a word: "Sifo."

"Where is the department chief?" Dillal asked.

"Oh. I thought you'd know. Dr. Harcourt . . . umm . . . retired a while ago. I've been—that is, Dr. Woskyat coordinates the place most of the time and I kind of pick up the slack when she's not in. But . . . uh . . . I guess, it's pretty much on you, until there's an official change."

Dillal nodded. "Show me the bodies, please, Starna."

Starna sucked in a breath as if Dillal had poked him with a sharpened probe. "Oh. Yes, sir. Back here." He pivoted around on one heel, wobbling a bit, and started toward the rear of the lab. He peeked over his shoulder as if making sure Dillal was really there.

He was.

"You've been here before, haven't you? I mean . . . before. When you were . . . umm . . . what your rank was . . ."

"IAD—Investigation: Assistant Detive."

"Oh. Quite a jump from IAD to Inspector."

"So I'm told."

Dillal's quiet tone hadn't changed, but Starna clammed up as if he'd been chastised, and led the rest of the way to autopsy prep without another word, his bony shoulders slightly hunched.

The prep room was empty of the living, but fully occupied by the dead. In addition to the victims of the Paz da Sorte murders, there were a few more prosaic med/legal deaths: suicides and accidents that needed looking into, and so long as someone was paying, GISA would look.

Starna led Dillal to a section of the room that had been separated from the rest by a set of long work tables. Sixteen covered gurneys were lined up inside the cordon in two columns of eight, head-to-head with a walkway between, like ancient tombstones. "We have them prepped and laid out, but no one was sure if you would do the post yourself or not, so . . . they haven't been touched otherwise. Their effects are in the cabinets on the far wall." He took a sheet of flimsy off the nearest work table. "Let me give you the temporary passcode."

The inspector nodded at the proffered information, and then gazed at Starna with the slightest tightening of his eyelid. The mechanism in his left eye clicked twice. "Thank you. I'd like to look them over before proceeding any further, but I can do so on my own. No need for anyone to stay and assist me."

Starna bit his lip and stared down at the inspector's hands. He nodded, then turned and walked a little stiffly out to the main lab. This time he didn't look back.

Dillal removed his jacket and folded it over the end of one of the empty tables. Then he returned his attention to the corpses, moving slowly toward them. He put his hands out to each side, just far enough to brush his fingers over the ends of their resting places. His finger-nails raised a low hiss from the steel surfaces. As he passed each pair of bodies, the information monitors over them lit.

By the time he'd walked to the end of the row, the rest of the morgue was empty and the only light came from the dust-choked windows and the glowing displays that shone down from above. He sat at one of the computer terminals and composed a message, then turned on voice recognition before he returned to the dead.

Dillal lifted each covering and studied the bodies, read and annotated every file: who they were, where they'd lived, where and exactly how they'd fallen on the blood-soaked floors of the jasso. He stood for a long while looking down at the only victim who'd fallen face-up. He closed his eyes tight for a moment before covering the boy, and going to the middle of the rows of bodies.

He stood there, turning back and forth, staring at the monitors above Robesh and Leran—the couple from the back of the gaming room. He went to them in turn, examined their hands closely, dictated further notes of wounds, bruises, and broken fingernails, responded to messages, took additional samples, again and again, until it seemed he could think of nothing more to do.

Then he put the dead to rights, washed up, and attended to Andreus's medication instructions.

One final look, then he grabbed his jacket and left the room in darkness.

Just a few steps down the corridor he found a door with his name beside it. The plaque was crooked and shabbily made, but he touched it and the lopsided wreck of a smile crept onto half of his face.

He waved his wrist over the scanner; the door gave a reluctant click and opened by a grudging half-centimeter. The lights came up automatically as he walked into the room—stark, but shadowed at the corners—and he slapped the wall unit to turn them off again, letting the light of street lamps and OLED signs from the road outside provide moody illumination through a wide window high in the wall. He closed the door and went to the long desk that ran under the window, haphazardly stacked with equipment. He tapped the computer terminal awake, and entered commands modifying the presets for the lights, the security system, and his access to the network. Then he stood in the flicker of descending darkness, assembling diagrams of the crime scene as one monitor after another lit with fast-multiplying information, images, files, messages . . .

CHAPTER SEVEN

Day 1: Evening

Matheson didn't remember passing out. After tripping at Public Health, his brain had stopped logging anything. When he got home he still couldn't fill in the hours he'd lost. He remembered leaving the skimmer . . .

And now he couldn't find his blasted mobile. "Damn it!" he muttered, scrambling through his discarded clothes and equipment. The flat was only one room, with the shower and toilet behind the free-standing "wet wall," so there wasn't much to search. The Peerless was one of the few—no, the *only*—truly nice thing he'd still owned, and he didn't own much, now. *It's probably wiped clean and making its way to a shop on the shadier side of Angra Dastrelas to go home in some tourist's pocket.* Panic stabbed him. The Peerless was supposed to be nearly un-hackable, but he'd still be in as bad a state as some of the people he'd rousted out of doorways if GISA files were leaked from his device, company promise or no. "Merry hell."

Still tired and muzzy-headed, he leaned with slumped shoulders into the ledge of his home net console and logged in, intending to beg Equipment for a replacement he could afford, and report his own as lost. On the top of his queue was a priority-flagged message from Dillal—or rather from "CIFO, Insp J. P. Dillal"—with the subject "PIRep & PMDD." *I could pretend I haven't seen it . . . but he probably knows I have.* He grumbled and jabbed the message.

"I have your mobile. Please come to my office to retrieve it. We will discuss the Preliminary Investigation Report when you arrive."

Matheson typed, "Just returned from health center. When should I report?"

A reply appeared in seconds. "Now."

He stared at the display, trying to think how to respond. He didn't exactly live next door to GISA HQ and "now" seemed a bit . . . peremptory.

Another message appeared in a few minutes. "Correction: within the hour. Attend to personal business first."

Matheson wasn't sure exactly what Dillal meant by "personal business," but he decided it included a shower, a clean uniform, and food. He put on his full kit, including baton, shock box, and the jacket he rarely wore on rounds, and headed out.

Both the humidity and the temperature had dropped for once, now that the sun was beyond the western horizon. The conditions were still less comfortable than he—raised in environmentally controlled rooms—liked, but he'd have to get used to it.

He reached the mutant growth of the GISA building—*it always looks like some kind of cancer overrunning an ancient church*—slightly itchy, and unsatisfactorily fed on noodles purchased from a street vendor and slurped down while standing at the stall. Dillal's message hadn't given a room number and the post of CIFO hadn't, practically speaking, existed before he'd pulled the inspector out of the hospital, so he went in past the main desk.

The SO on Information duty scowled at his question, and wrote on a slip of flimsy. "Everyone's looking for that room today."

Matheson raised his eyebrows. "Really?"

"Yeah. Saw the man himself a few hours ago." The ofiçe shook his head with a look of revulsion. "Not what I was expecting."

What does that mean? Matheson cocked his head with a frown.

The desk man made a face and gestured to his own eye. "You know . . ." Then he looked again at Matheson's ID, his expression going sour. "Oh. Yeah, of course you know." He snorted. "And by the way, you're off patch duty, or you'd have been late for briefing. Lucky you."

"Off? Where and when am I supposed to report? What am I supposed to do?"

The man only pushed the slip of flimsy across the desk with one finger as if Matheson carried a contagious disease.

"Oh," Matheson said. He wasn't sure what the desk man's problem with him was, but he surely had one, judging by the slight sneer he now wore. "Yeah," he added absently, taking the note. He turned away without saying more. The exchange irritated him, and he wondered if it was just his conscience pricking him for being put off, himself, by Dillal's appearance. *It's disturbing if I think about it. Am I trying* not *to think about it . . . ? Like pretending that the Dreihleat isn't a ghetto or that out-system tourists couldn't get away with murder around here?*

The last thought was still buzzing in his head when he reached the inspector's office. He stopped outside the door and stared at the small name plate on the wall beside it, right below the security panel. It wasn't engraved, or even object printed, only flat-printed like a temporary tag for a conference room: "Inspector J. P. Dillal, Chief Investigating Forensic Ofiçe."

Matheson looked around. The corridor was deserted at this time of day, but it certainly wasn't officer country. It was ForTech, just off the hallway that connected Security Office and Investigation Office. It made sense to put the man who linked investigation with forensics in the Forensic Technology wing, yet it struck him as a slight. The air near the labs and morgue seemed tainted and everyone walked a little faster to get past it. Even for a rush job, the sign beside the inspector's door was halfhearted.

Matheson sighed and touched the security panel, offering his ID. For a moment, the scanner did nothing—*is it broken?*—but then it flashed a green light and the door lock clicked. "Come in," said Dillal's voice from the tiny speaker.

Matheson pushed the door open and walked through.

Sign- and street light poured through the window into the otherwise unlit room, leaving dancing colors on the walls—reminders that Angra Dastrelas operated all day and night, spinning dreams and crushing lives. Matheson shook himself, trying to shrug off sudden bitterness. Dillal watched him from in front of the work table that ran the width of the wall under the window. The shifting illumination sparked the stubble of his hair and left colored trails along the edges of the incisions and the uncanny shape of machinery melded to his skull. The prosthetic eye gleamed red in the shadow of his face. Matheson shuddered.

Dillal held Matheson's mobile up against the light. The colored light limned the edges and made the rest a black blank. "It fell from your pocket loops at Public Health."

Matheson drew closer through the gloomy office and took the MDD, relieved to have it back. "Thanks for picking it up."

"How do you feel?" the inspector asked.

"Fine, sir," Matheson replied, trying to push aside the new disquiet that gnawed at him in Dillal's presence. He'd been too tired to remember exactly how strange the inspector was, but this was something different . . .

"I doubt that, but it's good of you to lie." The inspector's voice held a slight edge.

"I was told I'm off patch duty. Is that true?"

"Yes. I requested it. You were there when I did so."

"Was I? I seem to be having trouble . . . What exactly am I doing now, if I'm not a Security Ofiçe pounding a patch with the rest?"

"You work for me. Until this is over, at least. But you're wasting time. Don't you have better questions to ask?"

Matheson had one, though it probably wasn't much better. "Sir, could a tourist have murdered those people at the Paz da Sorte?"

"A system-hopper?" Dillal clarified.

"Yes."

Dillal looked at him without speaking for a moment. "Why would you consider the possibility?" His voice was still cool, but less sharp, and it relieved a little of the room's candy-colored surreality.

"I . . ." Matheson hesitated. *No, it's a stupid idea.*

The inspector tilted his head slightly and the right side of his face frowned. "Be blunt."

Matheson took a deep breath first. *What the hell.* "This city— Angra Dastrelas—is known as the place you can get anything, be anything, do anything, if you know the right people or have enough money. Maybe someone decided to see if they really could get away with murder."

Dillal nodded. "That's good. Wrong, but a step in the right direction."

"What? Why?"

"You're thinking beyond what's been shown to you. That's good. To the rest: Your hypothesis doesn't account for the chilling effect of a capital murder charge, or the rest of the facts already in hand. What connection would an out-system visitor have had to the victims that would account for the break in the pattern of the crime?"

The break—? Oh, the unbound couple. Matheson frowned as he thought it over.

Dillal continued. "Most of the victims were local business people and they had all been robbed. The Dreihleat operates on cash and blind e-transfers only, and Spring Moon is particularly lucrative. So, the victims would have arrived with heavy pockets, knowing they would be welcomed after hours, to mingle and relax with their own kind. But none of that is relevant to a thrill-killer. While the money might be attractive, the rest is too messy for an opportunistic thief, and too much trouble for a system-hopper with a mind to murder. There's also the element of community knowledge, which a tourist wouldn't have. So, it's far more likely that the criminals were also local Dreihleen. They would know who would be at Paz that night and that they would carry their day's receipts with them—because no Dreihle trusts a Corporation bank. Like their victims, they would have access to the club after hours, giving them the ability to enter quietly and wait for an opportune time to bind and rob the other patrons, exactly as they did. Do you concur?"

Matheson thought it over. "I don't know the Dreihleen like you do, but that sounds right."

"Good. I also believe at least one of the gang is among the dead."

"Why?"

"It's the only thing that makes sense of how the crime played out." Matheson stared at him.

Dillal made a noise in his throat that could have been a cough or a chuckle. "Consider what you already know—the evidence we've collected, the sequence of events so far as we know them, timing, the victims themselves—and build from there. Imagine what happened. *How* it must have happened. Put yourself in the room."

Matheson tried, but he could only see the blood-spattered jasso and the bodies. "I can't. They're Dreihleen and I'm a . . . an out-system stranger with less than a month on the ground here. How can I imagine otherwise?" He shivered.

"It's part of this job—to recognize and fill the voids, putting the pieces you have together to discover the shape of those you don't."

Matheson peered at him. He'd been trained as a street cop, not an investigator—certainly not one working for a planet-owning corporation—and he wasn't sure how to do what the inspector was asking.

Dillal snorted impatiently and motioned to an adjustable stool Matheson hadn't noticed just beyond the window's illumination. "Take off your uniform coat—discard SO Matheson. Discard Santos's 'this is the way it is,' and the narrow, physical rote of the Academy. This is not *chasing* a criminal—this is trapping him by the application of your mind, what you know, and what you infer."

Self-conscious, Matheson shrugged out of his already-limp jacket and draped it on the back of the stool.

Dillal darted forward, snatched the jacket, and threw it on the floor between them. Matheson stared in surprise and started to bend down to pick it up.

"Leave it," Dillal barked. "Leave that man—the SO—on the floor, and come with me."

Matheson blinked dumbly at the inspector. Was he still asleep? Because he couldn't imagine any other way this could be happening.

Dillal took him to the morgue. He turned on the lights and Matheson was grateful. The thought of stumbling into one of the bodies and destroying evidence, or putting his unguarded hand into a gaping chest cavity or an open skull unnerved him. He shuddered. It hadn't occurred to him at the crime scene, where everything had been chaos and he'd been too tired to do anything but what he was told. Here, he needed light.

The inspector led him though the bodies, neatly laid out and awaiting attention in their chilly beds. Dillal touched each ID tag and read the name aloud as he progressed, his rolling tone more Dreihleen than Central, "Anza, Tchin, Shimtan, Coupa, Initol, Initol, Leran, Tchillanin"—He pronounced the name "T'chil-HA-nin" with an aspirated hacking in the back of his throat on the H-sound—"Nole, Tonitol, Eshprito, Cheshe, Zashto, Anza, Dohan, Robesh. These are our dead."

Matheson frowned, taking it in. Dillal noticed and tilted his head the slightest bit as Matheson spoke. "Two Anzas, two Initols . . . Are they related or do they just have common names?"

Dillal gave a flickering smile. "They are related. Hanzo Initol owned the Paz da Sorte. Inela Initol was his wife—she kept his books and managed the bar, where she was found. Loni Tonitol was a cousin of Hanzo's—you noticed the similar name, I think—he was probably on duty as the bouncer since he was a large man and business tends to be a family thing in the Dreihleat. He was also found in the bar. Tina Anza owned the restaurant and bakery in front of the Paz da Sorte on the main road. The food spilled on the barroom floor came from his kitchen. During times when jassos were less tolerated by the law, the restaurant was its cover and there was a door from the kitchen that opened on stairs down to Paz, rather than using the current door on the alley. The staircase door was covered over years ago."

"How would you—? Oh, the Dreihleat was your patch."

Dillal gave a minute nod.

"What about the other Anza? Husband?"

"Tina was male. A widower. Stocha Anza was his son—fifteen years old. The youngest victim. Also found in the bar room, next to the oldest victim, Mahale Eshprito. He was seventy-two."

Matheson cringed at Dillal's curiously flat recitation. "Why more men than women? In a club, shouldn't there have been more female customers?"

"In another jasso, certainly. But this was after hours for the local business owners, and the majority of them are male. Businesses involve the whole family in the Dreihleat, but it's rare that the women own them outright and alone, even when widowed."

"Why?"

"Family, usually, but between clan and kind, Dreihleen society can be cruelly labyrinthine. For now, concentrate on the crime before us. We have established they were all killed between 0130 and 0230. But by your report, you were there by 0232 and didn't trip over their murderers in the doorway. What time did Santos split from you?"

"Didn't you ask him at the health center?"

"I'm asking you." Dillal sounded calm, but Matheson detected a stiffening of his shoulders under his suit jacket—it was a paler color than the one he'd worn from the hospital, but it still hung like he'd lost ten kilos.

Matheson had to check his log, though he knew it would have been recorded on the routine hourly upload, which Dillal could have accessed through the GISA network. "0211."

"Only twenty-one minutes. How long would it take to walk from where you two parted ways to the doors of the Paz da Sorte at your— no, at Santos's normal pace?"

"Six to eight minutes, depending on weather. If the sidewalks are slick with that sap the goldwood trees drop—like they were my first two days here—it takes longer."

Dillal seemed irritated by his answer. "The goldwoods aren't in high sap now so . . . eight minutes or so? After all, Santos isn't in excellent physical condition for sprinting soundless as a spider."

Is that from a poem? Matheson didn't know the source—if it *was* a poem at all. He pushed the distraction aside.

"Let's assume, then," Dillal continued, looking at the bodies arrayed around them, his posture still a little stiff, "that Santos didn't walk any faster than usual. In fact, given his reported injury, he probably walked slower, pausing and looking back to ensure you weren't following him."

"Are you accusing my TO of murder now?"

Dillal raised his head and pivoted to face Matheson, pressing his balled fists down on the autopsy table between them. That only half his face wore any expression at all did nothing to soften the disturbing effect of his ire and his words stung all the more. "Not your training officer, not your partner. Not any longer. You are seconded to me. Your former routine is no more. You are my hound—faithful, dogged, silent until you find scent worth pursuing. I entrusted the future of this investigation to you by attaching you in the field and I expect you to meet that measure. To discard your sheltered naivety, your disillusionment, and your high-minded assumptions. Do you understand?"

Matheson was taken aback and found himself pressing against a counter behind him without realizing he'd moved. "Sir."

Dillal softened his tone a little. "You must abandon everything but the job, and proceed with me. This is your future with GISA and you must exceed their expectations or we both fail. *Do* you understand?"

Matheson had to catch his breath and swallow before he could reply. "Yes, sir. I do understand."

The inspector stared at him for a long moment, then made a soft huffing sound, the tension in his shoulders falling away. "Not quite. You're angry with me and suspicious. You have a right—I shouldn't have led you into this when you had no idea what the situation truly was. But you are not yet corrupted by this system and this is not just a murder case—this is a trial. I need the best, the least biased, the most willing assistant I can get on my side. Or there is no chance of this case being solved."

"You could have just said so!" Matheson scowled at Dillal. The man might be out of his mind, but he cared about the case—which was more than anyone else seemed to.

The inspector waited a while, then sighed and threw up his hands. "I was wrong to co-opt you without explanation. I apologize. Does that satisfy you?"

"Not really," Matheson replied, then he looked aside. "But it'll do. I didn't exactly get what I wanted here and I'd be stupid to pass up this opportunity."

"No one gets what they want, here. And my point was not to accuse Santos of murder—the timing does not allow it."

Matheson looked back at Dillal, whose head was turned sideways so only his natural eye was exposed. All trace of his volatile temper was gone and he seemed uneasy. "Do we proceed?" the inspector asked.

Matheson took a deep breath, smelling the cool air and chemicals of the morgue, and braced himself. *He's a few steps sideways of normal, but . . .* "Yeah. We do. I guess I'm your dog."

CHAPTER EIGHT

Day 1: Night

Dillal nodded, and when he spoke again, his voice was much quieter, and slower. "Then, having eliminated Santos's direct involvement, let us start with who died first." He glanced at the nearest body and folded the sheet down only low enough to reveal a young woman's head—Venn Robesh—her golden-rose face sickeningly misshapen and burned a dark, blood-streaked brown on one side. One hazel eye was completely missing as if it had been forced out of her skull while the other stared. Her long black hair had been unpinned and laid in a careful coil beside the head block.

Matheson wanted to turn away from the horror of it, but he couldn't. *I've seen her somewhere . . . before the jasso, before . . . this.* It haunted the corners of his brain with the same disquiet that he felt walking almost anywhere in Angra Dastrelas.

Dillal stared at the mutilated woman, half his face turning downward in a scowl. Matheson could hear the mechanical clicking of the inspector's artificial eye. "Can you bring up the scene schematic and reference stills of the Paz da Sorte rooms? They're in the file."

Matheson finally tore his gaze from Robesh—*Mother of stars. She's just a girl, no more than a teenager!*—and used his mobile to locate the file in GISA's database. He directed it to the large central monitor above the empty dissection table.

"Well done," Dillal said, looking up at the screen as the thumbnails unfolded.

Matheson wished he felt smug about it, but he couldn't wipe out his anger, or the horror and frustration that swept him when he looked at the dead. He centered the schematic of the murder scene with the appropriate sets of stills linked to various hot spots in the picture and the information bar situated on the left. He tapped on the name "Venn Robesh."

"Not yet," Dillal said. "Just study the schematic for a moment. Then tell me how this crime proceeded. As you see it."

Matheson looked at the bird's eye view of the crime scene. Three rectangles: a wide, but shallow one for the entry; then a larger, nearly square one representing the bar; and, at a right angle, another almost three times as large representing the gaming room with a long, narrow box showing the position of a single step down from the bar. A small row of blocks represented the washrooms and office on the far side of the bar and vestibule, but they contained no markers—nothing of value collected. There were twelve body icons in the game room; only four in the smaller bar room; none in the tiny foyer. Ten of the markers in the game room made a fat, curving line down the middle of the long axis between the gaming tables, each shape lying mostly under the next like fanned playing cards, while the remaining two were separated, crisscrossed near a gaming table closer to the back of the room and the plastered-over door Dillal had mentioned. The four icons in the bar room were untidy, without any apparent pattern.

Matheson glanced at Dillal. "You already have an answer and just want to watch me jump the course," he said.

"Yes."

Matheson couldn't refuse. "All right . . ." He stared at the schematic a moment. "Presuming that the couple—Robesh and Leran—are the first victims—"

"Why do you presume that?"

What? Matheson stared at the inspector in confusion. "Because you—"

"No." The correction came gently this time. "Not because I say so, or because I show you a body, but because the facts and your own observation tell you it's true. Go on."

Matheson looked back to the monitor, taking a few breaths to clear his mind—and his irritation. "'Explain the anomaly and explain the crime.' All right. All the victims are bound except Robesh and Leran. If they weren't part of the gang, they would have run when the shooting started, but their positions and the defensive wounds suggest that they were . . . talking, or arguing with each other. Or . . ." He turned to Dillal as a detail edged into the front of his mind. "She had a broken fingernail. That's odd for a woman who was so well-dressed. Is there debris under her remaining nails?"

Dillal nodded and turned the edge of the sheet up to reveal the woman's right hand, not exposing more of the naked body than was necessary. He lifted the hand carefully—the death-stiff joints resisted a little. "She had Leran's tissue under her fingernails," Dillal affirmed. "She may have broken the one fingernail off in his cheek or jaw."

"You found it in his skin?" Excitement sparked in Matheson's chest, smothered by instant guilt.

"No," the inspector said, and walked a short distance down the double column of corpses to fold back the sheet covering Leran's head. Matheson recoiled at the sight. He'd seen it before, but the damage seemed obscene in the bright lights of the morgue: the head distorted by the passage of a bullet that had exited through the bottom of the man's face, leaving a mangled red void where the mouth and jaw should have been.

"Denenshe Leran," Dillal said. "Called 'Denny.' Petty criminal— the usual sort of stupid crimes that stupid boys get caught up in."

This time Matheson didn't have to bring up the files; the information bloomed onto the screen, apparently at the inspector's whim. "I haven't found that part of his face," the inspector continued. "I may not. Although I suppose there's a possibility we'll discover it among the other scene evidence, if centipedes didn't devour it." As if it were detritus dropped carelessly on the floor. Matheson winced at the thought. *People as bodies become objects, parts of objects scattered like bits of broken machinery in floods of fuel and lubricants, not limbs, faces, blood . . .*

Matheson's stomach turned uncomfortably and he covered his mouth a moment, thinking of the way Robesh's face was ruined by the heat of a pen torch. "If he were part of the gang . . ." He raised his eyes to read the monitor rather than look at Leran's face. He hadn't been as pretty as Venn Robesh and the clean tidiness of the room only made their wounds more horrific.

Matheson read, "Petty theft, misappropriation of skimmers, second-degree assault, fraud, a couple of gambling charges, some public misconduct—what does that actually mean around here, anyway?"

"Could be park-bench rabble-rousing, roaming outside the Dreihleat during a curfew lock-down, but more likely it's being a bad sport about losing bets, or aggressively soliciting street games."

"So Leran was a street punk and a con-artist with a sideline in putting the arm on tourists for short cash . . ."

Dillal nodded. "That was my assessment."

"If Robesh knew him or she just didn't want to be touched . . . Merry hell . . . He knew her. *He* killed her."

"Why do you think so?"

"She wouldn't pick a fight with a stranger if she thought she was going to die for it. All the other victims are so neatly tied up it's like they went along with it. But Robesh didn't. She fought. She fought with this man well away from the rest." Matheson glanced at her destroyed face and away again. "That's a contact burn. He put the pen torch against her temple and—" He squeezed his eyes closed, trying not to imagine how the heat of the plasma would have flash-boiled the fluids in the girl's skull that then rushed to exit through any opening or weakness—the entry wound, the eye socket . . . He took a shaking breath and forced his gaze back to the schematic—*just diagrams, just information, not people.* "But why kill them all?"

"You have the answer." Dillal said.

"I don't know—wait!" He pointed at the inspector. "You said it. You said these people were businessmen and they came to the club with their money in their pockets. So this was a robbery. But why didn't someone else raise a fuss about being robbed?"

"It's easier to bow the head. The Dreihleen—and the Ohba also—feel that they, as a people, stand alone, surrounded by enemies, oppressed, discriminated against, and disenfranchised without legal cause. Even the honest work they can get outside the ghettos is limited and poorly paid—unless they choose prostitution. They dislike and distrust GISA and wouldn't have reported such a crime to you—not even to Santos unless it was unavoidable. Other Dreihleen would understand that. These people did not expect to die. They only expected to pay the robbers and then exact justice their own way, later. It's one of the reasons the trade societies, the clans, exist. They aren't simply gangs, but cooperatives that protect the businesses and people of the Dreihleat. As GISA does not."

Matheson closed his eyes. "Would the Dreihleen have concealed this? The murders." *How many of the people I walked past every day might be clandestine killers, or culpable?*

"No," Dillal said. "A single killing, especially the result of a clan's determination of justice, might be concealed or obfuscated. But not this. This is beyond the Dreihleen's tolerance. And that is why these sixteen are all dead."

Matheson blinked at the inspector. "I don't understand . . ."

"Think, Matheson. If Leran is part of the gang, it makes perfect sense. They are collecting victims, they know your rounds, they mean to get out before you and Santos return, but Robesh fights and Leran kills her. Perhaps an accident, perhaps not, but then a bullet—an old military-issue projectile from an old style of gun—enters his head at the rear of the right parietal bone—"

Images appeared on the monitors above the bodies, conjured somehow by Dillal, and coming faster and faster as his speech sped up. Matheson looked back and forth, almost unable to keep up.

"It comes from above him and angles down and left, from a distance, as if he were shot by someone much taller, or someone standing in the archway between the bar room and the gambling floor—on the step between them. None of the victims have gunshot residue on their hands—Leran has some compound I haven't identified yet, but it's not propellant, and he was killed with the same gun as some of the bound victims. It's not self-defense and the shot that killed Leran was not an accident. The robbers became murderers and all the witnesses had to die or the Dreihleat would turn on them. Every friend would become an enemy, every stranger a possible assassin. They had to run before you and Santos returned. They had to kill them all and run!"

"But we didn't hear anything or encounter anyone!"

The flow of images stopped and Dillal replied with his usual reserve. "You were chasing a pickpocket and the thing was quickly done—look at how neatly the dead lie in the gaming room. As if they had no time to panic."

"But not those in the bar! They must have been killed in a hurry as the gang left."

Dillal nodded with the small lift of one side of his mouth that

Matheson mentally tagged "approval." He was almost embarrassed at feeling pleased. He shook his head at himself in disgust.

Dillal saw it. "Why are you displeased with your conclusion?"

"Not the conclusion that bugs me, it's—" Matheson shook his head again and glanced back up at the monitor displaying Robesh's information, watching the images of her face as it had once been. Memory struck him and linked to a dozen connections like flash fire. He felt dizzy and grabbed the edge of the nearest table to steady himself. "Oh. Blackness and burn . . . She's the Julian girl."

"The what?"

"I knew she seemed familiar! Merry hell, this can't be . . ."

"Explain," Dillal said.

Matheson glanced at him, then strode back to the lockers of personal items. "Which one is hers?"

"Third from the end, second row. What are you looking for?" Dillal added, crossing to him.

"The clothes! The shoes!" Matheson dug into the locker and took out the sealed bag of Venn Robesh's effects. He started looking for gloves or spray seal and Dillal handed him a can of the sealant from a drawer nearby.

Matheson covered his hands and wrists and opened the bag. He pulled out the dress—once a shimmering white shading to pearl gray, the shoulders and front were now drenched in blood and brain matter. He dug out the shoes and put them on the nearest work table with care, flattening the dress beside them with gentle hands. "The Julian Company—it's a . . . well, they run very high-end resorts, and also own lines of luxury cosmetics, jewelry, and clothing. This girl—Venn—I couldn't cross the jumpway-to-orbital transfer station or the space port without seeing her face on commercial banners and float ads all over the place. I should have recognized her earlier but the damage to her face . . ." The truth was that he'd tried not to notice or think about the presence of the company that was named for his great grandfather.

Dillal gave a grunt of agreement and drew closer to study the dress. "It's Regausa silk."

"I know. This dress must be a sample or a costume kind of thing. It's got the logo all over it—see this sort of . . . frond of gemstones at the shoulder?"

"Trench diamonds. They're Gattian—as is the silk—but no Dreihle girl could afford such a dress," Dillal said.

Matheson nodded. Beyond the unsettling presence of his family's financial interests, there was, more immediately, the girl herself: Robesh's outfit was the sort of thing that sold for staggering prices in exclusive boutiques next to the swank casinos on Cove Quay, produced in sweatshops in places like the Dreihleat and Ohbata a few at a time with painstaking skill for low pay. Robesh didn't have the hands of a seamstress. Even with broken nails, they were elegant and soft. However she'd risen to this, it hadn't been by manual labor. "All right," he said. "But the shape—that's an abstraction of the Julian logo. It's repeated on the skirt. And on the shoes. She was a sort of walking advertisement."

"But she wasn't in the Dreihleat to attract customers for the Julian Company. So why was she in Paz and with whom?"

"Leran?"

Dillal shook his head, wearing half a frown. "No. That doesn't fit. But Gil Dohan might. He owned Dohan Sewing."

"It's in the Dreihleat? I've never heard of it."

"Not on your patch. It's on the eastern side."

"If Venn Robesh was related to Dohan or works for him—"

"She's not related, except as all Dreihleen are in community. She may work for him, but Dreihleat businesses pay their Dreihleen workers under the table, so there's no record for us to connect. We would have to confirm her connection to Dohan ourselves, as well as confirming or eliminating a connection between Dohan and the Julian Company." Dillal gave Matheson a thoughtful look. "What do you know about them?"

"Julian? They're well-positioned—wherever there's something that draws the rich, you'll find the Julian Company busily pandering to them. I'd presume that's why they're developing a presence here. But since you didn't know about them, it must be recent." Matheson closed his eyes, shunted his personal feelings aside, and thought aloud, "The ad campaign must be a market-opener—a wedge. That's their usual strategy in a new market."

"This is family business."

Matheson flicked his eyes open, startled, then turned his gaze aside in discomfort. "Yes."

"I understand," said Dillal. "Why did Robesh stand out to you?"

"She was . . . exotic." His face burned until he expected to combust. "I thought she wasn't real, just a simulation, because she was flawless. Luminous. Like she was polished."

"Flawless," Dillal repeated, as if making note of the term. "Was her picture shown outside Gattis Jumpway?"

Matheson looked at the inspector. "I'd never seen it anywhere else. It was as if . . . she was Gattis. I admit, it gave me a false impression of what this place would be like."

"The face of Gattis was a seventeen-year-old Dreihle girl with little formal education or opportunity . . . What a loss. We'll have to discover how Leran and our Julian Girl knew each other."

"Why?"

"Because if we know that, we may know why Leran killed her, and from there the rest of this knot may unravel. But it will be bloody.

Homicide—even an accidental one—that occurs during the course of a robbery—"

Matheson knew the law. "It's first degree homicide and everyone willingly involved before or after is held equally guilty. They were already double-murderers. Fourteen more wouldn't make their burden in law any worse."

"Not most places. Here, it carries a mandatory death penalty. Aggravated murder. That is why, Matheson, no tourist would have been involved. Yes, one might get away with murder here, but not mass slaughter. Because we would hunt him, as we will hound these men, to the bitter end."

Matheson looked at the floor, then up at the monitors sparkling with the ever-rotating images of the dead as they had been, and as they were now. They glimmered above him like blood-spattered stars, and deathly silence folded around him until his ears rang with it. Scattered objects no more, but ghosts assembled to haunt him, suddenly joined with faces streaked in gore and mud the color of ripe plums . . .

The unexplained vision shook him. Then it was broken and chased away by the sudden intrusion of Dillal's cold voice.

"We begin tomorrow." Dillal's expression was grim. "I want you to speak with Santos. Irrespective of his injury, he'll be off shift for a few days until we can say he's cleared of any connection."

"Then . . . you didn't talk to him already," Matheson said, shocked to sharpness.

"I didn't say I had."

"You gave me that impression."

"You *took* that impression. I didn't correct it. Matheson, it's not my intention to mislead you, but to make you think more precisely and logically. To be rigorous, not to assume anything. That's why I had you discard your uniform jacket—so you would feel less like an academy man, or like Santos's trainee, thinking the way he wants you to. I need you to think like Eric Matheson, not like Security Ofiçe Matheson. A whole man, not a calculator, nor a recorder." He stepped closer, bringing an odor of disinfectant, mint, and medicine, and started to reach for Matheson, but drew his hand back suddenly, pushing his clenched fist into his own gut. "But I also need you to think here." He jabbed a finger again into his chest. "And here." He reached high and tapped his fingertips against the unshaven side of his head. "Not just here."

Then Dillal stepped back. "You're still an SO, in fact, but you're my IAD in practice, and that requires you to reason without a mental straitjacket. Do you understand?"

Matheson nodded. "I get it. But why send me to talk to Santos? We're not exactly close, and if he was the district bag man, he's not likely to tell me about it."

"That's not what I want you to discuss with him. It's immaterial unless it did bring him into collusion with the gang. All you need to do is find out when he actually entered the jasso and what he saw and did."

"Then you'll take the Dreihleat . . . ?"

"No. You'll have to carry on with that as well. I can't set you to work here—the forensic material is my purview—so the legwork falls to you until I've cleared my immediate end, though we'll both be at a disadvantage. You'll need to collect whatever the general canvass turned up and pursue anything promising. It won't be as simple as walking your rounds—you'll be alone and the SOs on first- and mid-shift won't appreciate your presence on their turf any more than some of the Dreihleen. There is also the matter of the tunnels."

"'The Tomb?' I've heard about it, but I haven't seen it yet."

"Remnants of the terraform. Commonly used by black marketeers and criminals. Don't pursue any leads that point there without me or a Dreihle you can trust with you. There's no communications, no cameras, no help—if you go in alone, you won't come out. The Dreihleat is a difficult place."

Matheson considered the unnerving feel of his first days. "It's better than the Quay."

Dillal raised an eyebrow, but Matheson volunteered no more. The inspector continued, "Orris's report is in the database, but Neme has yet to file her canvass report. Begin there."

Matheson was tired in spite of himself and wanted to go back to bed. He doubted that either of the senior detives was still in, but he trudged down to Investigation Office—"I-Office"—anyway. It lay on the opposite side of the building from Security Office with ForTech crushed between like an uneasy referee under the spire of the admin tower. *Funny how no one upstairs ever complains about ForTech's weird smell . . .*

I-Office was far from deserted. He could hear shouting and a scuffle before he even reached the doorway, and had to move quickly to the side to avoid being tripped or hit by flailing limbs as he passed through. Several rough-looking young men and women—Ohba and mixed—were cuffed to the intake rail. They watched the brawl in the middle of the room and shouted encouragement broken by spitting and insults. One female IO in uniform, Neme, Istvalk, and one more plainclothes struggled to separate two young men: one Dreihle, one Ohba. The Ohba, short, burly and carnelian red from his hair to his bare feet, slipped a blade from his loose shirt and thrust a solid jab at the other guy. Only a sudden backward pull by Neme and the IO saved his taller, slimmer Dreihle opponent from a knife in the gut. Matheson had no time to move before it was over.

Neme let go of the man she'd helped haul away, and spun suddenly into the broken circle of violence, ramming her elbow into the nose of the man with the knife. He reeled back a step, but didn't go down, in spite of the bright blood that burst from his face. He jerked forward, but Istvalk and the other investigator held him back. Neme reached behind her back and drew a smaller version of the standard shock box from her waistband. "Back down, meathead," she said, holding it up.

"*Nor o-sum,*" the Ohba snapped, wrenching his arms against the pull of the men struggling to cuff him. "This one is not being scared of a sandworm bitch protecting caddis flies." He kicked back at his captors and lunged.

The Dreihle behind Neme flinched back, but managed to spit at the Ohba from between his clenched teeth as he did. The heavier man lurched free and dove forward as if he'd go right through Neme to get to his opponent.

Neme swayed aside, slapped the shock box against the Ohba's neck, and pushed the button.

He let out a harsh shout and fell to his knees.

"You dirt-eating moron," she said. "Assault with deadly in a room full of cops? Are you that stupid?" Then she glared past him to the plainclothes who'd lost hold of him. "And you, Sojan. You're a bigger pile of crap than your prisoner."

"He's just another fucking hump!" Sojan yelled back. "How'd I know he was going to go jumpwise?" He was Central brown, taller, and older than Istvalk, but he sounded younger when he whined.

"You brought him, unfettered, into a room with a dreck and you didn't think there'd be a blow up?" Neme shouted back. "I should put you in the box with both of 'em!"

Half the cuffed audience at the rail catcalled and stamped, and she wheeled to glare at them. "Stitch it closed or I'll have you all shocked and locked before you draw another breath!"

One of the young women—dazzle-eyed and twitchy from drugs—strained forward against her confinement and jeered, "The hell you will, y'blue-assed bitch!"

Neme narrowed her eyes and darted across the space between them. She shoved the shock box hard under the offender's chin. "The hell I will," she said, staring into the other woman's face with her teeth bared.

Matheson felt cold when he thought of the woman down and bloodied. He started forward.

But the copper-skinned girl was all bluster. She cowered down into an uncomfortable huddle, her arms attached to the intake rail and her face averted. Neme took a step back and looked at the line of now-quiet detainees. "Who's next? I'm kind of enjoying kicking your punk asses, so go ahead. No . . . ? Fine."

Sojan and the female IO had wrestled the groggy Ohba to his feet and cuffed him while Istvalk took possession of the Dreihle.

Violence seemed to balance on a knife edge in the room as Neme turned back toward the Ohba and his escort. "Get that piece of shit out of my sight, Sojan, and clean up your mess."

"*My* mess? What about Istvalk? It's *his* filthy yellow intake who—"

The Dreihle started to speak and Neme stepped back and slapped him. "Trap up! You and your damned mouth started this." She shot a glance at Istvalk and muttered, "Get him done before I lose my temper."

Then she turned back to the IO and Sojan as she tossed the shock box onto a nearby desk. "I don't give a cat's crap why you didn't process your half-assed gang of *met* warehouse-breakers through S-Office like you should have, or why Istvalk is sitting on our canary-yellow friend like a duck hoping to hatch him. I only care that you're the blighted moron sollet-brained enough to bring trouble on my watch because you never, ever, *ever* bring multiple perps directly into this room without a sit check. Get me? So, finish up and get your flea circus out of here or I'll boot your ass to Belcourso myself."

Sojan's face went crimson. "Fuck you, Neme," he replied, but he still helped the IO drag their prisoner out.

The tension drained from the room as quickly as it had built.

"Yeah, there's a line for that," Neme muttered. She turned away, looking down at the sleeve of her blouse that was splattered with the Ohba's blood. "Crap." It reminded Matheson of Venn Robesh's ruined dress—the pale, pearly gray material was Regausa silk just a few shades lighter than Neme's skin.

Neme stalked back to the desk where she'd tossed the shock box, and threw herself down in a chair. She picked up a white packet and removed a brown cigarette, lit it, and leaned back. A curl of fume rose off the narrow cylinder clutched low between the unadorned ring and middle fingers of her left hand.

Matheson watched her smoke with her eyes closed for a moment before he walked toward her. "Shit," she muttered, and coughed as he drew close.

She twitched her head up as he stopped, and gave him a pinched glare. "Hullo, rook," she said, drawling out the greeting as she turned her chair to face him. "Feeling better?" She drew on her cigarette so the tip glowed cherry red, her mouth hidden behind her cupped hand.

"Yes, sir." He felt nauseated, though he'd never tell her so, and noticed that her hand closed into a loose fist near her cheek as she let the smoke rise up from her mouth like a curtain. It smelled like burning driftwood thick with a harsh tang of blue salts. Salfrin. Not illegal, but not a vice he'd expected from a woman whose family had a seat at Corporation House.

Neme pulled a sour face and raised one dark blue eyebrow. "Social call?"

"No, sir. I'm collecting the prelim and canvass reports on the Paz da Sorte case."

Neme rolled her eyes and pushed her chair back to get room to cross her ankles up on the desk corner. "I already sent that to the CIFO," she said, sneering a bit on Dillal's title.

Matheson didn't challenge the lie. "Yes sir, but I need an official sign-off and your prelim report."

She snorted. "You're wasting my time. It's a cat shit case and if your precious inspector can't pick a couple of goldenrods and tie it off already, what's the fucking point of his existence?"

Matheson bit his lip as she stared at him, leaning back in her chair. "Same as yours, I expect. Sir."

Her smile twisted. "You better watch that mouth of yours, Matheson. Some people around here don't appreciate smart-assery. Unless it's my smart ass they're kissing." She rested her head against the chair back and smoked, looking boneless and limp.

Matheson kept his mouth shut and tried to remember the medical uses for Salfrin while he waited her out. He couldn't imagine that Neme suffered from any debilitating conditions, any more than it seemed likely she was a recovering Wire addict.

"Why should I sign off on these reports?" she asked without moving from her sprawl. "It's a routine bit of dreck violence. No one gives the least crap about this case. Except your whip." She sat up in a flurry of spilling flimsy. "And how is he? Still 'fine, sir'? All hybrid vigor like a mongrel dog."

Matheson didn't reply.

Neme barked a laugh. "What? No response? Hasn't gone and died on us—I can only hope."

"No. Sir."

"Then fuck off."

"No."

"Spine?" she asked. "Oh, no. Wait," she continued, looking around as if the idea had only just occurred to her, though Matheson knew she was ganking him. "Evidentiary procedure. Doesn't matter a whore's damn if I sign off or not unless this pile of cat shit actually comes to trial." She raised her eyebrows. "Does it? So, our mechanical man actually found something. Bugger me—it works!" She rolled her eyes and went back to smoking, pausing a moment to pick a minuscule shred of Salfrin off her lower lip.

Matheson waited. Istvalk had finished with the Dreihle and stood to walk him to holding as Sojan returned with the IO. From the corner of his eye, Matheson could see all three of them watching what was going on between him and Neme. She surely didn't care what they thought, but even she had a superior officer to answer to—Investigation's Chief Superintendent Dominic Belcourso, who wasn't known for his easy-going nature—and Sojan could damage any complaint Neme forwarded if he could say he'd seen her obstruct or damage someone else's investigation.

Neme knew it as well as they did, and the corner of her mouth crooked in a cynical smile. "What in hell are you doing here, anyway, Matheson? Some hopper-brained idea about serving the greater good?" She coughed up a derisive laugh. "That's nothing but ego gas. There is a thin line between cops and criminals, and this end of the law—in fact, any end of the law—is not a noble profession. We are one half of the reciprocating machine that cuts humanity into chunks and spews it out to feed the pigs in their diamond-studded pens." She took one long, final drag and ground out the stub of her smoke on the side of the desk, letting the detritus fall into the trash chute below. Damn her—he'd seen cigarette butts in the Paz da Sorte alley that looked the same and if they didn't have her DNA on the lip ends, he'd eat them.

Matheson cast a significant look over her expensive clothes and back to her face as she peered at him with narrowed eyes. Neme leaned farther into the desk and glared up at him, her jaw working sideways a little. "At least I know what color the shit is on my trotters," she said. "And where it came from." She put her hand up. "Give me your fucking mobile."

Matheson hesitated.

"What? Now you don't want me to sign off?"

"You have a terminal."

She turned her head to regard the terminal with contempt. "That piece of shit? I'd rather use yours. Unless you don't really want my hash . . ."

Matheson took the MDD from his pocket and handed it to her. Neme looked it over. "Peerless. Nice. I had one of these. It's still running in an eel pit somewhere under the Verdan Archipelago." She thumbed the screen on and waited while Matheson unlocked the input and opened the appropriate files.

Neme swiped through to the GISA interface and hashed through the verifications and report upload in short order, without much pause to check that they were the right documents. Then she tossed the mobile back at Matheson with a casual flip of her wrist that made the device arc in a flat spin toward his face. "Keep me in the loop—I want a front row seat."

Matheson caught the mobile clumsily with both hands and slipped it back into the loops on his chest pocket without a comment. He added a perfunctory "Thank you, sir," as he turned away.

Neme made a harsh sound, like a warning bark. "Matheson."

He turned back and found her pointing at him.

"You will keep me informed," she said. "Technically it was my opener, my case. Current protocol says you copy me every file. And if you don't, I will make your job hell."

"Sir. I don't understand why you're interested in keeping tabs on a case you were glad to hand off. One you think is a waste of time and effort."

"Entertainment. And I don't want to have to play catch up when it drops back onto my desk."

"You assume Inspector Dillal will fail."

Neme gave an ironic lift of her eyebrows. "You're a bigger idiot than I thought. Crawl back into your kennel, puppy. The dogs in this yard are too rough for you." When Matheson made no response and didn't leave, she added, "Piss off."

She didn't move until Matheson had started walking away.

CHAPTER NINE

Day 2: Thursday—Morning

Santos hadn't responded to Matheson's messages—all his attempts to talk had been rebuffed so far. It was frustrating. Matheson wanted to get the case moving, but it felt as if he wasn't making any headway at all and the total freeze-out his partner—former partner—was serving him was more than just annoying. The thing that rankled most was the doubt the inspector had planted in his mind about Santos, but it was there now, and it niggled like a loose tooth.

It was the niggling that got Matheson out of bed much earlier than he'd intended, but six hours' sleep would do, and he was awake by 0540. His schedule was upside down after the fainting episode and Matheson was finding the change disorienting, but useful. The Dreihleat woke up early too, and if he couldn't get to Santos, he could at least start on that.

Fog floated off the canal in the Dreihleat, making the ground a mystery, but thinning quickly as it rose. The speakers and agitators hadn't braved the gloom and there were fewer drunks and drug addicts in evidence than he usually saw on his own shift, but the streets were getting busy with people on their way to legitimate jobs or slinking home from shadier ones, shopkeepers opening up, and bands of workmen—both paid and GISA detainees—taking down the viewing stands for the previous day's races, and mounting banners and setting up platforms for the Ice Parade that evening. Automated drones dumped the materials at designated beacons, but the workers did the labor—scut-work, pointlessly corrosive.

One of the detainee workers kicked and swore at a Dreihle child who crept close to investigate his tools. The SO overseeing the group looked bored and did nothing even when the sound of a boot against flesh wrung a sharp yelp from the child.

Matheson turned and started toward the altercation. A Dreihle woman dropped her broom and darted from the stretch of sidewalk she'd been sweeping to drag the child away. But once out of the overseer's sight, the woman slapped the child around the ears and sent it to pick through a drift of trash she had swept into a pile beside an alley mouth. No one else took any notice at all.

He paused at the edge of Yshteppa Park and watched the fish sellers—both men and women—removing baskets from the goldwood saplings. The fish scales clinging on the branches left an odd, oily smell on the air. Supposedly, Ohba gardeners had discovered that the adult trees developed their distinctive glitter by absorbing minerals from the scales. Matheson thought that as unlikely as Santos's contention that half the stink was rotten memories of Yshteppa Dome, which had stood on the spot for fifty years of the terraform, a safe home for the workers, until it had been collapsed for clearance, killing the Dreihleen and Ohba council arguing about settlement rights inside. Another contribution to their eternal spite. "Everybody's gotta have someone to hate," Santos had said.

The fishmongers slung the baskets over their shoulders and walked along the canal toward the docks at Fish Market Basin. They'd carry the best of the catch to the high-end hotels and restaurants, the rest going to whoever got there first. The whole job could have been automated and managed by a handful of human workers, but people were cheaper than machines and required less maintenance in the swampy tropical air. Santos joked that they were easier to recycle too, and Matheson watched the Dreihleen around him, uncomfortable with the sudden memory of the morgue—unwanted people and parts, like lost articles no one seemed to care about. He shivered and walked with the crowd toward the basin, the mist creeping around them.

The database had given a nearby address for Denny Leran's aunt and uncle—his only known residence. Matheson wasn't expecting a lot of luck in that quarter, but he had to start with something, and folks around the fish market didn't sleep late. He went down Rua dos Peixes in the moving fog and a cloud of morning smoke spiced with the skunky redolence of weed and Salfrin that trailed behind the fish-mongers as they muttered a running patois of Dreihleen mulched with Central English. The fog in the shadow of the crater made the crowd into ink-wash splashes at five meters and hid them completely at six; their voices seemed like the whispers of ghosts.

They passed the coffee house Matheson had visited just a day ago, and he saw a pair of first shift SOs—Jora and Halfennig, he thought—walking toward him. They were laughing over something and the larger of the two, Halfennig, elbow-hooked one of the passing crowd and coerced a smoke from the Dreihle, who never met his eyes. *Less than five meters away—they can't help but see me.*

Matheson hesitated, creating an eddy in the stream of people as they flowed around him. Dillal had warned him S-Office might be hostile. Cold crawled up the back of his neck and he had an urge to get out of the way. He turned and headed into an alley, thinking he'd go around the block to come out below the other SOs, and hoping he'd made his move quickly enough.

Someone called out to him and he swore under this breath, "Merry hell." He turned toward the two approaching ofiçes—he didn't like leaving his unprotected back to them. They stepped apart to block the path from the alley back into the street.

"Hey," Halfennig snapped, pinching out the smoke and stowing it in his chest pocket. "What are you doing out here? This isn't your shift."

"Not your patch either," Jora added. He was shorter, darker, and stockier than Halfennig, with a bit of extra weight that amounted to nothing in a fight. From the looks on their faces they figured Matheson's taller, thinner frame just made him more breakable.

"Sure, it's my patch," Matheson replied. "Third shift. With Santos."

"Not any more," Halfennig said. "We all know what happened. We had the morning walk. Santos is on leave and you—what are you on?"

"Seconded over to I-Office," Jora said as if it was on a par with fucking goats.

"It wasn't my request," Matheson replied, raising his hands.

"You should have refused the honor."

"Why?" he asked, and the word was out of his mouth before he realized he shouldn't have said it.

The other two SOs exchanged amused glances before stepping forward together and shouldering him backward. They pushed him against the wall and closed in, blocking escape to either side. He could fight out, but it would hurt—probably fine with them.

Halfennig leaned in, pressing one hand against Matheson's shoulder and pinning him to the blue stone wall. "You don't abandon a partner, rook."

"S-Office stands together," Jora added, emphasizing his points with sharp finger-jabs. "You turfed your TO to the snoops."

"I only told them what happened—it's not a knock on Santos that he went jumpwise."

"You made him look bad. Now you're stepping across to do I-Office's grunt work? You're letting us down, boy."

Matheson tried not to flinch in anticipation of a blow, but he could tell by Halfennig's chuckle that he'd failed. "You're new here, but you're catching on," Halfennig said.

"Get right or you're gonna regret it."

The SOs stepped back and turned away, walking off into the thinning crowd. Matheson leaned back against the wall, breathing slowly while he wrestled his temper. He wouldn't whine to Dillal—what could *he* do?—and complaining to Security Office's Chief Superintendent, Lorca Feresintavi, would just make his position within S-Office worse. He didn't need that. He wasn't going to stay on the bottom rung forever—he'd move up or he'd move out and either way, he knew how to keep his head down while still moving forward. *I made it past Callista; I'll make it past them.*

The distance from the coffee house to Fish Market Basin at the end of the canal wasn't much, but the change in the neighborhood was vast. Tourists didn't visit the Dreihleat fish market unless they were shady or stupid. The stalls were busy during the morning, just a few steps up from the canal, and the reek of fish viscera and fast-moving tropical rot disinclined most people to linger any longer than they had to. After hours the area became the haunt of small-time drug dealers and black marketeers, lurking in the shadows of the stalls they'd tagged as their own or under the canvas of the narrow canoes moored at the steps. Matheson suspected that the shady dealers had arrangements with the daytime vendors to use their space, or there would have been trade society rumbles every night. He and Santos had made only the most perfunctory of passes through the market when they were on shift and it was rare that they'd seen anyone. There was always evidence that someone had been there, though, and Matheson suspected they vanished into the cliff tunnels as patrols approached.

Now the market was busy with regular business, conducted in gestures and muttered haggling, cut through by the calls of boom-tail terns and the splash of scarlet cormorants. The sun was struggling to pierce the fog, making the shadows blur and wash into the mist. He checked for trouble and turned down Canoe Street, putting his back to the fish market. Half the homes and shops on Canoe were within the crater wall, facing a row of freestanding buildings on the other side of the narrow road. The road was quiet, with only a few people moving about while a hollow-ribbed hound slunk after a razor cat hunting in the shadows.

The address he sought was near the end of the road, on the cliff side. Doors, windows, and staircases had been carved into the scarp with industrial plasma torches. The process had sealed a hard sheen on the gray-blue stone surfaces that time and use had only scuffed. Here and there rougher excavations and changes had been made with cruder tools that left the habitation looking like a sand castle that had been attacked by inattentive woodpeckers.

Leran's aunt and uncle lived on the level above their racing canoe shop. The picto-sign on the wide roll-up door was a painting of a pair of sollets—Gattian sea mammals that looked like someone had bred a spotted seal with a rabid wolverine—fighting for a basket of fish. Now that the big canoe race of the season was over, the workshop was closed, and Matheson hoped to find the boatwright at home.

It was a long, steep climb to the apartment. *Must be hell in the rainy season. Surely, no one with another choice would live up here?* Shutters of selectively permeable canvas stretched on painted frames covered the windows, but the door at the top of the stairs was open. Matheson looked through, staying carefully outside, and called, "Hello? Anyone home?"

A Dreihle man emerged from the gloom at the rear of the room. He stopped a short distance into the light, slightly turned away from Matheson. His dark hair was graying at the front and secured in a knot at the back of his head with a skewer-and-net kind of arrangement, and his once-fine clothes were stained with fish and crackled varnish. The low light didn't account for the dulled marigold color of his skin or the curving blue lines that Matheson could barely see on the far side of his face. The man stooped a bit and didn't say anything, his gaze flicking nervously from Matheson to the wall, then back to him, and away again as if searching for a way out. He blinked frequently, as if he could clear Matheson from his vision.

Matheson identified himself, started the recording on his mobile, and said, "I'd like to speak to Temote or Chanan Vela. About Denenshe Leran. Are you Temote Vela?"

For a moment the man said nothing then he backed a step farther from the door, giving a jerky nod. "That I am," he replied, his voice cracked and buzzing, his teeth locked tightly closed around his words. He crossed the room in a furtive, crabwise fashion, and made a fluttering motion with his hand, indicating Matheson should come in.

It was surprisingly cool and dry in the stone apartment and much more spacious than Matheson had expected. He paused a few steps inside, watching a small lizard slip along the wall as his eyes adjusted to the low light. The main chamber led to halls and grottoes that crawled into the rock as if the whole cliff were honeycombed with excavations old and new. He corrected his assumption. *So, the cliff houses are an honor, not a curse. But why for a boatwright?*

Once Matheson was inside, Vela closed the door and seemed to breathe easier. He pointed at an arrangement of two tall, reclining-board couches and a spindly table that sat in the shadows near the back of the room. "You're please sit," he said and walked with Matheson.

Vela stepped aside at the last minute to fetch a tall glass to join another one that sat sweating condensation onto the table top beside a squat ceramic pitcher glazed brilliant red.

Matheson couldn't remain standing—that would only make Vela more nervous. The couches were something to lean into more than sit upon, but Matheson did his best. Being tall himself, he knew the indignity of unfolding from the ground or a low chair and the odd couch was surprisingly comfortable. "I'm sorry about your nephew, Mr. Vela," he started as Vela poured him a glass of cold tea and remained standing. Matheson could finally see the tattoos on his face clearly: not a trade society mark, but an abstract wave that swirled from ear to cheekbone and crested over his eyebrow.

Vela shuddered, shifted his gaze to the table top, and turned his own glass slowly. "Is . . . fair."

Matheson frowned. "Fair?"

"Denny . . ." Vela shook his head. "We're sorrow for the rest."

But not for your nephew. "Did you know why he was at the Paz da Sorte? Did he usually go there?"

Vela shook his head again, and glanced at the door as if expecting someone. "I'm not would—'Twas not his kind."

"Was he acquainted with a girl named Venn Robesh?"

Vela looked more distressed than ever, squeezing his hands tight together and bowing his head. "Venn . . . they're know each other." The words struggled out.

Matheson watched his distress with a slight tightness in his own chest. "Could he have gone to the Paz da Sorte to meet her?"

Vela repeated the same abrupt, jerky head motion as before.

"How did her know her? Were they a couple?"

Vela's gaze flicked continually around the room, then toward the door.

"You're expecting someone?"

Vela's head-shaking stopped abruptly. "My wife—"

The door opened, throwing gray sunlight into the back of the room. A Dreihle woman came in with a basket propped on her hip, murmuring words Matheson didn't know. She stopped and stared at him for a moment, taking in his uniform. Then she rushed across the room, letting her basket fall to the floor as Vela turned toward her. Delicate fabric and long, glittering beads spilled across the glassy stone surface as she threw herself into Vela's arms.

She muttered in Dreihleen as she beat her closed fists against his chest. Matheson recognized "Denny" and a handful of terms that meant "dead," "police," "friends" . . .

Matheson stood, but Vela made a swiping gesture through the air with one hand as he reached for his hysterical wife.

Vela grabbed her shoulders and held her from him, not controlling, but begging. "We're hush, Chanan! None're crawl here. None yet. Hush!"

"Hush? Hush—what would you?" They exchanged a hard look between them, Chanan trembling in her husband's hands.

Then she turned sharply, wrenching herself from his grip and flying at Matheson, pushing him toward the door. "Go, dehka! Get out! Get out!"

"Mrs. Vela," he objected. He had to back up a few steps to avoid her flailing hands against his chest and shoulders. He looked to Temote and back to Chanan. "Mr. Vela, Mrs. Vela . . . I know this is difficult, but anything you can tell me about why Denny was at Paz, how he knew Venn or anyone else there—"

Chanan's lips pulled back in a grimace and a chilling, choked howl started from behind her clenched teeth. Her shoulders and abdomen caved inward, as if the noise was slowly crushing her body. The sound went on and on without pause, rising hysterically as she sank to her knees. She reached for her head and clutched her gray-streaked hair in her fists, clawing it over her face, tearing it out in knotted hanks and reaching again. Vela lunged past Matheson and dropped to his knees as well. He hugged his wife tight.

Her collapse made no sense to Matheson and the sound tore across his nerves like electric feedback, but he started toward the Velas with his hands spread wide—as non-threatening as he could manage.

"Go," Vela said without looking up. The word seemed to wrench from his throat as his wife struggled in his arms, venting her distress. "He's bad son brings shame, misery. We're have no black for him. For Venn, we will bleed." He turned his head toward Matheson, glaring as if he held him responsible for his wife's fit, for the deaths, for all of it. Then he swerved his hard stare aside, toward the doorway as if the sight of Matheson was too much to bear. "We're not speak more to you. Go!"

He could not stand the piercing sound of Mrs. Vela's pain any longer—even if there had been a chance of getting any more information. He might regret the decision, but Matheson nodded and murmured, "Perhaps later. I'm sorry for your loss." *Damn, what a stupid thing to say!*

Vela made no reply as he bowed his head to his wife's while she twisted and howled in his arms.

Matheson could still hear the strange, clogged shrieking when he reached the street, echoed by a tattered dog.

There were several dozen Dreihleen in the lane, but they all turned their gazes aside as Matheson looked at them. One young man with a badly scarred tattoo on his upper arm dashed toward the stone staircase that led to the Velas' apartment. Matheson barely recognized the clan marking under the scar. He hadn't noticed a similar tattoo on Vela or his wife, or a matching mark on the doorway, so why was the boy heading there?

He whirled and lunged to catch the young Dreihle's arm. "GISA Ofiçe! Stop where you are!" he snapped as he caught the bone-thin wrist. He pulled out his ID and jerked the youth back around to see it.

Except for the tattoo, there was little to identify the teenager from hundreds of other young Dreihleen out of work in the ghetto—too thin, and his features not quite set in a face dark golden yellow under sun-streaked brown hair. The boy glared for an instant, then jerked his head aside and turned his gaze to the ground, trying to twist his arm out of Matheson's grip. Matheson held on and the boy muttered something that was probably an insult.

Matheson leaned toward the boy. "Denny Leran," he said. "How do you know him?"

The boy shook his head with the same sharp jerk Vela had used and breathed harshly through his nose.

"I only want to find out who killed your neighbors. If you tell me which clan he ran with, I have somewhere to start."

"None."

"Unlikely. Maybe . . ." Matheson racked his brain for the name that went with the nearly obliterated symbol on the boy's arm, "*Tzena*, like you."

The boy made a hacking sound in his throat. "Go jump, dehka."

"The longer we're seen talking together, the more likely it is that your clan will think you told me something."

The boy wiggled and tried again to jerk away. "Unaff," he muttered. "Belong to no one." His voice wobbled at the edge of despair. "Leave go!" He shot a look over his shoulder. "Please!"

"One thing, just one thing that connects Leran to Venn Robesh or what happened at the Paz da Sorte." Matheson glanced the same way the boy had and put his badge away. "Or don't you care?"

Halfennig and Jora rounded the corner. When they spotted Matheson and the boy, they started running toward them. *It's a short block . . .*

Matheson shook the boy. "Speak up and I'll let go." Though he would let go anyhow—he didn't want to put the kid in the line of anyone's wrath if he could help it, and certainly not theirs.

The boy turned his head up, staring at Matheson, his eyes startled wide and black, face bloodless. "They're no friends!" he gasped.

"They weren't friends?"

The boy just jerked frantically against Matheson's grip. "No friends!"

Matheson scowled as much in confusion as anything, but he let go of the boy's arm and the kid wrenched away, bolting for the stairs up the cliff wall. He ran up the steps, leaning forward and paddling with his hands at the steep stairs ahead. He scrambled upward, past the Velas' flat, and then, with a sudden turn, into a rough hole half his own height, and vanished.

The first shift SOs pounded past Matheson and up the stairs, but couldn't catch up to the boy and wouldn't fit through the hole he'd slipped into. They began searching along the carved gallery, looking for another entrance.

While they were occupied, Matheson turned and ran back toward the fish market. He was sure the boy knew his way through whatever labyrinth lay throughout the cliff face far better than Jora and Halfennig—even if they could find a way in that would accommodate men their size. And he doubted any of the residents would be helpful to the SOs.

So Venn and Denny had known each other, but the kid who claimed no clan affiliation had said they weren't friends. But if they were *ex*-friends, they might be *ex-lovers* and that could turn a calmly planned robbery into a crime of passion. He hadn't connected either of them to Dohan, yet. He'd try his luck a little longer in the Dreihleat, but he'd have to dodge the first shift SOs to do it.

Have to get out of sight before those two vent their frustration on me. He knew the area only at night, when the daylight businesses were closed, and the streets were filled with shadows and the people who preferred them. He'd be damned if he'd be chased out, but he still needed to go to ground until they passed.

The mist was thinning slowly as he turned up Rua dos Peixes and sprinted toward the park, then ducked into the first alley he knew cut back to a smaller street on the other side. Matheson didn't doubt he could outrun either of the older SOs in the open, but the Dreihleat's narrow streets didn't qualify. Slinking would have to do.

Matheson slipped through the door of the coffee house and pushed it closed, turning to watch the street as he did. So far, he was in the clear. He walked into a shadow out of view of anyone coming up the road from the fish market, and turned to look toward the counter.

A Dreihle woman in loose-fitting work tunic and trousers with many pockets stood by the end of the counter, staring at him. She was thirty or even forty with a bright ocher complexion that was only slightly creased around her eyes. Her black hair had been pinned up in several thick, looping braids, leaving bare her long neck and narrow, hawkish face. Her eyes seemed to spark and glitter as she cast an assessing gaze over him. *She's not turning her head*. Instead, she met his own disconcerted stare for a moment and it seemed to Matheson that he'd brushed a live wire.

He blinked a few times, trying to shake off the unsettling sensation, and she cocked an eyebrow, giving him an amused smile.

She turned toward the back of the room and said, "Minje."

The man Matheson recalled from his earlier visit shouldered his way through a swinging door at the back of the counter, carrying one of the large samovars in front of him with a ceramic teapot balanced on top. The two murmured together as they settled the urn and teapot. The woman seemed to ask a question. The man raised his eyebrows and shrugged. The woman gave a crisp nod, then walked around the counter and through the door behind it.

"Right man," the man said, turning to Matheson with his head down and glance sliding upward as the door flapped closed.

Matheson returned a nod as he walked to the counter. "I'm hoping you might help me."

"Help? What help you're want? This about Paz?" His voice was as accented and buzzy as ever, but Matheson was getting an ear for it by now.

"Yes."

Matheson reached to hashmark the recording on his mobile, but the man put up his hand, shaking his head. "This for him?"

Matheson frowned. "Him?"

"Z'Inspector."

"Yes."

The man shook his head some more. "Not if anyone else will know I'm say't."

Matheson peered at the man, thinking. "Would you talk to me if I don't record it? Confidentially?"

The man rubbed his bottom lip with the side of his index finger as he considered. "Is a thing you can do?"

"I can." He needed the link between Robesh, Leran, and Dohan—there would be corroborating evidence elsewhere, if the first link was good. "I'm Matheson," he offered. "What do I call you?"

The man paused, making up his mind. "Called Minje," he said, touching a barely visible brown tattoo of a tiny, chirping bird on the crest of his left cheekbone.

It was all he was going to get. Matheson nodded. "All right. I'm looking—"

"Eat first."

"What?"

"You're stand here, asking, I'm troubled. You're eating, is only breakfast chat, heh? And you're still watch for th'morning walkers."

"Jora and Halfennig." *The whisper-and-rumor net's faster than message streams here. No wonder you never see a Dreihle with a mobile.*

Minje nodded with a smile. "You're go sit," he said and turned to stick his head and shoulders past the swinging door.

The café's furniture was a mix of everything from cushions on the floor to the tall, leaning couches, and broad rails fixed to the wall for resting cups on while standing. Matheson chose an ordinary chair and small table that allowed him a view of the street.

What's the relationship between Leran and Robesh, exactly? The Velas were worried about friends . . . Denny's friends? What their own friends will think of them for talking to me? And Minje the same? And still no connection to Dohan—

The fabric that had fallen from Mrs. Vela's basket . . . and the beads bright and glittering, just like the trench diamonds on Venn Robesh's dress. There wasn't any record of Mrs. Vela's employer, but maybe . . .

Matheson looked up as Minje set a small plate down in front of him. "Do you know who Chanan Vela works for?"

"She's take sewing." Minje's voice seemed too loud in the empty coffee house.

"For whom?"

"Only one's pay Dreihleen for't—Dohan." Minje nodded. "Him who's die at Paz."

"Dohan's factory's not on this side of the Dreihleat, so why would he go all the way to the Paz da Sorte?"

"Z'big man—Paz's his kind."

"A business man."

Minje shook his head. "You're not been here very long, heh?"

"A month."

The other nodded and hummed. "Gil Dohan's heaviest kind. He's show his weight."

Loni Tonitol had been muscular, but none of the murdered Dreihleen had been fat. "His economic weight," Matheson guessed. "His power in the Dreihleat because he owned Dohan Sewing. Was he always . . . heavy?"

Minje tilted his head to the side and glanced at the woman who'd come back into the room to walk toward them. "He's grow lately. Very proud's Gil Dohan."

"I'd like to know about that growth. And how he knew Venn Robesh and Denny Leran. I need to speak to his family, his managers—"

Minje's scowl was adamant. "Won't speak to you."

"Why not?"

Minje cocked an eyebrow as if Matheson was being particularly dense. "Grief."

"There has to be a way . . ." Matheson muttered, more to himself than Minje.

Minje tick-tocked his head and seemed about to say something, but the woman stopped beside him and gave him a stare and a sharp "go away" lift of the chin.

Minje hurried off and the woman put a shallow box tray down on the table. She hefted a large teapot out of it and poured olive-brown liquid into two handleless cups. Matheson watched her hands: working hands, long-fingered, but calloused, strong, and permanently stained around the cuticles. He gave himself a mental shake, and forced his gaze up.

He offered a smile and said, "I usually drink coffee in the morning."

She gave him a sideways look. "We're gossip, we're drink tea," she said. "And you're not let that grow cold," she added, pointing at his plate. Her voice was more musical than Minje's, quieter, but still throaty and slow-moving. He found it more alluring than he should.

"I need information more than I need food."

She made a faint dismissive noise and looked pointedly at the dome of pale dough on his plate. "You're eat, I'm tell."

He sighed and took a bite. The pastry was still warm, filled with flakes of sweet barbecued eel.

"You're a police," she said. "You're chase this thing at Paz." Sounds buzzed against her teeth: "Zis" and "ting."

He swallowed hastily. "Yes, Mrs . . ."

"Only Aya." She put the emphasis on the second syllable, as she studied him from under her lashes. "You're ask about Dohan. Why you're want to know?"

"I want to know how he connects Denny Leran to Venn Robesh."

She waited until he'd taken another bite, then the near corner of her lips lifted in approval. "Sewing floor babbies." The first word came out "zo-ing."

Matheson gulped tea, burning his tongue a little, and asked, "What?"

She picked up her own cup and sipped before she answered. "Women're bring their children when they're work the sewing floor. They're all together since."

The front door opened and Matheson looked up, half-expecting Jora and Halfennig.

Minje was walking to meet the small, chattering group that had entered the café—Central tourists, not Dreihleen. Older women, up early and bored silly enough to brave the Dreihleat alone, but keeping to the main roads, because although they were foolish, they weren't stupid. Good. They'd make his presence less obvious.

"I was told Robesh and Leran weren't friends," he objected.

"Who's say so?"

"A boy."

Aya gave a slow, one-shouldered shrug. It reminded Matheson of Dillal and he frowned before he asked, "Did you know any of the victims?"

She nodded, sipped, then ran her fingers around the rim of her tea cup as she replied. "Loni Tonitol was teach me to bake."

"Loni?" Matheson had difficulty imagining a bouncer working in a kitchen.

"Used to buy pastry from Tina Anza, but cost dear. When Stocha's too young, Loni's help out. He's learned to bake, taught me." Her voice grew a little tighter as she clenched her jaw harder. "Z'a kind man. Not clever." The creases around her eyes deepened and she turned her face down.

"Did you know the Initols?"

"Neighbors," she said and sipped more tea.

"Any of the others?"

She turned her head just enough to frown at him for a second or two. Any hint of flirtation had died out. "Only customers. Dodi Zashto and Balandor Tchin, they're bought coffee, said good morning, but no more. Near the park's busy. Perhaps others are come, go, is not in my mind." She stopped looking at Matheson from the corner of her eye and turned her attention to the chattering ladies now seated near the door. Minje was bowing over them and they were noisily charmed. A few Dreihleen had paused on the sidewalk, as if weighing the advisability of coming inside.

Aya shifted, blocking his view out the window as she reached for her tray. "I've work. And no more for you now."

"I can ask you later?" She piqued his curiosity. Minje just seemed chatty, but Aya he couldn't figure and he thought he might like to.

She tilted her head and gave him a measuring, Dreihle-wise glance. "How you're one who's chase this? Is not work for patrol walkers."

"Just got stuck with it. The inspector needed an assistant and I happened to be standing still."

"You're not care how's done?"

"I care very much. Which is why I didn't say 'no' to the job."

She made a faint noise in her throat. Then she picked up the tray with its pot and her cup and walked back to the kitchen.

Matheson puzzled about her and stared out the window. One of the Dreihleen came in but the rest—one unusually broad-shouldered—had turned and walked on. Matheson finished his breakfast, paid, and left, thinking about the Velas, Venn Robesh, and Denny Leran. The connection wasn't solid enough yet.

Matheson had looked, but seen no sign of the first shift, and he'd gotten about a meter past the alley behind the coffeehouse when Jora caught him by the elbow. Halfennig body-checked him so he pivoted and swung into the filthy backstreet wall, sending a flurry of scampering motion through the shadows. Jora let go at the last minute and Matheson managed to turn and get his shoulder to the surface instead of his face.

"You have a hearing problem, rookie?" Halfennig asked and smacked Matheson's outside shoulder, turning him and jolting him into the plaster.

A rough patch scraped across the bridge of Matheson's nose as a stiffened hand jabbed into his right kidney. He sagged against the wall, gasping in pain, and knocked his forehead against gritty plaster that crumbled away from rough blocks of pale blue stone. He hooked his fingertips into the uneven surface, holding himself up and away by millimeters so he could suck in more air than moldy plaster dust and dirt sour with garbage.

"You ought to watch where you're going, Fishbait," Jora said. "You could get hurt, wandering around where you shouldn't be. Smart guy like you should be able to stay out of other people's way. Didn't appreciate what you did back on Canoe."

Merry hell . . . "It's a murder investigation," Matheson snapped, and caught a mouthful of dust that made him cough.

Halfennig gave him a quick rap on the back of the head. Matheson's left eyebrow split open against the pitted wall and he could feel blood start to flow. It stung and he covered his mouth until he stopped coughing.

"Yeah, but you ain't with I-Office, are you?" Halfennig asked.

Matheson turned and glared at them as blood ran into his eye.

"Find a dreck to take the fall and get back to your own job," said Jora. "Hell, we almost caught one for you, till you fucked that up."

"That kid? He hadn't—"

"You're not hearing me," Jora cut in. He reached to rap Matheson on the forehead.

Fuck it. It was easy to snatch the shorter man's hand aside and shove him around, twisting Jora's forearm up behind his back. "I don't want to fight with you or the rest of S-Office about it, but I'm going to do the job I'm assigned, whether you like it or not."

He shoved Jora toward Halfennig, who stepped out of the way and came forward swinging. Matheson dodged, but with Jora turning on his other side, he didn't have much room and took the blow at the edge of his ribs. It hurt, but it was glancing and wouldn't stick. Jora came in on the other side and hooked a fist toward his kidney. Matheson turned, deflecting Jora's hand, and landed a blow on the smaller man's sternum.

Jora staggered back, his blank expression narrowing toward real anger. *Shit.* Startled, Matheson didn't turn to counter Halfennig and the other man hammered him into the wall. Matheson put his arms up to protect his injured face and got served a couple of quick blows at his lower back. He gasped. One of the men swept his legs from the side and gave a shove. Matheson went to his knees and huddled to the wall. *It's not personal—better to swallow pride than teeth.*

The two SOs blocked him in again, but didn't strike. He could feel Jora looming over him. *Must be a rare treat for the little bastard.* "Just trying to help you, Fishbait. Nobody but Dillal gives a crap about this case and nobody gives a crap about him. So, find your way out of I-Office before he goes down and takes you with him."

Matheson held his tongue and kept his head down until he heard them walking away. Fighting them had been stupid. They were already chatting and laughing as if nothing had happened. Matheson was sore, but he got to his feet and turned to watch them go.

"Merry hell." He swiped the trickle of blood out of his eye and winced at the renewed sting. A few curious bystanders glanced at him and then aside, and even the oiled geckos clinging to the wall scrambled farther away.

He brushed himself off. In a fair fight, he might have stood a chance, but it wasn't a fight: it was a warning, telling him where the boundaries lay. He hated losing, but he didn't need the whole of S-Office on his back, and it wasn't something to be settled with fencing foils or target pistols.

He found a half-clean washroom at the edge of the park and took out his annoyance on his injuries. Once he'd scrubbed, and splashed enough cold water on his face, the cuts stopped bleeding. The bruises were mild—just enough to serve as reminders. The graze on his nose was trivial and the cut on his forehead didn't show too much through his thick, black eyebrows—they were the only feature that stopped his face from verging on pretty. *Maybe I'd look more interesting with a scar . . .*

His family was artificially perfect, gene-managed, and carefully bred. *Like champion dogs.* The result was unpleasantly uniform—every child tall and slim, same blue eyes, same hair, same skin—and it didn't help that he looked like the scruffy, male version of Callista. *Someone'll probably fix that for me if I stay here long enough.*

Bruises or not, he had work to do. The connection was spotty in the Dreihleat—even the Peerless had occasional trouble due to the low microtransmitter density—but public washrooms had automated systems that required a datalink. Crouching in the privacy of the stall between cleaning cycles, he teased his MDD into the GISA database stream and formulated the best query he could for Gil Dohan and any connection to the Julian Company. He'd keep working on Leran and Robesh himself. And Santos.

CHAPTER TEN

Day 2: Afternoon

Starna hovered at the edge of the autopsy field, restlessly shifting while Dillal and Dr. Andreus conferred over one of the bodies. They'd been engaged without respite since the early hours and Dillal continued to ignore the med/legal technician while they finished up.

The doctor stripped off her gloves as she talked and removed the base coat of spray seal on her hands. "The variation in the fatal wounds is interesting. Some are very neat, efficient—one or two shots to the head and it's done. Others look like the shooter was unsteady or scared. Then there's the plasma burns—also very messy, but they'd take some nerve, since they required contact for ten to fifteen seconds. The four victims from the bar room were all gunshot, but the gambling room victims are a mix of plasma and bullets. Wouldn't even call it a slaughter—that would have been cleaner. I don't see much else that's relevant to your investigation."

Andreus studied Dillal for a minute before she added, "So unless something pops on your tox reports later, it's just what you see. Eshprito's is the first case of advanced PPL I've ever seen, in person. The Dreihleen pulmonary physiology and breathing habit is like yours, and that compensated for the decreased lung capacity and stiffening of the tissue, but he was in bad shape. If he hadn't been shot, it would have been a race to see if the secondary effects got him before old age did. Maybe a bullet in the eye was a mercy." She seemed to be waiting for something from the inspector, but he didn't give it and she finally shook her head. "This planet breeds the most fascinating ways to destroy people. And all in the name of a good time."

Dillal's expression was unreadable. "Are you willing to sign these off?"

Andreus sighed. "As soon as the paperwork's up. But it's not going to help you much. Ballistics isn't my field and plasma burns have no identifiable signature. You'll have to look at the details and test materials yourself—as designed," she added. "So far, this poor bunch of bastards present nothing beyond the stupefying obscenity of wholesale human slaughter. I've seen worse, but I thought I was done with that crap when I came to Gattis."

"Let us hope that you are, now," Dillal said.

Andreus gave him a sour look. "If the administration doesn't turn some of its policies around, this place could get bloodier than Kora."

"Kora's was a civil war that broke along political lines. Wasn't it?"

Andreus snorted. "Politics, genocide . . . It all looked the same from the med tent." She peered at him. "I don't like the look of that subcutaneous graft. Are you using the meds I prescribed?"

She started to reach for his face and Dillal flicked her hand aside. His mouth tightened and he gave her as much of a glare as half a face was capable of.

Andreus gave an annoyed huff and turned her back, saying, "You'd better talk your tech down before he makes the whole lab uneasy. He's been glowering at us for twenty minutes." She began cleaning up.

Dillal picked up a tray full of bloody bullets, each in its own dish and tagged with the ID of the body it had been removed from. He stared at the misshapen slugs for a moment, then carried the tray to where Starna was standing with his hands thrust into his lab coat pockets, shoulders forward, unconsciously rocking on his heels.

Dillal held out the tray. "Clean these and take samples for metallurgy. Hold any results until I tell you otherwise. Then send them for ballistic analyses and match tests against the bullets taken from the scene."

Starna blinked at him, his gaze flitting from the tray to Dillal's left eye. His scrawny throat worked as he swallowed. "Can't you—?"

"No. Not every test runs in my head," Dillal replied with a hint of scorn. "What else did you want to say?"

Starna frowned. "What?"

"You've been waiting impatiently—I assume for me and not for Dr. Andreus."

"No, sir. I mean, yes, sir." Starna's hands erupted from his pockets as if he had no control of them. His eyes widened in annoyance. "Look, this request for shoe impressions is clogging my work queue. The scene techs have no problem—they do it all the time—but S-Office is being frisky." He clasped his nervous hands together, ending their fluttering, as he clenched his teeth and raised his eyebrows expectantly.

"Frisky?" Dillal asked.

"Non-compliant in a deliberately semantic way."

Dillal nodded. "Ah. They don't like the nature and implications of my request."

"No, sir, they don't. I don't understand why they're being so obstructive—"

"Have they ever been responsive to such requests?"

"They've never had a problem in the past." Starna dropped his gaze to the tray in Dillal's hand. "The requests I sent seem to be faring better than yours."

Dillal gave one of his fast-twitch smiles. "Then send mine again under your cover. You and I will have to work around it until the division comes to its collective senses. It's more important to get the prints for clearance now, than to fight over the boundary of my authority. S-Office lost that battle before it began. Start on these and keep the results to yourself."

Starna frowned and took the tray. "Yes, sir."

The tech hurried away and Dillal turned to remove his own gloves and the spray seal from his hands before retiring to his office. Dr. Andreus lingered, scowling, and followed him after a quarter of an hour, when Starna and the rest of the busy lab techs and med/legals seemed to have forgotten her.

Stop worrying about Julian. Matheson had too many distractions: if not the family, then Aya kept slipping into the front of his mind. Her cool self-possession teased him when he should have been concentrating on his job or staying off-scope of pissed-off SOs.

He'd crossed over to the far side of the Dreihleat to Dohan Sewing, his paranoia growing as he dodged his colleagues. He'd found only one unlocked door at the factory and the piecework manager had been the only person in the small office, hurriedly stacking packages and gathering his keys. "Factory's closed," he'd insisted over and over. Then he'd shrugged from further questions, leading Matheson outside so he could lock the door and run away with his head down. It was no good chasing the guy. Matheson followed up on the canvass reports for a while, but found no leads to anything useful, nor any connections between Leran and Robesh, or Dohan and the Julian Company. *Julian. Damn them . . .*

Frustrated, Matheson headed for Santos's apartment in East Quay. He went on foot because exertion usually calmed him, but it wasn't much of a tonic this time. He passed the elegant block of Corporation House, sitting on the landward side of the road as if observing the immaculate white expanse of expensive shops and hotels on the water side. Two silent rows of young errand runners sat on either flank of the side door—Ohba on the right, a smaller number of Dreihleen on the left. Their blue-and-gold jackets were folded over their arms or across their knees to keep the creases crisp in the rising humidity. Sweat settled on their faces, but the girls and boys—none older than twelve or thirteen—all sat as stoically as statues, watched over by a pair of door guards from the cool of the security gateway. Eyes shifted to watch him pass.

Matheson threaded through a stream of well-dressed shoppers outside Emporia. *Julian will be in there or the White Hotel, if it's anywhere.* As he walked past, he saw some of the patrons were trailed, not by the expected automated package drones, but by older Ohba or Dreihleen runners, somber-faced in their sweat-inducing livery.

Ohba pushing whispering, long-nosed machines snuck out to erase the blue sand and shoe marks left on the white walkway, then disappeared again behind inconspicuous doors. No one but the eagle-eyed doormen seemed to notice them. One Ohba woman, brown-red as a pomegranate's rind, stooped to pick up a fallen e-credit chit. The nearest door guard darted forward and snatched it from her. Matheson watched the doorman return the chit to its owner. Whatever tip he received, he didn't offer to share it with the cleaner, who had already retreated.

Matheson paused to look up and down the long white row of Cove Quay. There were no detainee work crews here. The whistles of doormen calling for skimmers or ground transport, and the chatter of the wealthy at play wound through the sound of water, genteel commerce, and the rail of seabirds against the electromagnetic repulser grids. It was the same in a hundred other places he'd been when he was one of the customers, instead of one of the cops. Except that here the overlooked workers—who didn't talk or laugh, but waited in subdued and watchful rows beside the service doors—were Ohba or Dreihleen.

The doormen, guards, desk clerks, and shop assistants weren't. A few tall Dreihleen and striking young people of mixed race clung to the arms of obviously wealthy companions. When they spoke, their voices were brittle. They came and went through hotel doorways, passing their hands discreetly over the waiting palms of guards who offered no other acknowledgement or thanks as they pocketed whatever they'd been given and held the doors open only long enough.

Matheson watched it all for a minute. No one met his eye. *Is it the uniform or the color of my skin?* An unaccountable chill crawled up the back of his neck and he moved from the static, white walkway to the slideway, anxious to move faster.

He passed quickly into the middle- and working-class neighborhoods on the northeast. There were fewer people on the streets here at this time of day—maintenance was mostly automated and unemployment was low in East Quay—but his paranoia lingered. No one gave him grief, but he kept thinking that if he turned the wrong corner, the blank, disinterested expressions would become fierce. They wouldn't, of course. This wasn't the Ohbata or Centerrun, where kilometers of microtransmitters regularly went mysteriously silent and the evidence of crimes vanished as quickly as water into sand. *I'm a cop. I'm perfectly safe here.*

Still, he found himself jogging, in spite of overloading the capability of his CoolTherm undershirt.

The building was a well-built multi-story condo stack near the working waterfront of East Quay with a view of the cove—if you leaned out a bit to see around the two other buildings between it and the water. Santos's was a corner unit high enough up to catch a faint breeze. It was nicer than Matheson's fold-out single room by a long measure, even if the area did have a stronger odor of sea water and industry than his. *Corruption pays well.*

Matheson didn't bother sending another ping to Santos, he just passed his ID through the electronic outer door and coded it open. He was not going to let Santos or his wife put him off again. *What'll they do? Throw me out the window?*

The door gave way and he went up to the appropriate floor in the dry cool of the elevator. His uniform shirt and singlet had unstuck from his back by the time he reached the unit he wanted.

He didn't bother with the courtesy bell but pounded on the door. "Santos! It's Matheson. C'mon! Let me in."

Santos's voice came shakily from close inside the door. "I don't want to talk to you, Fishbait. I'm fuckin' fine without you. Just fine. Go the hell away."

"I'm not going to," Matheson shot back. "You know what a pain in the ass I am—you tell me so often enough. I'm going to camp here for as long as it takes. You know I have to ask you questions." He remembered a discussion they'd had about the various senior ofiçes and added, "Better me than the blue-haired harpy." Santos didn't like Neme any better than Matheson did and he hoped Santos didn't know she was no longer on the case.

The door unlatched. "Can't get rid of you, can I?"

Matheson leaned through the doorway cautiously and glanced around. Santos stood nearby, clutching a cylinder of beer and looking unsteady on his bare feet. "No. Can I come in or are you going to brain me with that?"

Santos peered at him, swaying a little. His brown complexion was mottled from drinking. "Don't know. What's with your face?"

"I had a business meeting with an irresistible force."

Santos grunted. "You can come in, but I'm not talkin' to nobody but you. You don't got that bitch behind you, do you?"

"Neme? No. I'm alone. She's not even on the case anymore."

"She's not? What? What happened?" Santos asked, backing toward the living room. Being relieved of the specter of Neme hadn't soothed his nerves any.

Matheson eased inside, looking down both arms of the entry corridor, just in case. Three pairs of footwear lay in disarray beside the door. "I'm supposed to take your work boots for elimination when I go," he said.

Santos shrugged without turning. "Whatever."

Matheson followed Santos into the main room. It was sunny, but cool with forced dry air that smelled of meat stewing with hot pepper and onion. He glanced around and saw a large sitting room, a small dining area that led to a balcony in the window corner, and a kitchen counter that divided the space facing the bank of windows. Santos's wife lurked in the kitchen, out of easy earshot, but able to keep an eye on both men while she worked.

Christa Santos was a round, muscular woman about fifty, under average height, and with the bearing of a queen. If she wasn't pure Ohba, she wasn't far removed. Her skin was a russet color only a little lighter than her auburn hair. Given the deep-seated hatred and continual violence between the Ohba and Dreihleen, it struck Matheson strange that she'd marry a cop who worked in the Dreihleat. Yet there she was.

She turned to stare at Matheson, her eyes a startling shade of leaf green. She narrowed her gaze, looking him over as if assessing his threat level. Finally, she gave a dismissive snort and returned to her work. He turned to find a seat close to Santos, listening to Christa in the kitchen making a steady noise that sounded like a knife thumping into a butcher block.

Santos was a little older than his wife. At the moment, the difference seemed like a decade or more, though Matheson knew it wasn't.

Before their last night on patrol, he'd seemed solid and massive; now his shoulders sagged and his fat hung like bagged sand, as if he'd lost fifteen kilos overnight. He was wearing deeply wrinkled uniform trousers with a blue shirt unbuttoned over a CoolTherm singlet, all stained with yellow blotches.

Santos had sunk into an overstuffed arm chair that looked like it was slowly digesting him. Several dozen drink cylinders had piled up at the chair's side. "You gonna ask me questions about that night. At Paz."

"Yeah," Matheson replied, sitting down on the edge of the couch that matched the chair.

"Who's on it?" Santos demanded, staring at Matheson with rheumy, red eyes.

"Who what?" Matheson asked.

"Who's the IOC?"

"Orris was IOD."

Santos shook his head and leaned forward, fighting his way out of the chair's embrace with a panicked expression. "No! I know Orris was Investigation Officer of the *Day*. Who's in charge if not Neme? Who's the Investigation Ofiçe in *Charge*? Who?"

"J. P. Dillal."

A fresh waft of hot spices and a sharp scent of citrus floated into the room on the harsh clatter of pots and pans against the stove grates.

"The *CIFO*?" Matheson noted that Santos made a word of the acronym. Dillal seemed to be the only person who used the initials or full title. "Fuck! They're gonna crucify me. I didn't do *anything* to those people. I knew them! I wouldn't—" Santos turned his head aside, clenching his eyes and mouth shut as if fighting the urge to vomit. In a moment, he gasped, catching his breath, but he didn't turn back to face Matheson. He looked toward the kitchen and the bright windows beyond. His words came out wet and slurred from drink and misery. "I knew the Initols and that thick cousin of theirs, Loni. And they didn't mind—" Then he turned his head and glared at Matheson. "You're gonna ask if I killed them. Well, I didn't!"

Matheson shook his head. "I wasn't going to ask that."

"No? You're not working with the CIFO?"

"I am, but that's not what I was going to ask you. I know you didn't kill those people—you didn't have time."

"That's all you think is going to save my neck? That I didn't have *time?* What *do* you want to know? How I did it?" Santos's voice rose to a hysterical pitch.

"No. I just want to know what time you really entered the jasso."

"I don't know what time! I was with you, Mr. Meticulous. What's your log say? Whatever your log says, that's what it is."

"It doesn't matter what my log says, Santos. Show me yours."

Santos took a drink from his beer, hands shaking. "I ain't got it."

"Because you broke the screen on your mobile, so you didn't hash the incident. But the auto-upload should still have gone through eventually, even if it couldn't reach a connection at the time."

Matheson paused and watched Santos, who said nothing. Matheson's gut twisted in disgust—as much at what he was about to do as at Santos. "I can't find the file. It was never uploaded. There's no record of your movements after we split. We don't know if you were in the building or if you stayed outside as you said you did. *I* know you didn't kill anybody but that doesn't mean you weren't involved."

The older man's face was red and damp now, his mouth tight as he held something in, but his hands were trembling. Still he kept silent.

"Did you break the mobile on purpose because you knew—?"

"It was an *accident*!" Santos said, choking on the words.

"A convenient accident. Because you were planning ahead."

Santos's expression twisted into sodden bitterness. "You're thinkin' like fuckin' Dillal already—you think I'm some kinda master criminal."

"No. I think you had something you needed to do that you knew I wouldn't like—or that the Initols wouldn't like me to see. You had to pick up the protection money and you didn't want to cut me in or make the Initols nervous, so you made a reason to send me the long way. I notice you're not limping now."

Santos lurched a bit in his chair and glared.

"Even broken, the mobile should have uploaded your position, it should have given you an alibi, but it didn't—I did." Matheson let his voice grow louder as he talked, keeping his gaze on Santos the whole time. "You made sure I knew exactly when we parted—you made me hash the time. You put *me* on the hook for the upload reports. You didn't *need* an alibi—or you didn't know you would—and that's the only reason I don't believe you were in on this thing. Because no matter how greedy you were, you weren't stupid enough to implicate yourself in murder. So why didn't the upload run?"

Santos had gone pale and his face was slick, but he didn't reply.

"Why didn't it run?" Matheson repeated louder, leaning forward.

Santos shook his head, squeezing his eyes shut.

Matheson rose to his feet so he loomed over the older ofiçe. "Why didn't it run?" he demanded.

Santos surged to his feet and flung the beer cylinder against the nearby wall with force enough to flatten the stiff thermal film and spray chilled liquid onto the surface in two brown fans. "Because I shut it off!" he shouted, staggering from the motion. He grabbed the back of the chair to keep from falling and glared at Matheson. "I shut it off, you smartass bastard," he muttered thickly, "to keep you from finding out I was pickin' up the bag. 'Cause you're so fuckin' pure." Then he turned unsteadily and looked toward the kitchen.

Matheson glanced the same way and saw Christa Santos step out carrying a heavy frying pan. Hot oil dripped from it onto the floor, sending black smoke curling up from the tiles. Her expression was wary and she watched Matheson like a guard dog. He turned back to Santos, hoping Christa wasn't easing forward to smash his head in.

Santos waved her off as he held onto the chair with his other hand. He swayed a little in place and his eyes weren't quite focused. "Happy?" he muttered.

Matheson waited until he heard Christa put the pan down on the stove. "No," he said. "It'll go against you, but it's better than what I thought I'd hear."

"Like this could get worse . . ." Santos said and turned to drop back into his seat, shivering from his dying rage and boneless with drink.

Matheson took a long breath to pack down his own adrenaline and leaned his weight against the beer-stained wall. "Tell me if I'm off base here," he started. "Even if we hadn't had that incident with the pickpocket, you'd have found an excuse to fake an injury so I wouldn't question your dodging your extra shift later or splitting then so you could head to Paz alone. Maybe the mobile breaking was a lucky accident, maybe it wasn't, but either way, you'd have my log to confirm you were injured and on rounds like you should have been. You knew I wouldn't ask any hard questions because, while I may be naive and too by-the-book for my own good, I'm still a rookie and you're my TO."

"Yeah."

Matheson glanced away for a moment and sighed. "You lied to me and you set me up. You're just as corrupt as everyone else in this stinking system, but you're not a killer." He turned back to Santos. "So help me prove that you're not. Tell me when you entered the Paz da Sorte the first time—I know you did because you were way too close to jumpwise over a locked door. I don't have to know the exact hash time, just how long it was before you called me to rejoin you. Twenty minutes? Ten minutes? Five?"

Santos rolled his head against the back of the chair, his eyelids fluttering, his speech slowing. "About six, seven minutes maybe. I had a key. I unlocked and . . . the lights were off. But I could smell it, and it was so still in there . . . I knew it was somethin' bad. Somethin' real bad."

"How far did you go into the room?"

"I didn't. No. Like . . . maybe a step or two. I didn't leave the tiles, 'cause I could feel 'em under my feet and I thought, when I started feelin' dizzy, that they was broken and sliding around. So I got out and locked it back up. And I called you, and then I ran to the end of the cross-alley and threw the key down a drain. Man, you almost got to the door before I did. I thought you were gonna notice, but you didn't say nothin'."

"The drain." Matheson repeated, feeling foolish for not checking it himself, though ForTech would have. "I thought you were pacing, like you were impatient for me to arrive."

"Wasn't impatient. I was scared what we were gonna see. I didn't want to go back in there."

"Did you see anyone else in the alley or nearby before or after you went into the jasso?"

Santos shook his head miserably. "No."

"Do you remember who was in the club on our earlier round? Did you look inside?"

"I didn't. You remember: we walked on by 'cause there wasn't nothin' looked fishy. I wish I had looked, but I didn't want you to notice nothin' was different. So I didn't."

Matheson nodded. He remembered it the same way. "All right." He straightened from the wall.

Santos stared at him from under drooping lids as if he had no energy to move—and no desire. "I didn't kill them," he said.

Matheson fixed his eyes on his TO's face, though he had an itchy desire to check on Christa. "I know that."

"Yeah. Well. Bully for you. That's not gonna help me, much. With the CIFO on it, it's gonna be a rush job. If they can't find someone else they like, they're gonna say I did it or covered it up. They're gonna hang me up and say it was me, and they're gonna slam the lid on this case like the lid on my coffin. And if this don't all go their way, they're gonna come after you too, Fishbait. You better keep your head down or that face is gonna be the least of your hurts."

"'They' who?" Matheson asked, thinking of Jora and Halfennig, and the sort of people his family utilized to get around "obstacles" in their way.

For a few trembling seconds, Santos seemed frightened, then he narrowed his eyes, and replied, "GISA and their butt buddies. The rich guys out on the Quay. They don't want this investigated. They want it swept into a box and dropped in the sea. Better yet, hung around some Ohba's neck so they can call it an ethnic thing and wipe 'em off the face of the planet."

"Why?"

Santos closed his eyes and a tear that was at least as much alcoholic depression as it was water leaked down his cheek. "C'mon Fishbait . . . you think it's any kinda coincidence that sixty percent of the internees in the camps on Agria are Dreihleen and Ohba and the rest are mixed? And most die in their first two years? The cits don't get sent—they contract when they're too damned hard-up to get out. Gattians? Never, fuckin' *ever* go up, no matter what they did. That whole continent's a friggin' death camp so Gattis Corp can cover up their dirty deeds."

"*What* dirty deeds?"

Santos just rambled on. "Why do you think they got the CIFO on a Dreihleat killing? Because they give a shit about dead yellow guys? They give a shit about money, just like any other corporation—'specially when they own the whole friggin' planet! Do whatever they want, and stick the blame on someone else. CIFO's a blind and Pritchet and his Corp House friends'll squeeze him till he gives 'em what they want. That magic answer-ball forensic crap don't work. You think they picked Dillal for his skills? They picked him 'cause he's trash they can threaten and screw over and then flush down the crapper when they're done with him and ain't nobody gonna care."

Matheson clenched his teeth, holding back his frustration and anger. "You're wrong. No matter who thinks they can pull his strings, the inspector's not going to let someone roll him over."

Santos shook his head. "You're exactly as fresh as you look."

"Damn you, Santos. I'm trying to help you, but if you don't believe I can—we can—then to hell with you."

Santos struggled up from his chair, shouting, "To hell with me? To hell with you! I got my feet on the ground—the ground of Gattis as it is, not as I wish it fuckin' were in some fuckin' college-boy universe where bad shit only happens to bad people! This is a screwed up world where the guys with the money and the right DNA run the game and everyone else scrambles to get what they can before the guns swing their way. And don't you give me that crap about the charter—the charter's the fuckin' problem, you highbrow jackass! Guys with power don't like to share!"

"I know that!" Matheson shot back. "If you think I don't, I'm not the only jackass in the room. And this may be just one rotten case that means nothing to anyone but me and Dillal, but I will do everything I can to make it go right!" He was breathing hard and he hadn't thought he meant it until the words were out of his mouth. He sent a paranoid glance toward the kitchen, looking for Christa, but she only stood behind the counter and stared at him with a blank expression.

He turned back and watched Santos's anger fade to sorrow. The older man shook his head. "Fuck me. They're gonna jam me up and hang me out to dry. You, they're gonna cut into little pieces and throw off the Pillars like chum. Fishbait, boy. You're fucking fishbait."

Andreus had removed the ocular from the prosthetic frame, twisting it out of Dillal's head with a device that looked like a black, three-clawed bird's foot. Dillal hadn't flinched as her hand pressed against his cheekbone, but it came at the cost of a close-bitten bark of pain. She served him a narrow-eyed glare as she cleaned the frame without gentleness, and then stepped back, putting the eyepiece aside for a moment.

She pointed a finger at his face. "You are pushing far too near the edge. Let me be perfectly clear about this: When something goes wrong that close to the brain, the progress from illness to death is swift. An infection could kill you and even *your* extraordinary immune system won't save you. If the implants don't integrate properly and your body rejects them, you'll die. If the system over reaches and becomes invasive, you'll die. I watched it happen to your predecessors and let me assure you that none of these are pleasant ways to go. Your chance of surviving a surgical deintegration is better than any of the previous subjects, but at this point it's still less than ten percent. You should have had six weeks supervised recovery. You had two. If things go well, you might be stable at week three. If not, catastrophic failure becomes more likely."

"I know the risks."

"Yours, maybe, but this is not just *your* potential failure. I cannot afford to send yet another body to the incinerator." She turned aside and bent over the eyepiece on the office table, illuminated by a single harsh light. "I knew you were lying to me. Pride or fear, which is it?"

"Inexperience," he said.

All the display screens in the gloomy office flickered in an ever-changing array of information, test results, reference photos, in-process responses, autopsy diagrams, dossier files, messages, mobile uploads . . .

"You're blaming this on a lack of *instructions*? You didn't wait long enough for instruction and calibration and you didn't ask for any. You can do all of this, self-taught"—Andreus waved one hand at the screens—"which is more than I thought the interface was even capable of, but you wouldn't admit you didn't know how to clean the ocular. And you palmed Starna off with routine work so you could hide this from me."

"From him—I apparently have no secrets from you, Doctor."

"Damned right you don't. What I know about you—"

"Is no worse than what I know about you," Dillal finished as the displays shifted to a fast flicker of images more graphic and horrifying than what lay in the morgue next door: field hospital hillocks of roughly amputated limbs and ruined organs, patients with bodies desperately reconstructed in ways far removed from nature, prison camps and small settlements in rubble and flames, mass graves . . .

Andreus watched the screens for a moment, her face hard. "A field surgeon doesn't always have a choice about who lives and who dies."

He gave her a hard smile. "Not always." The screens went black, then flickered, one by one, back to their busy scan of case notes and message pings. Two red pips flashed on the message queue as the doctor turned her back.

Andreus finished with the eyepiece and carried it to him, glaring. "Do you want to prove how clever you are and put this back in, or do you concede that I might know what I'm doing?"

The door chime issued a lock override warning. The name "Ference Pritchet" appeared on the central display and the door swung inward, letting the brighter light from the corridor into the room. Dillal and Andreus both looked toward it.

The man on the other side of the opening ducked a little as he entered, passing his hand over the light controls as he did and bringing the illumination up.

Andreus turned back and spread her left hand across Dillal's face to press her fingers against the prosthetic frame. She snapped the ocular into it with a sharp twist. Pritchet sucked his breath through his perfect, white teeth, wincing in disgust, and turned his face aside.

Andreus looked up as she took a step back from Dillal. "Pritchet," she said, offering a grudging nod.

Dillal shook himself and ran his fingers over the edge of the ocular frame as he turned to face GISA's Angra Dastrelas Regional Director.

Pritchet dwarfed the CIFO in any dimension, a head-and-a-half taller, more than twice as wide across the shoulders, and built like a statue of an athlete meant to be seen from a distance. His lapis blue hair fell over tawny eyes in a carefully styled cowlick. At sixty-two, was well aware of the powerful image he projected and he salvaged his moment of weakness by planting himself in the center of the small room. A checkerboard of ID crystals was barely visible below the crisp edge of his left shirt cuff as he crossed his arms.

"Dr. Andreus. Come to check on our . . . ?"

"Experiment?" she offered. She shifted her gaze to Dillal who turned his head to watch her. "He's better than I expected at this stage. In fact, he's quite a piece of work."

Pritchet kept his focus on her. "Excellent." His voice held no real enthusiasm. Then he fell silent.

Andreus picked up her kit, leaving the claw-like instrument on Dillal's desk, and exited without further comment.

Pritchet pivoted slightly to face the inspector. He studied the smaller man for a few seconds without obvious reaction this time. "What is your progress?"

Dillal raised his eyes, not his head. The slight clicking of his prosthesis drew a shudder from Pritchet. "Fair."

Pritchet raised his eyebrows. "Fair? Not solved?"

"It will be."

"When?"

"Soon. It hasn't been even forty-eight hours yet."

Pritchet raised his chin a little and grunted. "You have a week, barring unforeseen circumstances, and the clock is already ticking. Quick and prosecutable results are the object of this project. Don't disappoint me," he said and turned away, leaving Dillal alone in the office. The lights sank back to their preset gloom.

The inspector turned back to the display screens and opened the message queue. The red priority pips were both from Starna within the past hour. There was no information attached, just a request for attention. Dillal sent a ping back and the tech appeared in his open doorway within five minutes.

Starna stood just outside, still wearing eye shields, his hands fisted in his coat pockets. "Sir?"

"Come in and close the door."

Starna entered and closed the door like he was sealing his own doom. He seemed to cringe, waiting for Dillal to speak.

Dillal outwaited him.

Starna drew his hands from his pockets and rubbed one thumb hard into the palm of his other hand. He clenched them together tightly enough to make the muscles in his shoulders and neck tense.

"I found a latent. It's a partial—probably won't get anything from the database on it—but it has a trace. I held it, as you said, but . . . should I run it?"

"Bring it to me."

Starna started to turn, then spun back. "Sir . . . it's not Dreihleen."

Dillal tilted his head slightly. "And you know this without running complete analysis?"

"Genetic biochem was *going* to be my specialty, once." He pulled off the shields and met Dillal's gaze for the first time since he walked into the office. "The relevant markers were obvious. It's Ohba."

Dillal glanced aside, as if distracted by something Starna couldn't see. "Bring it to me."

Starna squeezed the eye shields until they cracked. "You knew."

"I need confirmation," Dillal said, returning his gaze to the tech. "Without logging into the system that is open to anyone who wishes to look."

"You think someone . . . is spying?"

"I'm sure of it."

Starna frowned, dropping his eyes. "Director Pritchet's never come down here, before."

"I imagine not."

"The lab's almost empty. Everybody's heading home."

"And you?"

Starna hunched his shoulders and crossed his arms over his chest as his head went down a few degrees. "No."

Dillal took half a step back, studying the man in front of him. Starna didn't look up.

"I'll come into the lab in a few minutes."

CHAPTER ELEVEN

Day 2: Evening

Santos had been scared, angry, and drunk, but that didn't make it easier to shake off what he'd said. It rang with uncomfortable truth. *That only means* he *believes it. He's not* that *good a liar and he held something back.* The whole conversation worried Matheson long after Santos had slipped into incoherent muttering. He'd given up trying to get anything more, and had started to leave, but Christa had blocked him at the door. She'd held her silence till then, but her expression was less hard, if no less fierce while she studied Matheson. Then she'd picked up the boots Santos had worn on duty and held them out.

"You are being his friend?" Her voice was slow and dark.

Matheson had taken the boots with care and put them into a thin film bag from his pocket. "I'm trying. It would be easier if he'd told me everything—and told me sooner. Do you know what he didn't say?"

She'd shaken her head. "Nor."

That was all she'd offered and then locked the door behind him as he left.

Now he hurried back toward the office, frustrated, angry, and anxious. If what Santos believed were true, nothing he or Dillal did would matter, and that wasn't acceptable—he'd agreed to be a blood-hound, not a catspaw.

Matheson didn't run this time, but he wanted to. Once he reached the GISA building, he took the long way to ForTech to avoid S-Office. His mobile pinged with database search results that only made him more tense.

As Matheson entered the lab, a raw-boned man wearing a lab coat passed roughly by, barely mumbling an apology on his way out the door. There wasn't a med/legal or technician left in the place. He checked his mobile, but, no, he hadn't lost track of time—it wasn't much later than he'd thought and he wasn't sure why the place was abandoned so early in the shift. There was only one figure far to the rear of the room and even at a distance, Matheson recognized Dillal.

The inspector was at one of the dissecting stations, staring down into a sample dish, with his right arm crossed over his chest to support his left elbow. His left index finger was stretched against his stubbled temple, while his right eyelid drooped sleepily. The cybernetic eye, however, was wide open. Matheson kept his distance.

In a minute, Dillal closed his eyes and shook his head, stepping back from the work bench. "What is it, Matheson?" He sounded tired.

"I talked to Santos. He admitted to entering the jasso earlier—he did have a key—but he said he didn't go any farther than the tiles. I also got his damned boots—"

Dillal pointed to the side. "Leave them there. I'll have Starna deal with them tomorrow."

Matheson put the bagged footwear on the table Dillal had indicated, then walked toward the inspector, saying, "There's something else."

Dillal nodded absently, turning and opening his eyes—the natural one was bloodshot and even the prosthetic seemed dull. "Yes. I saw your query on Dohan."

"There is an unpleasant connection, but that's not the only thing that causes me concern."

"Concern?" Dillal asked. Then he blinked a while at Matheson, frowning, and cocked his head. "What particular venom has dripped into your ears?"

Matheson felt he was about to step into the abyss. "It's about you and this project . . ."

"Ah. Then this is not a discussion for the lab," the inspector said, and turned to walk out of the room. He stopped and waited for Matheson to follow him. "How were you injured?" he asked.

"What?" Matheson replied, jarred into movement by the change of topic.

Dillal rubbed a finger along the bridge of his own nose. "Injury. How."

Matheson's face felt stiff as he answered, "Accident. I slipped."

The inspector growled and walked out. He stood impatiently, then locked the lab door behind them with a swipe of his wrist across the sensor, and a keyed command. "Don't lie to me. If you prefer not to reveal a personal detail, say so, but if you force me to pick through every word you speak, you're of no use to me."

"Use is exactly the question raised," Matheson said. He didn't want to discuss the origin of his scraped face, whether or not it was relevant.

Dillal waited a moment, then shrugged and turned away. He led Matheson into his office and collapsed into a chair beside the array of busy information screens. He covered his eyes with his hands. "Tell me," he said. "I have no time to drag it out of you."

"I don't like to be maneuvered."

"I know. Explain how that's relevant."

"Santos thinks you're a dupe. Look: He admitted to the protection scheme and breaking away from me to make the pick up—you were right on that—and I'm convinced that he had no part in the robbery or the murders. But he was resistant to speaking and he was upset, until I said *you* were the IOC—then he got scared."

Dillal lowered his hands and looked at Matheson, dusty light through the high, filthy window falling in stripes across his face and illuminating his red hair. "Of me?"

"Of getting spaced. He doesn't believe that you'll be allowed to solve the case—or even that you can—but that the office of CIFO is a political blind to make sure certain cases get closed as the corporation sees fit. He believes you—and by extension I—are nothing but pawns to Corporation House."

"And you believe that also?"

"I don't want to, but he's not a great liar and he's convinced to the point of panic that if no one . . . *politically expedient* is arrested quickly enough, he'll be framed for it and shoved out the figurative air lock. I said I'd see this through, but I will not be party to that."

The inspector didn't raise his voice. "Nor would I. We both know he's not involved. Why should I do such a thing?"

"Because you'd be given no choice."

The inspector made a harsh noise in his throat. "Trash can't be brought lower."

"What?"

"Santos thinks my ambition can be used against me. That having given me this position, Pritchet and Corporation House can manipulate me to their own ends. But my ambition rises from vacancy—there's nothing to take away, nothing to threaten me with. And they hardly know you exist, as yet. It's true that if a solution doesn't appear in a timely manner—as it seems it will not—the case may become a political talking point at Corporation House. But before that pressure is brought to bear, we have a more immediate problem."

Matheson scowled at the inspector's quicksilver change of topic. "Sir?"

"Forgive me," Dillal said, scrubbing his hands over his face and back into what remained of his hair. "I may be jumping at shadows. Starna has turned up some disturbing results and Director Pritchet is observing our progress. My progress. He can't observe it in this room, however."

"What did this tech find?"

"Ohba DNA."

A chill coiled in Matheson's guts. "In the scene materials?"

"On one of the bullets—no other sign on scene so far—but if that one fact becomes known, it will play to the corporation's desire to call this an ethnic crime."

"Does this change—"

"No." Dillal leaned forward in his seat and stared into Matheson's face. "I stand by our original scenario, but it does mean our immediate goal is not so much solving the crime, as finding the suspects—or compelling evidence that points to them—before Pritchet and Corporation House shorten our leash. That will require confidence—yours in me, mine in you—and the security of this room. We won't have the further luxury of second guessing." He offered a fast-flickering smile. "I promise you I won't be pushed to an *expedient* solution, though the road to the *right* one may be unpleasant. Now, what else do you have to go forward with?"

Matheson took a slow breath, catching up before he spoke. "I may have found the connection between Robesh and Leran—they're both children of women who worked for Dohan Sewing. It's likely they played together at the factory as children and would have known each other at school."

"Such as it is for Dreihleen."

Matheson frowned, but let the inspector's comment pass, for now. "My database query also returned a registered contract between

Dohan Sewing and the Julian Company. So that confirms the origin of the clothes Robesh was wearing when she died. Speculation is that Dohan was in the Paz da Sorte to show off. Taking the model for his new line along would fit with that, but it's unconfirmed and we don't know if Robesh worked for him or for Julian."

The inspector's ocular clicked and he narrowed his eyes. "Why does this Julian business continue to distract you?"

"If the company is involved, that would . . . complicate the issue. For me."

Dillal was silent a moment before he spoke quietly. "Discard your personal demons. We must proceed quickly and the company's involvement is unlikely to have any weight but as a drag on your attention."

Matheson was not entirely reassured, but he replied, "Yes, sir."

"What else have you turned up?"

"Not much. One possible confidential informant, plus a woman I haven't been able to interview properly yet, and an unaffiliated kid who said Robesh and Leran weren't friends. My feeling is they were lovers and had a falling out, but that's also unconfirmed. I could go after the boy—I didn't get his name and he slipped off into the tunnels."

"Find a definite suspect or lead before chasing unaffs into the Tomb. The Dreihleen mourning ritual may be a problem, however."

"In what way?" Matheson asked, warily.

"The families may isolate themselves, but the tradition is rather old-fashioned and the festival also complicates the situation—people who must work to eat can't afford to hide behind blackened doors."

"I haven't had any slammed in my face yet."

"You will. But don't let it stop you—there is always the kitchen gate and your ID pass code. Delicacy must be balanced against our need to move quickly."

"It seems a little disrespectful."

"*That* is a line you'll have to walk for yourself." The inspector glanced back to his displays and stared at them as if even he didn't know where to start. "We have a race we must win and there are many obstacles."

Matheson let himself out of the office, disturbed by the inspector's distraction and obvious exhaustion. *Confidence . . . I'll have to fake it.* If this went to hell, he was the least of the people who'd be on scrap heap, but without the inspector, his own position was as tenuous as a rowboat's in a gale.

The Quay was getting busy with the upcoming night's festivities. Within hours, it would be even denser in the Dreihleat where the "more authentic" celebrations still played to the locals and tempted the hardcore culture mavens into its clogged streets. Not to mention attracting those who thought a night slumming was more thrilling than mixing with the pack of well-washed and well-heeled.

The crowds thickened as the late afternoon wore on toward the promise of the Ice Parade—a strange celebration of the passing of winter that centered on building lavish sculptures from water fast-frozen onto a skeleton of volatile fuse creating complex, but brittle shells that were filled with treats and gifts. The sculptures—called "floes"—were carried with much pomp through the neighborhood, business, or shop that had sponsored or built each one and then set on an appropriate street corner atop augmented-thermoelectric chilling platforms to counteract the tropical heat. The artistic icebergs were then destroyed by Suvil—the Great Breath—personified by Suvilen: a crew of costumed dancers and acrobats who would tumble and caper through the area with live torches, setting fire to the fuses in each ice sculpture so that they shattered into sudden clouds of ice crystals and a rain of gifts. According to Dillal, it was all as made-up as a fairytale, but that lent it a sort of lunatic charm.

Matheson had never experienced the event in person—he wasn't sure of the attraction of being pelted with ice and cheap gewgaws and the distraction factor would be high—but if he weren't on the job it might have been fun. The camaraderie of celebration, infectious excitement . . . he missed that. He hadn't made many connections on Gattis yet and under the new-guy-on-duty workload his personal pursuits had dwindled down to the solitary habits of his pentathlon days. The downside to the parade was that the whole town would be in the streets, one way or another, and there'd be no chance of finding one specific Dreihle once the floes and their attendants appeared. But he had a window before that and he had to take it.

He checked his information again. Gil Dohan had been a widower who seemed to have changed his attractive female companions as often as his clothes. The scanty Dreihleen media streams had hinted that he plucked his conquests from his employee pool, but no one had ever raised a fuss. *But who would they complain to? The trade societies? Doesn't seem likely.*

As he searched the eastern half of the Dreihleat for Dohan's friends or family, crowds carrying drink bags and unlit fireworks were already forming on the sidewalks or creating knots around the floe platforms erected to hold the sculptures sponsored by the flashiest casinos and shops on the distant Quay. Matheson noticed that the large commercial platforms attracted few Dreihleen—only those with a sharp and hungry look to them. The pickpockets and street rats would attract SOs, who might be as unpleasant as Jora and Halfennig. The last thing Matheson needed was another run in that could give Pritchet or Belcourso an excuse to pull him out and interfere in the investigation.

Hyper-vigilance slowed his progress and wore on his nerves, so it took longer than he liked to reach Dohan's home: a tall, narrow stone house on Estrada Seda, as far from the musty, noisy environs of the fish market as anyone could get in the Dreihleat. He stood across the road and frowned at it. Detached, single-family houses were rare in the city and more so in the ghetto, and this one was elegantly tall and narrow—a far cry from the low, square, utilitarian construction in most of the Dreihleat. But none of that was what made his mind reject it.

It doesn't have a door. At the top of the steps from the street there was only a blank, black wall. Matheson went up and put his hand on it. Stiff paper, thick and rough-textured. An empty stone box as tall as his hip sat on the top of the stairs, but there was no sign of a door or opening that it might conceal. He retreated to the road and walked to the end of the block farthest from the major intersection—a floe platform had been erected there and he preferred to stay out of the crowd's surge.

Turning the quieter corner, he found a service alley that crossed behind the Dohan house, among others. He went up it warily, early evening filling the narrow space with purple shadow that rustled with lizards. A black-on-gray razor cat perched high atop a wall, watching intently. Matheson gave it and its lethally sharp talons a wide berth. One small cat wouldn't kill a man his size, but pissing it off would still be painful.

Further down the alley he found several service porches, all with doors locked tight. He knocked on the door at the rear of the graceful blue stone house, but no one came to open it, though he saw a movement in one of the upper windows. He tried using his ID override on the electronic security pad but it was an archaic one that barely acknowledged his existence. When the door clicked, something inside slammed it back into the locked position and he heard a metallic thunk, as if a steel bar had been dropped into heavy braces. He called out, "GISA Ofiçe! I need to speak to you about Gil Dohan," but no one responded.

A next-door neighbor stuck her head out of a window, but pulled back inside as soon as Matheson turned her way. He jogged to her door and knocked. He identified himself and called out, "I'd like to talk to you."

The door creaked open and a young man peered out. Dreihle, early twenties, athletic, and blank-faced. He said nothing, just stared at Matheson from the corner of his eye.

"I'm trying to solve the murder of your neighbor and the others who were killed at the Paz da Sorte two nights ago. Do you know anything about Gil Dohan's movements that night? Or how he was connected to Venn Robesh?"

The man turned his head, but his expression didn't change. He looked past Matheson and quietly shut the door.

"Merry hell," Matheson muttered, and pounded on the door again, fruitlessly.

He tried each door down the alley and met with doors that never opened, and more that closed again without any questions answered. He returned to Estrada Seda and tried each door facing the road. Only a single Dreihle, a woman named Eshvelen Zehan, replied to his queries.

He guessed her age at sixty. Her skin and hair were all the same honey blond color and it lent her a delicate, faded look. "For Gil's marry we're all hoped," she said out of the blue. Her brown eyes were wide and wet under pinched brows as she stared at a bit of air just to the left of Matheson's elbow. "His mother, his sisters are alone now."

"Are they in the house?"

"In the house," she agreed.

"Do you know if he went around with a young woman named Venn Robesh? That night, or at all?"

Eshvelen closed her eyes, washing a flood of withheld tears down her cheeks to drench the hint of a sad smile that twisted her mouth. He wasn't sure if she nodded or if she merely bowed her head as she backed away and shut her door. She was the last piece of luck he had.

He exhausted the neighbors for two streets in each direction, but got no more out of the few who were home or willing to speak to him. Most of the doors remained closed as the sun fell.

Street lamps came on, their lights turned down to a low golden glow that shed no real illumination, the better to highlight the torches of the Suvilen when they arrived. Matheson shook his head—he was at the end of his chances for the day and he hadn't learned one more useful thing. *Damn it!*

He was tired—he'd been on his feet for fourteen hours—but leaving still felt like retreat. He'd have to cross most of the ghetto to get to the west bridge gate over the canal, which was the closest to his flat. *Nothing for it.* Matheson started walking, staying away from the thick crowds along the twisted route of the parade as much as possible, but still walking in the edges of the darkness, past alley mouths and doorways rank with drug smoke, sex, and piss.

He moved away from the major thoroughfares when he could, shaking free of the already-liquor-lit holiday crowds and the rising noise punctuated with incidental firecrackers and barking dogs. He worked his way around the parade route, crossing only where he could dive into another road or alley on the far side without being swept up in the entourage of one floe or another as the sculptures began their illogical and noisy progresses from refrigerated warehouses and restaurant freezers to their short-lived glory at their assigned street corners. It was beautifully insane.

He could have given up and fallen into the celebration, yet he found himself avoiding it. Instead, he saw more black-papered houses and boxes of stone. He frowned and made notes for tomorrow, mumbling to the mobile as he walked. He turned down Rua dos Peixes, wondering if Minje might still be behind the counter at the coffee house—if Aya might be there. They both knew more than they'd said.

There was a crash of noise, cymbals, shouts, a scurry of startled cats, rats, and lizards, and a wheedling sort of piping as a band of costumed acrobats burst into the street from one of the alleys. Disoriented, Matheson spun to see where they'd come from and felt a moment of inappropriate panic as he was grabbed by his elbows.

He was whirled wildly by a laughing pair of the revelers who dragged him back toward the road he'd just escaped. By their slender builds he knew they were Dreihleen beneath their face paint and bright clothing, but they had no reticence about touching him or looking at him and they gave full-throated, open-mouthed laughs more raucous and loud than he'd ever heard in the Dreihleat.

For the slimmest of moments, their motley and makeup faded in his mind to grim faces streaked with blood. He stared, frozen in his unreasonable shock. The nearest Suvilen seemed to find him particularly amusing, spinning him like a top before they dashed away, passing him like a baton to other dancers and tumblers who poured out of nearby doorways and alleys. Torches flared as the noisy mob dragged him toward the nearest floe.

The floe exploded in a burst of colored sparks that lit the ice shards as they tumbled into the air and then rained back down amid the clatter of deci-*real* tokens and cheap baubles wrapped in twists of colored foil. His horror broke, and Matheson stumbled backward into someone, nearly falling as the crowd surged away to snatch up the fallen treasures. He was put back onto his feet with a shove and an ungentle poke in the ribs.

CHAPTER TWELVE

Day 2: Night

"Fool," a Dreihleen voice spoke near his ear. "You're not know to turn your back? You're admire the floe *before* th'explosion."

The crowd was squealing and scrambling after the loot of the floe as the Suvilen moved on and another floe exploded with a crackling roar farther away.

"No," Matheson replied, jarred back to himself as the bizarre procession moved on.

"Is no wonder you're look as you do, then."

He shook his head clear and squinted as his eyes adjusted to the weird, moving light cast by the torches of the Suvilen between the dimmed street lamps. "I got caught in the Great Breath—who knew it had a childish sense of humor?" His voice trembled more than he liked to admit and he peered at the figure in front of him.

It was a Dreihle woman and her loose hair swirled around her as she looked sideways at him, her face mostly in shadow. She cocked her head "Do not all zephyrs? Only children, after all."

"I'm afraid I don't understand." *I know you . . .*

She gave him a more direct gaze, though she was still slightly turned away. She was within ten centimeters of his own height, which put her eyes surprisingly close to his in the sudden flow and crush of a crowd moving past them to follow the Suvilen. Those eyes seemed to spark and glitter. *Must be the reflection of fireworks and torchlight.*

But it was her—Aya. He noticed a faint scent of spice and coffee, sparking inappropriate thoughts, and his breath hitched in his chest.

The passing crowd shoved them together for a moment, then she stepped back as the crowd loosened around them. The awkward contact left a fleeting impression on Matheson's skin through the sweat-moistened layers of his shirt and singlet that made the hairs on his body stand up as if magnetically attracted to her. *Don't. Don't think it.*

She looked aside as if checking her own thoughts. Then she repeated, "Children." Her voice was so low he had to lean toward her to hear the word, threaded with bitterness. "Suvilen crews," she added. "But for z'torchmen, all children. We're almost cancel th'parade, but how we're do that to them now? Say, 'this last thing you're love, we're take that away too'? 'Yes, your uncle's shot in the head, and your neighbor, your friend's mother, so you're go cry in the dark and we're take away th'only thing's give you hope. Spring's canceled. No Great Breath, no hope, no rebirth. Sorry!'"

Matheson blinked at her, trying to get words out straight. "You're one of the few people I've met who's angry about what happened."

She scoffed. "Then you're not look very hard." She glared at him, and then reared back, looking puzzled. "Why you're bleed? They're not so rough with you."

He wiped his eyebrow with the back of one finger. "No. Suvil's not so rough—more of a rollick." He glanced at his hand—even in the low light, he could see a dark smear of blood on his knuckle.

"Rollick?" She chuckled. "Is sound like sollets're doing. Now, come, or someone's think I'm one who's make you bleed." She grabbed his forearm and tugged him along.

He followed in her wake, bemused, as she dragged him across the dim road and down an alley to a door that she unlocked with a hurried code combination and a press of her palm against a scanner plate on the door itself. *Sophisticated system for a back door*. The portal made a clanking sound and cracked open, then she pushed it wide and pulled him through behind her.

Inside, low lights along the floor and ceiling molding shone just bright enough to bring the largest objects out of the gloom. Aya locked the door behind them and led him deeper into the room, saying something he couldn't understand.

The illumination rose to a moderate glow, but no brighter. The revealed room was a small industrial space like a kitchen with two long work tables and a wrap-around counter holding a row of three identical machines beside a large device that looked like a washing machine with a bad attitude. The room smelled as she did, of coffee and spice and some exotic flower. Everything was scrubbed clean, put away, closed up, and wiped down for the night. Even the floor that was one smooth, continuous pour of angelstone was without a speck or stain. Speckless perfection was the nature of angelstone, but in this light and shut suddenly from the revelry outside, it seemed uncanny, like a computer model that verged on the surreal.

"What is it about women in kitchens today?" he muttered, turning to look at her in the light. He stopped and blinked, shaking his head. "This is . . . the coffee house?"

"Where else I'm take you? Public Health?" she said, drawing him to an old stone sink set down in the rolled steel counter. "You're prefer, I'm send you."

"Umm." He stumbled over his tongue as well as his feet. "I'm . . . ah, no. It's dark in there."

She lifted an eyebrow and looked askance at him.

Matheson shook his head and regretted it. "Never mind. I'm tired."

She took a cloth from a cabinet and moistened it at the faucet. Even the water had a scent—fresher and colder than what came out of the spigot in his dingy little flat. She put her hand on his chest and pushed him toward the counter. "Sit."

"On what?"

"Stool behind you. What? You're think I'm knock you down?"

"I think you very well could," he answered and sat, aware of the strength of her shove and the hard competence of her hands. She was poised and slender as a whip, with few curves that weren't muscle. Light shone through her thin dress when she moved around the room, and he tried not to think too much about her shape and feel. *And she could probably break my neck if she took a mind to.*

He shook the bizarre thought away. It might be true, but it was as unlikely as it was gruesome. He concentrated on her hair, instead. There were strands of copper in the blackness of it, and sparks of metallic red. *Dye? Bits of foil flung by an exploding floe?*

She put one hand on his shoulder and applied a little force. "You're lean back over the sink." *"Z'zink." Sounds like Christa's knife striking into the butcher block.*

"You're not going to kill me, are you?" he blurted. "Because it's been that kind of day."

She clicked her tongue and pushed him back. "Been enough killing here," she said, and dabbed at his eyebrow with the wet towel. "That's how you're get this?"

He liked listening to the pleasant lilt and buzz of her voice. Since he seemed to be capable of nothing but idiocy at the moment, he didn't reply to her question.

She nudged his hip with her knee and rubbed the swollen skin around his cut eyebrow enough to regain his attention. "Heh?"

"I had a meeting with an immovable object."

"Kind that's talk or kind that's not? I'm not believe you're clumsy—were perfect this morning."

Matheson gave a rueful chuckle. "Perfect is my least-favorite adjective, especially when applied to me."

"I'm not you." She finished dabbing the blood off his brow and frowned at it for a moment before she went to another cabinet. She returned to his side with a small container. "You're tilt your head more back. You're not want this in your eye."

"What is it?" he asked, trying to let his head fall back without the rest of him tumbling off the stool.

"Alum—stops bleeding."

"People bleed a lot in here?" He leaned too far and slipped off the stool, landing in a self-conscious, laughing heap on the floor. "You're going to retract that not-clumsy comment. I'm a disaster."

Aya laughed, covering her mouth with her free hand. She helped him up and moved the stool so he could lean back against the counter without another collapse. "Is not disaster . . . a small pity, like a fallen cake."

"A cake? That *is* a pity. I'd like to be more interesting than cake."

"You're lay your head back." She didn't laugh, her smile settling into a more serious expression as she pushed aside the damp hair clinging to the abraded skin of his brow. Her hand was cool and he resisted giving in to the shiver that started on his scalp and scurried down his neck and spine.

"Not so stiff," she chided. "Th'alum's not sting you. Is mostly for cooking. Also for pickles and pricked fingers. You're close your eyes." She continued brushing his forehead and studying him.

The way she rolled her Rs and clipped off the end of "pricked" made him smile. He shouldn't, but he did as she told him, letting his head fall back until it rested on the counter. His eyes slid closed. It felt dangerously good. She traced her finger over his unbroken eyebrow and down his nose. Then cool powder touched his skin. He felt her lower her head close to his, heard the soft sound of her breath as it stirred the air against his temple. She held him still a moment. He could imagine her lips near his brow, her eyes searching his face . . . Then she blew across his forehead and lifted him up again.

He came all the way to his feet, shaking himself out of the seductive floating feeling that had gripped him. "What was that for?"

"I'm blow away th'extra powder once the bleeding's stopped."

"Oh, I see."

"You're not see—had your eyes closed."

It was a lame joke, but he chuckled anyway. He couldn't think what else to do that wouldn't be horrendously ill-advised. "You've been too kind." This was a strange conversation and a bit disturbing. He almost felt dizzy and groped to steady himself against the counter.

The alum container tipped off the edge.

Aya snatched it from the air and turned to put the canister away. "You're not remember me," she said over her shoulder.

He scowled "Of course I do—from this morning."

She shook her head and turned back, looking grave.

"I do remember you," Matheson replied, his mind spinning through the possibilities of where or how they'd met before that morning.

She gave a dismissive little "huh" and turned aside again.

He took a step and touched her shoulder, then jerked his hand back, appalled at himself. "I do. You had come in the front door and stood aside as I walked out. It was hard to see your face with the light shining through the window. You were just a beautiful woman in the morning sun."

"Not's beautiful as Venn Robesh."

Matheson stared, dumbstruck, at her. She couldn't know what he had said about Robesh.

She looked directly at him, her eyes still holding a strange glitter and spark. "You're had asked who I knew, asked about Gil Dohan, but . . . everyone's know you're gone to Velas, asking about Venn and Denny. Words're fly quick here. I'm know how this," she added pointing at his cut eyebrow and then running her finger along the side of her own nose. "You're the police asks for Dohan tonight. You're ask all day, though you're say's only work. The rest, they're come, they're go. You're here. So."

Something cold settled in the pit of his stomach. "You came looking for me?"

"Found you. Did not look."

Outside, the clash of cymbals and the squeal of the pipes passed, accompanied by the too-loud laughter of the Suvilen and the calls of drunken tourists.

He dragged her closer to him, perhaps rougher than he'd meant to. She narrowed her eyes at him but didn't pull back. He peered straight into that narrow gleam. "Tell me about Venn and Denny. Who did they know?"

There was a decent view of the Ice Parade route from high up the old theater steps—not much detail, but an overlook of moving torches and glittering explosions in between the buildings. Dillal stood on the landing with his arms crossed, leaning one shoulder into the wall as he watched the streets below. He was dressed like a tourist. No one had paid him any attention when he'd walked into the Dreihleat with his head down behind a gaggle of hoppers, nor as he'd made his way up the stairs. The door from the backstage opened and a middle-aged Dreihle man stepped out, dressed in work clothes. He was taller than the inspector and had a small tattoo, shaped like a lily, below his right eye.

"Zeno," Dillal said, barely turning his head.

"*Trahna* . . . Cousin," Zeno replied, hesitating.

Dillal gave a snort and continued in Dreihleen, but he didn't clench his teeth around his words as Zeno did: "I'm 'Cousin' today, am I? Is that honor from them or from you?"

Zeno raised the barest of shrugs. "It's I greet you, but them who speak. They ask if you've caught the red tars that did this thing."

"No."

Zeno continued quietly, "Why not? Why do you dawdle? It should be done."

"You sound just like Pritchet, except you've made the culprits a different color. The trade societies presume that if a wrong of this magnitude is done, it must be the Ohba who did it, heh?"

"It is as 'tis."

"No, it isn't. We have no reason to suspect any Ohba were involved in what happened at Paz."

"Then it goes unsolved."

Dillal turned and glared at Zeno. The starlight slid across his face; Zeno twitched in shock and took a step back. "Why do you imagine I would let that happen?" the inspector demanded.

Zeno stared a moment before he turned his head a little aside and replied, "'Tis the trade fathers, not I. GISA has no care for us. They'll not pursue hoppers or cits who harm Dreihleen."

"If it were one death or two, the trade fathers might be right, but this is beyond what can be swept aside as a cost of doing business. And still they don't say why they think *I* would let it go that way."

"Why would it be otherwise, Cousin?"

"That you can imply two such contradictory things in the same breath astounds me. I am not 'one of them.' I haven't become a monster in two years—though the trade fathers may think I've always been one. Yet *you* still call me 'Cousin' as if you remember that I was born less than two-hundred meters from this spot. Which is it, Zeno?"

"'Tis not for me to say."

"Cat shit. I know what the societies think of me, but what of *you*? You were like an older brother when I was a small child—you stood beside my mother and my sister, then. You were a friend—or at least friendly—when I was a young ofiçe trying to deal fairly here. Now you keep your distance as if I could infect you, though by the reckoning of the societies, you're not much better than I—useful only to carry messages to the unclean."

Closing his eyes, Zeno sighed and hung his head. "Have pity, Djepe. I am not like you. I've no place but this."

Dillal growled and turned back to look at the street, clutching the railing. "Say their piece."

Zeno opened his eyes and took a long breath before he said, "If not the red tars, then find another, soon. Or we shall."

The inspector's eyes narrowed with a faint click. "I don't intend to let the corporation or anyone else dictate the result of my investigation, nor to let the societies play into the corporation's hands by allowing you to kill your own."

"Intentions count for nothing." The words sounded hollow in Zeno's mouth.

"Mine do. I will find the parties who are guilty *in fact*, not merely those who are convenient. Not for the corporation and not for your society chiefs, either. I've seen the agitation, the riots, the deaths in the agricamps . . ." His voice didn't rise as he spoke. "I know that if this isn't closed soon it will be another cause for violence one way or another, and that only benefits the corporation—no matter what the rabble-rousers and park bench revolutionaries say. Gattis Corporation and Corporation House have divided us, turned us on each other, preyed on *all* of us—Dreihleen and Ohba—for more than two centuries. They created the Agria Corps for the sole purpose of crushing us faster and laying the blame on someone else. Anyone can read the history of it—if they're allowed to learn to read. If they're given access to the net instead of tucked away in blacked-out ghettos where they become their own prison guards and executioners out of fear and hate. We have lost our history. When the charter is reviewed, it will all come out, but it won't matter what they've done to us if there aren't any of us left."

Zeno's face pinched in misery as he stared at Dillal's back. "I don't know if 'tis true, Cousin—I can't read your books—but I see us breaking apart: the trade from the free, those who will bow from those who will not . . . I listen to the speakers in the park. They're just as bad as the rest. Some tell us to hold to our tradition, some to revolt, some tell us to withdraw, others tell us to speak . . . Only this terrible thing has drawn us back together, and I'm afraid. I do not want to see more of us die. And I don't know what to do but carry messages and duck my head."

Grim and weary, the inspector muttered, "Know a man by his ideals; but measure him by how he stands up to his friends." He turned to study Zeno. "Tell the trade fathers that I will find who did this—whether it serves them or not. They needn't worry that I'll dance to the corporation's tune either, since it's as poisonous to me as it is to the Dreihleen and Ohba both. But warn them of this: I won't tolerate any trade society justice, nor any further interference with my assistant. They should help me find who did this before the corporation uses it as an excuse to do here what they've done in the penal camps of Agria. And if they won't, then be damned to them."

He walked down the stairs with a deliberate tread. His shoulders were rigid and his grip on the railing was tight the whole way. The crowd in the street below the theater closed around him, hiding him from sight. He swayed, held up for a moment only by the press of other bodies. But he kept his feet and made his way out of the Dreihleat by the east gate, his stride slowing once he was several streets away.

Aya sent Matheson to the closest work table while she prepared a pot of tea. "Talk less well without tea," she said.

He leaned against the table—he'd fall asleep if he sat. "Does it have to be a particular tea?" he asked, more to say something while she was turned away than because it was of any importance.

"Tea has moods. Not coffee. Coffee has personality—usually very loud, like tourists. May sweeten it, but can't change its nature."

She brought the pot of tea, small thick-sided bowls, and a plate of pastry, and set it all on the counter between them. Matheson eyed the small balls of flaky dough with suspicion.

She set her hip against the counter and chuckled. "Won't hurt you."

He gave the pastries a sour look. "They look like escudos."

"I'm make them."

"You made the escudos . . . Of course. Because Loni taught you to bake."

Aya shrugged. "Make them when I can. Make everything, if I can. Even grow flowers for tea—sweet jasmine, mum, aminta, rose. Cost's too high if I'm not."

Aminta, that's the spicy honey fragrance. "You own the shop—or your husband does?"

She shook her head. "Not married." *Marret.*

"Oh. I . . . thought . . ."

"What you're think? Women aren't run businesses?"

"I was told business is a family thing among the Dreihleen."

"'Tis, if I'm cleave to family. But I'm have too little left and I'm not bow to kind, so they're leave me be. I'm have Minje—though I'm angry with him for giving th'escudos, but what I'm do? They're not kill you."

"Not quite," he said.

The tilt of her head spoke volumes of irony as she looked him over. "Thought I'd not see you again. Just an ofiçe running errands."

"But you said you knew it was me asking questions today and you knew I was the same clueless fool who wandered into your shop two days ago."

"Word said a tall *shashen*—black hair, blue eyes."

"*Shashen?*"

She hesitated, then said, "Foreigner."

"System-hopper."

She shook her head. "Hopper is temporary, is selfish, sees nothing but their own desire. Shashen is . . ." She looked straight at him. "Stranger."

Her eyes still fascinated him. They were brown—ordinary brown, he reminded himself—but he kept being caught in them whenever she gazed directly at him. Most Dreihleen looked aside. *Except Minje, and I don't look into* his *eyes and watch for stars.*

Matheson turned his head aside to break the spell. "Venn and Denny. Tell me about them."

He did not watch her pour the tea.

"You're want to write it down, what I'm say?"

He braved a glance and she made a gesture of scribbling in the air, lifting her eyebrows in question. He chuckled. "No. The mobile does that," he added, looking at the device where it rested in the loops of his chest pocket. "Crap." He'd forgotten to hash the incident, though it hadn't been clear it was an interview when he'd found himself joining her for tea. He pressed the hash key and noted the flicker of the recording indicator.

She placed a cup by his elbow and looked at his pocket. "My name's Aya Leyhan." She gave her last name the harsh throaty sound he'd heard Dillal use in the morgue.

"Spell your last name," he said, wondering . . .

"L-L-I-A-N."

He'd guessed right. "Go on. Venn Robesh and Denenshe Leran."

Aya shook her head. "Nine thousand of us in Dreihleat Ang'Das. Can't know everyone, but Venn . . . She was Suvilen, was a festival dancer, was an admirable star in our sky. But still Dreihleen, and no future but house service, sweat labor, or sex. Denny Leran—petty, cruel boy—was best she could get. He's got money, but she's not like what he does."

"What did he do?"

"Crime. Small things—thief, card cheat, mugger . . . I'm tell Minje I'm not like chancers in the shop. They're make hoppers think Dreihleen're low." Chilly anger sharpened her expression and sent a shiver down Matheson's spine.

"But Leran came anyhow?"

Aya growled under her breath. "Is hard t'keep all trash outside and Minje's softer than I. But s'better for business he's work the counter and I'm work here—or I'm sweep away the good with the dirt."

"I see," Matheson said. Her manner hinted she was capable of worse. He paused and redirected his questions. "So Venn and Denny were lovers. Did that change?"

Aya gave a derisive cough. "He's never love her. He's treat her as property. Then she's become Beauty of Gattis and Denny's no longer the cat that's stalk the yard."

Matheson scowled over the phrase. Aya made an endless circle with her finger against the tabletop. "He's keep her frightened, keeps others away."

Matheson nodded. "How often did they come here?" he asked. "Did she have other admirers?"

"Weekends, morning perhaps, they're come separately. She's listen to speakers in the park, come for coffee afterward, for talk it over. She's not a fiery girl, very quiet. Always the men they're want t'charm her, buy her coffees. They're care nothing what she's feel about speeches, only want t'be seen with her. But, Denny . . ." Disgust edged her voice. "Always his talk's how pretty she is, how she's his, then how she's stay with him, how she's help him. She's never say yes, but she's go with him from fear. The more she's come t'listen in the park, the more she's say no and Denny's get angry. They're fight and she's break from him. Several times. Denny's temper's violent. He's tell her she would be a whore. He's tear her dress and say what he's do t'her for the price of a coffee."

Matheson's stomach clenched. "What did he say he would do?"

Aya closed both her hands around her bowl of tea.

"Did he threaten to kill her?" Matheson asked.

She shook her head, glaring at the counter. "Is always sex. Violent. Degrading. Things a prostitute's not do. Only someone much lower, someone broken." Her voice quivered slightly and her fingers had clenched tight around her cup.

Matheson felt a shameful satisfaction that Denny Leran was dead. "None of those things happened to her."

"Only murder." The same rolling R and hard D that Minje had used on the word days ago: "mare't.dair." She rested her hands on the counter and the tea bowl chattered. The muscles at the corner of her jaw shifted.

"I suppose it's not a consolation that Leran is also dead?" he asked.

Aya squeezed her eyes closed and the trembling turned to shaking, pale-lipped rage.

He wanted to tell her Denny had died for hurting Venn—shot in the head like a rabid animal—but then he'd have to tell her that they'd all died because of what Denny had done.

"There's no—no consolation," she started, her voice harsh and cracking. "No relief. In this. I'm not love them. They're not mine. But when we're killed like animals—And no one—Who's not—who can't—"

She broke off. Her cup dropped to the floor with a heavy thump, splashing the cooled tea across the sugar-white angelstone. She turned her head sharply away and down, pawing at her hair and drawing it over her face like a thick curtain as she bowed over her grief and fury. She didn't tear her hair as Mrs. Vela had done, but her body shook with one high, choking shriek that seemed to go on continuously without breath drawn. The sound seemed to tear something out of her and cut through him as well.

He couldn't see her face, but he knew from her posture that she must be burying it in her long-fingered hands, half smothering herself. *I'm to wait . . . wait, don't touch, don't offer, don't interfere until asked . . .* But she wasn't exactly a witness and her screaming made his own chest ache. *Screw that!*

He stretched his hand out toward her shoulder. "Aya . . ."

She collapsed into a crouch, tucking her head to her knees.

Matheson knelt down, reaching for her.

She wrenched around to face him, raising her head and hands. The look on her face made him recoil. Then she shut her glaring eyes and covered her mouth with her fingers. She drew a loud breath through her nose and slumped to sitting on the floor, her back against the counter's footing.

Her tension escaped on long breaths and she wiped her face with the backs of her wrists. Then she glanced at him, eyes a little wide and wary.

Matheson put out one hand. "Are you all right?"

"I . . . am sorry," she said, putting one of her hands in his and starting to pull herself up. "My anger's not for you."

He helped her to her feet and stayed closer than he should have. He handed her his untouched tea. "I hope this mood is better."

She gave him a small smile and took the bowl. "*Felje.*" She sipped, then stood taller with great effort. Her hair was tangled, but she left it alone. "You're . . . have more questions?"

He'd almost forgotten. "No. I think we're done. Though I may have questions some other time."

"Is fair," she said, and nodded. She put the tea bowl on the counter and gazed into it, resting her hand beside it.

Matheson turned off the recording and put his hand over hers. "Thank you for your help. I'm sorry it was so . . . terrible."

"We're all grieve, but the ones who did this, they're profit by our grief. Our terror. Who's spoken to you but me and Minje?" she asked.

"Only Vela and a neighbor of Dohan's. Your neighbors are reluctant to talk to a . . . shashen about it."

Her smile was bitter. "Most won't. They're cling to silence and pain, hope it will disappear—blow away like flowers dried in desert air. I'm not cover my door in black paper and hold out the world."

Black paper, like the seamless sheet that had hidden the Dohans' doors. Blackened doors. Dillal could have been more specific, exhausted or not . . .

"It's getting late. I should go," he said, excusing his frowning silence.

She looked at his hand and he started to draw it away, embarrassed. She caught it and held on, then turned her gaze up to his. "Your touch's not burn me."

"You shouldn't—*I* shouldn't touch you . . . like this." He had a squeezing, dropping sensation in his chest that felt like a heart attack and he had to swallow hard and force himself to breathe.

She said nothing and didn't let go.

"It's unprofessional," he managed to say. A paltry, transparent sop to ethics that parts of his body were giving no sort of damn about.

"We're done with that. I'm want you should stay."

"I shouldn't."

"Shouldn't is not won't."

Matheson made himself move, withdrawing his hand from hers. He was breathing too fast, and sure that he was shaking, but he couldn't see his hand tremble. *This is a bad idea . . .* "I can't."

She turned her head and glanced at him sideways. Not as she had before. Now it was deliberate. She offered him a small smile. "A good police. Won't take advantage of a woman who's broken."

"You're not broken. You're angry and I think you might be a little . . . confused."

"Not confused. I'm know what I'm wanting." She gave a quiet snort and reached up, touched his eyebrow. "You're bleed again."

"It's becoming a bad habit of mine," he replied.

She chuckled low in her throat and handed him a cloth from the counter. He pressed it to his brow before blood could drip into his eye. He was grateful for the excuse to withdraw before he got in too deep. But those depths were tempting.

"Then don't make people angry."

No, and especially not women with eyes like yours. If he were smart, he would leave—he was a little too attracted by her knowing gaze, the sense of something dangerous coiled in her depths. He started to back toward the door. If he had more questions, it might be better to send them by message, no matter how tight Pritchet's schedule was.

Aya cupped her hand around the back of his neck, stopping his progress. Her long fingers brushed his ear on one side, eliciting a shiver. She stepped close and pressed a chaste, closed kiss on the corner of his jaw. Or it should have been chaste if he had not let his arm curl around her and if he had not been thinking about all the other places she could put her lips.

"Right man," she murmured into his ear, but she didn't let go.

He didn't either, and in spite of himself he knew he wasn't going to.

She took the bloodied towel from his hand and urged his head down until she could kiss his cut brow.

He tightened his arm around her and turned his head, trying to catch her mouth under his. She evaded him, lifting her face as her hands swept down his back. His lips brushed her throat instead. If that's what she would give him, that's what he would take. He pressed his free hand between her shoulders, drawing her closer while he kissed his way down her neck.

He wasn't going to leave and he wasn't going to be a right man after all.

CHAPTER THIRTEEN

Day 3: Friday—Morning into Afternoon

No nightmares, no sudden starts to waking as he had for the past few months, and Matheson wasn't sure where he was when he opened his eyes. He couldn't hear the whine of struggling ventilation fans, the air didn't have the musty stillness of his flat, and blood-orange light moved across the high, planked ceiling. A wisp of white flicked across his view—a bit of gauze borne on a breeze perfumed with rose petals and cut grass.

Aya's loft above the coffee house. Even as he turned on his side to find her, Matheson knew she wasn't in the clean, white bed with him. He sat up, blinking the tailings of sleep from his eyes. He hadn't expected to spend the night, and he'd had other things on his mind when he did, so he hadn't paid much attention to the room when they'd come upstairs. He'd heard the distant sounds of the celebration in the street and the light had had a peculiar, moving quality that reminded him of camping in the woods, and the second-hand streetlight through Dillal's office windows. Now he looked out toward sunrise with nothing but air between him and the light.

The room had no eastern wall, only a few support pillars. Ahead of him, more than half of the old building's roof spread open, contained only by tall posts hung with bird netting and fluttering streamers of colored fabric. A dense perimeter of potted plants ringed the open roof edges in greenery and blossoms. Aya had her back to him. She used a silicone rake to turn petals that lay strewn across stretched cloth set on the sun-struck expanse of rounded rocks and gravel.

Matheson was rooted in place as he watched her moving, swaying slowly forward and back, sideways a step, then forward and back . . . The low morning sun burnished her and the light dazzled in her black hair as it hung loose down her back. He remembered the heavy, almost rough feel of it against him, and the taste of tea dust on her skin.

She turned, leaning her rake into the corner where the covered section gave way to the open roof garden. She reached high upward, stretching, her shirt pulling taut across her small breasts and riding up to show a hint of her waist. Her feet were bare under her skirt and she curled her toes into the white pebbles. She looked ecstatic and it left him breathless.

She turned her head and saw him. Her hair partially obscured her face, but he could still see the wicked curve of her smile as she looked him over sideways. She caught his eye, her smile widening a little, and turned her head away as if beckoning him to her.

There seemed little point in dressing, so he walked out to her as he was. He started to put his arms around her and she turned, sliding into his embrace so her back pressed to him from chest to groin. It was arousing, but he didn't want to be teased. He wrapped his arms close around her waist so she could feel him more firmly against her. "Do I stay or go?"

"What would you?"

"You know what I would. The sun's barely touching the crater's lip and the streets are still full of fog. Even my boss wouldn't notice if I spend another hour in your bed. But it's not up to me, and if you tell me to stay this time . . . are we starting something or are we just fucking?"

She tilted her head with a mild shrug that exposed the long line of her neck. "Fairzee-mairzee."

"What does that mean?"

"Is . . . either/or . . . some of each . . . as you like."

"You keep putting this back on me," he said, and bit lightly up the exposed line of her neck, "but 'as *I* like' starts this way . . ." He turned her to face him, hauled her in hard for a kiss, but she turned her head aside. He exhaled against her cheek, letting her go. "And you keep doing that."

She took a half step back, pressing her lips hard together, and lowered her head. It was hard to tell in the ruddy dawn light, but, was she blushing?

Frustration—that's what this irritation is. "Have I done something wrong or are you just toying with me?"

"Neither," she muttered.

"Then what is it? I'm attracted to you and you don't seem to despise me. We're good in bed, but if this were just about sex, I'd have left last night. Or you'd have thrown me out. So why do you always pull away when I go to kiss you?"

She looked up from under her brows. "We don't . . ." She rubbed one folded knuckle against her closed lips. "We don't."

"You don't *kiss*?"

"Not—Dreihleen don't . . . with the tongue." Was she disgusted? Embarrassed? Flustered? Not Aya—poised, shiver-inducing Aya. Not after what they'd done.

He peered at her, thinking aloud. "Dreihleen don't open their teeth . . ."

"Killing cold can't pass closed teeth."

"It's not cold here. At least not this part of Gattis."

"Is a very old saying."

He nodded, keeping his train of thought to himself. Gattis hadn't been hospitable in the early days—they'd had to drop in sealed environments like Yshteppa Dome for the surface workers. The Dreihleen must have been among them. And they'd learned to keep their mouths shut or die—you had to drag words from them and they still came out sideways. Only children ever smiled widely or laughed out loud. "And you don't open your mouth when you kiss."

She shook her head. "Only whores."

A telling word to choose since Dreihleen, though small in number, held the highest profile among Gattis's licensed sex-workers. Gattis Corporation raked in millions of *reals* annually from the trade—it was regulated, paid well, and was generally safe—but it was still distasteful.

"Swimming doesn't make you a fish," he said.

Aya gave him a sharp look.

He should walk, but he wasn't ready to give up—merry hell, even with her glaring at him he still wanted to drag her back to bed.

"You kissed my cheek, and I've kissed you . . . all over. But it doesn't make me a sex worker."

"Is not the same."

"You're right—it isn't a business transaction. It's a pleasure I want to share with you—like you shared with me."

She looked curious. "You're . . . enjoy that?"

"I'm a man—I think it's fairly obvious when I'm enjoying something." He caught her nearest hand and drew her closer so he could whisper into her ear, "But I also enjoyed hearing you moan when I put my mouth on you, feeling you shudder . . ." He slid his own hand along her arm and under her hair at the back of her neck. "Let me kiss your mouth."

She closed her eyes, turning her face away.

He sighed and let her go, contenting himself with pressing his lips to the height of her cheekbone, where the sun had set small wrinkles below the corner of her eye. "Then show me something else. Something you like."

She gave him a wicked sideways glance. "I'm already show you what I like," she said, sliding one hand down his chest.

"Oh, we'll get to that," he said, catching her wrists. "Teach me something new. I'm an eager student."

Aya hummed speculatively and looked him over. "You're say."

"I've always done well at oral exams."

"Is too easy for you."

Matheson smiled and let go of her hands. "Whatever you will— I'm at your mercy."

"You're will be . . ."

He caught his breath.

Dillal frowned at Starna and the tech shivered, dropping his gaze. "I'm sorry sir, they run much slower on the old machines that are off-circuit. It will take a day to get a complete sequence. Ohba is all I know and if there's no record of the individual in the database—if he or she is a phantom—the best I'll be able to do is specify the family line, and I'll have to match that by hand as it is."

"That will do."

"This would be easier if we could use the database . . ."

"I've already told you. This must remain discrete, isolated from the system. Any request to the database through normal channels will be noted and the result will be open to anyone with access to these case files. Which includes Detive Neme and Director Pritchet. Can you not imagine what will happen if this is known to either of them?"

Starna looked ill and nonplussed. "Yes, sir. I mean, no, sir. Oh, blight it all!" he shouted, looking up, shoulders hunched as if expecting a blow. "Yes, I know what will happen! I grew up in Centerrun! One of my uncles died in the race riots! When you're like me it's not good enough to be 'good enough.' It's not good enough to keep your head down. Yes, I understand. Yes, I do. So do you." He clapped one hand onto the opposite forearm, clutching his red-brown skin as if he would tear it off. "You don't let this stop you. Why should I?"

"I don't allow it to break me, either. Or become an excuse."

Starna clenched his jaw and leaned toward the inspector, glaring. "You don't—"

The door chime sounded and Starna yelped as if he'd been jabbed with a needle, whipping around to face the office door.

Dillal called out, "Come in, Matheson." But the inspector wasn't watching the door—he was watching Starna who turned back with his eyes wide. Dillal served the tech a hard look and a minuscule shake of the head.

The door unlocked and the inspector's acting IAD entered, blinking against the dimness of the room as everyone did. The lithe, light-skinned young man was uncharacteristically mussed, unshaven, and a faint scent of woman and crushed leaves clung close to his skin. He paused and frowned at the other two men, as if he could read the tension between them. "You called me in?"

"I did." Dillal's gaze hadn't left the technician. "Get some sleep, Starna. The tests will run on their own."

The tech looked away, ducking his head. "Yes, sir," he replied, turning to brush past Matheson with more force than necessary on his way out the door. He didn't raise his eyes or apologize.

The tall ofiçe took a step back and watched him go with a bemused frown. He turned to the inspector with the expression intact.

Dillal tilted his head. "Santos's sole impression is not a match."

Matheson blinked and looked relieved. "Oh. I suppose that's good."

"Why?"

Matheson looked confused. "I . . . like him, so . . . I am glad he's not, apparently, a killer."

"But you never thought he was."

"No, I didn't. But confirmation in evidence does make me more comfortable with my gut feeling—which you seem to want."

The inspector shrugged. "It was expected. Other problems with the forensic evidence were not. Scene contamination . . ."

Matheson heaved an irritated sigh and rolled his eyes. "Merry hell. Neme's cigarette ends."

Dillal gazed at him sideways. "How do you suppose that?"

"She smokes Salfrin. I noticed a couple of days ago and thought some of the lip ends we found were crushed out the same way she does hers. I should have mentioned it before."

"It matters less than the as-yet-unidentified Ohba DNA. And as I've had a discussion with the Dreihleen trade societies—who want this closed as swiftly as Pritchet does—there will be even greater pressure to make a case from nothing if this information comes out. It's not enough simply to eliminate someone—we need a positive lead. Your report from last night wasn't complete."

"It wasn't?"

"There was an interview file that was improperly closed. It never uploaded. Was there something useful in that?"

Matheson blushed and looked aside, missing Dillal's quizzical lift of one eyebrow. "I'm sorry, sir. I didn't realize it didn't go. I'll send it now—"

He reached for his mobile and the inspector waved it away. "In a moment. Thus far, your reports are hollow—filled with facts and interviews, but devoid of conclusions or observations that link information into a pattern. I remind you: it's not your ability to record that is important but your ability to think. Summarize your report for me now. Surely something stands out?"

Matheson gave an irritated shake of his head that let a curl of disordered hair fall into his eye. He flicked it away, flinching as his fingers hit the scab in his eyebrow. "It was frustrating—you didn't brief me very well about Dreihleen mourning. I could barely get anyone to talk to me about Dohan—only the one woman who said she'd hoped Dohan would get married. I'm not sure if she meant that he was considering marrying Robesh or if it was just a neighborly opinion that he should have settled down. Another woman—that's the file I missed sending—was able to make a more decisive connection between Leran and Robesh and described some prior instances of violence between them, but her information is too removed to *prove* a motive—only to imply that Leran was jealous and possessive toward Venn. The woman wasn't able to name names or make a connection to other possible suspects. I'm developing another informant, but he won't speak on the record, and this latter woman probably knows more than she's said, but—I don't know how to deal with the screaming . . . or crying, if that's what it is. I'm not sure if it's a cultural thing I need to be careful of or if I'm being snowed in. There's nothing in the brief or the protocol—"

"Describe it."

Matheson shifted on his feet and replied slowly, "Mrs. Vela and this latter woman both did it—a sort of screeching and tearing at their hair, which they pulled over their faces. It went on and on, like they didn't even need to breathe, just . . . screamed."

Dillal nodded, his expression remote. "*A Trizesh*. It's a . . . howl—at the injustice of loss. Part despair, part rage. The mechanism of the long breath that makes it possible is specific to Dreihleen physiology. Usually, only other Dreihleen witness it."

Matheson reared back and looked confused. "Why would they . . . ? In front of me? The Velas did seem anxious to get rid of me, though I still don't know why. But that doesn't seem to be the case with the other woman."

"It's an unlikely action to take just to drive you away, but it is a very odd coincidence." The inspector looked thoughtful. "The community hasn't been assaulted like this before. What happened at the Paz da Sorte attacks the core of the community, makes them feel vulnerable. Perhaps you were simply the last pebble that brings down the Pillars."

Matheson frowned at the floor.

"Tell me about this morning," Dillal said.

The younger man jerked his head up and looked startled. "This morning, sir?"

Dillal looked him over, his prosthetic flickering a red gleam as he drew a breath through his nose. "You came from the Dreihleat, and plainly you did not sleep at home."

Matheson glanced down for a moment before meeting the inspector's gaze. "That was personal business. Sir."

Dillal cocked his head slightly and the corner of his mouth twitched. "So I see." He paused, seeming to recompose his thoughts several times before he spoke again. "We're on a tightrope with this investigation, Matheson. Be careful."

"Of course, sir."

The inspector shook his head. "There is no 'of course' to it." But he didn't elaborate. Instead he cast another glance over Matheson and seemed uneasy with the other's disheveled state. Then he looked away. "Clean up and carry on. We need to connect Leran positively to sur-

viving perpetrators, whoever they are. So far, ForTech is failing on that
front and we have only five days left."

Matheson headed down to the Security staff room. Neme and Orris
were walking up the hall toward him and he passed them without
making eye contact. Then he heard Neme stop and wheel before her
voice rang out, "Hey. Rookie. Pull up."

Ignore her . . . but he turned back, resigned to field whatever
unpleasantness the senior detive wanted to throw at him. She closed
the distance between them as he gave a minuscule nod. "Sir." Orris
leaned against the wall a couple of meters away, waiting for her with
an expression of annoyed boredom.

"Your reports are late." Neme glanced at Matheson's face and
smirked. "Bad guys playing rough?" Her nose twitched and she cast
an assessing glance over him. "What have you been into, puppy?"

"I've been working the Dreihleat but the inspector's been in the
building. If you had a question about the reports, you should have
gone to him."

"I shouldn't have to go to your whip. I'm on your distro list and so
far, not one damned report."

"PIRep and lab reports—" he started, but Neme cut him off.

"I hear you have a dead perp and some lab results no one's going
to like."

A chill wound up Matheson's spine.

"Let me suggest," she continued in a low voice, "that if you are
holding back your reports because your investigation touches too
close to home for certain people, or on information the administration
would prefer to suppress, you will much prefer to have me as an ally
than an enemy."

Matheson glared at her. "Sir. I'm not certain what you're implying."

"Get me your reports—all of them—or I will rain hell on you like a summer firestorm in northern Agria."

"You'll have to take it up with the inspector, because I can't help you—no matter how much hell you bring."

Neme gave him a narrow look and snorted. Then she turned on her heel and strode down the hall, giving Orris a brusque "come on" gesture. The older detive shot Matheson a curious glance, but turned and went with her down the hall toward the central tower.

Neme wanted the reports, yet she already seemed to know things he'd only just learned. It bothered him all the way down to the lockers.

It was just past shift change, so there were about two dozen SOs in the room taking their time before heading home. Matheson ducked his head and slipped through the crowd to his locker, once again avoiding anyone's eye as he went.

He dodged most of the usual jostling and the occasional jabbing elbow he'd been subject to since his first day. It was basic hazing, but he disliked it nonetheless. The aisle near his locker was mostly deserted and there was an odor that made his stomach roll. He was sure he wasn't going to be amused when he found out what the source of the stink was. He wedged his shoulder against the frame as he reached to unlock the door, bracing himself for more casual shoves and elbows in the ribs. The door popped open as soon as he lifted the latch. A gush of rotting fish offal sprayed out. The noxious garbage blinded him and he stumbled. He tripped backward over the bench between the rows of lockers and tumbled head first into the next row. His arms and legs tangled in the bench and open locker doors as he tried to thrash back to his feet. He heard a smattering of rough laughter and clenched his teeth in anger, then gagged as he inadvertently swallowed rotten fish. He clawed through the slippery effluvia to grab the bench and pull himself over it, then sit upright enough to free his hands and wipe the worst of the crap out of his eyes and mouth.

"Funny. Fishbait," he muttered, spitting. He was still blind and not sure how big his audience was. "Very funny." He stood slowly, determined not to make a bigger spectacle of himself, and turned toward the showers. He was fuming, but he'd be damned if he'd wear rotten fish, even though he had nothing clean to change into. Better a wet uniform than that. His restrained anger made him even more unsteady on the muck-covered floor, but he went forward with deliberate steps. "I get it, you sick bastards."

Someone walked up behind him—someone wider, but not taller than he was. Halfennig? Tyreda? He couldn't tell—there was too much stink of rot to tell if the man behind him smelled of the Dreihleat fish market or of citrus soap. "No, you don't get it," the man said.

The lights went out and Matheson felt two men scoop him up by the armpits and haul him forward. He felt others brush past him as he was dragged, but they didn't intervene. "Hey!" he started to yell.

A hard fist rammed into his belly. He coughed out the last of the vile liquid in his mouth as the breath was forced from his lungs. Now they dragged him more easily as he slumped, gasping, between the two unseen men.

There was a dim blue glow ahead—the creeping of exterior illumination through the light pipes into the shower room. *Merry fucking hell*.

They threw him hard against the dull green slate of the shower stalls. He barely got his arms up to protect his head from impact with the wall. It was an inside corner—had to be the first corner on the right where the cleaning hose poked out of its wall socket. *Shit, shit, shit*.

"No—" he started, but he didn't manage the whole word before someone jabbed him in the kidneys. He lurched into the wall, reopening the cut in his eyebrow. His feet slipped out from under him on the wet floor. Someone slapped the side of his head. He lost the rest of his balance and bounced his face off the wall as he fell. His nose broke as he scrambled against the tiles. Warm blood ran down his chin and neck and into his left eye. He rolled back into the corner, groping for a purchase and finding none.

"Someone wash this shit out of here. Fuck, it stinks." A jet of icy water bored into his chest as he curled on himself. The water almost seemed to hold him in place and he gasped, unable to catch a full breath in the battering cold. Shadows passed through the drenched glow from the light pipes.

Someone—or more than one—rocked his head and chest with a few more blows. Then the hard nozzle of the hose swung into his gut. He doubled over, crouching into a semi-fetal position and bringing his arms up over his head.

"No, no, no . . . we ain't done with you," someone whose voice he could have identified if his brain was working, growled into his ear. Big hands shoved past his defense and grabbed his shoulders, yanking him upward with a shaking motion that uncoiled Matheson's pain-weakened limbs. "You don't get to roll up and hide just yet."

The looming shape in front of him kneed him in the groin.

Matheson let out a breathless squeal. The man dropped him back to the wet slate floor. "Now you can be a fucking bug."

The hose slammed across his back and sides, across his hips . . . He lost count of the blows, then the kicks. Distantly, he noted that the nozzle never struck him again and they avoided any further damage to his face.

When they stopped, he wasn't sure how much of his body was still attached to the rest. What didn't hurt was dead-numb from the cold water. Someone crouched down beside him—he could make out the person's bulk through the blood and swelling. No face, just a shape.

The shape began talking, punctuating its points with a jabbing finger against Matheson's broken nose. "You don't upset the natural order here, Fishbait. You don't step over your brothers and sisters on the street. You don't snoop and pry into their business and stab them in the back. You don't suck up to Investigation. You don't jump the queue. And you don't go grass. Get it, Fishbait?"

Matheson wasn't sure he could answer, but he managed a weak nod and a moan of pain.

"Good, becau—"

His interrogator might have said something more, but the lights flicked on and another voice roared into the hollow staff room "What the fuck is going on here?!"

Matheson could hear the SOs who'd beaten him scuttling away like cockroaches.

"What are you stupid motherhumpers doing? Shit! Get the hell out of here! Get out!"

The owner of the voice drew closer, shouting and, from the sound of it, handing out a few blows of his own. The shouting man stopped near Matheson. "Shivering Suvil on a stick. What the hell . . . ? Matheson? What the fuck?"

The man hunkered down and hoisted him partially upright, then leaned him back to sit against the shower corner.

Matheson blinked, but couldn't clear enough of the blood out of his eyes to be sure who he was looking at. He was shivering too hard to raise his hands and wipe his own face.

"You look as bad as you smell. What is that stink?"

"Fishbait," Matheson muttered. The word came out slushy due to his bloating lip and broken nose.

The man dabbed at his face with a moist cloth—it felt like a clean-up wipe from a scene kit. Matheson whimpered as the solvent stung his cuts and the motion of the rag disturbed his nose and the quick swelling around his eyes. When the wipe was withdrawn, he blinked again.

Orris. All Matheson managed was a lisping mumble.

Orris stooped to put his shoulder under Matheson's and drag him to his feet. "C'mon, c'mon . . . you need to stand up and get to Public Health. What the hell happened?"

"Stepped on toes," Matheson tried. It came out "shept on doesh."

"You should file a complaint."

Matheson shook his head and regretted it. His brain felt loose in his skull and everything else had to be bruised, torn, or broken. He was nauseated and his mouth still tasted of rotten fish and blood. He gagged and spat blood onto the wet slate floor, grateful that he hadn't expectorated any teeth as well.

Orris straightened him up again, wearing an expression of suppressed disgust. He maneuvered Matheson to another corner of the shower and propped him in it. "I hate to do this, but you stink, rook. Grab hold of something for a minute."

Orris turned on all the closest shower heads. The water came out cold, but soft at first, then warmed up and turned into little needles that stung Matheson's skin right through his filthy clothes. He squirmed and worked his way out of the water on shaking legs, clutching at control handles and ledges to hold himself up.

Orris stood in the shower room with his arms crossed over his chest, watching him. When the senior detive was satisfied, he turned off the sprays. "Well, you still look like shit, but you don't stink like it. Who stomped you?"

Matheson shrugged wordless denial. *Just want outta here alive.*

"You're a fucking moron, rook. Your fellow patch pounders beat you into a heap because you . . . what? Had to question your TO about his part in a crime? Better you than someone else."

Matheson tried to shake his head, but the motion darkened his vision at the edges and brought nausea wrenching through his gut. He twisted aside, holding tight to the nearest ledge, and threw up. There wasn't much to lose, but it still hurt like fuck. Memory of the taste of Aya's skin and the flavor of tea was drowned in pain and humiliation. "I'm," he said, still trying to clear his mouth, "out of order."

"You need a doctor."

"No. No report . . ." That would only sideline him and turn attention that Dillal didn't need on the investigation.

Orris looked disgusted. "You are sollet-screwing stupid. You're playing by their rules!"

"Uh-huh." Matheson straightened out enough to rinse his mouth and face in the nearest shower spray, letting the bile he'd cast up run down the drain.

"You going to the health center now? Before you kill yourself?"

"No." He stumbled as he tried to walk away and Orris caught him, putting a shoulder under his armpit again to brace him up.

"Fuck you," the older man said. He wrapped his near arm around Matheson's back and pressed the business end of a standard issue shock box against his side. At contact, the effect would be concentrated and narrow as a knife blade—before Matheson passed out it would feel just like one, rusty, dull, and tearing viciously through his intercostal muscles. "You're going to the doctor if I have to drop you in your tracks. You can walk or I can haul you. I'll even fox the report if that's what you want."

Matheson tried to resist one more time, pretty sure it was useless. "Dillal—"

"Gas that. You can talk to your damned whip when you can say his name without dribbling blood. Now, come on."

CHAPTER FOURTEEN

Day 3: Evening

"I've got the family lines isolated, but I can't get any farther without the database to match through."

Dillal didn't look up from a bloody mass he was separating with meticulous strokes of a pair of forceps. "I told you to sleep."

"I can't. You need this. You need *me*." Starna was shivering, pupils huge, eyes wide, speaking too fast. A trickle of blood had dried just behind his right earlobe and in a thin line running halfway down his neck.

"I do not need you, and this information is not worth your life. I can run the matches through births and deaths myself, though I believe I already know who I'll find."

Starna didn't seem to have heard him. "But look! I'm a few minutes' work away from getting the name!" Most of the med/legals and techs remaining in the lab had turned to look at Starna as his voice rose. "If you'll just let me access the records—"

Dillal dropped his forceps and turned so quickly that Starna jumped back. "I ordered you to go home and sleep. You chose to ignore my orders," he said in a low, sharp voice. "You are not fit for work."

"I don't need sleep—" the tech shouted.

"Not when you're riding a hit of Wire, of course not! Do you even understand the concept of tainted evidence?"

"I'm not—"

Dillal swiped his fingertips behind Starna's ear and held his hand up between them. Particles of dried blood clung to the skin and under his nails. The sight struck Starna dumb; the only sound in the lab was the hushed whine and click of the inspector's ocular. "As bright to me as a luminous tide," he said. "Do you doubt that I can see it, or smell the chemical signature in your blood?"

Starna shook and panted, his gaze darting around the room as if he were frozen in place and looking for someone to save him. No one stepped forward.

"Leave your work with me and go home before all your research is too compromised to use," Dillal said. "You're no use to me in this state. And if you can't curb your habits, you'll be no use to me at all."

Starna quivered, then swung around and bolted from the lab. The only sounds were his footsteps and the spinning of machines.

Matheson was not a priority, no matter how much water and blood he dripped on the health center's floor. An automated freight lifter had clipped an inbound worker transport from Agria as it had set down, and his injuries barely rated a towel until the desperately broken were attended to.

A cranky PA got to him after a few hours and poked him with devices he couldn't even name. "You'll be fine," she said. "We've loaded you up with viral bots that will speed the healing process. You're going to be very stiff, sore, and tired for about two days, and really hungry. Then you'll be pretty achy for a few more days after that. Just sleep, eat, drink a lot of water, and take the pills. How did you say this happened?"

"I didn't."

"Ah . . . well . . . ." She reached out and re-set his nose with a pop that made Matheson yelp and weep sticky pink tears. "There, Mr. I'm-not-going-to-turf-my-friends. Don't worry. You'll be as pretty as ever—just a little lump in the middle is all."

Like the mattress that Matheson was longing to get horizontal with. *And to think I imagined a broken nose might be rakish . . . I'm an idiot.*

He hated the place more with each visit and he couldn't even enjoy the billion-*real* view. After a few more hours of watching him to be sure he didn't pass out or piss blood, they sent him home.

The various chemicals he'd been anointed, injected, and sprayed with were doing their jobs fairly well and he could see out of both eyes by the time he reached his flat's door. He was achy, itchy, and dopey and he wasn't sure his brain was hooking up the signals from his eyes correctly.

The short man waiting by his door had turned so his face was largely in shadow, hiding all but the unnatural shape of his skull and the red spark of light reflected through the lens of his gold eye.

Matheson stared at him. "Inspector?"

Dillal moved away from the door and gestured Matheson toward it. "We'll talk inside." He seemed tense and annoyed.

Matheson unlocked his door and waved the inspector in ahead of him, wincing at his own ill-considered motion and moving slowly. He closed and double-locked the door on the inside.

Dillal went to lean against the counter that did dual duty as food prep and wash bowl. He didn't take the only chair, and his fingers brushed over the pommel of the broken fencing foil Matheson had left wedged between the counter and the food storage unit. *What must that tell him?* Matheson tugged the latch on the side of the narrow, mostly empty shelf unit to let his bed down from the cabinet. The platform unfolded with a low hiss and he dropped to sit on the edge of the neatly tucked mattress, stifling a grunt.

"What happened?"

Matheson drew a breath that shot spikes of red pain through him, and flinched. "I think the SOs don't like my . . . promotion. Or you. Or maybe specific SOs don't like it."

Dillal gave a small shake of his head. "That's why, not what."

Matheson blinked at the inspector, thinking it over before he opened his mouth again. "Technically, the report says a practical joke went over the pole and I fell in the shower room trying to wash off the mess. That's not exactly the whole of it."

"And not the first time."

"No."

The inspector shook off his annoyance and made a low grunt. "Tell me how it really went."

Matheson's muscles objected to every breath in or out and every motion required to speak or keep him from toppling over, so he spoke slowly. "Well. Got the shit beaten out of me by members of S-Office after someone left an over-pressured bladder of fish guts inside my locker. I opened the locker, the bladder exploded. When I headed for the showers, unknown individuals turned off the lights and escorted me roughly to the shower room. They beat me, doused me in cold water, and told me I'd overstepped. Then came some vague threats and a list of actions I wasn't to be caught doing. Apparently I've turned on my fellow SOs by working for you—or possibly for questioning Santos—maybe both. I step out of line again, and they'll make sure I live up to the nickname 'fishbait.'"

"And you intend to do nothing to redress this threat."

"How? File a report with Feresintavi and have it get worse? Give the admin a reason to pry into your investigation? I want this job. And I don't want to get my skull beaten in. Seems like my only choice is to keep my mouth shut and dodge."

"I can take care of this."

Matheson shook his head and regretted it. "No. My sister was right—I've been protected too much. Only things I've excelled at on my own merit are frivolous physical endeavors. Imagined that by becoming a cop I was pursuing something worthy. Had this infantile idea that I could make something better. But I was just running away from *them*. So here's where I'm digging in my heels. I won't be put on a desk and I won't dump you in the shit. Santos said no one really cares about the deaths of a bunch of people with yellow skin, but I do. You do. I may not be a regular cop, may not have ended up where I wanted, and I may be in over my head, but I don't want to let go. I want this case. I won't screw it or you by whining to the Chief Supers or Pritchet."

Talking was tiring and he wanted to fall backward onto the mattress, but he wasn't sure what the inspector was going to do or say next. Matheson stayed upright, leaning forward onto his braced hands. His forearms were bruised from protecting his head, but they weren't broken, and the distance lent by the medical cocktail he'd been given let him ignore the discomfort of the posture once he was in it—so long as he didn't breathe too deeply.

Dillal watched him a moment, probably cataloguing every injury and drug in his system. The inspector turned his gaze aside after a while and ran his fingers over the broken fencing foil. "How did you spend your free shift before your last rounds with Santos? Not sleeping."

"No," Matheson said, shaking his head and feeling woozy. "I don't sleep well. Haven't in . . . I don't know . . . months. I have nightmares—anxiety dreams—sure I've done something terrible. Wake up, thinking I'm falling. Falling into mud and blood and just . . . deep black nothing. So if work doesn't let me sleep, I work out. Broke that on day two. Y'know, I've had that thing for years and it shattered against a target—not even in competition." *I sound drunk.*

Dillal made a thoughtful sound in his throat. "I'll hold your complaint for now—"

"Haven't made one," Matheson objected.

"Not officially, but I know," Dillal said. "I need you and I am . . . relieved that you wish to continue. There are some . . . developments I have to deal with that may prove dangerous."

"Dangerous in what way?"

"Starna's genetic trace connects to someone I once knew."

"In the Ohbata? Thought your patch was the Dreihleat."

The inspector gave a minuscule shrug. "Regardless, it must be addressed immediately and I can't ask that of you."

"I've got a feeling you don't want to go, either."

"No. And there are internal issues to manage as well."

"Yeah . . . Neme cornered me about reports."

"I expect no discretion from that quarter—she'll get them when I'm ready to let her have them." He touched the unnatural curve of machinery embedded behind his left ear. "Filing reports via the cybernetic interface is slightly faster than typing them, but still time consuming. Also, I did discover Robesh's missing fingernail. ForTech had scraped tissue off the carpet in both rooms and the shattered remains of the nail were in one of them. It was definitely Leran she fought with and no one else. I have yet to pinpoint the residue on his hands, though."

"Maybe it was clean-up wipes," Matheson said, ideas falling out of his mouth without filtering first.

Dillal cocked his head. "Why do you think so?"

"No other residue on his hands, but he killed Robesh. Contact range with a short-plasma. Wouldn't the plasma kick back particle jets? And if not, the pressure release from the . . . umm . . ." Matheson felt sick, unable to shut off his imagination completely, no matter how tired he was—or maybe because he was so tired and hurt. "When her head . . ." He stopped and swallowed hard, feeling the motion all the way up the back of his neck and across his jaw.

"Ah!" Dillal murmured. "The steam ejecta should have left some residue on his hand."

Matheson nodded unsteadily. "If there was spray seal and he wiped it off his hands in a hurry, could have left some partially dissolved on his skin—in the creases of fingers or his wrists. And everyone forgets their forearms."

"Mixed with the ejecta, the seal and solvent might appear as one deliberate compound. I'll look again. The solvent won't break down DNA evidence and the speed and volume of the ejecta may have carried viable tissue out along with the rest. If Robesh's DNA is in that sample, that will confirm Leran as her killer absolutely."

"Just leaves us to figure out who killed *him*."

"Also why petty criminals in the Dreihleat were using spray seal during a crime they would not have expected to come to GISA's attention. Or why they had it at all."

"Mm-hm," Matheson agreed. He nearly fell backward as he nodded.

Dillal shook his head. "Stay out of the Security staff room from now on. You'll have to work from my office and pick up the investigation in the Dreihleat as soon as possible. It appears that your presence stirs up something which may benefit us, however difficult the situation becomes."

He couldn't argue—Dillal's state at the beginning of the investigation had been worse than his currently was—and the inspector was already heading for the door as if there was nothing else to discuss. Maybe there wasn't, though he did wonder how a dead man had wiped spray seal off his hands. A disconnected thought popped into the front of his head as he struggled to his feet and followed Dillal to the door. "A key. Did they find a key in the sewer sweep?"

"A key to what?"

"The jasso's door. Santos said he had one. Dropped it down the drain."

Dillal stopped and gazed into the distance. Things moved under the skin above his left ear. "You mentioned it in your report. I haven't examined all of that evidence yet, but I shall when I return." He continued forward. "Till then, I hope you'll sleep. We must find Leran's companions in this crime, but not at your further expense."

The inspector turned back as he reached the doorway. "There is a chance I'll run into difficulty and be unable to call for help. The Ohbata is worse than the Dreihleat—nearly stripped of microtransmitters, and hard links exist only in the worst possible locations for me. If I'm not back in the morning, send Neme."

"Why her?"

"Because she'd never refuse such an opportunity to embarrass me."

CHAPTER FIFTEEN

Day 3: Ohbata Angra Dastrelas—Night

Dillal stood in a shadowed doorway at the very edge of it for the best part of an hour. Only the industrial port development was uglier than the Ohbata but the port had started that way—unadorned function without any softening grace. This part of the ghetto had made itself out of decline, dirt, and shadow. Long rows of shattered hothouses and the upthrust of silos gave the place a feral look—like a jaw full of cracked and ragged fangs.

A crazed pane of glass distorted a flicker of movement that continued in warped progress across the front of what had been a forcing house long before the city had grown to fill the bowl of Trant's Crater and clutter the shore of the cove with white towers. Other small motions answered from other broken panes along Biol Road, flickering and vanishing at angles too oblique to be reflection. Dillal watched from the corner of his right eye. He kept his head turned and a length of dark fabric pulled over his left eye to keep the light from striking the polished surface of the ocular.

A short, stocky figure emerged at the end of the forcing house and turned from Caine Passage onto Biol. Dillal, dressed in dull brown as ragged as the ghetto, slipped from his hiding place and darted into another shadow, following the figure. When Dillal reached Caine, he turned and stepped into the shade of the forcing house. No new flurry of tiny signals erupted along the frontage of broken windows.

He found a door in the dirt of the wall, and twisted and jiggled its handle in a peculiar pattern until the latch gave way. Then he ducked through the narrow doorway, closing the door behind him.

The old forcing house still smelled of earth. Rogue plants—procullus, hair fern, and climbing aminta—had worked their way through the floors, growing toward the broken windows in search of light and casting shadows behind. An array of hand-grown OLEDs stretched across the top of the windows, dangling their strange electronic fruit down the inside of the remaining panes. Dillal darted past an observation post that looked out on Biol through the cracked and dirtied glass, and along a twisted aisle of sharp-bladed sedge. Swags of honey-scented aminta drooped from the ceiling beams, pale orange blossoms swaying as unseen creatures scuttled through the leaves.

The avenue of wild plants meandered through the building until the path appeared to come to an abrupt end at a rusty steel door that had grown shaggy with moss and mildew. Dillal pushed his scarf down around his neck and squatted. He studied the edge of the door for a minute, running his hands over the filth-crusted frame and wall beside it. A crevice near the floor yielded and he dug his fingers through the rotten foliage behind it, groping until he flipped an ancient manual override mechanism loose. It turned by reluctant fits and the door made a squealing sound that caused Dillal to raise his head and look over his shoulder.

No one came to investigate and the hanging plants remained still, rustling only where the breeze passed through the broken glass. It took three complete revolutions before the seal on the door gasped and the locks gave way with heavy thumps. He gave a thin smile, pushed the door open wide enough to squeeze through, and leaned his weight back against it on the other side until it sighed closed.

A ramp sloped down into darkness. The walkway curved gently

and his sure footsteps didn't echo on the hard surface. The muffled passageway stank of mold and at two hundred meters in, his net connection failed. He ran his fingers over the left side of his head, pressing, but it didn't return until he'd backtracked upslope several meters. He turned and walked back down. In less than a kilometer, he reached another door in the depths of ear-bleeding silence.

Built like the first, but in much better repair, the door took little effort to open and he emerged into a small warehouse. He checked his connection again, but it remained dead. The subtle clicking and whining of his eyepiece shifting through its settings was the loudest sound in the room.

The large space was poorly lit and thick with the odor of waterproofing and packing grease. Nitrogen-purged crates were stacked on chain-elevator racks that rose to within two meters of the lofty ceiling. He walked along the corridor created by two parallel racks, checking some of the labels on the crates as he went. He found a gap in the stacks where something had been removed and looked hard at it before moving on. His footsteps were accompanied only by the faint, asthmatic wheeze of the ventilation system.

"Bomodai?" he said.

No answering sound. He drew a small, slim gun from an inner pocket of his ragged clothes.

He stepped out from between the racks, sweeping for trouble, and looked around the cleared staging area, drawing a slow breath through his nose. He turned his head sharply right, making a visual search, then ran a few steps past a loader.

An Ohba woman lay on the floor in a swirl of ruddy brown robes a few shades darker and duller than her own skin and the thick, drying blood that had pooled around her. The bloody footprints of a small razor cat led from the puddle into the shadows. A wheeled work counter stood about four meters in from the locked loading door with another standard door beside it. Blood had splashed at head-height onto the shelving to the right.

Dillal made another search of the area gun muzzle first, checking each of the aisles. The cat's eyes glowed at him from under a pile of crates, but aside from the busy scurry of disturbed rats, there was no sign of anything else alive in the room.

He scowled, walking closer to the body and putting his gun away. He crouched at the edge of the stain, touched the blood, and raised his fingers close to his ocular, which clicked for a few seconds. Then he looked back at the dead woman.

Several bullets had passed through her cheekbone and brow and made the left side of her head an unrecognizable pulp. Dillal gathered a tattered bit of his sleeve over his hand and rolled the woman's head a little toward him to examine the less-ruined side of her face. The corpse's muscles resisted, but gave way, and a renewed odor of death filled the air. He looked at her face, then put his free hand over his eyes for a moment, his mouth compressing into a hard line.

He rested back on his heels and looked her over, his hands hanging between his knees until he tried to reboot his connection one more time and ended cursing it under his breath. He gave a resigned grunt and leaned forward once more. He checked the ruined left side of her face again. A dark shape had flattened against the remains of her orbital ridge. He stared hard at it, then touched it lightly with his covered hand. It fell to the floor—a misshapen bullet. He tilted his head slightly.

A door crashed open behind him. He rose and turned at the same time, reaching for the gun in his clothes.

Two men and a woman, all bulky in full SO uniform, crowded through the doorway. The moment they saw Dillal, they raised weapons already in their hands and shouted conflicting orders—"stand still," "get down," and "who the fuck are you?"

Dillal quirked an eyebrow at the weapons pointed at him—only one was the standard issue shock box. He let the fold of fabric fall away and raised both open hands to chest level, the ID checkerboard in clear view on his wrist. "I am Inspector J. P. Dillal, CIFO," he said, his voice calm and clear as he looked from one to the next.

"Like hell," the man at the front and center replied. "Bong mets don't make Inspector." The slur raised no response from Dillal as he shifted his gaze to the other two SOs.

The woman scowled, while the remaining man—the farthest back, clearly the youngest, and the only one carrying a regulation weapon—looked nervous and uncertain. The right corner of Dillal's mouth lifted in a fleeting smile before he returned his attention to the man who'd spoken.

"Not usually, but I am an exception and this is my crime scene."

"You haven't called it in—whoever you fucking-well are."

"You know there are no accessible microtransmitters this deep into the Ohbata, and the building's shielded. If you have an uplink, or there's a hardline nearby, call it in yourself. Then you can scan my command array and confirm my identity," the inspector offered, twisting his left hand slightly so the dusty light in the room glided across the crystals embedded in his wrist.

The two SOs in back exchanged nervous glances.

"And get close enough that you can do to me what you did to that bitch?" the first one asked. "I don't think so."

"This woman has been dead for hours. So, unless you imagine I'm as irredeemably stupid as you, I'm clearly not her killer."

The SO in front took an aggressive step forward, gun outthrust as if he could stab the inspector with it from a distance. "On the floor!" he shouted.

The man at the rear took a step back, his hands starting to fall. The motion caught the first SO's attention and he turned his head to snap at the man behind him. "What are you doing?"

"I don't like this . . ." the younger man started.

Dillal dove toward the distracted SO and rolled forward. The woman behind him had no shot that didn't endanger one of her companions and the men were too slow to adjust to the target closing the distance to them. The inspector hit the first man at the knee. Then he regathered his feet under him and kicked forward. The lead SO shouted and lurched backward into the younger man who was hesitating behind him.

Staying down, Dillal swung around, lashing out at the woman's legs and catching her just behind the knees. She buckled with a shout of surprise as the other two fell in a heap together. They wouldn't be off balance for long, but the opening was sufficient for Dillal. He rushed through the doorway and into the poorly lit street outside, his dark and ragged clothes blending him into the night shadows.

He ran, dodging objects that should have caught or tripped him, and turned sharply into another alley, drawing up short in the sudden glare of half a dozen small flares. He didn't have time to speak or draw his gun before one of the figures in the dark grabbed him, clamped a hand over his mouth, and yanked him into a darkened doorway while the flares all went out. The man put his mouth to Dillal's ear and rumbled, "Still, or this one is letting the sandworms have you."

The inspector made no protest, dropping his head and going limp in the man's grip. The man almost dropped him in surprise. Dillal twisted and lunged to escape but his captor reached out and snatched him back, his fingers digging into the inspector's shoulder hard enough to make him flinch and drop to his knees without a sound. The man in the dark jabbed his thumb into the nerve nexus behind

Dillal's right ear and the inspector crumpled face down, unconscious in the shadowed doorway.

The SOs rushed past the alley, the woman splitting off to check the narrow passage. She ran the length, more focused on reaching the end than taking good stock of the alley itself, and turned to rejoin the other two on the next block.

The owners of the pocket flares stepped out of the shadows. One of them searched Dillal, removing the gun, compact shock box, and half-a-dozen e-credit chits. Another hefted him up and over a shoulder like a sack of grain. The group turned to walk the other way, disappearing in shadow and darkness with the whisper of sand blowing over stone.

Dillal was awake before his escort came to a halt, but made no further move to extricate himself. They made their way through a labyrinth of unlit passages by the light of flares and starshine through broken glass. The man carrying him dropped him without ceremony into a shaft of light. Dillal rolled and landed in a crouch on soft ground, raising the salt-and-sulfur smell of shed insect carapaces, dried dung, and iridescent fish scales.

They were in one of the rooting sheds in the Sand Trap—an old First Settlement agri-base, abandoned and now reclaimed by the Ohbata gangs that ran less-savory agricultural ventures. He kept his head down—letting the scarf obscure his face, shoulders hunched against an expected blow. He saw the legs of perhaps twenty people— Ohba by the shape and color of them, stocky, with skin and hair in varied and beautiful shades of red, bodies swathed in layers of ragged brown cloth. So long as he remained in his current posture and clothes, he didn't look much unlike them.

He swept his gaze side to side as far as he could without raising his head. They were in a large clearing among the rows of plants slumbering in the darkness beneath the opaque vault of the roof, the light a bright spot from above. It was a short distance into the darkness, but a long way to safety. He grew still, gaze focused on the feet of someone who walked to the edge of the light, but stopped short more than a body length away. Male, heavy, elderly, moving at a majestic pace under draperies edged in black. What skin was on view was decorated in designs of tiny, raised dots that shifted from black to white and back as he moved, bringing apparent life to the suggestion of animals and plants on his hands and feet.

"This is being what?" The elder had a low, round voice that seemed to strike the ground like the reflected peal of a great bell.

The reply came from behind Dillal in the Ohba's odd English. "Bong met. These are taking it from three sandworms who are then coming from Bomodai's warehouse. The auntie is dead."

The feet in front of Dillal shifted as the man started to turn away. "The thing has been at killing Auntie Bomodai. It is deserving the same."

"Uncle Fahn," the man behind Dillal objected. "Something . . . is being wrong with its face. The uncle is looking—"

Uncle Fahn turned back and stomped one foot with great deliberation, kicking up dust. "We are not being concerned that its face is turning you white, Maani. Kill it."

Dillal uncoiled and stepped quickly forward. He was within arm's reach of Uncle Fahn and nearly two body lengths away from the man who'd carried him into the Sand Trap.

At Fahn's height, but less than a third his girth, Dillal stood very straight, his head up defiantly. He looked coolly at the old Ohba, who stared back with an expression of growing disgust and horror. The dotted suggestion of a few white birds appeared at the edge of one cheek and vanished again.

Dillal clasped his hands together at his chest and bowed over them. "This one is at your mercy, Grandfather." Then he straightened, dropping his hands to his sides.

Uncle Fahn gestured and the men closing on Dillal from behind stopped and fell back a step or two. He said nothing more for a long moment, glaring at the man in front of him, unable to settle his expression. He reached out and grabbed Dillal's jaw, tilting the younger man's face with a rough twist of his decorated hand. He glared at the golden orbit of the inspector's mechanical eye and the unnatural shape of his skull. "What has the corpse walking been doing? It is not being content with killing our son, but is making itself newly repulsive. It is turning now to killing the rest of us?"

Dillal continued, "I mean no harm to the Ohba of the Green Houses and I did not kill Bomodai. I came to speak with her and found her murdered."

Fahn did not shift. "It is being grateful that it would not then be having to kill the auntie itself."

"I would no more murder the auntie than you would."

Fahn threw him aside like rotten fruit and Dillal stumbled to his knees, catching himself with one hand before he could be dashed to the ground on his side.

Fahn closed the distance in an instant, clutching at Dillal's face, digging his strong fingers into the skin around the ocular frame. The big old Ohba bent over him and growled between bared teeth. "What will it be doing if we are ripping its metal eye from its head?" he asked, shaking Dillal and drawing blood that seeped down the younger man's cheek.

"Die, I suppose," Dillal replied as evenly as the violent motion allowed. "I will die, as you have so often wished. And you will have killed a senior investigator." Fahn stopped shaking him, but did not let go as Dillal continued, "Those three ofiçes who were chasing me will be quick enough to point the finger at you—they must work for Jolongodi, because you would never bed with the corporation. Between it—that wants any excuse to wipe the Ohba off the face of Gattis—and him, there won't be much left of you. If you still want to kill me knowing that, then do it. Do it and give them what they want."

Fahn bellowed with rage and flung Dillal away from him, backing a step, as if distancing himself from the idea as much as the man in front of him. The inspector hit the ground hard, his breath knocked from his lungs. The rest of the Ohba standing in the shadows muttered and swayed.

Dillal lay as he'd fallen for a moment, blinking, while Uncle Fahn raged. "Our son is dead because of this corpse and its whore of a mother! We are solitary in the heart of us—this one's wife, all this one's flesh, is dead—yet it is still being here, this worthless piece of yellow shit! We should have been having the corpse's mother torn to shreds before it could be born!" He ripped down meters of the hanging aminta, shredding it and sending its perfume into the air as he screamed. "We should have been having it strangled as it was being shat from its mother's womb!"

Dillal sat up slowly, drawing his knees in and leaning forward until he could rest his uninjured cheek against them. "She died soon enough," he said quietly, pressing his left hand over his prosthetic until it clicked back into place. "And my father died for believing things could change for all the colored—for Ohba and Dreihleen and even for mets—not because he loved a woman whose skin was a different shade than his. I apologize for my tenacity in remaining alive—I know how my existence offends you."

His grandson's calm seemed to have infected him as Fahn drew closer and finally replied. "Nor o-sum. Why is it being here now?"

Dillal rolled to his knees and stood slowly, taking a long breath and keeping his eyes cast down. He replied so quietly that Fahn had to lean close to hear him. "You've heard of the murders in the Dreihleat."

"A good start being made on removing their stain from our planet."

Dillal shrugged. "Some were shot. It appears the bullets were acquired from Auntie Bomodai. I have let no one know of this." He raised his eyes to Fahn's. "I came to ask her who bought them. To tell her to flee until the killers are caught."

"Why is it doing this? The auntie was never having any more liking of it than we."

"Nor I her, but I do not wish for this to become the cause Corporation House wants to destroy the Ohbata."

Fahn narrowed his eyes. "What matter is this being to the corpse walking, when it has been selling itself to the parasites? We are knowing what it has done. We are knowing what it is."

"You do not. Little as you like it, I am my father's son."

Fahn growled a warning. "It is treading on the grave . . . We are hoping that it, too, will be found now with its skull being smashed open in the Agrian desert."

Dillal closed his eyes and sighed, then looked at the ground bedside Fahn's feet. "Grandfather, do you want me dead so much that you would sacrifice everyone here for it? If I cannot solve this before word leaks out—as it will—that the Ohbata was involved, the case will be taken from me and summarily closed as a race-related crime. No one else will even try to find the truth. And you know what will happen after that."

Fahn stepped back, peering at Dillal with a speculative expression. Dillal shifted his own gaze to watch Fahn, but he didn't turn his head.

One of the Ohba stepped out of the shadows and leaned to whisper into Uncle Fahn's ear. Fahn scowled, whispered back, then waved the other away.

He turned back to Dillal. "It is claiming it is being here to do a favor for the Ohba. We all are knowing death well enough to concede it is not then murdering Auntie Bomodai. But that one is dead nonetheless and the corpse must answer. It is doing nothing but bringing bad memories and the stink of death, but we shall be having truth."

Fahn glanced at the patrol who had brought Dillal there. "Maani, Gant. Be taking it to the pools." Then he returned his gaze to his grandson for a moment.

Dillal stood as expressionless and unmoving as stone.

Fahn chuckled. "Go willingly, or we will be having Maani break its legs and be carrying it where it must go." Then he turned and walked away into the dark, trailed by the man who had whispered in his ear.

Maani and the teenage boy grinning brutally beside him closed in behind Dillal. The boy, Gant, unslung an elderly rifle from his back and prodded the inspector forward. Dillal clenched his teeth and went ahead of them into the darkness between the rustling plants.

The building was a long, low, cement-printed block at the edge of fields that had gone feral. Water still ran through the pipes and troughs of the old hydroponics tanks. An office and control area hung above the work floor, up an extruded cement staircase, its walls low and full of broken windows. The constant, swift flicker of monitors connected to a hardline data feed illuminated the mezzanine and cast inconstant shadows down onto the water flowing in the troughs. Fish flashed between the fronds of water poppy growing in the nearest trough and sent ripples across the surface.

Dillal balked just past the doorway. Gant shoved him forward and the inspector spun around. "I have done nothing deserving this. I did not kill the Auntie, nor bring that fate down on her."

"So it is saying," Maani replied, taking a step closer to Dillal that caused the slimmer man to step back nearly to the trough's edge. "But we shall be washing the truth from its lies."

"I haven't lied—" Dillal feinted left. Maani intercepted his reversal as Gant stepped in and drove his rifle's stock hard into the inspector's gut.

Dillal doubled up with a cough of expelled breath. The two Ohba spun him around and shoved him toward the trough, muscling Dillal's upper body over the edge.

"Can it hold its breath as long as the caddis flies?" Gant asked. Then he gave a short laugh, and shoved the inspector's head into the water between the water poppies' broad leaves.

A gold-and-white spotted fish as long as his arm swept past Dillal's face in alarm, scraping his cheek with a sharp-edged fin. Dillal shut his eyes and mouth in a tight grimace, but he didn't fight.

Above the water, Maani and Gant scowled at his still back, then looked to each other, letting their grip slacken. Dillal kicked back sharply, hitting Gant's thigh, and then turned aside as he rose, getting his back to the trough. Water ran down, washing thin blood from the cut on his face and leaving him soaked. While the boy was still off balance, Dillal threw himself forward and butted him hard just below the sternum. Gant buckled backward as Maani jumped forward to grapple Dillal from the side. Gant scrambled up, trying to bring his rifle to bear as the door opened behind him. Maani grabbed Dillal by the upper arm and yanked him back toward the door. Gant grinned with a hint of malice and curled his finger in from the trigger guard.

Fahn put a heavy hand on Gant's shoulder and the boy stiffened.

"Gant. We are having another purpose for the corpse than painting our walls."

Maani held Dillal's arm tightly. "It is not then being proved by water."

Fahn nodded. "Nor o-sum. We are having something to be showing the corpse. We may be changing its mind about its masters and its . . . friends." He turned and walked toward the stairs.

Dillal made no move until Maani walked him forward. Gant fell back to follow, keeping his rifle trained on Dillal's back. No one saw Dillal's flickering smile as they drew closer to the whisper of the hardline.

The mezzanine formed a long, narrow room crowded with controls and monitors along the low walls that overlooked the floor, and a few locked cabinets against the back wall. A data suite had been cobbled from dissimilar parts and mounted to the counter about a third of the room's length from the door, its screen providing the room's weirdly flickering light. A skeletal chair of metal and stretched netting sat alone before the display.

Dillal curled his lip and allowed himself to be prodded to the chair. As soon as Dillal sat, Fahn handed Maani a freestanding drive cube about twenty centimeters on each side, and motioned to the lockers with his head. Maani walked across the room to retrieve something as Fahn watched. Gant slung his rifle, stepped up, and held Dillal's left wrist against the chair arm, taking a wire tie from his pocket to secure him. The inspector didn't pull his arm away but snapped his head toward the boy and snarled at him with bared teeth. Gant flinched.

"Touch me again, and I break you."

Gant lurched forward with a furious expression and Fahn stopped him with a glare. Gant narrowed his eyes and stepped back, the wire tie hanging loose.

Dillal shifted his gaze to Fahn. "I came voluntarily. You needn't tie me. Unless you mean to torture me further."

Fahn offered only a knowing smile. "Maani."

Fahn's lieutenant stepped forward with the drive cube and a cable, and connected them to the comm unit. Then he stepped back to Fahn, drawing a small, homemade shock box from his clothes.

There was a noise on the staircase outside and the three Ohba turned toward it. Gant moved to cover the door as it opened to a new-comer, who blurted, "Jolongodi's sandworms—"

Dillal snatched the cable out of the comm box and lifted it toward the socket behind his left ear. Electricity sparked to his wet skin, then the display flickered and returned to its previous busy scan while Dillal closed his eyes a moment, frowning.

Fahn and Maani started toward the runner as Gant lowered his gun. The Ohbas spoke together in low whispers for a minute or so. Then Maani glanced back toward Dillal and let out a surprised yell.

The inspector came to his feet and whipped around, the cable trailing from behind his ear. Gant lifted his rifle. Dillal heaved the chair at him. It knocked the gun's muzzle upward, smashing into the boy's face and Gant staggered back, bleeding from the nose and forehead. The runner on the landing jumped back and Maani jumped forward with the shock box held out toward the left side of Dillal's head.

The inspector turned aside, raising his right hand between the box and his skull as Maani pressed the discharge button. The arc hit Dillal's hand and seemed to spin him back into the counter, yanking the cable loose from the socket behind his ear.

Dillal, with his right arm hanging loose, scrambled onto the counter and threw himself through the nearest empty window. He tumbled over the edge and vanished, followed by a splash from one of the tanks below.

Maani started for the window. Gant, swiping at his bloody face, headed for the mezzanine office door and shoved the newcomer aside. Fahn joined him. They both looked through the doorway, searching for Dillal.

Gant turned his gaze. "Door!" he shouted, and brought the rifle up as he spotted Dillal near the building's exit. Fahn put his hand over the near sight and pushed Gant's rifle down. "Still."

Dillal bolted outside.

"Uncle!" Gant complained. Maani and the newcomer also stared at the elder man.

Fahn watched the door swing closed behind his grandson. "Let it run. The corpse will be doing our work for us."

All the other men stared at him, but Fahn only turned up a sharp, white-toothed smile.

CHAPTER SIXTEEN

Day 4: Saturday—Morning

The drugs let Matheson sleep later than he'd meant to and gray illumination through the light pipes made his flat feel like it was under a dozen centimeters of dirty water. He'd fallen asleep in his clothes, sprawled across the bed face down—that had been easier on his back and sides, but he'd done himself no favors with his broken nose. He got upright slowly, wincing and swallowing pain, stuffed his stained and stinking clothes into the disposal chute, and made his gingerly way behind the wet wall. The tepid shower loosened some of the stiffness in his muscles and joints, but left his skin stinging as if he'd bathed in salt water.

The anti-inflammatories had reduced the swelling of his face and joints, but they'd had little effect on the cuts and bruises. The small wound on his eyebrow had gotten larger and now gaped a little. He poked it and winced, setting off a series of sharp pains across his face and down his neck. He looked like shit, felt worse, and the idea that scars added character was a load of crap.

He started dressing, but could barely stand the touch of cloth on his skin. He swore and flung the bed up into the cabinet too vigorously, regretting the motion as every muscle cramped and ached. The bed banged into place, dislodging one of his three hoarded print books from the shelf. He cringed at the noise, which brought a clattering response from the neighbor on the other side of the wall—like acorns thrown down a hollow metal tree. He'd never seen this neighbor and had thought the flat was empty.

Matheson leaned against the counter, persuading himself that, once dressed, he wouldn't notice the discomfort so much; he hadn't considered how much it hurt just to pull the clothes on. Even the lightest things he owned chafed and pressed too much. The weight of his belt on his hips was misery, and he was glad he didn't carry the weight of a personal firearm too—not that he had the seniority or assignment to exercise that option. He slipped his feet into light-weight shoes, unable to face the discomfort of bending down to lace his boots, much less pick up his fallen book. He hoped this stage would pass quickly, but he wasn't optimistic. There was too much to do to give up and curl into a fetal position on his bed for the rest of the day . . . and it would probably hurt more to undress again and lie on his side than to keep on going. He bribed himself with the prospect of seeing Aya.

As he exited the flat and locked up, he banged into his mysterious new neighbor and hissed in pain. The other drew back, scowling, as Matheson turned stiffly.

Russet-skinned, just under average height, bearded and burly, the man was swathed in black draperies that covered his head, looped his neck and shoulders loosely, and then trailed to the ground behind him. He had a design of small, raised white dots on the back of his right hand, and he moved silently on bare feet. Matheson wondered what—if anything—the man had heard of last night's conversation and if he'd just never realized he had a neighbor, before. He'd never heard any noise from the far side of their mutual wall before this morning's Pelting of Disapproval. The thought of the solemn Ohba's bare feet made him shudder with a sudden vision of icy water and furious electricity.

"I'm sorry. And about the wall this morning," Matheson said. "I . . ." He didn't really want to explain it, so he stopped trying. "I'm just sorry if I disturbed you."

The man looked him over with brilliant green eyes, casting his gaze from top to bottom slowly as if he noted every bruise. Then he smiled, showing Matheson a handful of stained teeth. "O-sum," the man replied in a low, gravelly voice. "Nor o-sum." He turned away, chuckling to himself, to glide off down the open hallway.

Matheson remembered the terms from one of his cultural brief-ings—*O-sum* meant "nothing" or "worthless," *nor o-sum* would have been "less than nothing" . . . or "less than worthless." *So . . . was the noise "nothing" or am I nothing . . . ?*

The encounter was strange and Matheson had an urge to find Dillal as quickly as possible.

Matheson found the inspector in his office and thought the man looked worse for wear himself: eyes puffy, the left ringed in small, oozing scabs and bruising, a long nick on his cheekbone, and a raw patch on the side of his right hand and wrist that looked like an electric-discharge burn. *He looks as tired as I feel.*

"No key," was the first thing Dillal said.

Matheson frowned. "What?"

"I've been unable to find a key of any kind in the materials taken from the run-off drain in the Paz da Sorte alley. It's not impossible that a rat or some other animal carried it off if it was shiny and light enough."

So, what had happened to it? Had Santos not, in fact, thrown the key away? Dillal seemed to be less bothered by the lack than Matheson was, though that could have been because he was obviously preoccu-pied with something else. But Matheson believed Santos. The man had been terrified and had no reason to tell him more falsehoods once he'd started on the truth. Matheson let it lie for the time being, probing for whatever might be bothering the inspector.

"What about the chemicals on Leran's wrist?"

"Still processing. But if it is seal and solvent mixed with the brain ejecta, who used the wipes? Leran was dead."

Matheson was pleased that he'd had the same thought, although his present discomfort made him question every memory of the night before. "Some other member of the gang must have done it," he suggested.

"It was someone with a remarkably clear mind, considering that the situation had reversed completely in minutes. And yet . . ."

"You keep saying that whoever planned the crime is clever."

Dillal scowled. "But not as clever as he thinks. Cleaning off the spray seal would have been intended to make Leran appear just another victim, but it was sloppily done. He didn't think as far ahead as he should have—that appears to be a consistent weakness of our mastermind."

"That's a grand term for him."

"I don't doubt that he'd think it perfectly apt—criminals frequently hold higher opinions of their intelligence than evidence supports. Though not all . . ."

Matheson started to laugh and regretted it.

Dillal shook himself and said, "You'll feel better tomorrow."

"They said that about today."

"I won't expect to see you here, so you can start in the Dreihleat with whatever leads you turn up today in the blocks around the Paz da Sorte and Dohan Sewing. Robesh's home address is nearby. The neighbors should be able to tell you more about the nature of her relationships with Dohan and Leran, and who else she may have spent time with. That may lead to at least one other member of the gang. It's possible they may even be in the area, trying to appear unconnected to the crime, rather than slinking off into the tunnels."

"Playing innocent bystander so no one will turf them?"

"Calling no attention to themselves. They had a plan and it went awry, but if no one left alive knows they entered the Paz da Sorte to rob it and walked back out as killers instead, they may think that we won't connect them to Leran."

Matheson nodded and flinched. *How come I never noticed how many muscles that takes until they're all screaming?*

"I've sent the addresses for Robesh and her parents to your mobile. Start there and work outward."

Relieved to be dismissed, Matheson started to go, then turned back. Was his brain as sluggish as his body? "Last night . . ."

"What of it?"

Matheson hesitated. "I may have misunderstood."

"I doubt it. Ask your question."

Matheson looked stiffly back at the door, reassuring himself that it was closed. "You . . . said you were going to the Ohbata . . . ?"

"Yes."

Matheson did not glance at the inspector's burned wrist, but there was no avoiding the new lacerations on his face. He held his tongue.

Dillal cocked his head slightly. "The contact I had hoped to meet was dead."

Matheson frowned and the inspector nodded. "Shot. Four to six hours before I arrived. I believe she was the arms dealer who supplied the ammunition used at Paz—and she appears to have been killed with the same bullets—but I couldn't confirm it." He held up his burned wrist. "I ran afoul of old enemies and had some difficulty extricating myself—the damage is less dramatic than it appears."

"Are these enemies connected to the case?"

Dillal shook his head. "They would have killed me if they were."

"And it's no coincidence that the arms dealer is dead, is it?"

"There's no evidence one way or the other—and I couldn't gather anything other than the immediate scene impressions and chemical intake—but it would be unlikely."

"But ForTech will have something."

"No," the inspector replied, bitterly. "By the time it was reported, the scene was scrubbed, the body gone. I had no communications, and I wasn't there officially, though I may have given some people that impression. I hadn't truly expected such a development and it's my own mistake for letting the situation get the better of me." He shook it away. "Regardless, this information must remain between us, for now."

"Yes, sir."

The inspector glanced back to his displays. "We have a great deal to manage in three days. Concentrate on finding Leran's associates in the Dreihleat—they must be there or connected to someone there." Dillal's tone was grim. "The mourning period and your condition make this more difficult, but we must find something to buy us more time or to close the case without bringing in the Ohbata evidence. Exploit every contact you have—even those you think you shouldn't."

"Sir?" Apprehension crawled up Matheson's spine.

The inspector sighed and turned back to him. "Your informant, and the woman you're sleeping with, even the unaff boy if you can find him without entering the Tomb unescorted. At the same time I remind you to be wary of them. There are factions within the Dreihleat that will use you to their ends as much as Pritchet would. Until you know where each of these contacts stands, you can't entirely trust them, but we have no choices left."

Dillal closed his eyes a moment before he continued. "I . . . have a habit of silence that is difficult to break and I can't possibly tell you everything you need to know about this planet, this city, these people. I must rely on your intelligence, observation, and training. I've done what I can to make your job easier, but it's still yours alone for now— though I wouldn't forgive myself if you came to grief for lack of information I could have provided. I have a few more tests that may give us something, but they may not provide it quickly enough to satisfy Director Pritchet. We *must* turn up a new lead, and therefore I apologize for throwing you into dangerous waters ill-prepared. I'll join you as soon as I can."

Tiny shocks of panic brought cold sweat prickling on Matheson's too-sensitive skin. He dropped his gaze and nodded, unable to meet the inspector's eye. "Yes, sir."

He knows I slept with Aya. Why didn't he say anything before? I didn't either, but still . . . Dillal probably knew that Minje was the Confidential Informant Matheson was developing as well. The inspector knew them both and had put them in Matheson's path when he sent him to the coffee house that first day. He'd also said Minje was useful to know . . . So, the inspector had wanted him to use Minje and he wasn't angry about Aya, but he warned against them. *There's got to be some twisted history there and I'm not sure I want to know it.*

Matheson cursed under his breath and made his way to the Dreihleat. All the businesses that didn't cater directly to tourists were closed for the weekend and the area was thronged with both visitors and locals celebrating Spring Moon. There was no one at the clothing manufacturing company and no one nearby seemed to know anything helpful. The Dreihleen turned aside and shook their heads. He thought his battered face and uncomfortable posture did as much to make them back away as his questions. He was worn down, tired, even though he'd barely started. He tried Robesh's address in an old-style open-stack building a lot like his own, but found no one home and began canvassing the building, in hope that someone wasn't out celebrating.

It was well after noon when he found an elderly couple by the name of Tzeren one floor down from Robesh's flat. They were uneasy in his presence, not wishing to give their names at first, but shocked about what had happened to their beautiful neighbor.

Finally, the wife turned her head toward Matheson, keeping her face lowered and her gaze aside. She spoke so softly that he had to strain to hear her. "For Dohan's I'm do the training, until I'm too old. I'm work with Lele—Venn's mother." Matheson had to listen with all his attention to decipher her words in the low, lock-jawed Dreihleen accent that turned "worked" into "werrk't." "Very pretty. Venn's so like her. So young . . ." She wiped welling tears from her eyes and pressed her lips tight for a moment.

"She worked as a model, didn't she?" Matheson asked. "Venn, that is."

Mrs. Tzeren nodded and sniffed. "Fitting model—pretty figure, so pretty . . . Everyone's keep Venn in their eye. Company man's almost fall in love with her." She gave a small, trembling smile. "He's say she's model for all the line—so perfect. For her family's very good. She's not have t'go into service or prostitution."

Matheson coughed to cover his surprise. "Why would she? Was the family—?"

Mr. Tzeren interrupted, irritated enough to meet Matheson's eyes. "Is legal and such pretty girl should have chances better than sewing for half-*real* a day. What other chances we're having if we're not criminals like the red tars who're kill our neighbors? Heh? How we're to rise if we're treated as animals only fit for work to death, only prey for criminals and Corporation too?"

Mrs. Tzeren put her hand on her husband's shoulder, murmuring in his ear. He dropped his head, angry tears running from his eyes as he muttered, "Is not right."

She tilted her head toward Matheson. "Venn'd good chances. Dohan . . . so proud of her, he's take her everywhere, show her off in the Julian dress."

"Is that how she ended up at Paz that night?"

Mrs. Tzeren ducked her head lower to the side. "I'm think so. I'm think . . . he'd thoughts of her."

"What sort of thoughts?"

She lowered her head farther and shrugged. "Maybe marry her . . ."

He started to nod, but given Mrs. Tzeren's posture, Matheson doubted there was anything so honorable as marriage in the thoughts Venn's philandering employer had entertained. "Maybe not?"

Both the Tzerens flinched but said nothing.

Matheson shifted the topic a little. "And Denenshe Leran? Did you know his mother or his aunt from the factory, too?"

Mrs. Tzeren kept her eyes on the floor. "All family kind. But Denny . . ."

"Was he one of the children, there at the factory?"

She nodded. "All th'children together, also. I'm not know how he's grow into what he was."

"What was that? What was Venn and Denny's relationship?"

Both Tzerens turned their mouths down. "Bad. Denny," said Mr. Tzeren, his voice harsh, "he's not best for Venn, but won't let her free. He's cruel to her. A wild boy. His friends . . . bad dogs."

Matheson frowned over the phrase. "Who were some of these bad dogs? Were any of them sweatshop babies? Do you know their names? Any of them?"

The old man hesitated, then his wife shook her head and he followed suit.

Matheson tried to pry more information out of them but the Tzerens were done—something restrained them from saying all they knew. Working for Dohan would have brought them under the protection and pressure of a trade society, but Mr. Tzeren seemed too angry to be bowing to the clan. Could it be one of the factions Dillal had mentioned? The constant irritation of pain shortened his temper, but he took what they were willing to give and left before the aggravation got the better of him.

Dillal redirected a file from his official message queue to an offsite directory less easily hacked and deleted all record of its movement. Then he left and locked the office behind himself. Even on the weekend there were dozens of Directory-level employees heading up via the central lift to log in and keep GISA's endless flow of paperwork from jamming up like a neglected watercourse. He waited with his left hand cupped over his mechanical eye, head bowed. Anyone would have thought he was upset or exhausted, but no one paid him any attention beyond a quick glance that turned away as fast, or faster, than it had arrived.

He sighed a little and brought his hand away from his face, studying it a moment, as if he wasn't sure it was his. A moist red smear glimmered on his palm. He rubbed it away with the fingers of his other hand.

When the lift arrived, Dillal stepped in, keeping his head turned to the left, staying left, putting himself as far from the other passengers as was practical in the small space. They all alighted well before he reached his destination. Stopped at the top floor, he passed his wrist over a scanner next to the elevator's door and the panels opened for him. He stepped out, bypassing a desk occupied by a stunning Gattian woman by turning right and going straight to the large goldwood doors at the end of the glass-paneled hall.

The woman started to rise and chase after him, but checked herself as a message appeared on her console. "Insp. Dillal directly to RD Pritchet's office." She glared after him for a moment, then returned to her work with a disgusted grumble.

Dillal touched the door with his left hand, the ID crystals in his wrist turned toward the glowing surface. The doors swung in with majestic grace, dwarfing the inspector in the gap. He strode forward, his gaze trained on Pritchet, who stood between the large goldwood desk and the unbroken curve of windows that stretched floor-to-ceiling and wall-to-wall several feet beyond it.

The director turned away from the view and waited for Dillal to come to him. He didn't sit or invite Dillal to do so, but put one fist on his desk and leaned on it, looming over the inspector. "What's going on with this investigation of yours?" He kept his voice civil and low, but he didn't sound pleased. "The file's been open for four days."

"Three and a half."

Pritchet gave a dismissive snort. "Irrelevant. Why haven't you closed it yet?"

Dillal didn't tilt his head back to look at Pritchet, but turned it sideways and watched him from the corner of his eyes, the prosthesis tracking just a bit slower than his normal eye and casting a bright reflection across the RD's face as it moved. "Because the crime is not solved."

"I expected more of this project, considering what we've invested in you." Pritchet gave up trying to intimidate Dillal and sat down behind his desk. Dillal remained standing, turning his head to follow Pritchet. "Surely with your . . . skills you should have been able to round up a bunch of Dreihleen clan boys by now."

"It's not that simple."

Pritchet laughed. "Oh, please. What's so complicated? Find a dreck who'll cop to it and close the damned case. Unless by complicated you mean this is an inter-racial problem . . ." He eyed Dillal significantly.

Dillal returned a flat expression. "It is unlikely that the GISA Directors and their friends at Corporation House have thought through this idea they've put into your mouth further than their own agendas. Any racial element is incidental to the true focus of this case—which is capital murder and should be addressed with all due gravity. If you will allow me to do my job rather than attempting to pull my strings like a marionette, you and the board will be adequately satisfied with the blood of the guilty soon enough, and not that of more innocents. Significant progress is being made, but with sixteen victims from a community that is resistant to police interference and resentful of government intrusion in their lives, the case is, as I said, complicated. But solvable."

Pritchet frowned slightly and looked askance at him. "There is a rumor—it's not just the board who's talking—that there's a racial element involved, beyond the mere fact that it happened in our Dreihleat." He leaned forward. "Dillal, I, personally, put a great deal at stake with you. Not just with the project—my project—but in picking you specifically. You are a risk in yourself."

"I'm aware of that. I also know that the qualities that persuaded you to choose me are what make me disposable and an easy scapegoat if you need one. If I fail, I expect the worst. Therefore, I won't fail."

"Well, you'll have to start not-failing on a tighter schedule. The board and a lot of other people want this off the books and they are very concerned with the rumors that have started grumbling around— not that they've ever been happy with the issue of the ghettos and their residents. Just give me something I can take back besides 'It's complicated' and 'we're working on it.'"

Dillal closed his eyes a moment, the mechanism above his left ear making its unnatural ripple beneath the lengthening red stubble of his hair. A small tear of pink liquid formed on one of the fresh cuts below the metal rim of his eye socket. Pritchet winced and turned his gaze aside.

Dillal reopened his eyes. "I'll have something for you tomorrow. I have a metallurgical test finishing up that should tell me the origin of the bullets used in the crime."

"Bullets? Surely a projectile is a projectile?"

"These were unusual."

"They'd better be downright rare."

"The preliminary results should be on my desk by now."

"Not just rattling around in your skull with all that . . . ?" Pritchet waved one hand vaguely.

"Yes and no. I could read the results aloud right now, but I think you'd rather have the summary when I'm done with the complete report."

Pritchet looked disturbed at the idea. "Tomorrow," he said, uncertain.

"Or sooner."

Pritchet still looked unconvinced, but he waved Dillal away. "Better be sooner."

Dillal left quicker than he'd arrived, covering his left eye with his hand as he went.

CHAPTER SEVENTEEN

Day 4: Afternoon and Evening

The Robeshes lived at the top of a cement-printed box stack that was old, unfashionable, and half-covered in aminta vines. There'd been no security system at the main entry—just two graceful, green cerm-glass spires topped with fluttering ribbons to frighten off birds. A flight of black-winged macaws had taken roost at the corner anyway, spattering the wall, vines, and ground below with the evidence of long residence. A lone Dreihle girl in tattered, sweat-dampened clothes had been scrubbing at the mess on the walkway, creeping forward by centimeters as the cleaned sidewalk behind her gathered new shit.

She hadn't looked up as Matheson paused to ask her about the Robeshes, only shaken her head and returned to her unending task.

The climb to the flat was misery. Aging ventilation fans muttered and shushed in rickety mounts, barely moving the thick air in the stairwell, and Matheson reached the landing aching, panting, and mentally cursing the slack lift maintenance in the ghetto buildings. He took a few deep breaths, loosening the pain-knotted muscles in his neck and shoulders so that he didn't hunch like an ape. There wasn't much he could do about the bruises but try to ignore them.

The interior doors were all dull-colored fireproof types with hardened security shells that didn't match one another. The residents had placed various identifying objects and air-scrubbing plants at their thresholds, and with the mismatched doors the hallway had a pleasantly eccentric look. The Robeshes' south-facing unit at the end of the hall broke the effect.

Like the Dohans', the Robeshes' door and bell were completely hidden behind smooth black paper. A tall straight spray of dried maiden grass stood in a jar to one side beside a small box of rough slate holding a pitiful collection of black-edged envelopes and small black-wrapped objects. A young Dreihle woman peeped out of the next doorway and gave Matheson a disapproving glare before turning her gaze down. She didn't return inside, but seemed to be waiting for him to leave.

He took a step back, studying the paper-covered doorway. The residents wouldn't answer his knock any more than the Dohans had, and buildings like this didn't have kitchen doors to try. *How does anyone get in to bring food or carry in the mourning gifts? What about the funeral? The bodies'll be released in a day or so and what'll they do about that? Not leave them with GISA.*

Matheson walked forward again and put his hand out flat on the paper, pushing slightly. The paper shifted back with a grating sound and he looked down to see a line of dust on the floor. It was mounted on a removable board.

The woman in the next doorway started to come out and stopped as he turned to look at her. She jerked her head down and tried to sidle behind her shaggy-leafed procullus plant. Matheson closed the distance and pulled out his ID.

"I'm SO Matheson. I need to speak to your neighbors about the death of their daughter."

The woman backpedaled, trying to duck through her open door, but Matheson swung around her and blocked the way.

"You must be a friend, since you're looking after them. Help me, or I'll have no choice but to open that door."

The woman gave a violent shake of her head. "Shouldn't!" Her voice squeaked in anxiety.

"I don't want to. I understand that they're in mourning, but I have only days to discover who murdered Venn and the rest. That must be worth a great deal more than the silence of a black paper cocoon."

She twisted her shoulders aside as if he'd tried to touch her, her expression curdling with disgust. "None should speak with you, dehka! Yours is no help for us!" Her low voice was venomous.

He peered at her, but he didn't back off. "If you think doing nothing would be better, you're wrong. The trade societies can't fix this."

"Clans're no more help than you—bow to the corporation you work for."

"That might be true—I don't know—but *I* don't bow to anyone. If not me, who do you think will find the people who killed your neighbors' daughter?"

"Some are martyrs for justice—"

Merry hell. "Martyrs? Venn and the rest didn't give themselves up for a great cause—they were murdered by criminals for their own ends. That's no form of justice I—"

"The world will change because they're killed. People are see how th'corporation and men like you do nothing t'avenge our cousins."
Cousins? Real or rhetorical?

Irritated, he pushed the distraction aside and snapped, "I would do anything in my power to find the men who killed them—regardless of what the corporation, the trade societies, or any park bench revolutionaries think. It's my job, and I'm only asking you to help me do it."

She drew back until she was pressed to the wall and looked sideways at him, snorting sharp, angry breaths. "Is easy said . . ."

"So's the thoughtless parroting of other people's ideas. If you actually want justice for Venn and the rest, I am a far better bet than hoping that the world will change before next week. Talking to me can't make it worse, but stopping me can. So . . . you want to keep on arguing in the hallway or will you help me? Or should I override the door?"

She glanced at the floor, her mouth setting in a hard line. Then she looked toward the Robeshes'. After a moment, she said, "They're can't help."

"Can't or won't?"

"Lele's sick. She's . . . she's hurt herself when she's hear about Venn."

"Hurt herself? Why isn't she in the hospital, then?"

The woman scoffed. "Hospital? Think Dreihleen can afford hopper's doctors?"

"It's public health."

"Went to Public Health. Pumped her stomach, sent her home." She glared at him again. "Think I lie?"

He shook his head. "No, but it doesn't help me. I want to know how Venn and Denny came to be in Paz at the same time, who they were with, and why they went. I know they grew up together, but why did she keep seeing him after the things he'd threatened to do to her? What did they have in common that kept drawing them together? One of Denny's bad dog friends?"

She only glared at him.

He turned and looked at the black-papered door. "I guess I'm going in alone."

The young woman bolted to get between him and the barrier. She was quick, but he'd had his fill of being polite and it only took one well-placed foot to trip her.

She fell against the black panel and it crashed against the door hidden behind it. Matheson stepped past her as she scrambled to her feet. She swung around, raising her hands like claws. He checked her with his forearm and stared her down. "I wouldn't advise it. I'm not in a good mood."

The blackened door toppled forward and they both had to jump out of the way.

A bleary-eyed Dreihle man in rumpled clothes stood in the revealed doorway. "Rela," he started, his voice querulous and low. He was middle-aged with dark hair hacked unevenly short, streaked with gray, and his skin had a sickly cast that turned his complexion an ugly khaki. He had the air of a sleepwalker, but as he focused on Matheson, he fell silent.

Rela turned back. "Trahna, Cousin," she said in a rush. "Apologies. This . . . ofiçe's come t'disturb you. I'm try to keep him out."

The older man nodded. "Is nothing, Rela." He looked at Matheson. "For you I have nothing."

"Sir, I doubt that." He produced his ID, hashed the recording, and continued, "Are you Con Robesh?" The man nodded again, leaning as if exhausted on the doorframe. "I'm trying to discover a connection between your daughter, Venn, and Denny Leran that would explain *why* they were both in the jasso that night and who was with them."

Con flinched at the words as if they were blades stabbed through his chest. "Venn . . . was in every eye. Our little beauty. Who'd not wish t'see her?"

"I've been told their relationship was abusive, on-again-off-again. Off at that moment. Is that true?"

Con Robesh nodded, keeping his eyes down. "Rela," he said. "You're go to Lele."

"Cousin," she objected.

Con turned an angry expression on her and ground the word between his teeth, "Go!"

Rela ducked her head and scurried past him, into the apartment.

Con beckoned Matheson closer with a crippled hand. "You serve nothing here."

"I serve the law—"

"Law's grind us to death. Is not for Dreihleen. I'm waste my breath t'speak t'you."

"If you tell me what friends they had in common, I may find the people who murdered your neighbors. If I can understand why Venn and Denny argued at Paz—"

"How you're know what they did?"

"Evidence. They were together, away from the rest. He killed her."

Con sucked a breath through his teeth and shuddered, squeezing his eyes shut. "He's not good enough for Venn—she's want better. Thought they wanted the same, but two can chase same idea to different ends."

"What was it they chased?"

Con shook his head again. "Is not for you."

"Then who believed as they did? Who was with them? Who were their friends in common? Where can I find them?"

"You'll not change it," Con said, a tear escaping from his eye. "My wife's try t'kill herself, but this nor you won't bring Venn back. Will not unmake th'unfair world." The older man's voice shook.

"The people they knew in common may be as responsible for your daughter's death as Leran was."

"Nothing more for you, dehka. Cannot bleed two colors." Con stepped back as tears flooded onto his cheeks. He started to shove the door closed.

Matheson blocked it with his leg and shoulder, swallowing a

jolt of pain as the door rammed against his still-tender bruises. "I can change it—not the world, but what the world believes about the deaths of your daughter and your neighbors. If you know who killed them, tell me."

"You'll carry nothing," Con said, his voice breaking, and rammed the door into Matheson.

Matheson flinched and jerked away from the sharp impact. The door slammed shut as he pulled back and the bolts clanked home. He stared at the door and its fallen screen of black paper. *He knows—or suspects—who was there, but he's not going to say. At least not to me.*

Venn and Denny had believed something in common, if Matheson could find out what it was, he could find their mutual friends—mutual killers.

The howling began as he walked toward the stairs.

A Trizesh . . . Except for the register, it seemed no different from the pained cries of Chanan Vela or Aya . . . except that Mrs. Vela had fallen apart suddenly and the others had built slowly to their collapse. *Which one of them's yanking my chain?* The thought distracted him as he hit the street and he had to push it aside. He needed to find the "bad dogs" who might connect Venn and Leran to someone else and he looked among the weekend tourists for the petty criminals, the grifters, the pickpockets, and drug dealers . . . but each time he saw someone he recognized from the street, they faded back into the crowds before he could get close. Even black-and-blue and without his uniform, he looked too much like a cop.

He returned to Canoe Street, but the Velas' apartments were empty and the neighbors gave no leads to where they'd gone or when. If he hadn't been played, it was a damned strange coincidence. What had made Chanan Vela so desperate to get rid of him? Temote had made the first connection to Venn, but there'd certainly seemed little love lost between the Velas and their wayward nephew.

Matheson stared up at the crater wall. The unaff boy had vanished into a hole near the Velas' door. *Does it connect to the Tomb?* He'd have given a week's pay to find that kid and learn what else he knew about Denny Leran, but he doubted he'd have the luck to simply stumble on the boy this time. Putting the word out might do more harm to the boy than good for Matheson—he wasn't sure what the status and relationship of the unaffiliated was to the bad dogs and trade societies, but the scarring across the kid's tattoo had looked deliberate and painful, as if he'd been cast out as much as cut loose. That would be why Jora and Halfennig hadn't hesitated to go after him.

Matheson was nearly out of options, but not quite: Minje—chatty, quick-eyed, "useful" Minje . . .

Matheson waited at the edge of the park, watching down the road until the foot patrol had walked past. Not Jora and Halfennig, but he didn't know which of the other SOs had attended his beat-down and he wasn't going to chance it. He looked at his mobile and marked the patrol's check time for future reference.

The café was quietly bustling. Tourists and locals mixed together under the buzz and mutter of Dreihleen conversation and both Aya and Minje were occupied. Minje had the floor and glanced up as Matheson entered. The man blinked in surprise, then scowled and jerked his head toward the counter where Aya was working, casting his gaze quickly the same direction. Matheson shook his head and received a puzzled look in reply.

He found a stretch of unoccupied ledge near the back wall. Several Dreihleen stood nearby, resting their cups on the flat, narrow wooden rail at waist height to them. They'd turned sideways to look out the window, or put their backs to the room for privacy. He didn't recognize any of them as they made space for him. He started to lean against the rail, but the first touch of the hard edge through his clothes made him wince. *Merry hell, but that hurts.* Standing still he was more aware of his weariness, ground in by the constant ache of motion against injury.

Minje walked past him with his arms full of used receptacles. "What's bring you this time, right man?"

"More damned questions," he replied in a low voice, as much from frustration as discretion.

"You're ask z'wrong folk these questions?" Minje gave Matheson a pointed stare.

"No. I had a disagreement with a shower."

"Heh. You're fall in the shower?"

"I had help."

Minje grunted with a knowing nod. "Is usual, this help?"

"No. Why would you think so?"

Minje shrugged. "You're a police. If you're good police, z'other police don't like you. If bad police, bad dogs challenge you."

Matheson looked sharply at him. "Tell me about the bad dogs—the ones Denny Leran knew that Venn Robesh also knew."

"Why you're ask me?"

"You know a lot you don't say."

Minje closed his eyes and shook his head. "Can't say." He opened his eyes again, glancing around and then back to Matheson with raised eyebrows. "Is not good for you," he whispered.

"It's not good for the Dreihleat if I don't find them," Matheson replied as quietly.

Minje narrowed his eyes, then shrugged and turned away with his burden of dirty dishes.

Matheson stared after him and tried not to look at Aya while he waited, but she caught in his mind even when he kept his eyes off her. When he gave up and glanced her way, she returned a tilted scowl. Her eyes glittered with sparks even at a distance and he made himself look away. He didn't dare talk to her yet, not when he was wondering if her rending howl had been sincere.

He saw Minje check in with Aya twice, receiving obvious sharp retorts from her. She was no busier than Minje but she didn't make an excuse to come and talk.

When the crowd thinned, Minje came back, bringing a large mug of tea. "She's say you're drink this," he said. "Is for your pressure kisses." The words sounded like "prezher kizziz."

Matheson frowned. "My what?" he asked, taking the warm, heavy cup.

Minje brushed a fingertip under his own eye. "Bruise. Somebody's break your nose, heh?"

"That's just what shows."

"Your cousins're do this?"

"Cousins? Dreihleen use that word a lot, but they can't all be related to one another. So, what's it mean, really?"

"Is family. Kind. Is also family's not your blood—is an honor-word."

"I see. Yeah. My cousin ofiçes did this to me."

Minje shook his head. "Bad dogs. You're not quit?"

"No," Matheson snapped.

Minje smiled and tucked his head down, chuckling to himself. "Heh. I like you, right man." His expression sobered as he looked up again. "You're tell me what you're afeared."

"It's not a fear, it's an inevitability. If the inspector and I can't break the case in two more days, we'll be out of funding and it'll be summarily closed. GISA will just pick someone expedient to blame and give Corporation House the excuse it wants to suppress the ghettos.

And then what? You fight a superior force and die, or do you all stand still and allow yourselves to be transported to the agricamps? Neither makes any sense and yet . . . I spoke with Dreihleen who know—or suspect—who did this but won't tell me. Why? Why would a man who is so torn apart by this that he *howls in pain* keep that to himself?"

"Is keeping that's make him howl, maybe?"

"How can telling me be worse?"

Minje offered a sad flicker of a smile. "You're not Dreihleen. There's much worse than t'lose one beloved."

"Yes, and apparently talking to me is one of those worse things."

"Is not you."

"I know it's not me—it's what I don't know." Matheson closed his eyes and shook his head—sometimes it seemed utterly clear why this was happening, and then it slipped into shadows and doubt. "Dillal says you're useful and I need to find the intersection of Denny's bad dog friends and whatever crawled out of the Tomb that makes a parent willing to let his child's murder go unsolved."

Minje frowned silently a while. "Denny Leran . . . he's not my kind."

"Not your clan?"

Minje nodded. "Not my society—not any society."

"He's an unaff."

Minje shook his head. "No, no. Free. Has friends in two, three societies. His mother, his uncle . . . all different societies. Unaff . . . they're . . . ghosts among the lost. Denny's friends I'm not know—could not say."

Matheson considered the phrase in silence.

Minje watched him a moment, then said, "Kind nor corporation's not the only thing can hurt us."

The clans had pressured Dillal to close, so if not them, what? "It's like something swimming under the surface that I can't see, but I know it's there," Matheson muttered to himself.

Minje looked unhappy and stared at the mug Matheson hadn't touched yet. "You're should drink."

Matheson picked up the cup mechanically and tasted the brew—it was bitter and smelled like sour apples. Aya's tea . . . *Truth or lies? She says the tea's helpful. Maybe it is, but what if it's like water poppy seeds?* "Is this like the escudos?"

Minje made a rueful face. "Sorry—should not have given them you. Cousin Aya's tea's safe."

The warmth of the tea was surprisingly pleasant, even if the taste wasn't. Minje was puckish, but was he dangerous? And Aya? There was a tangle. If she wanted to harm him, she'd had ample chance while he'd been thinking with his dick. But, there were more ways to do harm than sticking a knife in someone. *What the hell.* Matheson nodded stiffly and drank some more tea. There were gaps in everything and the solutions glimmered like dust motes he couldn't catch. Perhaps one answer would lead to another.

"What about the unaffiliated?" he asked. "Would you know them?"

"Some. Who you're look for?"

"I don't know his name. A boy about fifteen or sixteen. I saw him down near the Velas' home—near the tunnels." He tapped his own upper arm with his free hand. "He has a Tzena society tattoo on his shoulder that's been burned or cut—scarred over. He seemed to know Leran and Robesh at least enough to say they weren't friends."

Minje narrowed his eyes in thought. "Weren't friends? Is that he's say, this boy?"

"He said 'they're no friends' actually."

"What question you're asked him?"

"Just trying to find a link between Denny and Venn—before I found out about Dohan Sewing."

Minje glanced over his shoulder toward Aya. She stood beside the counter glaring at two Dreihleen men who seemed to be arguing. Minje looked away, his gaze skipping around the room before it came back to Matheson. "Zanesh," he said, looking troubled. "He's not mean Venn and Denny's not friends. He's mean they're *knowing* Friends."

"Friends . . . I don't understand."

Minje shook his head adamantly. "And I'm not say more."

Matheson sighed in frustration "How 'bout his last name?" Matheson asked. "Zanesh what?"

"Don't know."

"Then how can I find him?"

"Can't. Unless you're go t'Agria. He's arrested."

"Merry fucking hell!" Matheson swore, thumping the nearly empty mug on the rail. The boy might as well be dead for all the chance Matheson had of finding him in the work camps, even if he had time to look.

A few of the lingering customers stared at him, then looked away—hopper and Dreihleen alike.

"What about the tunnels?" Matheson asked, lowering his voice again.

Minje's expression was grim. "Full of knives and voices. You'd not pass alive."

"Knives and voices?"

"Violent ones and politicals. They're work together too much now."

Dissent that went past rhetoric to physical confrontation—that would be the reason for Angra Dastrelas's notorious riot response protocol. Matheson shivered with remembered nightmares and felt an idea slip into place. *Politicals . . . the corner speakers. They were always here on weekends. . . . "Two people can chase the same idea to different ends . . ."*

Minje leaned closer to him. "Finish your tea. Wait for quiet. Then talk t'Aya." The Dreihle gave him a long, thoughtful look. "Is not wise to feel like you do."

"What?"

Minje picked up the mug and started to go. "Care less, hurt less."

Matheson scowled after Minje as he walked away. He stuck to his bit of the now-empty cup rail, convincing himself he could talk to Aya without either shaking her for the truth or thinking of her under him, wrapped around him . . .

He glanced toward her and saw she'd leaned toward the two men at the counter and her face held the same cold anger he'd seen flicker in it the night before. She spoke to them in Dreihleen. One of the men took a step away from her while the other glowered back. She spat a word at him and the man turned sharply away, stalking toward the door while his companion scurried alongside. She stared at them until they'd gone, then flicked a warmer glance at Minje as he stopped beside her. They exchanged a word and she gave a small nod.

She left Minje to the cleanup, and walked toward Matheson—swaying the way she had on the roof, raising exactly the ache he didn't want, and an equal pain that worked against his doing anything about it.

Aya stopped in front of him, turning her head a bit sideways and looking at him from the corners of her eyes. A strand of her hair fell past her ear. "You've habit of injury? Tea helped?"

He started to say no, but it wasn't true—he was still sore and tired, but the all-over pressing, rubbing irritation had faded and only the deepest aches were obvious now—at least while he was standing still. "Not a habit, just the result of being stubborn. And yes, the tea helped." *Should I question her or take her to bed? And will I survive it if I do?*

She cast her glance over him as if she could catalog his bruises through his clothes. "Minje's worried for you—likes you."

"So he said. What about you?"

She put out her hand. "Should talk elsewhere."

He didn't move. "I think it's safer if we don't."

She raised her eyebrows at him, then waved at an empty corner couch that was screened from the door. "Sit?"

Matheson didn't even look. "I'd rather stand."

"Where patrol sees you?"

He gave it a moment's irritated consideration, glanced toward the windows where he could see the Gattian sky beginning to darken and stripe with sunset clouds, then said slowly, "Bugger them." *What more can they do? Break some bones next time? Kill me? So long as I don't put any of them under the gun, they'll get over it.*

Aya's smile had a knowing quirk. "You're have more questions?"

"I do." *How to start . . . ?*

The room settled toward silence as Minje walked the last customers to the door and locked it behind them. Then he called out, "I'm clean up, heh?"

Aya raised her head with a jerk. "In back, Minje. I'm clean here."

Minje frowned at them. "Cousin—"

"What? This *ofiçe* will rob me?" she asked, her voice heavy with irony.

Minje looked at Matheson as if considering it. "More worried what you're do to him," he said.

Aya gave him a chilly stare, then turned back to Matheson. "I'm frighten you?"

"You scare the life out of me."

Aya glanced at Minje and nodded at him to leave. Minje shrugged and headed for the back room, casting a frown at Matheson as he went.

Matheson stood stone still, tangled in suspicion and desire that stabbed like thorns. Even his aches were less persuasive than they had been. "You have me alone, after all."

"Is better."

"It's not a good idea."

"Is't not?" she asked, raising her hand to touch his face.

He flinched and his back hit the cup rail. Sharp pain stabbed through his ribs and he cried out. The twinge bloomed into a throbbing that made him gasp and clench his teeth, no matter how he resisted. He clutched the rail to hold himself up.

Minje ran back into the room and to Aya's side, but he looked at Matheson. "You're new injured?"

"No. Just hit something," Matheson said between gasps. "Merry fucking hell that hurts . . ."

"Work room," Aya said, starting to slide her arm around him.

The brush of her arm across his back spread the fiery ache all across his skin and he sucked in a hard breath, holding back another flinch that would only make it worse. "Don't. Please, don't . . ."

"Fool." She peered at him. "What's not hurt?" she asked.

Matheson had to think, sorting the current flare of agony from the simmering aches and the general irritation of his skin. "Not much," he had to admit. "But nothing bleeding this time."

"Minje, the boiler, then go. I'm look after our good police."

Minje snorted. "He's no worse when you're done, heh?"

Aya snarled at him.

Minje ran back to the work room while Aya and Matheson followed more slowly. He'd thought he was improving, but the flare of pain put the lie to that. He was relieved to prop himself on the edge of a stool, though resting even part of his weight against it sent knives of pain up his spine and through his hips to his groin. He laid his forehead against the cool steel surface of the work counter, keeping his broken nose clear of it. "Fuck . . ." He felt drained as the immediate wash of pain subsided.

"Ofiçes're do this to you?" Aya asked.

She didn't seem to include him in the scorn she heaped on the word *ofiçes*. "Yes."

"Show me."

"No."

"Coward."

"Not. Just . . . No. Too much to do."

"You're not rest, you're not heal."

"What's that saying? 'I'll rest when I'm dead.'" He tried to rise.

She pressed her palm between his shoulder blades. The strength of her arm and the pain of the pressure conspired to make his knees buckle. "Will be soon enough, you're not taking care now."

"How much will it matter if I can't get answers that fit?" he asked as he gave in and turned his head to rest his cheek on the cool counter.

"What questions you're have, now?" she asked, walking away.

"Can I trust you?"

"That's your question?"

"One of them."

Someone made a snorting noise and the boiler hissed loudly. "I'm go," said Minje. "You're want I should open tomorrow, Cousin?"

"I'm do it," Aya said. "I'm throw this fish back if it stinks."

Minje chuckled and Matheson heard him leave through the back door. Silence held sway a while before Aya spoke, and little pieces came together in his mind. Rela and Minje and the boy . . .

"You're think I lie to you."

He couldn't see her, but he was aware of her standing nearby. "Not a lie, just not the whole truth. You and Minje must know which of the political or revolutionary groups frequent your own café, so you're both aware who Denny and Venn knew in common, you just don't want to tell me."

"Why you're think their friends're anything t'do with Sunday speakers?"

"You said so—Venn came to listen and Denny would find her here, so he knew where she was because he knew what she was doing and with whom."

She made a sound in her throat that was cut off by the louder sound of the boiler, the splash of water, and the hiss of steam. Then he smelled herbs and something medicinal, sharp. She walked behind him—he could feel the warmth of her there.

"This helps your pressure kisses," she said, laying something hot and wet against his back.

It felt like a soaked towel and he gasped as it pressed on him. It stung. Then the heat began to work, soaking into his muscles like the water into his shirt. He sighed in spite of himself. "Nothing will ever feel this good . . ."

"Sure of that, are you?"

"Yes."

"Even though you're not trust me?"

"I want to. I've been trying to put this together," he said. He felt heavy and tired and let the words run out of him. *Let me be right about her. Mother of stars, let me be right . . .* "What is worth letting the deaths of family, neighbors, and friends go unpunished? Worth the risk of the corporation's further caprice and oppression? It's not just a crime—it's linked to something bigger that could be *threatened* by solving the crime. Hope's a vicious thing . . ."

Aya stepped around to peer into his face, bending down until she was almost close enough to kiss. "Hope's vicious? Hope's all we're have."

He closed his eyes a moment and nodded slightly, his cheek rubbing the warming steel counter. He looked at her without raising his head. "Which brand of hope are you buying?"

Her eyes narrowed.

"That's what politicians sell—even street corner politicians," Matheson said. He knew them—they were no different than his family and their highly polished cronies. The back-garden politicians, the street corner activists, and park bench revolutionaries, all the weavers of false promises were the same except for the gloss on their suits. He had grown up beside them, been raised by them. "They peddle it like drugs—first fear, then hope. Such desperate hope that it is worth the blood of innocents."

He closed his eyes against unexpected tears and a growing tightness in his throat. "I can't begin to imagine what it's like to be the father of a dead child, and every Dreihle I meet seems to be related to too many ghosts. It's a terrible price, but some people are willing to keep paying it on the promise that this wretched system is going to get better. Isn't that it? That's why Con Robesh won't tell me who his daughter knew—even though his wife tried to kill herself over it, even though it tears him apart. That's why the Velas have disappeared, why Dreihleen won't answer my questions. Someone sold them this idea— this belief, whatever it may be—and they know that someone close to it killed their families and neighbors."

He heard her take a sharp breath. "You're think we're monsters." Her voice had an odd catch in it.

"No, but I think that whoever did this isn't worth protecting. They didn't just rob these people. They didn't kill them by accident— they *murdered* them, calmly and systematically while their victims

235

were helpless on their knees. And now they hide in the center of the trust and belief they've betrayed." He imagined the hundreds of thousands of Dreihleen dead over two centuries, like ghosts on a battlefield.

"Only three people knew of this evidence—SO Matheson, me, and you. And now, somehow, Director Pritchet and the sharks at Corporation House. This slip threatens the investigation." The inspector didn't seem angry, or cold, just as tired as the man in front of him.

The street signs and sunset shining through Dillal's office window painted transient colors on Starna's face, his eyelids drooping in despair. "It wasn't me." He opened his eyes and stared at the inspector. "I swear it. I would think you, of all people, would—"

"Excuse you? Because we are both mets? Solidarity among the muddied class?"

Starna bowed his head. "That's not all of it. You know how hard it is to get ahead here when every part of what you are—bi-colored, addicted, ambitious, all the rest—is another mark against you, another reason to keep you out. It all piles up and you think that if you—if *I* were just one less bad thing it might be forgivable, might be possible . . . But I am as far up the ladder as I'll ever be. I was . . . content with that until you came here."

Starna raised his head and gazed at Dillal. His skin had the dusty pallor of illness, his eyes sunk in verdigris shadows. His hands shook with a slight tremor and he crossed his arms, tucking his hands into his armpits to stop it. He waited for the CIFO to respond, but the other man remained silent.

"It sounds as if I'm confessing," Starna said with a weak laugh. "As if I'm justifying this leak you think I'm guilty of. Or blaming you. I'm not. I'm doing everything I can—everything you're willing to give me—but I could be so much more to you."

Dillal shook his head. "There is no more. I can't save you. I can't lift you past the same difficulties I've overcome to get here—I haven't got that power and this fight isn't won by favor or trickery."

Starna glowered. "I haven't lied or betrayed any confidences. I haven't asked for favors. Only recognition. Which I would expect—yes, expect—from someone as much like me as you are. I've worked for everything and I didn't go crying to Pritchet to get ahead."

"But my problem remains."

Starna looked slightly panicked. "What are you going to do?"

"Nothing. I can't ask for a security review based on the transmission of information I will not admit exists. I'm neatly trapped unless I can serve up an appropriate perpetrator before Corporation House falls on me."

"You need a scapegoat."

"That would satisfy most of the sharks and even Pritchet. But it won't satisfy me."

"You'd still be the CIFO. You'd have another chance to make things right."

"There's more to make right than one case, but this one does offer a crack in the wall. If I can solve it *properly*, the wall may eventually come down. Which is why this . . . leak disturbs me so."

"It's not me," Starna repeated, giving Dillal an earnest look, "but I'm still no use to you because I'm unstable and addicted and one of us."

Dillal put his hand out as if he could stop the tech's stream of self-recrimination. "Starna. The problem is not who you are or what you are. It's what you're willing to become. For *one of us*—even with your skill, ambition, intelligence—you must be willing to risk everything or nothing can change."

Starna closed his eyes again, breathing heavily and turning his face away. "You think less of me because I'm not . . . able to make that leap."

The inspector shook his head and snorted. "*Willing*, not able—and I would have to despise most of the planet if that were true. But you and everyone like you will remain as you are and where you are if nothing changes."

"I'd rather open a vein than continue in this hell."

"More than two hundred years," Matheson said. "Cold air and pressure kisses . . ." Maybe he didn't have all the pieces—or he was standing too close to see the picture—but he knew the pattern the scattered objects formed. "The Dreihleen have always been here, haven't you? The Dreihleen and Ohba are human—not some other race brought here to work—and you've been here since the beginning, even before the Gattian First Settlement families." *It's all of a piece.*

He opened his eyes to peer at her curiously. "Aya, why would Venn's choices be limited to prostitution and sewing? Those weren't your choices . . ."

Aya let out a harsh snort. "She's not read or math! Most Dreihleen are work from time they're eight, or families starve—no time for school. I'm lucky my mother's teach me before she's die, or I'm work for Minje, not him for me."

"Most Dreihleen can't read, can they?"

"Of course they're not! Corporation's not provide schools here, just like they're not give us access to th'net except by hardline that's choked stupid. If we're learn, we do it ourselves."

"The corporation keeps you ignorant and isolated and too busy just staying alive to rectify that. And that's why you don't—can't trust me. Why the Dreihleen won't speak—Merry hell . . . You *need* us to fail."

238

Aya stepped very close and stared down at him, resting her hand on his shoulder. "What you're saying?"

"Blackness . . ." Sickening despair choked him. He squeezed his eyes shut against it, as it dragged on him like the cooling weight of the cloth against his back. He squirmed under it and groaned. "This thing . . . if we solve it, we'll destroy something so precious it's worth the blood of innocents. But if we don't, it's the beginning of the end for the Dreihleen, and the Ohba after them."

Aya pulled the cloth away and he heard it thump into the sink. He struggled back to his feet, still achy and unsteady. Her gaze bored into him. "Tell me why you're say these things." Her voice was low and sharp as the edge of a blade.

He held onto the counter edge and returned her stare. "You know why. The Dreihleen—all of you—are plodding toward your death, keeping your heads down and hoping for some way out of it. That's what your Sunday speakers offer—that desperate, precious, killing hope. One in particular—whoever he is—is tied up in this. The irony is that whatever he's offering isn't salvation or safety anymore. It's poison. It's put all of you at the corporation's mercy. And believe me—corporations have none when their own survival is at stake. If Dillal and I don't solve this case soon, GISA—on behalf of Gattis Corporation—will simply arrest whoever they want and make them disappear forever.

"But if we solve this case, it will destroy that idea, that speaker, who's given you all such hope. If it's not him, it's his close associates who've done this and taking them down will destroy that hope—that's the only thing that makes sense of this entire, horrible situation."

"When you're find them, what you're do? What you're do that's not as bad as the corporation will do?"

He cut off his rising fear and panic, closing his eyes and catching his angry, aching breath. Why did he care so much that she should believe him, talk to him? Not just for the case, not just because he didn't want to think he'd been had. "I am not the corporation any more than the men who did this are the revolution—or whatever it is they represent. They murdered your neighbors. They did it in cold blood, and whatever cause they may support, their actions made it filthy. It will never be clean or noble so long as they are free. You were angry enough to howl over the injustice of it. I can see how furious you are about the whole screwed up system that caused this. You know who these men are—" Of course she did! Of course! He'd even said it and not really realized . . . but now the light was on and it illuminated so much.

Matheson grabbed her by the shoulders. "Mother of stars, Aya! Tell me who they are! You *have* to know—you and Minje run this shop where they sit and talk. You know who, and you know what they've done. If they are taken quickly the cause won't be harmed, but the longer we have to wait, the worse it will get—Pritchet changes the rules every day." His frustration only made the pain in his muscles worse. He felt it crawling over him, tightening his neck and shoulders, driving a pain like a spike through his head and making him dizzy.

Her eyes sparked with strange color in the work lights as she looked into his. "You're ask if you're can trust me. What answer you're have now?"

He thought about the Ice Parade and the rooftop. "It's yes. Or I wouldn't ask for your help." *In spite of everything that I don't know.*

The corners of her mouth lifted a little. "I'm tell you names, but you're have to stay and wait."

"Why? Don't you understand—"

"More than you. You're ask me to betray Friends, but is only the bad dogs you're need. I'm not throw them all to the cats. And I'm not throw you to them either." Then she plunged her hands into his hair and kissed him.

Shocked, he let her go, but she held on. He pushed her back. "What are you doing?"

"I'm kiss you." It had been a terrible kiss, abrupt, unschooled, and messy, but the touch of her against the only parts of him that weren't bruised sent his imagination places his body was incapable of following.

"Why?" he demanded. "You don't—"

"I'm kiss you so you're know I'm true and you're trust why I'm ask you to wait."

He peered at her in confusion. "What?"

She put her hands on his chest and closed her eyes a moment, seeming to listen for his heartbeat through her palms. "Is not safe you're go where they are. They're kill you whether I'm show you or not." She looked at him again. "But you're wait until morning, they're come to you—is Sunday."

The park was less than a block away. "And the kiss . . . ?"

"I'm trust you with my breath."

CHAPTER EIGHTEEN

Day 5: Sunday—Early Morning

There was no sun yet, only the faint glow of Angra Dastrelas marring the sky from below the crater's lip. Matheson peered at it between swollen eyelids.

Aya had persuaded him to stay. He'd laid on her bed and let her minister to his aches and injuries until he couldn't keep his eyes open any longer. Now he felt better than he had a right to, but his shoulders and hips were still too bruised to let him sleep on his side or back, so he'd bunched the pillow under his chest and now lay with his head hanging forward. His neck was stiff and made crackling sounds as he tried to ease his position.

Aya's cool fingers stroked up his spine and into his hair at the base of his skull, then dug into the tight muscles. He grimaced, but didn't object.

"Your sleep's bad," she murmured.

"I never sleep well, even when I haven't been used as a sparring dummy."

"Were much quieter when you're in this bed before." She continued massaging his neck with one hand and her voice floated up beside him as he kept his face turned toward the mattress.

"The situation was different."

"You're wait for me to tell what I'm promise, a piece I'm cut from myself, from my neighbors."

"Aya," he said, sighing. "I don't ask out of a desire to harm them. If you can't bring yourself to tell me, I can't force you—I won't—but I have to find—"

Her hand stilled on his neck. "I'm say, I'm do. But I'm not do this for you. I'm speak *because* of you. What I'm do *for* you's protect you from youthful stupidity. You're understand?"

"You think I'm an eager idiot who'd rush into the Tomb and get killed. Or cause the deaths of people you care about."

"You're think with your passion too much." Her low voice held a bitter edge. "And I'm think of what hope I'm sold, how it's beautiful, but chewed inside by worms. Hope's all we're own of dreams in daylight. We're hold hope or we're die. But I'm raise my head from blind dreams and I'm see blood behind us and more ahead. What we're want and what we're do for it's cost too dear. It's not hope that's kill us—it's the worms within. I'm help you pluck them out, but not more."

He turned his head with care and looked toward her. Beneath the sheltering shadow of the loft's roof, she was only a shape beside him. "You cleave to the ideal."

"I'm not let it go—but I'm see the difference between where we're go and how we're go there, and who we're follow."

Matheson smiled a little.

"I'm not spend you as well," she added. She took a long breath and let it sigh away. "In the morning, you're find two men—Hoda Banzet, Osolin Tchintaka. But not now. Promise you're wait."

"I've held to that promise. Dawn's only a few hours away, so why do you ask me again?"

"You're have your names, you're go—for your work, for your inspector. I'm want keep you longer for myself."

"For yourself?" The idea staggered around his head.

He heard her nod more than he saw it in the deep gloom. "First I'm see you, I'm think you're pretty."

Matheson grunted in ironic amusement. "Pretty . . ."

"But too young and perhaps foolish."

"No doubt of that."

"But each time we're speak, there's fire in you. Even when you're say things that bring me anger, pain, there's fire and it's leap to me like a spark. Close by you, I'm foolish, too. You're too bold—"

"I'm too bold?"

"You're try to kiss me."

"*You* kissed *me*."

"Before."

"When I was pretty."

After a minute, she whispered, "I'm refuse you and fear you'll go. But you're stayed and asked for something of me. Is not as others do and if you're pretty or not's no part of why I'm ask you to stay now."

The conversation hung in the dark while Matheson lay in silent astonishment. "You would be the first person ever who doesn't care what I look like, what I have, or who I'm—who I know." He'd almost said "related to."

"Where you're come from that you're know only selfish, stupid people?"

"Someplace I left."

"And you're come here, to find criminals who murder their own?"

"That wasn't exactly what I was *looking* for . . ." He shifted, taking his weight on his forearms, even though it sent sharp pains up his shoulders and across his back.

Aya rearranged herself beside him and stroked his back as he settled into a new position. His eyes closed again as he drifted toward sleep.

"How you're not believe this thing's done by strangers?" she whispered.

He was too sleepy to hold onto his thoughts and let them sneak out. "All Dreihleen," he murmured. "Denny and Venn knew who killed them. Trusted him . . ."

"How're you prove it?"

"The wounds. Dillal knows . . ."

"Santos is dead." The text message woke Matheson at 0527. "Orris may wish to question you."

The day was still only a suggestion on the horizon, drawing dim shapes on Aya's walls. The MDD's luminous screen was the brightest thing in the room and he saw the message clearly as he lay on his stomach in the bed. Matheson snatched the mobile off the floor and struggled upright to sit at the edge of the bed, wincing and stifling his grunts of discomfort.

Aya turned in the bed beside him, her fingers trailing over his hip. He held her hand a moment as he caught his breath and forced himself awake. Then he let go and carefully wiped the grit of sleep from the corners of his eyes, feeling the complaints of body bruises and the tenderness around his nose. At least nothing felt like it was tearing apart now.

He stared at the message and his breath hitched painfully. "No . . . no, no, no," he mumbled. "Merry hell." He rubbed his eyes again, but the words didn't change.

Aya sat up, turning to him and touching the back of his neck. "Eric?"

"I—" He was dumbstruck—couldn't form a sentence that made any sense. "Wait." He shook her off and stood, staring at the mobile, blinking and trying to think.

She got out of the bed, too, and came to stare into his face, confused. "What is't?"

"I can't—"

He walked out of the loft and onto the open roof, into Aya's
garden, still staring at the message as if it would mean something else
if he looked long enough. He started entering a reply. "What . . ." He
broke off and tried again. "Where? And what about his wife? Is she
all right?"

In a moment, his mobile blipped: request for a voice conversation
from Dillal. Matheson heard Aya step onto the white gravel behind
him, then stop. He checked that the camera was off before he tapped
"accept" and sat down on the edge of a bench among the potted plants,
feeling suddenly dizzy. "Sir?"

The background was noisy, but Dillal's voice sounded low and
immediate, as if he were speaking directly into Matheson's ear. "Mrs.
Santos is well, but upset. She's being escorted to her family home. She
discovered the body perhaps forty minutes ago when returning from
the harbor fish market. Orris notified me as a courtesy, since Santos
was also of interest in our case."

Matheson held back a dozen questions, shaking his head and
trying to put them in order. His last conversation with Santos had
been bizarre at best, but still . . . "How?" he asked after a moment.

"Hanged."

The word jolted him. "*What?*"

"Orris is inclined to call it suicide."

"What about you?"

There was a long silence while the sound in the background
changed, dropping to near-silence and then rising again to the sound
of wind and distant traffic. Dillal grunted as something thumped and
clattered near him. "Without an autopsy, strangulation by hanging

does *appear* to be the cause. His neck wasn't broken, though he did fall, judging by the abrasions."

Matheson didn't manage to mute his microphone before his rush past Aya and to the toilet to vomit. He could too easily imagine the scene and he wished it was as easy to purge from his mind. He gagged over it for a few more seconds. He started at the touch of Aya's cool hand on his back. He waved her away before rising unsteadily to rinse his mouth and face with icy water.

He had kept hold of the MDD and the sound of wind reminded him that Dillal and Aya were still listening. He went hot and cold in mortification, ducking his head and slipping past her. "I'm sorry," he mumbled as he stumbled back outside. There just wasn't enough air . . .

"It's early in the day for gruesome revelations," Dillal responded. "Luckily for you, only I heard that. *Un*luckily for me."

No, not just you. The thought made him wince, as much as his gratitude that Aya didn't follow him.

Apparently Dillal hadn't put the mobile down—maybe he couldn't. *Is this conversation coming directly through the cybernetic link?* Matheson wasn't sure if he should admire that trick or find it deeply unsettling.

"What do you think of this?" the inspector asked.

"Me? I don't know . . ." He felt off-kilter between Aya's comforting refuge and Dillal's grim recall to reality.

"I'm not asking for a technical evaluation. You spoke with him recently. Did his state of mind seem bent to this?"

Matheson squeezed his eyes shut, dredging for memories that seemed suddenly slippery. "Uh . . . he was distraught. He thought he'd be blamed in some way for the situation at Paz. He was panicky and distressed, but he was also drunk."

"Would he take his own life over that distress?"

The weight of unresolved sleep was falling away and Matheson sighed. "I'm not sure. I suppose it's not impossible." He rubbed his face with his free hand but stopped short, flinching at pain, and feeling the rough scratch of whiskers against his palm.

"'Not impossible'—there's a useless phrase," the inspector said. "Once again, without your brain getting in the way, does it ring true to you?"

He gave only a moment's reflection—Dillal had ragged on him enough about over-thinking. "No. It really doesn't."

Dillal heaved a disgusted sigh. "But it will stand as suicide unless the examiner finds otherwise, which seems unlikely."

"Can't you rule on it? You're the CIFO, after all."

"That is what Orris is asking also, but it would only further complicate our case."

Matheson's brain was still sluggish. "How? Aside from being unable to question him at trial."

"Would that not be complication enough?"

"You're laying another of your verbal traps for me, aren't you? Sir."

"Not this time. But I do fear there is another sword waiting to fall if I misstep here. I can't take the Santos case without bringing scrutiny on its possible connection to ours and I can't let it be summarily closed as a suicide if it *is* connected." Dillal growled and added, "Send me your report on yesterday as soon as you can."

"I will. Sir, I did make a breakthrough—"

"Then follow up—I can't speak further now. I'll want to see you as soon as Orris is finished with you—if it comes to that." The inspector closed the conversation and the downward "ping-ping" sounded from the mobile's speaker.

Matheson sat on the bench, at a loss. The inspector was pissed off about Santos, but Matheson was, for the moment, adrift. There would never be a return to walking his rounds with Santos—or anyone else. This case loomed as all he had and might be all he would ever have. There were too many people whose lives were crushed or hanging in the balance. It wasn't just his career or Dillal's at stake. He shook his head and thought about dead people, about the victims at Paz, the anonymous arms dealer in the Ohbata, the unaff kid, about Christa Santos coming home and finding . . . He had forgotten to ask how long Santos had been dead. He hoped it had been hours, not minutes. Though it didn't make him feel better thinking of Christa walking right past her dead husband in the morning darkness. The cool dawn air was full of the roof garden's scents and sounds, and he knew Aya was nearby, but none of it seemed to mean anything. He shivered in horror and his mobile fell into the white gravel at his feet, unnoticed.

The fog off the Cove was starting to thin in the street below as the morning breeze moved between the buildings, trailing the smell of industrial saltwater and fish. Higher up, the wind whispered along the balcony rail, but wasn't strong enough to move Santos's body. Dillal dropped his hand, which he'd cupped over his left ear. Then he stared at the body and didn't turn immediately when Orris stepped onto the balcony and accidentally splashed into a shallow puddle of water spilled from an overturned planter.

"What d'you think?" Orris asked, crossing his arms over his chest and tucking his hands under them.

"Of what?" Dillal replied.

"This. Situation, COD . . ."

"Death by ligature strangulation."

"So, he hanged himself."

"Probably." Dillal's voice was flat. "His hands and neck don't show much sign of his having tried to remove the rope."

"Much?"

"Very little—any ForTech med/legal could tell you this. Most hanging victims panic at some point and try to loosen the ligature. You see scratching at the neck and abrasion on the fingertips. Even suicides do it."

"And that's what you'll sign off on."

"No."

"No?" Orris stepped around and stood close in front of him so Dillal was forced to look up. "Why not?" The older investigator had to squint as the rising sun hit him in the eye and glanced off the front of his faded jacket. He shaded his face with one hand as he glared at Dillal.

"Santos was connected to my investigation," Dillal replied. "I can't certify death for one of my own suspects. It would be fatal to the legal standing of the case. Pritchet wouldn't be pleased."

Orris didn't raise his voice or change his tone, but he said, "Dog-bugger Pritchet. We don't have enough staff to certify this and close it today, unless you do it now. It's a ball-cutting shame, but this isn't a major case—it's just a miserable, friggin' suicide—and I'd like to clear it and get back to the rest of my load."

Dillal shrugged. "I know a doctor who would step in to certify, if you're in that much of a hurry."

"I am. Who've you got?"

"Dr. Andreus. She's always on weekends at the health center—no seniority. It shouldn't be a problem."

Orris nodded, looking grimly pleased. "Good. Thanks. I can wrap this up and let his widow get on with mourning."

"It's a pity."

"Fuckin' tragedy, but it happens all the time."

Dillal nodded, but made no further comment. He walked through the balcony door and Orris followed him back inside. Dillal made for the main door and stopped short. Then he turned back, his gaze directed to the floor as if he were uncomfortable.

"Despair, I suppose."

"What?" Orris asked, walking a little closer.

Dillal looked up, the metallic lid of his prosthetic eye blinking out of sync with the natural one and setting a tear of thick, pink fluid at the incision's edge. "Matheson reported that Santos was despondent about the Paz da Sorte case. This, I suppose, is the result. We've both walked that patch and feel nothing. Why did Santos take it so hard?"

Orris gave him a strange look, as if he thought Dillal had lost his mind. "Well . . . your reasons would be different from mine, but it's not like anyone's heart breaks over leaving the Dreihleat. Santos never left."

"Why not? He'd been in Security Office a long time—you worked with his unit when you first transferred from Agria Corps, I recall. He must have had chances."

Orris heaved a sigh and folded his arms again. "To tell the truth, and meaning no disrespect to the dead, Santos was a fuck-up. Hit his personal ceiling and couldn't get over it—though I suspect the grease didn't hurt. But he was stuck there and when this jasso murder went down, he wouldn't have seen any way back up. Especially if he had anything to do with it. Did he?"

"He hadn't the time to kill them, if that's what you mean."

"But you said he was a suspect, so he must have been involved."

"Possibly."

"Y'know, if it was racial, that could have been the problem—or the cause. His wife's Ohba."

"I thought as much. It must have given them difficulty—him working in the Dreihleat, forming connections with the enemy, so to speak."

"It would wear a man's soul right down to the nub. He drank pretty heavily—or at least he had been, judgin' by the trash."

Dillal grunted and turned away, letting himself out the door.

Matheson had been sitting a while when he began hearing people moving on the streets two stories below, but he didn't bother to wonder what they were doing. The white stones on the roof clicked as Aya walked across the open garden. She had put on a dress—a thin white thing that billowed in the breeze coming up with the sun over the edge of the crater. She draped an equally light blanket over his shoulders and sat beside him. He shivered again, though it wasn't cold and the wind wasn't strong enough to chill the moisture in the air.

He sat still and tried to breathe, but it felt like a weight had settled on his chest and his breath came in hard jerks and pants that sparked pain across his bruised back and ribs. He closed his eyes and felt a harsh burning at the lower lids that was not only lack of sleep. His mouth crooked at an unexpected pang of grief. *This can't be right. This isn't right!*

"Eric?" He opened his eyes slowly, saw the motion as Aya tilted her head, but couldn't make himself turn to look at her. "What is't?"

He had to lick his lips. It was hard to speak at all and his tongue felt heavy, his brain thick. "He's dead." His voice shook and he noted it as if it were someone else's. "He died this morning."

Now she put her hand on his shoulder—a touch barely discerned—as she leaned toward him. Her face creased in a puzzled frown. "Who?"

"My partner. He's dead." It didn't seem real. But the inspector wouldn't lie to him about this. Santos was dead.

Aya took a sharp breath through her nose and stood, rearing away from him. It startled him and he turned to her in concern. She looked thunderstruck.

"Dead?" she asked. "By what?"

He stumbled over it, not wanting to say, but wanting to push the idea out of his own head and get rid of it. "He hanged himself." The words seemed to crush a cold void in his chest that grew larger as Aya's eyes grew wider.

Matheson shook himself. There was someone else to worry about, now, someone else to deal with. His voice sounded mechanical in his ears. "I'm sorry. I didn't realize you must have known Santos. He'd been here a long time, so I should have guessed."

She closed her eyes and swayed. He pulled her down to sit beside him on the bench and she lowered her face into her cupped hands, her hair falling forward. She shook for a minute and Matheson had no better idea what to do this time than he had the last time.

She raised her head suddenly, but kept her face forward. She didn't even turn her gaze to him Dreihle-wise. "I'm know him. But I'm not cry. I'm . . . thankful."

"Why?"

"He's one takes the *real-protezhão.*"

Matheson knew half the word—*Real* was the Gattian monetary unit—but the other word was too far from one he recognized . . . Aya frowned at his incomprehension and made a gesture for money, rubbing the tips of her first two fingers and thumb together.

"Protection money. Merry hell. You too." Matheson closed his eyes and put his hand over them. Even knowing it was true, he hadn't *wanted* to believe it of Santos, poor dead son of a bitch . . . but his disgust was suddenly stronger than grief. "He's dead, but there'll be others."

"I'm already pay the morning walkers this month. I'm not do it, they're burn down my shop. Even Minje and the kind are not stop them."

His emotions were in chaos. He turned to her, guilty by association. "Aya. I'm sorry."

"Why? You're make these men? You're send them here?"

"No. But it's all part of the same system. The system I work for, the system the Sunday speakers rail against—rightly. Yet I've asked you to betray those people . . ."

She scowled, casting him her sideways glance. "This you're not saying last night. You're not believing it but for the pain you're feel now. You're think one crime's excuse another now?"

"No! Maybe! Blackness take it, I don't know!"

Her expression softened and she put her hand on his cheek. "Is hard for us. You're understand now why we're buy hopes from park benches. Why Robesh is not tell you who Venn's follow like her own heart's beat. But I'm tell you who you must find—not for destroying hope, but for making it clean again."

"What am I becoming? A better cop, a worse one . . . or a tool for someone's revenge?"

"We're not deserve vengeance when they're murder our neighbors, poison our chances?"

Confusion tore at him and muddied his thoughts further. "Yes—No—I—is that what I'm pointed at? Is that what I can get? Without ruining something else just as precious." Matheson lowered his eyes. Now he felt hollow. "I don't know. I'm coming to think I don't know anything at all and the people I know best are all dead."

Aya leaned closer to him. "Is not true."

"I mean . . . the people I have come to know *about* are sixteen murder victims that I know better than my dead partner. And except for Venn Robesh and Denny Leran, I hardly know them, either. They are names and faces"—he shuddered, remembering Venn's face and Denny's—"disconnected from . . . a person. Ghosts that haunt me because it's my job to put them to rest—or try to. I don't *know* them, but I know you and you make me feel their loss and their desperation like a knife in my gut. And now there are two more—maybe a third. And there may be others—there may be a lot of others if things go wrong."

Aya peered at him. It was a searching look that seemed to take him apart and stare into places he didn't want to look himself. "You're trust your inspector?"

"I do. I have to. We're in this mess together."

"You're not think he's let you sink in it if it's save *him*?"

"Never." He had no hesitation about that but Aya seemed to be measuring his reply, weighing him against a standard he didn't comprehend. "We've each put ourselves in the other's hands. We have to solve this or we're both done for. Without Santos it's going to be harder. And if I can't find the men you told me about last night—"

"Banzet and Tchintaka."

He nodded and repeated the names. "Do you know if they did this? Or are they only names that lead to more names?"

"I'm not know if they're the ones go with Denny. But they're friends between him and Venn. I'm hope is not them, but they're all I'm know."

"If I don't find them, I may not find a solution in time. If Dillal and I are right, that could lead to the death of all of you, every Dreihle and probably every Ohba too, because you stand between Gattis Corporation's charter and its future survival."

Back in his office, Dillal found a report among his messages and read through it on one screen while composing a message to Dr. Andreus on another. Once again, he moved the file to a more secure virtual location and destroyed the original and all trace of it that he could reach. But he paused several times and reread sections—especially one that mentioned Fahn.

Dr. Andreus replied by voice while Dillal was composing a summary of the report for Pritchet. He touched his hand to the back of his left ear and winced as he made an adjustment to the socket there. Then he typed a command on his terminal, routing the call through his datalink. Only his half of the conversation was audible to anyone else and he kept his voice low. "Yes."

"I don't have time to play games with you, Inspector. What is it you want now?"

"Do you have a report on Santos yet?"

"No. The body only just arrived. But if you want me to make an educated guess, it's strangulation, as everyone else said—including you."

"Nothing complicating?"

Her annoyed sigh came through the datalink "At first glance, yes, but that doesn't change the COD. You didn't ask for a full autopsy, just certification of cause of death. I'm ready to certify strangulation by hanging. But I suppose you want all the details, don't you?"

"I do. And I've a small problem of my own."

"Yours isn't the only dead body I've got on my agenda today, so if you want this done with any speed, you'll need to come to the hospital and lend me a hand."

"Thank you." He tapped the keyboard, cutting off the voice call. Then he continued typing Pritchet's summary, scowling the whole time.

> . . . three different types of projectiles of the same caliber and com-
> position, but with varying design. This leads to the conclusion
> that the individuals involved in the murders at the Paz da Sorte

were unable to obtain consistent ammunition from any legiti-mate source and were placed in the position of accepting what was available from an illegal source or sources.

The combination of materials used in the projectiles is unique and is definitively identified as part of an ordinance con-signment used by outside military and mercenary forces supporting local units during suppression of the Cafala flood riots on the continent of Agria twelve years ago. A voluntary detachment of those troops remained for clean-up and debriefing. Agria Corps standard procedure did not require accounting for ammunition issued by non-Gattis units at that time. Thus, a significant cache of ammunition of this design and caliber could have gone missing without comment. The remaining question is, from whom did the perpetrators obtain the ammunition and weapons? Since both are military in origin, the obvious conclusion is that they were acquired illegally.

GISA's interest in this case will be best served in locating the undocumented cache, seizing it without delay, and interrogating those with knowledge of it with as little publicity as possible and an eye to apprehending not only the perpetrators of the Paz da Sorte murders, but any other parties who may be in possession of such illegal matériel . . .

Dillal read through the stultifyingly dull report and smiled. Then he directed the document to Pritchet, and rose once again from his desk.

He avoided both staff and private transportation and made his own way to the hospital.

CHAPTER NINETEEN

Day 5: Morning

The crowds in the street seemed like a mirage to Matheson. His thoughts fragmented—part still with Aya, part mourning Santos, while the rest was trying to get back on track with the investigation. The two men Aya had named should be somewhere around Yshteppa Park, but he didn't know what they looked like. He sent a database request for any records of Hoda Banzet and Osolin Tchintaka and flagged the inspector on it as well. Dillal wouldn't be able to do much with it while he was dealing with Orris, but at least the names would be in his queue.

Matheson hadn't noticed the crowd thickening and slowing until he couldn't move forward without elbowing the people around him. They glared at him with more open annoyance than he'd seen from Dreihleen before. One or two seemed familiar—*from the coffee house?* Most of the bystanders were as tall or taller than Matheson, blocking his view of all but the top of the obstruction—a banner that bore the "Relief, Redress, Revolt!" pictograms in bright red and the fleeting view of a man's head and hands as he spoke to the crowd.

". . . Equality among *all* races of Gattis!" the man was saying. The man's voice was clear and easy to hear.

Matheson frowned. *He's loud.* Odd among people with such an unusual way of speaking and so quietly that Matheson often had to lean in to hear them and pay close attention to every word. He didn't see an amplifier. Was this another trick of what the inspector had called "the long breath"? He craned his neck and tried to figure out how the man was doing it.

"We're not as worthy as any blue-skinned man or woman?" the speaker continued.

A few muttered answers came from the crowd, but the audience seemed unsure if they should agree or disagree.

"We're less human than people who're live on the Quay?"

Now a few of the crowd answered back, "No," and Matheson blinked at the direct reply. *They never just say "no" or "yes."*

The speaker asked them again, "Are we less human?" He wasn't saying anything that other rabble-rousers and street corner preachers didn't, but the man's passionate sincerity seemed to infect everyone near him. Was this the man Venn had listened to?

The crowd answered louder, more sure of themselves, "No."

"We're less worthy of fruits of our labor?" *This guy doesn't lock his jaw and they haven't noticed.* But they wouldn't, because he had them in the palm of his hand.

"No!"

Disquiet stirred the hair at the back of Matheson's neck and he stood quite still. He watched what he could see of the speaker, and studied the crowd without turning his head.

"Our parents and grandparents—all our ancestors from *before* First Settlement worked hard as anyone for this planet, heh?"

"Yes!"

"They're build this whole, mighty planet of wonders from Pillars of Archon to Verdan Archipelago, from vast plains of Agria to Exley Trench." The speaker spread his arms in the air as if he could hold the whole of Gattis in their compass. The crowd shifted and looked upward as if they, too, could see the whole world arrayed in the span of his arms.

In the gap, Matheson finally caught a full view of the speaker: standing on a small cargo crate, a Dreihle man no taller than average but with the look and presence of a stalking lion—and eyes that gleamed and glittered like Aya's did. For just a second, the speaker seemed to look right at Matheson before his gaze moved on from face to face, his mouth turning up in the smallest of smiles.

The man continued, "They're build this by sweat and toil. We should have less right to fruits of that labor—our labor—than blues and system hoppers and shashen investors?"

Every Dreihle in the crowd rumbled now, "No!"

"Is't right that color of our skin's dictate our fate?"

"No!"

The speaker continued, faster, inflaming the crowd, "Our children should be denied education because they're yellow, or red?"

"No!" the crowd shouted and Matheson cringed at the unlikely sound. *They're like the Suvilen—they've thrown off who they normally are.*

The speaker barely paused for their reply. "Our young men're turned slaves or criminals t'get by, our mothers and daughters t'servants and whores?"

"*No!*"

"This impropriety, this inequality, this *immorality's* forced on us by unfair laws, created by politicians and businessmen who're not *of* Gattis, enforced by weight of arms carried by foreigners and mercenaries—"

Cold certainty enfolded Matheson and he turned to work his way toward the edge of the volatile crowd. Every move he made brought dark, angry gazes to bear on him, and the nearest clear space seemed too far away.

"—whose only purpose is t'hold us down!"

"*Yes!*" the audience shrieked. All but those who stared at Matheson as he struggled to break out of their midst.

The creeping edge of panic tightened his chest as he pushed forward.

"We're not lie down! We're not be *held* down! *Pushed* down t'be raped and murdered and trampled like mud in the streets!"

"*No!*"

"We're lie down anymore?"

"*No!*"

"Will we lie down?"

"*NO!*"

"Then rise up!"

Matheson could hear the orator plainly even with his back turned and the growing mutter of the crowd around him. The sound sent a chill of dread over him, and the feeling of something he'd willfully forgotten writhed like a snake in the back of his mind.

"*YES!*"

"Rise up for *relief*! Demand *redress*! And when we're bear no more, *revolt!*"

The Dreihleen in the street let out a collective shriek of mob rapture that cut across Matheson's caution like a whip. The nearest people turned and grabbed for him . . .

Matheson swore and bolted, shoving people aside in a panic to break free. The unclear memory of something awful goaded him.

"This is live, cadets! This exercise is live! Keep your helmets on, keep your shields up! Go, go, go!"

They rush the doors, orderly, but fast, jumping the short gap to the ground and swarming forward, thrusting the crowd away with the force of inter-locking shields and strong young bodies. It's noisy as a bell tower in hell. His head rings and his vision narrows, discolored and jittery. He has no idea where they are, only that bodies under angry, shouting faces press against them—tall and short, thin and stout . . . so many, and all resisting their push, pushing back, battering at the shields with strange tools, and shouting. Shouting that quickly turns to screaming as they plant their shields on the ground, forming a wall, and aim through the ports in the interconnected plates.

Electricity cracks the air, ozone and burned flesh stinks in his nostrils. The crowd falls back, the stunned staggering away or being dragged by their nearest companions. The cadets raise shields and thrust forward, making headway through the human tide.

A pole thrusts through the port on his left, jabbing into his sideman's arm and sending the other cadet backward. He cannot hear his sideman cry out in the noise. The cadet beyond the fallen man discharges his stun baton at the person holding the pole and takes a step right. He takes a step left, locking the shield edges together again. The squad moves forward, shoving the pole bearer back until the man falls over, vanishing into the churning crowd.

The cadets surge forward. He feels softness under his feet and spares a reeling glance downward. He's walking on the fallen pole bearer. His stomach heaves, but it doesn't have to be because he's stepping on another human being. They've done three jumps in a day and the final orbital fall to—wherever in hell they are. He is disoriented, fatigued . . . jumpwise. They haven't stopped since sunup to do more than suit up and launch. Jumpwise, that's all it is. He pushes onward.

They all push onward.

The crowd resists. Someone brings a water cannon to bear, trying to hose the cadets back. They plant their shields, crouching and bracing against the pulse of water. A cadet drops a shock baton into the puddle and a chorus of new screams erupts from the crowd. They must be wearing leather shoes—or no shoes at all. He doesn't know. Only that the insulated soles of his own boots protect him.

He pushes forward, into the shouting, the crack of electricity, the stink, and the churning, sucking mud until his head is reeling. He can barely see—

everything seems to swim and waver in his vision, turning colorless and cold—and he hears nothing but roaring silence and the taut crack of static up his limbs that stabs at his brain.

He doesn't remember planting the shield, doesn't know why he does it, but he feels the ground against his shins, so they must be bracing again . . . Then the world swings and the ground kisses his face with azure mud blood stained the color of ripe plums. His vision narrows and darkens . . .

CHAPTER TWENTY

Day 5: Morning into Afternoon

Matheson ran, not back toward Aya's, but toward the canal—into the open where he stood a chance. He wasn't sure he could stay ahead of the mob. His heart beat too fast and his adrenaline was burning out after the shock of the crowd's turn and the terrible flash of shattered memory. His broken nose forced him to suck in mouthfuls of the humid air, thick with the stink of slow water and floating garbage. He cut across a corner of the park, then angled through the grove of goldwoods and toward Southern Star Canal—he'd swim the pestilential thing if he had to.

He swung around the door of the GISA checkpoint at the lock. Closed! No easy call for help and no easy way through. He'd have to take the bridge.

He didn't waste time to swear, but switched back through another section of the goldwood grove that cut across the mob's path. The crowd was falling off, but it was still a dozen or more. They formed a line to cut him off. *Shit. Shit! Can't outrun them . . .* He was flagging and the Dreihleen had the advantage of righteous indignation. He had only his fear.

He whipped left and down the steep, grassy bank that fell back toward the canal below the lock. He ducked, hoping he was far enough ahead to be out of sight for a moment, and threw himself at the staircase that led down to the footbridge. He leapt and caught the ornamental bars, hauled himself, shoulders aching and bruises screaming, into the sub-deck where the old lift mechanism had been before the recent rebuild. He drew his legs in and lay flat against the metal sub-deck, trying to slow his panting and shaking. He squeezed his eyes shut and held his breath as long as he could. It was foolish, but he was already playing the fool and he thought if he could make the blackness behind his eyelids dark enough, he might blot out the jagged fragments of memory that tore at him.

But, since the memories came from darkness, they played more vividly on his closed eyelids. As he shivered through the assault again, his pursuers passed him, clattering up the stairs over his head and across the canal, the din echoing in his head as the pounding of boots and the screams of the phantom mob as they fell. It just kept going. Over and over. Unreasoning terror held him rigid. *Don't find me, don't find me . . .*

He lay still in the sub-deck until quiet finally claimed his attention. The air had grown thick and felt too warm to breathe. The bridge deck above him had given up its morning cool. He listened, afraid to move and give himself away, but there was no sound of the angry mob milling near his hiding place.

He slithered out and fell gracelessly to the ground, too sore and too drained to manage a better exit. *How long . . . ?* He shot furtive glances over his shoulders. No one near. In the distance he could still hear sounds of anger and saw rising columns of smoke—though he could barely smell it. He didn't make a move toward it.

The sun was well up and the air was hot and thick, insects rising off the canal in motes that spiraled on the updraft from the hot metal bridge. He thought of Santos talking about the ramp-up in riot response and hoped the Dreihleen would wise up and disperse before—

The whine and hollow echo of incoming riot control squads cut into his thoughts. Matheson shuddered at the nightmare they brought back in slashes of memory. He checked his mobile. One message: Dreihleat West Gate Bridge Closure. He'd been cowering under it for almost an hour and had only ten minutes left to get out.

His muscles quivered with post-adrenaline crash and burned from bruising and abuse as he crossed the bridge out of the Dreihleat. Now he had seen the deep well of rage that tortured Con Robesh and simmered in Dreihleen silence and sideways glances.

He stepped off the bridge and paused at the stone markers at the edge of the ghetto. Then he looked back. No one followed or waited for him. His paranoia for the past weeks hadn't been without cause— it just hadn't been the one he'd imagined. He lifted his gaze toward Rua dos Peixes. *Aya. Is she safe?* Then laughter as bitter as water poppy choked him. The men she'd named must have been among that mob. Whether she'd known what would happen or not, she was safer without a "shashen mercenary" in her home—especially one who couldn't remember exactly what terrible thing he'd done somewhere or sometime.

The gate alarm gonged and the staunch metal gratings grumbled into motion. Matheson turned and walked away from the Dreihleat and the gate ground closed behind him.

He made his shaky way to a café that lacked a view of the canal and sat down to straighten himself out. His thoughts were tangled and terrifying. There was something lurking in his own mind that he didn't understand but the incoming tide of it was familiar and it reeked of devastation and ruin. He rubbed his hands over his face, wincing as his fingers passed over the scab in his eyebrow and pressed on his recently broken nose. Gattis was cutting him into pieces and throwing those pieces back like knives. But the place had set its hooks in him, as Aya and the Dreihleat and Dillal had also, and something even more horrific hid in the shadow of the Paz da Sorte investigation.

The health center's autopsy room had the distinction of a colored angelstone floor. Whether it was cast that way or had somehow shifted color, this particular floor was a pinkish gray—the color of macerated brain tissue—all the way through. The area beneath Dr. Andreus's work was dotted with red for the time being, but it would be as smooth and unmarked as the rest of the otherwise empty room once it was hosed off.

Dillal stood on one side of the table and the doctor on the other. She leaned back, working her shoulders as if they were stiff, and rested her weight on the counter behind her. She looked up from Santos's body lying open between them, and cast an assessing gaze over the inspector. "I don't know who I'll have to cremate first—him or you."

Dillal didn't raise his gaze from the body. "He has family awaiting the remains."

"I meant, you're not so far from being on this table yourself, inspector."

"You exaggerate."

"And we'll both know how much when you let me get a look at that. Don't think I haven't noticed that you're keeping the corpse in between us."

"I did mention I had a problem, but he is of greater importance in the moment."

"No. Your reason for existing is guys like this and if you die at this point, what happened to him and those sixteen people in the Dreihleat will just keep on happening." Her voice was sharp with annoyance. "You have to survive this or there won't be any further Forensic Integration Project—and I've worked too long and too hard to let you sink it with your belief in your own infallible immortality."

"There will be no further FIP if I don't solve this case, either. Which I cannot do if you won't tell me what you've discovered."

Andreus rolled her eyes. "Spare me the disingenuousness. You may not know the particulars, but you must have picked up the trace at the scene. I'm not flattered to be used as a blind."

"It was necessary or more people may die. ForTech is not secure and information has already gotten out that never should have. There's a woman dead in the Ohbata because of it."

Andreus glared at him. "How do you know?"

Dillal looked disgusted. "It could be a coincidence that she was the one who supplied the ammunition used at the Paz da Sorte, that she was shot with the same type of weapon, and that her DNA was identified in my lab only a few hours before. It is possible. If you believe in coincidence."

"It doesn't have to be a conspiracy, inspector, only a villain covering his tracks."

"That's all any of this is," Dillal snapped. "This system is nothing *but* villains covering their tracks. That's what brought you here."

"Not to hide," she shot back.

"No, you don't hide much, do you, doctor? There's a straight and bloody line of your work from Marshel to Kora to here." Dillal pointed at his gleaming left eye.

Andreus leaned across Santos's body and slapped Dillal's hand aside. He wasn't quick enough to turn out of the way and his fingernail cut across the welt that had developed under his eye. Sticky red pus splattered across the wall beside him. He flinched and took a step back.

The doctor walked around the table, glaring at him, and pushed him against the wall. Her angry gaze swept his face and then she stepped back. "Well, lucky you—it's only an abscess right now. But you're slowing down and that's not a good sign. Six weeks ago you would have caught my wrist and broken it before I had time to touch you. Tell me how this happened."

Dillal gave her a wary look. "I've told you I have a problem."

"Not like this!" She glowered at him and then settled back slightly. "All right, let's make a deal, here. We're both heartless bastards and we're not friends, but we aren't and shouldn't be enemies. Neither of us can weather a failure here. Neither of us wants to see this world in flames, and I believe we have some goals in common—though why you give half a damn what happens to these people after what they've done to you and yours is anyone's fragging guess. So this is my proposal. First—stop screwing with me. I'm your surgeon, I'm your ally, and I'm not going to go grass on you. Second—take proper care of the work I've done. You want this as much or more than I do and I've put a phenomenal advantage into your hands, so treat it with some respect. Third—when you need help that I can render, don't maneuver and manipulate me, fragging *ask*. Because if this relationship breaks down to a grudge match we will both lose. I did not slog through three different wars, blood, bullets, and bodies, medical and military tribunals, and dodge death squads to lose! Not this time."

Dillal scowled at her for a moment, a trickle of blood running down his cheek. Then he closed his eyes, his jaw working a little as he ground his teeth and thought. He shook his head and opened his eyes again, his expression neutral now. "Yes. All right. Proposal accepted. What's the rest?"

"You think there's more?"

"Plainly there is."

Andreus grunted and gave up a thin smile. "All right. Number four is tell me what happened to cause this while I take a look at your eye—and that burn on your wrist and whatever else you didn't bother to mention—and I'll tell you what I've got from Santos."

Dillal assented and Andreus cleaned up so they could move to her exam room. She had him strip to the waist and attached several monitor pads among the patches and tracks of scars on his back and chest.

Then she started to attach the data cable behind his left ear. The skin around the plug was slightly reddened and marked with small, charred black lines.

"What happened to the socket?" the doctor asked, peering through a magnifier at the area.

"Bad cable connection."

"What sort of analysis were you attempting to run?"

"I wasn't. It was a rather desperate improvisation and I've had to work around it. I haven't been able to retrieve the data I was hoping to save, but I believe it's still in the swap buffer."

She backed off and stared at him. "You did what . . . ?"

"If you'll complete your examination, this will make more sense."

"Will it?"

"The damage to the data socket and the burn on my wrist are related."

"And the eye?"

"Indirectly. Same incident, different cause."

Andreus gave him a hard look, studying him for a minute. "Fine." Then she removed his ocular and continued the exam.

"There's a crack in the lacrimal bone and another in the supraorbital margin near the frame attachment. I can't do anything about the cracks without detaching the entire frame, which would require a few hours in surgery and more downtime that I expect you'll say is unacceptable, won't you?"

Dillal raised his remaining eye to hers as she stood in front of him. "Yes."

"Well, the cracks will heal on their own, but the blood and fluid from the tissue damage are draining to the lowest point along the infraorbital margin and through the cracks in the lacrimal. That's causing the abscess under your eye. If you're still taking the drugs I prescribed, that should stave off infection there, so long as you keep this dry, but it may still drain for a while, even after I clean it up today. I can fix some of this, patch some new spray skin, but you need to baby those cracks for a while—don't go banging yourself around or putting pressure on your head or eye." She leaned in again and peered at his left cheek. "This damage . . . it looks as if someone tried to yank the unit out of your skull."

"He didn't try, he only threatened to."

Andreus stepped back and leaned against the nearest counter. "Who did this? What did he use?"

"His fingers."

"Fingers?" Andreus looked intrigued. "He must have extraordinary grip strength. Who was this?"

"My grandfather."

The doctor scowled at him. "The Ohba side?"

"Yes."

"That explains the grip. These marks in your skin around the frame are from his fingernails."

Dillal said nothing.

"The burn is his gift, too, I assume."

"Indirectly. I chose to leave before he had given permission. You'll see it goes a distance up the arm," Dillal said raising his right forearm between them for her to look at. The electrical discharge burn ran from below the smallest finger of his hand to his elbow. "There are two companion marks on my left shoulder," he added, resting his hand above them. The two bright red patches were in perfect alignment with the long burn on his forearm and directly below the data socket.

Andreus studied the geometry of the burns. "These didn't come from the data cable—they don't carry significant voltage."

"No. They're from a homemade shock box. I was wet at the time and feared the charge would damage the socket if it chanced to arc to the device."

"Not a cable . . ." Her eyes widened. "You attempted a data transfer directly to the buffer from a free-standing device. You are insane."

Dillal shrugged. "It was a very small drive, there wasn't much risk in it."

"Until your grandfather tried to electrocute you."

"One of his lieutenants did it when he noticed what I was doing with the drive. As I said, I feared the charge would damage the socket. My right hand was still free, so I blocked the contacts and the discharge traveled up my arm instead."

"What's on that file in the buffer?"

"I don't know. I had no chance to access it, but I assume it's unpleasant and damning or my grandfather would have no interest in forcing me to see it. I thought it better to take it and run than stay and discover what else he had planned."

Andreus watched him a while in inscrutable silence. "You really are a remarkable piece of work. Perfect specimen for this—the brain, the physiology, the sheer damned cussedness."

"I'm not familiar with the word."

"You know the phrase 'too stubborn to die'?"

"Yes."

"That's you."

He tilted his head as if accepting a compliment. "I believe you owe me some information in return."

"I'll tell you while I upload the buffer and clean these wounds."

"Upload the buffer?"

"You want access to the file don't you?"

"I don't necessarily want it in anyone else's hands."

"Tough. It won't go beyond this room, but I'm as interested as you. And I'm the only person aside from you who stands a chance of extracting it. That's my equipment in your head, so that's my price."

Dillal gave an annoyed grunt, but didn't object further.

The doctor cleaned up the cuts and burns before she turned back to working on Dillal's eye. "So, the interesting thing about Santos . . ." she started. "You already know this, don't you?"

"Not specifically. There was no viable blood sample."

"But you got trace indicators off the ligature and while we were in the morgue."

"Yes. But please amuse yourself before coming to the point."

She barked a laugh. "Hah! The report from that ass Orris claims Santos was a heavy drinker, but while there was a hell of a lot of alcohol still in his stomach and blood, there's no evidence he was a long-term user. He was drunk at the time, but not habitually. He also wasn't a habitual drug-user though there were drugs in his system—drugs the scene techs didn't find in his house—and also some they did. All together, the relevant substances create something we called 'deadman's dram'—"

The console on the doctor's table made a noise and she turned toward it. "Looks like that file is some kind of video, but my machine says the codex is broken. It'll take a little while to rebuild."

"Deadman's dram," Dillal prompted.

"What, you didn't look it up while my back was turned?"

"Data cable insertion disables the system antenna."

Andreus barked again. "Hah! It's a last-ditch, last-rights kind of thing. Developed centuries ago for terminal patients who were in extreme pain. We called it deadman's dram on Marshel during *that* war, but it's got lots of names: Snow's Elixir, soldier's rest, Brompton Cocktail . . . The combination of an anti-nausea component, like cannabis, mixed with a specific type of stimulant, alcohol, and an open-chain opiate, given in moderate doses, makes the patient comfortable and sociable for a few hours—even up to a few days—before they die. You've got a couple of choices of stimulant and opiate—which is great when you have to work with whatever you've got—so there's a small range of effect. If you mix in something sweet, it's almost palatable and an appropriate dosage is about ten milliliters, maybe fifteen to twenty milliliters for someone of Santos's bulk—less than half a shot glass full. There are better things, and it's almost unknown outside of field hospitals and backwater clinics, but everything you need is easily available on most agricultural planets. Now, a side-effect of this specific combination is that it makes the patient extremely suggestible while it lasts. In this case, the tonic would have been effective for a little over an hour, two at the most."

"Suggestible enough to persuade a man to take his own life?"

"That would depend on his mental state at the time, but it might not have been a very hard sell."

"And when did he die?"

"Between 0300 and 0500."

"He would have been talkative during that period also?"

"He'd have been willing to discuss anything an interrogator asked him, right up until he couldn't talk at all."

CHAPTER TWENTY-ONE

Day 5: Afternoon

Once his mind had settled, Matheson began picking at the investigation's threads. He had questions and possible ideas, but he'd been unable to contact Dillal, so he went to GISA HQ to find him. There was no sign of the inspector in the morgue or the ForTech lab, which was staffed by a handful of techs and med/legals. The lab was clean, but the hallways outside had been tracked with the powdery blue sand from Santos's neighborhood and the occasional sticky footprint made by spray seal solvent that some overworked scene tech hadn't wiped completely off their shoe. The thought clawed at Matheson and he started to turn away.

Starna caught him as he was nearly out the door and pulled Matheson into the small sample room off to the side of the main lab. The tech looked as if he hadn't slept or bathed in days, and long welts down his forearms and neck spoke of scratching compulsively until he bled. His eyes were bloodshot, the whites gone a tea-stained yellow where they weren't red. "Have you seen him?" Starna asked.

"Who?"

"The inspector. He was here. I missed him . . ."

"I haven't seen him, either."

"Oh." Starna's disappointment was deeper than reasonable and his breathing was ragged, but he didn't seem to have been running or physically exerting himself. Matheson frowned as Starna looked down and swallowed convulsively. "Tell him I couldn't . . ."

"Couldn't what? Starna, what's wrong?"

"Can't you tell?" Starna gave a broken, hysterical laugh. "*He* can. And I can't do it."

Matheson grabbed Starna by the shoulders and jerked him up straight. The tech was trembling, his skin too warm, but not sweating. "What is it you can't do?"

"I can't—I can't do . . ." Starna's gaze darted around Matheson, and he gave up a twitching, miserable smile. "I can't do what he wants me to do. And I can't match—can't match the sample. The other— that's what he expected. The rest. I can't." He spoke as if his thoughts were tangled in his head and he could only get them out by tearing them into pieces.

Starna gave a sudden short trill of laughter, and pulled out of Matheson's grip. The tech stood up straighter, lifting his chin, and spoke in carefully deliberated bursts, his expression weirdly amused. "Tell. Him. The sample. Was. Not. Viable. And I. Can't. Run it. Tissue. Solvent. Yes. The rest." He punctuated the chopped-up sentence with a tiny laugh. "Total failure. I can't. Do. What he wants. I'm. Sorry."

The apology seemed to unlock something and Starna sighed, closing his eyes for a moment, relieved. Then he spoke again, his voice calmer, but still a little high-pitched, and a slight tremor ran continually over him. "There is one thing I can do. So, I'll do that." He looked at Matheson and offered another crooked smile. "There can always be a goat. Tell him."

Confused, Matheson replied, "He'd rather hear it from you, I'm sure."

Starna grinned and laughed, quite normally. "I won't be here." He looked at the door and started past Matheson. "Excuse me."

Dumbfounded, Matheson didn't follow him immediately and by the time he stepped into the lab, Starna was gone. On the off chance the tech was wrong, he started to go check Dillal's office, but that was no haven either; Orris was prowling around outside the room. Matheson considered asking if he knew where the inspector was, but he didn't want to give the detive an opportunity to interrogate him. He was too unbalanced, too raw with respect to Santos, and too worried about his own investigation to let Orris paint him into the corners of another one. Matheson needed somewhere to run searches without being interrupted or beaten. If the inspector wasn't there to help him, he'd have to find another place . . .

S-Office. It would be abandoned—it was the middle of the shift and everyone who wasn't asleep or on patrol would be on riot duty. The irony almost made him laugh.

Matheson ran every search parameter and permutation he could think of—just knowing the men's names was no help in finding them unless he could identify them by sight or corner them somewhere they would have to go. Banzet was the more elusive of the two—he was nineteen and had no record in Angra Dastrelas, but he'd moved to the city less than a year earlier from Dreihleat Northcut. He had no local family, friends, or contacts, no clan affiliation, and his address was a general labor flophouse. Matheson would be surprised if he was still in residence.

Matheson looked further into the man's past. Northcut was an industrial town about three thousand kilometers northwest of Angra Dastrelas. Banzet's family owned a small machine shop that seemed to do one-off and repairs jobs too minor to interest anyone else. Matheson didn't see much about Hoda Banzet in the GISA Northcut Regional District files either, except a single warning for illegal assembly. The only file image available was a recent one from Banzet's travel papers, but the young Dreihle didn't look familiar and the name didn't pop anything else.

Matheson waded into the larger volume of material on Osolin Tchintaka. He'd been born in a contract camp on Gattis's other major continent, Agria, and moved to Ariel and Angra Dastrelas six years ago—free, but with the stigma of the camps on him like a stench. He had a long list of petty cons, theft, public disruption, misrepresentation . . . There was no mention of Denenshe Leran or Hoda Banzet on his record, but there was also no clan association listed.

Maybe "free" is almost like a clan of its own. Matheson imagined the three restless young men with no trade society ties floating around the Dreihleat, frequenting the same neutral territory, the coffee houses, the tunnels, until they inevitably met . . .

He sat and stared in the direction of the display for a while, his eyes unfocussed. They'd known the Paz da Sorte well enough to know the routine and that it would be open late. *If they were in with the "Relief, Redress, Revolt" movement, I can see how they'd be dazzled enough by that man to think a little robbery to support the cause wouldn't be unforgivable. Until things went wrong.*

Matheson blinked and rubbed his eyes, refocusing on the display and looking for Tchintaka's image. He hadn't spotted Banzet at the mob scene, but maybe . . .

Tchintaka's image stopped him cold. He tilted his head in disbelief and stared. "Merry . . . fucking . . . hell."

The orator who'd sparked the crowd into a screaming mob was Osolin Tchintaka.

Aya couldn't have known what was going to happen, couldn't have known Tchintaka's rhetoric would set the mob on *him* . . . Matheson's breath hitched in remembered panic. He forced himself toward calm with a few longer, slower breaths. He couldn't think enfolded in irrational reaction. He had to find this man—both men—and that meant going back into the Dreihleat in the midst of a riot. The thought almost made him ill.

He tried Dillal one more time and was surprised when the inspector picked it up as a voice call.

"Yes, Matheson?" He sounded a little irritated.

"I got some names and I'm following them up—Hoda Banzet and Osolin Tchintaka."

"Oso? I know him—knew him," Dillal corrected. "Politically active, rather a trouble maker."

"Yeah. He's one of those 'Relief, Redress, Revolt' speakers. Compelling—mesmerizing, really. I happened to be nearby when he incited a riot this morning. Had to run like merry hell to get out—"

"I've only just heard. Did you get any useful information from the encounter?"

"Not much—to be honest, I'm disturbed."

"Is this the same issue that disturbed you before?"

"No. Something different—it's weird."

"In what way?"

"I . . . uh . . . I can't say. I'm in S-Office."

"I see. Is it relevant, this thing?"

"I don't know."

"Then set it aside and concentrate on what you do know. Your contact named Oso and this Hoda Banzet. What do you have on him?"

"Banzet? He doesn't have any record except a warning for illegal assembly back in Northcut—it wasn't even a full booking. He's nineteen and moved here about eight months ago, so I figured he's probably part of Three R, just like Tchintaka, and sedition might have been his reason for moving."

"Northcut's a small community, much harder to hide in. And Leran knew them both?"

"According to my contact, yes. They were all of the same political bent."

There was a long pause before the inspector spoke again. "If the riot continues, they'll be in the tunnels—I see no sign of either name on the sweep lists. You'll have to take your contact as a guide. If you believe you can trust him . . . or her."

Matheson frowned a little. "I think so. And, I ran into Starna."

"In the Dreihleat?" Dillal sounded startled.

"No. Here at GISA. He's not well."

Matheson felt the weight of Dillal's sigh even through the distance of the mobile. "Starna is a gifted med/legal technician, but he's also a Wire addict, among his other problems. I had hoped he would try to overcome it."

That explained Starna's appearance and behavior—or might. Matheson hadn't seen many Wireheads, that he knew of, and fewer who seemed to be at the stage where their mental function was so fragmented and difficult to manage. "He said he can't. Or I assume that's what he meant. He said something about a sample that wasn't viable and so he couldn't run a match. And something about tissue, and something about a goat, and having one more thing to try. He wasn't making a lot of sense."

"Hell." Matheson had never heard the inspector swear and the mild expletive startled him. "I had hopes. Matheson, do you know where Detive Orris is?"

"I know where he *was*."

"Even better."

"I've been trying to avoid him, to be honest. I'm working in S-Office while the patch pounders are on riot duty because I figured I don't have time to be questioned about Santos if I'm going to find Banzet and Tchintaka."

"Indeed you don't. But I still need a sole impression."

"What . . . still?" Matheson was annoyed with his own annoyance over the petty detail.

"Yes. Still. I thought I'd captured one, but apparently not. It's become more important than I can say at the moment, though your two men are, also."

Matheson thought about it, but couldn't see how that was true. But if the inspector said so . . .

Dillal huffed. "Once again we shift our focus. But only for a moment. Banzet and Tchintaka must still be in the Dreihleat or the tunnels. They'll be unable to move to safer territory while the riot lockdown is in force. If you know where Orris's footprints can be found, get them and leave them with Starna before you return to the Dreihleat."

"Starna said he won't be here."

"Then send them to me and I'll find Starna or run them myself. I'm recovering video I salvaged in the Ohbata last night and that can't wait." There was a loud noise in the background and Dillal cut the connection abruptly.

Matheson wasn't sure why the sole impression was so important to him, but the inspector obviously knew something he wasn't willing to discuss yet, and it just increased Matheson's own confusion. It was a ridiculous errand, but Matheson knew right where to find Orris's prints, conveniently near ForTech.

Dillal finished his conversation as he dressed.

Andreus squinted at him. "You no longer need a microphone to talk via the datalink . . . How do you do that?" she demanded. "I didn't design that."

"I retasked the frequency sensors. While the socket was damaged I was forced to improvise."

"Huh," she muttered, shaking her head as if amazed. She turned to her console and started the rebuilt video, still looking thoughtful. Her expression died to chilly remoteness as the video rolled.

The camera never moved as the scene unfolded except to pan side-to-side and shudder at the beginning and end. Riot troops swarmed out from the transport beneath the camera and, finally, returned, as muddy, bloody, wet, and disoriented as their prisoners. The crop stubble in the field beyond had disappeared under water and mud. In the foreground, scattered bodies lay strewn across the cobbled administration plaza in swaths of water tinged violet by blue dust and red blood.

They watched it twice—it was only forty-eight minutes long. Dillal stared hard at the display. He ran segments of the stream again and again, growing more visibly agitated with each viewing. He replayed the opening shot—a general pan over the assembly of Dreihleen and Ohba men and women who'd been standing in the plaza as the transports arrived. He stopped and restarted that short segment three times.

Dr. Andreus also stared at the display, frowning. "Why this? That's . . . Camp Donetti."

"He wanted me to see it," Dillal replied, sharply, as the troops walked back toward the camera. "He said it would change my mind."

Shields were down, helmets pushed back, weapons slung, and the boys—the nearest group were all very young men—were either buzzing with adrenaline or staggering with exhaustion. Some halted where they stood, stripping their equipment as if they could shed the experience with it. Others seemed to revel in the mess and horror. One, left of center, fell to his knees, holding his empty arms in front of him as if he retained the shield and shock stick he'd dropped somewhere. Then he pitched forward, into the purple mud. His companions trudged on. He wasn't the only one to go down—just the one close enough to see.

An officer in a pristine uniform walked out from a transport and picked up the fallen man, raising his face out of the mud, removing the helmet to reveal sweat-soaked hair the color of coal, and wiping the worst of the muck out of the boy's mouth and nose so he wouldn't choke or suffocate on it. Then he dragged the young man toward the transport and they vanished together below the camera's view.

The video halted.

Dillal continued looking at the still display, blinking.

"That's the riot Gattis Corporation claims never happened," Andreus said.

"How are you sure?" Dillal asked, reaching for the display controls.

Andreus brushed his hand aside. "You weren't my only subject in the past couple of years, you're just the one that survived. One of mine worked the medical clean up on this . . . fiasco. You must know about this thing."

The inspector nodded. "Not at the time, of course, since I was already working with you. As you say—officially, it never happened and I heard about it only after the fact. Reverse the video stream one frame at a time. Please."

"Why? It's an agricamp riot. Bloodier than most, but no different than Cafala or Agria-Sud."

"It *is* different—one-hundred twenty people died and everything about it was hidden. Fahn didn't release this footage to the net, which would have caused panic at Corporation House, but he wants *me* to see it, now."

"The illegal troops here are pretty damaging," Andreus said, clicking backward through the frames. "I'm surprised he held on to this so long."

"He may not have had it all this time," Dillal replied as he studied each still frame. He seemed to be barely holding himself still. "Wait. What is that insignia?"

"Which one?"

"On the shoulder of the man going to retrieve the fallen boy."

None of the ground troops had any visible insignia at all but there was a small, subtle marking, light gray, at the shoulder of the unsullied officer's charcoal gray sleeve. Enlarged, it looked like two jagged saw sections on each side of a dome under the barely visible letters FSA.

"It looks like a lens cross-section," said Andreus.

"Show me the young man," Dillal demanded.

Andreus backed the video to the appropriate time hash and clicked through one frame at a time, until she found a clear shot of the kneeling man and zoomed in on his features.

The blood drained from Dillal's face and he scrambled out of the exam room at a full run.

CHAPTER TWENTY-TWO

Day 5: Afternoon Continues

Matheson didn't need Dillal's disturbing facility with the GISA building controls to check the ID logs and discover that Orris had swiped out almost an hour earlier. *Probably hoping to avoid the return of the SOs from riot control.* Matheson would have to do that, too. Men coming down from that kind of duty tended to be in one of two states: too amped to be reasonable; or too exhausted to care. Either way, he didn't want to be found anywhere near S-Office in the next twenty minutes.

He headed back toward ForTech at just short of a run in spite of the protests of his still-tender muscles. Dillal's office door was closed and locked. Matheson noted dim blue stains of sand sticky with spray seal solvent at the edge of the threshold where he'd seen Orris standing earlier. He dropped a marker and took an image of the footprints at the door.

Matheson kept clear of the prints and waved his ID over the scanner next to the office door. Without the inspector inside, he wasn't sure it would unlock for him—or how Orris might have gotten in, if he had. The lock thumped and he pushed the door open, staying just outside without bringing up the lights. There was still plenty of sunlight bouncing at second-hand angles into the room and he wanted the shadows in any case. The shabby old carpet was stained and threadbare in patches, but still thick enough to take an impression where someone had stood still a while—especially someone of Orris's weight. The hard part was finding it and making the impression visible as the carpet rubbed the last of the sand and solvent off the shoes. He could think of two places Orris would have stopped for a significant time—in front of the door and in front of the desk. He'd already found the prints outside the door. Matheson couldn't see any use in the impression at this point, but he'd do as asked and get back to the Dreihleat as quickly as he could.

He crouched on the threshold, wincing with the lingering pains of bruises and abused muscles, and took the Sun Spot off his belt—relieved at the loss of the small weight from his bruised hip. He turned the light on and adjusted the spectrum and temperature, then laid it on the floor so the beam spread parallel to the surface. Every uneven rise in the pile cast a dark blue shadow in the shaft of light. He got back to his feet, grunting at the discomfort that stabbed him as he rose to observe the carpet from a greater height, looking for a pattern in the light. It wasn't there—at least not in the section he'd illuminated.

It took several uncomfortable tries before he found one pair near the desk that was still slightly stained with blue dust and large enough that they had to be Orris's and not the smaller, lighter inspector's. Matheson laid a sheet of contour flimsy over the area with care and used the Sun Spot to heat the page.

The sheet crumpled a bit at first, curling on the edges and then sinking against the carpet like water trying to drain away. It clung and formed to the shallow indentations without pressing them flat, leaving a paper covering on the dents. Another adjustment to the Sun Spot illuminated the paper so the most stressed areas showed up dark red while the parts which had hardly changed were a pale pink. He dropped a marker, just as if the office were a crime scene, and took an image with his mobile. Then he knelt down and pulled the edges of the sheet up with firm pressure until it ripped free of the carpet, and he popped up with a grunt as the muscles in his back, arms, and abs complained at the sudden release from strain almost as much as they'd complained when he'd started tugging.

He sent the image to Dillal and started to go looking for Starna, but he caught movement in the corner of his eye and whirled, dropping the sheet onto the inspector's desk.

Neme was leaning in the doorframe with her arms crossed over her chest. He cursed himself for leaving the door open as she said, "Well, well. My unhelpful blackbird. What have you been up to, rook? Investigating the inspector? He is a slippery bastard."

"No." She wouldn't believe any explanation he could offer—not that he owed her one.

"I still don't get you. You have no reason to be here—and I don't mean standing in your whip's office like you got caught foxing reports."

"Just a rookie trying to climb." *I don't have time for this.*

She rolled her eyes. "You don't need to work. You don't need to climb—academy man with your connections won't be allowed to sink into the dark blue depths of Gattis's corporate shame."

"Maybe we're two of a kind, sir."

She snorted. "You and me? Poor little rich kids playing cops? Except I live here, and I'm known to be easily bored. You . . . you're a *Matheson*—all capital letters with the hypno-glitter effects scrolling at the bottom of the display. Even out here in the back end of the jumpways, we know our power celebs—hell, probably know them better here than anywhere because families like yours are meat and eggs for us. You should be swanning some Central System paradise in a uniform that's never going to know a speck of dust, not grubbing dirty murders in yesterday's clothes and sporting more pressure kisses than a terraformer with a faulty suit. Mummy and Daddy aren't going to be happy if you turn up floating in the Cove."

Matheson kept his tone casual. "My parents aren't particularly concerned with what happens in my life, and there's no reason to think I'm on anyone's hit list—unless it's yours."

"Me? You think I'm threatening you?"

"I'm not sure what you're doing. Sir."

"I'm trying to figure the angles. Dillal I get—he's an ambitious, motley sideswipe willing to take any risk in order to rise in our professional cesspit. Until the inevitable failure. I can wait for it. You, though . . . you could be dangerous."

She peered at him from the corners of her eyes with a speculative expression and went on, "Corporation House is looking down the barrel of Central System's big guns when the planetary charter comes up for review. We've had over two hundred years of laissez-faire what-the-fuckery and no one important here wants that to change, but it's going to, because once Central is here, they'll stay. The question is 'in what person or form?' I'm trying to decide if you're the family scout, the sapper, or the stick."

"I'm not following you."

Neme gave a disgusted snort. "You lie better when you keep your mouth shut. That's one for free. And here's another piece of advice— whether you're here to gather intelligence, sabotage the system, or put down roots and take over, you're not going to help yourself by fucking the boss's sister."

The ground seemed to drop out from under him and his ears rang as if all the air had been sucked from the room.

Neme laughed. "What? You didn't know? Well, there's a pretty slice. You should be asking yourself what *she's* after—'cause it's not just your firm, young body, slick. She's certainly had as good, or better in her time."

Matheson could barely force a word past his fury. "What?" was all he managed.

Neme suddenly looked wary and took a step back, into the hallway. But nothing blunted her tongue. "You're a fucking naif. She's my age and has no living family but your whip. How do you imagine a single Dreihle woman could have afforded to start a business on her own if she didn't spend a lot of time on her back, first?"

Matheson's nails bit into his palms as he clenched his fists and the sharp jolt of pain up his forearms was the only thing that gave him pause enough to stop him smashing Neme's face in. She wasn't the one he was mad at—not really—but he bulled toward her anyhow.

Neme jumped back and barely kept her feet, stumbling, startled, into the hallway. *Good.*

He lunged at her one more time, too aware that the halls were monitored, but unable to rein his temper in any further. He didn't quite touch her, but it was a close thing.

Neme caught herself against the opposite wall, but stood firm. Then she glowered back, ready and more than able to take him down if he came toward her again. She didn't say anything, just set her feet and waited for him to move in.

Matheson stood shaking in front of the doorway. He wanted to hit her, or scream at her . . . anything but holding still in the burning struggle of his confusion and rage. He managed to reach back and pull the door closed until the lock engaged, without giving in to his urge to damage the senior detive. He turned, unable to keep looking at her without breaking, and stalked away, stiff with unshed fury.

"Where is SO Matheson?" The inspector's voice was sharp and the SO at the information desk jumped at the sound.

He turned to regard the CIFO with a nervous stare. "I don't know, sir."

"Is he still in the building?"

The desk ofiçe clattered away at his data console. "I don't see any sign that he's swiped out, but—"

Dillal cut him off. "Has riot control returned from the Dreihleat?"

"They're coming back in now. Third shift is taking over with augmented patrols and . . ."

The inspector didn't stay to listen.

He ran down to S-Office, rushing into the staff room. There was no sign of Matheson. He bolted for the locker room. It was packed with SOs in varying states of undress—mostly stripping out of sweat-soaked uniforms and heading for showers or returning from them.

Jora came toward him wearing nothing but a sneer and reached for the inspector, saying, "Not officer country down here, turd biscuit."

Dillal snatched and twisted Jora's hand so quickly that the SO staggered and cringed. "Still yourself or I'll break you. Where is Eric Matheson?"

The men and women in the room stopped and stared at Dillal and Jora.

Jora gasped at the pressure on his wrist and fingers. "Haven't seen him. Thought he was under you, now," he added, making the term sound dirty.

Dillal spoke with chilly precision. "Consider your answer carefully: When did you see him last?"

"Fuck you, I said I haven't—" Jora's response broke off in a squeal as Dillal put more pressure on his hand.

"When and where did you see him last?"

"I haven't scoped on the bastard in two days!"

Dillal leaned close to Jora's ear, but he didn't lower his voice. "Two days? Not three?"

"Yes!"

"Where?"

"Here! Right, fucking here!"

Dillal dropped Jora's hand and the sudden release made the SO lurch down and sideways, into the sudden clap of the inspector's hand over his left ear. Jora's eyes rolled back and he tumbled to the floor in a dead faint.

Dillal looked up at the staring crowd of SOs. "Any of the rest of you seen my IAD today? Or 'seen to him' two days ago?" His tone was venomous. Hard red sparks reflected off his eyepiece as his gaze shifted over them all.

Even the silence held its breath until a third-shifter raised her head.

"I . . ." she started, her voice shivering. "I saw him a while ago in ForTech corridor."

Jora stirred a little on the floor and Dillal took a step away. His expression implied he'd just noticed something filthy near his shoe. He glanced at the nervous third-shifter. "You're Kyasdottir?"

The SO's nod could barely be told apart from her shiver.

Dillal gave a thin half-smile that did nothing to dispel the mood of the room. "Thank you."

Dillal turned on his heel and left. As the door closed, the SOs erupted in chatter. No one moved to help Jora to his feet.

Dillal ran to his own office next, but Matheson wasn't there. A stiff piece of contour sheet lay on the inspector's desk, but there was no other sign of the younger man. Dillal did not stop to check the ID swipe logs, only took the contour, locked himself back out, and went into the lab next door.

A handful of med/legals were still busy with evidence from the Santos apartment and other cases, but they were winding down for the day. Neither Starna nor Matheson was among them. Dillal caught the attention of a round, mid-brown woman who approached him with the wariness of a cat. Her hair and eyes were the color of dust.

"Jem Starna or SO Matheson," Dillal said, curbing his temper. "Have you seen either recently?"

She looked ready to flee, but swallowed before answering. "Uh . . . the SO was here earlier. For contour flimsy. Is that it?"

"I would assume so. Who are you?"

She flinched. "Dr. Woskyat. Can I . . . can I take that?" she asked, putting out a tentative hand for the contour.

Dillal glanced at the formed sheet as if he'd forgotten its existence. "Yes. Model this and run comparison against the prints from Paz da Sorte scene database." He handed the sheet to her, scowling. "This should be Starna's job."

"I'm sorry, sir. I haven't seen him in a couple of hours. He was here, but I don't know where he is now. He might have taken a break for dinner or . . . or something."

"Hope for his sake it is not 'or something.'"

CHAPTER TWENTY-THREE

Day 5: Afternoon in the Dreihleat

"I just want to know which it was—did you lie to me, use me, or set me up? Or all of them? Is that it? You kept me close to keep an eye on your brother's investigation for Tchintaka's benefit . . . ? And then you let them come after me. The man's a spellbinder—if the crowd had caught me, they'd have killed me! Is that what you wanted?" Matheson had hoped that running across town, crossing the eastern barrier, making his way to her on the roof would calm his temper, but it hadn't changed the sickening sensation one bit. He was shaking under the weight of his angry disillusionment and he spat out his words from between clenched teeth. "You play a remarkably cool game, Aya. And I fell for it."

Aya's expression was calm, but her posture was tense and wary. "I'm answer what you're ask. I'm find you when I'd things to tell you, and I'm think on what you're say. And is't a crime to be kind? Left you on the street bleeding, sent you away last night, would've pleased you more?"

The breeze across the rooftop smelled of cinders and smoke and the noise of the riot—now reduced to pockets of desperation—clattered in the distance. "That first night, you didn't come to render aid," he snapped. "You came to keep an eye on me—on the investigation."

"Why you're think I would?"

"For Tchintaka, for the *cause*. Because you're the inspector's sister, and I've got to wonder why no one said so! When I told you my partner was dead, you were shaken, but it wasn't over Santos—you said you were *relieved* to know it was him. You thought it was Dillal. Oh and I'm sorry—I've been mispronouncing that—it's 'dil-HAL' isn't it? Like your name is pronounced 'le-HYAN' because that's how Dreihleen names work when you're related. And I was too damned stupid to see it! You got close to me, seduced me, you picked my brain about the investigation and I didn't even wonder why. I believed you and now I can't trust one thing you've done or one word you've said—in bed or out of it."

"Nothing I'm tell you's a lie."

He stepped closer with every angry sentence. "The lies are in the things you *didn't* say! You didn't say Tchintaka is the heart of your revolutionary hopes." Nearly standing on her feet, he yelled at her, "I doubt it's a coincidence you practically sent me into his grasp this morning and he incited a riot that could have gotten me killed!"

Aya slammed her palm against his chest, jolting him back. Her expression was icy-sharp. "I'm not send you to be harmed."

Matheson took a step back, the near-hysterical edge knocked off his unreasonable anger, though the heat still remained. He'd known she was dangerous. Confirmation brought no comfort. "You made a damned fine job of it anyhow," he said.

"You're th'one's convince me to speak, Eric. You're know why we're hold our tongues, why we're bleed silence. When you're convince me our hope's corrupted, I'm tell you who're the worms you're seek."

"For your own sake!"

"What's matter when you're get th'answer you need?" she spat back.

"'What's matter' is that you manipulated me into your bed and used what I was idiot enough to tell you to protect your friends, so two more people died! And now more are dying and I could have been one of them."

"I'm tell no one what you're say in my bed."

"I can't believe that—you've played me too well. I was stupid enough to imagine that for once in my life a potential lover—you— had no ulterior motive, except simply wanting *me*. Merry fucking idiot that I am. But now, whether you've told them or not, I have no choice but to think you were using me to keep an eye on your brother's investigation to benefit your political friends! Why else would you use me? Why not go to him—"

"Because he's only half my brother and I'm hate him!"

She spat the words so furiously that Matheson was taken aback. He stared at her. She glared back at him, her face flushed as she took agitated breaths through flared nostrils.

A spike of curiosity let his anger ease to a simmer. "Then why did you care when you thought he was dead?" Matheson asked.

Aya closed her glittering eyes and turned a little aside with a frustrated growl. "You're not believe me, no matter what I'm say."

This is too much and I am too raw. "Aya, I wish I could. But I have been beaten, informed of my TO's death, menaced, chased, assaulted by some haunt of my own mind, threatened, and now I discover that the woman I'm . . . fucking is not who or what I thought. How can I trust anything when I'm standing on quicksand?"

"You're trust *him*."

"I've told you—Dillal and I have to trust each other or we both go down."

She turned back to look at Matheson, her expression tired. "And so you're also trust me. When I'm tell you of Hoda and Oso, I'm betray the Friends for hope of making them clean again. If you're not arrest them, if you're persuaded me to think wrong, all's done. I'm ruin every hope and the Friends are ruin me."

The way she said it rang a bell. "Friends . . . ?" Matheson asked.

Aya nodded. "Friends of th'Idea."

The Velas had spoken of "friends"—one of the few Dreihleen words he knew—and Minje said something about "they *knew* Friends". . . . *"Friends of the Idea" . . . and the Three R movement . . . How did I miss it?* "I see. But you did lie to me."

"How?"

"I told you the boy said 'They're no friends' and you said they had friends in common."

"They're did. *The Friends.*"

He laughed bitterly at himself. *That Dreihleen thing of talking sideways.* "And the Friends are Tchintaka's followers—which I didn't know. How does that explain the rest? You sympathize with Tchintaka— leaving aside whether you nearly handed me to him—and you claim to hate the inspector, but you almost collapsed when you thought he was dead. Tell me why."

"Because of him, our mother's die. How I'm trust such a one's only half Dreihle and half machine? What's his care for us? But I'm not expect to feel such pain for thought of him dead." She paused to close her eyes again and swallowed as if something had caught in her throat. "Or such doubt for the cause I'm always think's right. I'm even argue with Friends in my own shop. Is like a knife with no handle, this . . ."

Matheson stepped back, worn down with uncertainty, and the ache returning to his muscles. He wanted to believe. He took her hand and pulled her to the bench. "Sit down and tell me the rest." He stayed on his feet.

She sat, pole-straight, and looked out at the flowering garden. "I'm tell you the truth last night—Oso would be here and the tunnels're not safe for you alone. You're make me think of what he's done that should not have been done and see he's not a right man." Her voice became sharper as she grew more angry. "He's wear the face and we're all believe, but he's only a bad dog who's piss on what we're work for, and I'm shamed Friends're turn a blind eye. And if he's done what's done at Paz, I'm rather tear the heart from us and hand it to Djepe than go where Tchintaka's take us." She nearly spat these last words. "And that's why I'm tell you—and by you, Djepe."

"Djepe?" Matheson echoed.

She tilted her gaze at him. "Your inspector. Is his name. Our mother's name him for his father, who's arrested and died in Agria." She shook her head and stared out into her garden again. "She's not give him his father's family name—is Ohba and too dangerous here— but a Dreihle name that's like. Djepe Inza Dillal. I'm three when he's born. Ten when she's leave." She sounded bitter.

"Leave?"

"Die."

Matheson nodded. "And you held him responsible."

She shifted her gaze farther aside. "She's ill from his birth, never healed. She's not work. I'm work for my uncle—Minje's father. He's take us in, even after what's happen. And then my mother's die. I'm not want Djepe and my uncle's not like him in his house. So, I'm give him away."

"But you kept track of him."

She shook her head. "I'm not hear of him again until he's twenty and returns here as an *ofiçe*. Then I'm not wish to know more about him—not wish to see him or know him—but he's here, in Dreihleat Ang'Das . . ." She shrugged, but it was stiff and forced. "And I'm not trust him."

"Because he's with GISA or because he's half Ohba . . . or just because he's your brother?" Matheson's fury was gone and what remained was broken and sad.

"How you're trust an ofiçe when they're no better than bad dogs?"

"I'm not a bad dog. If I'm to believe what you've just said—anything you've said—then I have to believe you trust me. So do you?" It was all senseless and terrible enough to be the truth and he *did* believe it. But he wanted her to say the same.

Her brow puckered and her mouth turned down for a fleeting instant. Then she turned her head down and away from him. The gesture gave him an unwanted pang.

"You do." He sighed, resigned to it. Neme had been right. "You trust me because I'm such an eager, innocent puppy. And you played me. Maybe for what you thought was a good reason, but you did it anyway." He sighed. *Better get used to it—you're a cop and people will fuck you for their own ends.*

Matheson gazed at her garden a while in silence and out toward the rest of the Dreihleat while the midday sunlight fell on the roof like a hammer. He hadn't been wrong, but his common sense had gone jumpwise where she was concerned and he'd gotten the right answers almost by luck as much as work. *And I'd have solved it days ago if I'd just known what the unaff kid—Zanesh—meant by "friends."*

Matheson sat still beside Aya and rested his forearms on his knees, wincing a little from the bruises and the ache in his back as he shifted his weight. He could smell acrid smoke lingering in the air as the ghetto became unnaturally quiet around them, the last of the resistance being beaten away before the sweeping-up started.

"I think you've misjudged your brother," Matheson said. "He *is* a good man—better than me. He cares about the people who died at Paz and what's going to happen to the rest of you if this goes unsolved."

She scoffed, but it sounded uncertain. "You're know him a week."

He turned his head toward her. "And you don't know him at all."

She turned her eyes away.

"You're certain of the connection between Tchintaka, Banzet, and Leran? You didn't just drop me in the shit?"

"That they're know each other, that they're speak together often, I'm do—all friends together and all eyes for Venn. What they're say, I'm not know. I'm not listen. I'm not asked."

"So you've been in the Tomb."

She nodded, still not looking at him. "Many times."

"Could you help me find Tchintaka and Banzet? Given what happened earlier, I'm afraid that if they knew Leran as you say . . ."

Aya rose slowly to her feet. "I'm know what you're think—if they're friends, perhaps, they're murderers also—and I'm fear the same."

The windows of the coffee house lay shattered inside, goods and furniture scattered in the street like all the rest. Dillal strode through the maze of destruction and into the café by the broken front window, rather than the still-locked door.

Minje swung a length of construction bar at his head and Dillal ducked, grabbed, and shoved the taller Dreihle around and down by the momentum of his own motion. Minje rolled to get back up, but Dillal caught his foot and flipped him to his back. The inspector came down on one knee beside him, right hand drawn back to deliver a palm strike that would have smashed the other's nose.

Minje flinched, bringing his hands up to protect his face, which was already bloodied on one side. Then he relaxed flat on the floor with a loud exhale of relief. "Is you."

"Where's Aya?" Dillal demanded.

"Don't know. Been here five minutes. Thought you were looting." He sounded amused at the idea.

Dillal stood up, helping Minje to his feet, then started for the work room door.

"She'll not want to see you," Minje said, rubbing the back of his head and checking for damage.

Dillal turned back. "It's not her I'm after."

Minje raised his eyebrows. "Your pretty hound, heh?"

The inspector's expression was cold. Minje looked him over for a moment, cocking his head in curiosity and narrowing his eyes. His gaze lingered over the artificial eye and a small red patch below it on Dillal's cheek.

Then Minje shrugged again and pointed to the ceiling with his thumb. "The roof. If here they are. I'm clean up this mess. Hey . . . go soft—he's young."

"And blissfully ignorant, I pray," but Dillal's tone said he doubted it.

The inspector went through the work room and up the stairs swiftly, seeming not to care how much noise he made on the way. He burst through the door of the loft, nearly colliding with Aya and Matheson as they were walking toward it. They stepped back, startled, and Dillal stepped forward, an expression of restrained fury on his face.

"Sir?" Matheson started.

Dillal reached out and plucked Matheson's mobile from his pocket, swiping past the lock and several commands as if it were his own. Then he flipped the display side toward Matheson. "Explain this."

The riot footage from Camp Donetti started at midpoint and streamed forward. For the first few minutes, Matheson and Aya both frowned at it, confused. Then Aya backed away, her eyes wide, covering her mouth as if she might scream or vomit.

Matheson's face went slack, staring in horrified recognition, his breath coming in sharp, hysterical pants. When the water cannon came to bear, he flinched and gasped as if he'd been struck and wrenched his face aside, squeezing his eyes shut. His hands came up as if he could push the images away and he took an unsteady step back from the inspector.

Dillal didn't let him go. He closed the distance and snatched Matheson's hands aside. "Don't look away," he snapped. "You have no right to look away. You said you've been on Gattis a month, but this was more than a year ago. One-hundred twenty people died there. One-hundred twenty. All Dreihleen and Ohba. And they will die here, too, after today. So tell me why you were there. Or tell me this isn't you." He let Matheson go and flicked the stream to the end, to the freeze-frame of the young man's face as he collapsed in the mud.

Matheson buckled to his knees the same way now, folding on himself, covering his face with his hands as Aya leapt at Dillal, slapping the mobile from his grip.

She let out a grinding shriek, lashing out, double-fisted, at his throat. Dillal wrenched aside and took the impact on his shoulder, but it spun him and he dropped to one knee in the white stones at the verge of the garden. "*T'ulfeshté!*" she spat, taking another swing at him.

Dillal caught her forearm, deflecting the blow, but she'd locked her foot behind his other leg and swept it out from under him.

He didn't let go and she fell across him as he went down on his back. She rammed a knee into his groin. He doubled up with a ragged gasp of pain and she scrambled over him to Matheson's side, saying his name.

The young man twitched away from her touch, muttering, "No. I can't . . ."

Aya froze where she crouched, her hands fisted and arms rigid, watching Matheson curl tighter on himself as he shuddered. She ground her teeth and glared.

Dillal picked himself up, wincing, and stood near them, bowed in discomfort. "Do you believe in his innocence? Or do you want to defend him only because you hate me?"

"What's that . . . *thing* you're showed him?"

"Illegal riot suppression. Fourteen months ago on Agria there was a workers' demonstration at Internment Camp Donetti—they refused to work in the conditions of the camp any longer. They gathered in the common square and asked for relief. For redress. Does that sound familiar?"

Aya's eyes grew wide and horrified. She stared up at her brother.

Dillal continued, "They were locked out of their dorms, starved, left standing in the square during a storm. A few became ill, two died. That is where the official story ended—media claimed they returned to work. But that wasn't what happened. After five days, those still strong enough became violent—counseled to revolt by a visitor who disappeared in the chaos. So they tried to break into their own homes, into stores or offices for food. They found weapons—very few, but enough—and tried to force their way into the administration building. Troops arrived illegally from out-system without documentation or record and put them down. One-hundred eighteen more dead. No word of it ever passed beyond the GISA regional director and the agricamps."

"You're know about this?" she demanded.

"Some. Not all. Not until today. The missing visitor bears an uncanny resemblance to Oso, and this man—" Dillal added, pointing at Matheson—"my IAD, my hound, your lover—was one of those troops."

"We didn't know," Matheson murmured. "*I* didn't know."

Dillal started to squat beside him then winced again—Aya hadn't done any lasting damage, but it was enough for a few hours' discomfort. He sat on his knees instead and spoke in a scathing tone. "Explain to me what you didn't know."

Matheson uncurled a little. His posture was the mirror of Dillal's but he shivered and stared at the white pebbles of the garden as if they had become the violet mud of Camp Donetti.

His voice was hollow. "We were told it was a training op. Live, but insignificant. Legal. We didn't know where we were going or what was going to happen. We were one of many units inbound. I don't know how many. It's a blur—a nightmare I had for a while, then lost, and found again when I got here. I don't remember . . ."

"How is it that you don't remember?"

"Maybe I didn't want to. Maybe it's just . . . We scrambled through so many jumps, trans-orbitals, warp bubbles . . . By the time we were boots down we were all jumpwise." Matheson took several slow breaths, his posture loosening slightly. He shook his head. "Now . . . seeing that . . . I remember pieces—the push, losing my sideman . . ." his expression crumpled into confusion, and his breath and voice shook as he continued, "stepping over a downed man. But I don't know what I did to him. I remember water and shock sticks and screaming. I don't remember the chase-down. I remember kneeling, though I don't know why I did it. I don't even know how long—" He raised his head to look at Dillal. "How long was it?"

"Forty-eight minutes."

Matheson shook his head, his gaze drifting to a distant point. "It's a blank. Days' worth of blank. I don't remember forty-eight minutes or how long we were in transit, or even the date we left Fresnel."

"FSA," Dillal added. "Fresnel Security Academy. That was the insignia of the officer who retrieved you."

Matheson nodded. "There were three training officers . . . I woke up in the academy medical unit, told I'd taken a fall. I didn't have a head wound, didn't feel concussed, but I couldn't remember what had happened." He shuddered and took a long, settling breath. His gaze refocused on Dillal's face and his voice was stronger when he continued. "I had nightmares for a while—I told myself that's all they were—but they stopped. When I got to Gattis, I started feeling like I was under constant surveillance, like there was something wrong just out of sight, but . . . I thought it was the system, the oppression, the bigotry, or maybe even the signs of my family's tendency to stick their fingers into planetary pies and stir until the shit rises. But it's not them, this time. It's me."

Matheson felt wrung out and slightly dazed. He watched Dillal get to his feet and pace stiffly until he had to stop and lean against the door. He'd missed the cause, but from the look of it, the inspector had been hit in the nuts. Matheson winced sympathetically.

Dillal scowled at him for a while. "It's not you," he said, "though I wish I could say that it was."

Matheson felt less kindly about the egg-scrambling, and he wouldn't argue his own condemnation, so he stayed where he was.

Aya shifted a chilly stare between him and Dillal and came to her feet like a storm cloud rising. "Now you're neither blame nor defend him? Why? And why you're do nothing when this's happened?"

The inspector snorted and a flicker of disgust crossed the right side of his face. "I, too, was in training. I had no authority then and there is little enough I can do even now. What I can do I am doing."

"And that's what?"

"Finding the men who murdered your neighbors. Including Tchintaka if he is responsible. As he was responsible for this fiasco today and what happened at Camp Donetti—your darling revolutionary was there."

"How you're sure?"

Dillal pointed at the Peerless MDD still lying on the white stones. "I have the testimony of that recording, and of the files. He was there. He incited the riot that left one-hundred eighteen people dead! What more would sixteen in a jasso matter against his glorious, stupid dreams of revolution?"

Matheson's stomach clenched.

"You're not *know* he's t'blame for Paz," Aya objected.

"No, but you believe it yourself or you wouldn't have turfed him to Matheson. Don't worry," he added in an acid tone, "I'll not arrest him until I'm certain. But I will find out, and if it is him, I will take him."

They were oblivious of Matheson, locked in their mutual spite as he crouched there, unsure of his own claim on innocence. *They'll turn on me if I get between them. And I might deserve it.*

Aya snarled at her brother. "For your own dreams? Your own anger?"

"Anger is my natural state," Dillal responded. "It's why I am as I am—what I am. It's how I've survived. You are as responsible as I am for the monster you believe me to be."

"I?" she replied, raising her eyebrows. "I'm do nothing to you!"

"Nothing?" Dillal's tone was nearly too bitter to bear. "Leaving a child of mixed race alone in the Ohbata is a death sentence. You hadn't the fire in you then to bash in my head, so you left it to someone else."

"I'm a child—alone! My parents're dead—"

"As were mine. But you have a community, a place, clan and kind. I have a grandfather who wishes me dead and a sister who gave me to him."

"Not for that! And you're alive, still."

"Because I'm too stubborn to die, and I've too much yet to do."

"To find who's kill my neighbors, or to chase th'ambition you're give your eye for? Is Dreihleen who're leave here, Dreihleen who're under the boot of the Corporation's own you, Djepe. Not *ulfeshté* like you."

The heat of Dillal's anger drained away and, even at a distance, Matheson felt chilled as the inspector's fury turned cold. Aya's anger faded to horror as her words hung in the silence between them.

Quietly, Dillal said, "I am half Dreihle and no one owns me. You know nothing of my ambition, Aya."

CHAPTER TWENTY-FOUR

Day 5: Afternoon into Evening

Dillal regarded his sister with a somber gaze. "You think so little of me that you find it hard to believe I have a motive other than my own advantage. That anyone who is not pure Dreihleen bleeds as you do. You listen to Tchintaka's rhetoric—that those who are red and those who are yellow are equally oppressed—yet still cling to your bigotry like a drowning man clings to the wreckage that will drag him under.

"The color of my skin doesn't matter. I bleed the same as you—from the same injury, the same hate and fear. This system devours its own young. It's broken and can't be fixed by spitting in the Corporation's face. Bloody revolution is a romantic notion, but one doomed to failure. Violence only plays into the hands of Corporation House and gives it justification to destroy us—justification Tchintaka gave them at Donetti, and then he slunk away to hide when his plans went wrong. Once begun, the purge will only spread, until not a single native Gattian remains alive whose skin is not blue. Perhaps I am beloved of none and born to die, but I will at least make this life count."

"You're one man," Aya started. "How—"

"How?" Dillal interrupted. "By subterfuge. By whispering in the giant's ear, gaining its trust, and then slitting its throat while its back is turned. This system's destruction is my ambition, not to become the master of it as Tchintaka dreams," he shot a glance at Matheson, who'd almost thought himself forgotten, "nor hand it, drenched in innocent blood, to new overlords as Central System would do. This is why I've done everything I've done since . . . since Agria." He directed his gaze to the rooftop gravel and fell silent as if he had said something he hadn't meant to.

Shaken from his own thoughts, Matheson frowned. "Agria?"

"I trained there. Agria Corps. GISA Internment Control from the age of sixteen."

Matheson studied the inspector as the humid afternoon wind swept over the rooftop with a stink of destruction and the rattle of sweep transports incoming. "You're a subversive. A bigger idealist than I am." *And likely no more innocent. I see.* "You're a deeper, darker revolutionary than Aya."

Dillal glanced at him and shrugged. "More practical, perhaps. No less hopeful."

Matheson got slowly to his feet. "That," he said, pointing at Dillal's face. "That's how—that's *why* you chose to undergo . . . all of that."

The inspector gave a particularly bitter smile. "Yes." He touched the bloody mark under his left eye and ran his finger along the new patch of spray skin that covered the edge of the prosthetic frame. "This is my weapon and my lock pick—my way into the system that refuses to let anyone more colored than a blue sand beach rise above the bottom tier. I have broken myself, given up everything else so that I can burrow under the skin of the beast and turn it against itself. I didn't expect . . . this," he added with a small gesture between them. "Nor to have so little time to try." He paused to rub behind his left ear and up the back of his neck, wincing and shaking his head as if an insect had bitten him.

"If I can't persuade Pritchet that today's demonstration is unconnected to Paz and Camp Donetti, he'll have little choice but to let Corporation House do as it will here," he continued. "If we can't arrest—or at least name—the men who perpetrated the massacre at the Paz da Sorte before the Ohbata connection becomes common knowledge, the corporation will have its excuse to expand its action to all the ghettos. It will no longer matter that everything they've done to the Ohba and the Dreihleen is illegal. Troops will descend like the monsoon, and the charter's promises of equal shares to the native races will be nothing but a puzzle for future scholars to argue over."

Matheson stiffened, electrified with the connection that had finally come together in his mind. "The charter . . . Neme mentioned it, and Santos said 'the charter is the problem' and I didn't get it. The Dreihleen and Ohba are also native—or as native as you can get on a terraformed planet. The Corporation oppresses them, encourages the idea that they're immigrant workers, and tries to imprison or kill them so they won't have to pay reparations when the charter's reviewed in eight years!"

Dillal gave a small nod. "Yes."

Aya frowned at Dillal and said nothing. He turned his discomfiting stare to her. "I could have stayed in Agria."

She shifted her gaze aside, looking at the white pebbles on the roof, then at the mobile lying on them. She picked it up, turning it over and over in her hands before she stopped to stare at the display again. It was still frozen on the image of Matheson with the lavender hues of blood-soaked mud covering everything, every face and body, every weapon. She shut her eyes and turned her head away from it.

Miserable self-hatred chilled Matheson as he realized that she was refusing to look at *him*. She turned to her brother. "Is better you're not." Her jaw tightened. "I'm . . . can't like you. Can't change so quick as you're want me to. But I'm try."

Dillal stared at her, his expression keen with some difficult emotion. He closed his hands into fists at his sides, and then he looked away, breathing harshly. "You won't fail. You're too strong."

Then he turned toward Matheson with an irritable jerk of his head, hissing through his teeth. "That noise . . ." he muttered, touching the back of his left ear again.

A cloud of black-winged macaws rushed screeching into the hot air under the warbling of prox alarms. Dillal's gaze flashed up, over Matheson's head to the sky just above the rooftops. He looked horrified. "No . . ."

Matheson and Aya turned as the next sound hit—a whining roar and crash that shook the building under them. A white transport with GISA's orange star-and-stripe down the side bucked and wallowed in the sky, one engine cowl ripped open and spewing smoke. The spinning duct tore itself to pieces around the stabilizing strut of a much smaller package drone. The horrific vision Matheson had every time he went aloft on Gattis hung in front of him for a moment as the smaller craft was flung groundward in smoking chunks.

He stared, startled from his self-recrimination and aghast as the larger transport groaned and shuddered into a wing-over. It plunged toward the canal. A hard grip on his arm shook him, and he looked down at the inspector, who yanked him toward the door.

"It's sweep transport."

"What?" Matheson asked, still too stunned to think clearly.

"Prisoner transport," Dillal shouted as he yanked Matheson into the stairwell. "The Dreihleen swept up by the riot unit are in that lifter."

Matheson's "Shit!" went unheard as the building heaved and shuddered under the rolling impact of the transport hitting ground outside. He almost fell down the stairs following the inspector out to the street. His muscles and bruises protested, but he ignored them and ran toward Yshteppa Park.

The transport had hit upside down and gouged a shallow trench at the edge of the sloping lawn. A long line of goldwoods and grass leading to the canal edge had been ripped out before the skidding transport had hit the side of the bridge and spun into the water. One stubby stabilizer was crushed into the bridge structure and the vehicle had jammed cabin-down under the water's mucky surface. The exposed belly of the transport was blackened, but intact—no one would be crawling out of it through any lucky holes. If anyone was still alive inside, they'd have no option but swimming out.

A milling crowd of cits and tourists was already gathering along the opposite side of the canal. More people rushed to the edges of the accident track and closed in on the wreckage from the Dreihleat side. Matheson reached for his mobile, but it was still in the loft with Aya. The riot unit would have to call it in.

Matheson ran as fast as his aches would allow and got to the canal edge with the first of the mob. Dirty, bloodied civilians shouted and ran up and down the length of the wreck, looking for survivors or a way in. Matheson didn't pause. He kicked off his shoes and dove for the water, sucking in less air than usual as his bruised ribs protested.

He hadn't swum in months and he was sore but there was no other option. It was dark under the transport's bulk and the sunlight didn't penetrate far in water that was cloudy with blue sand and garbage. He kicked down and saw movement in the flickering illumination behind the transport's transparent front plate.

Matheson swam to the window. Water was only half way up the cabin interior—so some of the emergency seals were intact, but not all, and anyone inside didn't have a lot of time left to get out. Once the doors were open, the transport would flood quickly. He pounded on the window, and something bobbed against the clear plate. A boot . . . a leg . . . *Merry hell.* The pilot was still strapped in, head down below the rising water.

An SO in standard uniform—no riot gear, no helmet—struggled in his direction from deeper in the cabin, blood running down the side of his head and face as he stumbled and fell in the water. The SO dragged himself back up on the inverted pilot seat and scrabbled at the window in panic. He made a "help me" gesture. Then he pointed down and drew his thumb across his throat.

Matheson's lungs tightened with a need for air. He tried to make a reassuring gesture, but he wasn't sure the man inside understood him. He turned, swam toward the transport's nearest door, and grabbed the handle. It twisted and the hatch moved a little. Then it jammed in the warped frame. The pressure to breathe increased as he tried to force the hatch open. Bracing his feet on either side of it, he yanked upward as he pushed hard for the surface, every muscle in his bruised back screaming.

He felt the door wrench farther open as he shot upward, toward the chopped and scattered light. He didn't know if it was enough or if the man in the pilot cabin—or anyone else inside—could get out before the transport filled with water.

He broke the surface and gasped for air. His chest felt ablaze from the ache of his ribs and the burn of carbon dioxide in his lungs. He thrashed in the water, trying to orient himself, and spotted the inspector and Aya near the bridge. They ran toward his position, pushing people out of the way.

Three Dreihleen splashed to the surface nearby, up from the transport below. Then they paddled blindly toward the nearest way out of the canal. A body in GISA riot gear floated into the wake of their motion. More Dreihleen surfaced as Matheson swam for the verge.

Dillal knelt down and pulled him from the water. Matheson hadn't expected the strength of his grip and winced as the inspector's hand closed on his bruised forearm. Matheson shook his head. "Pilot's dead. Not sure how many left down there. Door's jammed partially open. Cabin's flooding."

"Can you go back down?"

"Not long," Matheson admitted. He panted and struggled against desperation and imminent failure. "Bruised ribs—can't breathe deep. Someone's gotta go in. Can't wait on extraction, now the door's open."

Dillal looked toward the Dreihleen gathered along the canal, but they began scattering as a team of SOs ran toward them from the south side of the park. He muttered something under his breath and stripped off his coat, shouting, "Aya! Dive!"

Startled, she looked up from helping a man out of the water, shot a glance toward the incoming riot team, and then did as she was told. Matheson watched her arc gracefully into the water and vanish below the surface.

"Stay here. Explain the situation." Dillal slapped his mobile into Matheson's hand. "I'll hear you if you call, but I won't be able to respond." He kicked off his shoes and dove.

Matheson waved the team toward him. They split, four pursuing the scattering Dreihleen, the other three running toward Matheson.

One of them took charge, stepping in front of the others and pointing them toward the wreck as he lifted the visor on his helmet. It was Charley Tyreda. "Get 'em up!" he shouted and then looked at Matheson. "What the fuck, rook?"

Matheson filled in the SO on what they'd seen and how fast the transport had gone down. "There are still people trapped down there, but I'm not in any shape to be much help—"

Tyreda made a face. "Yeah, I heard. Wasn't me—"

"I don't give a merry fuck about that right now," Matheson snapped. "Don't know how many are down there. At least one of ours still alive and trapped in the pilot compartment. Dillal and . . . uh . . . a bystander are swimming down—"

"That dreck girl?" Tyreda interrupted.

Matheson glared, hesitated a second before he said, "She's his sister."

Tyreda gaped and muttered, "Fuck me . . ."

"Just shut up and listen. Organize extraction and pick up. She and the inspector are going to get anyone they can out of the transport. So get the rest of your team back here—we have to get people out of the water as soon as they come up."

Tyreda scowled and cursed. "Shit. They're sweeps—we gotta arrest 'em."

"Screw that! These people will die if we don't get them to safety! *Merry fucking hell*, Tyreda," Matheson shouted at him, "is every SO in Angra Dastrelas a soulless, bigoted dogfucker, or just the ones I have to work with?" Then he winced and gasped around the pain that clutched his ribs and abs.

Tyreda put up his hands. "All right, all right," he muttered and turned to recall his team and request further assistance—wreckers and divers, more SOs, and a medical unit to deal with the injured.

Several more Dreihleen came up and were hauled out of the water by Tyreda's team. Then nothing.

"Where are they?" Matheson muttered.

"Don't panic yet," Tyreda said. "Drecks can hold their breath for-fucking-ever."

Matheson started to glare at him.

Aya broke the surface nearby with her arm around an SO Matheson hadn't seen before. He was pale and a dead weight with his riot gear on. Matheson wasn't sure the man was still alive. Then Tyreda and one of the SOs hauled him out and he coughed up water.

Two more SOs started roughly dragging Aya out as well. She fought, yanking one into the canal where she kicked him in the gut as she twisted away from the other.

"Let her go!" Matheson yelled, walked toward them, wincing again. "She's with me." Aya wouldn't appreciate his claim, but he didn't care.

The one still snatching at her looked up. "With *you?*"

Matheson glared at him. "Yeah. Are you fucking deaf?" He was taller than the SO and he knew he looked like hell, which he hoped was intimidating enough, but he took the baton off his belt and flicked it out to full extension just in case.

Aya splashed and shouted in the water. Matheson looked down to see the first SO trying to grapple her and shove her under. Matheson stooped and jabbed the man with his baton. The SO panicked and paddled at the water. Matheson was too sore and tired to rise, so he put his hand down to Aya instead. She took it. Her grip was like a claw.

"Where's the inspector? He's been down a hell of a long time." He sounded rough and angry rather than scared out of his wits.

"I'm go back." She took a long, deep breath and dove again.

A massive air bubble breached and churned the water, flinging bodies, trash, and wreckage to the surface. With a grinding screech the transport tore away from the bridge, then creaked and settled deeper into the canal.

Matheson lurched toward the water and dove in after Aya, but she bobbed back up beside him at once. "He's where?" she asked, wild-eyed.

The water seemed to boil for a moment longer, bubbles, bodies, wreckage all tossing on the disrupted surface. Some of the bodies flailed and moved weakly. One of them raised its head and swam toward them, towing another under its arm. Matheson was relieved when he recognized Dillal. Even wet, he was distinctive when the sun caught his face and ginger hair.

The man in Dillal's grip was the SO from the pilot compartment, but the inspector shook his head as he reached the wall between Matheson and Aya. "I couldn't leave him," he said, letting Tyreda and the newly arriving SOs pull the limp man from his arms.

Medical Intervention shoved their way through and began working on the man. Dillal, Matheson, and Aya crawled from the water unmolested. Dive and wreck recovery arrived with Medical. *Anyone still trapped down there's probably dead.* The thought left Matheson colder than his soaked state accounted for.

Matheson shifted and watched with sick fascination as Dillal pressed on the inner curve of his metal eye socket. Gory pink liquid ran from a bright red wound below the orbit's lowest edge. The spray skin under the inspector's left eye had torn, leaving the golden frame of the prosthesis partially exposed where it met his cheek bone. The surface was curiously rough and light scattered off it in dull sparks.

Dillal got to his feet and made a small beckoning motion with his head. Matheson and Aya followed him as he picked his barefooted way through the debris field toward the last standing goldwood tree on the canal side of the park. Dillal leaned his back against it. Aya and Matheson stopped close and faced him, though they didn't look at each other.

"Not an accident," Dillal said.

"No?" Matheson asked.

"The man I brought up was afraid of dying, but more afraid of me. When they retrieve the wreckage, they may find a steering beacon for the drone, but perhaps not."

Matheson scowled, thinking. "Do you believe there really was a beacon?"

"I heard it. I shouldn't have, but Andreus has been tinkering . . ."

"Who's do this?" Aya demanded.

"I can't be sure, but one has only to ask 'who benefits' to compose a rather short list."

Matheson nodded. The morning seemed days ago, but the memories cut like broken glass. "First Santos, then that . . . video file . . ."

"Santos didn't kill himself." Dillal put up one hand. "But we haven't time for that discussion now. I have to persuade Pritchet not to allow any further action against the ghettos."

"Why they're do that? Victims're Dreihleen, not hoppers or shashen or blues," Aya objected.

"And half-a-dozen GISA personnel," Dillal said. "Fear mongering is a high art at Corporation House and if it serves any faction's purpose, they will do it."

Aya lowered her face and stared at the ground. "So, you're go . . ."

"To speak to the regional director. The two of you must find Tchintaka and Banzet as quickly as possible. Don't linger. If I can offer any other focus to Pritchet's attention—better if I can offer him a perpetrator—we may at least stave off more violence and buy time to solve the crime properly, without giving Corporation House more fuel."

"The tunnels, then?" Matheson asked. He shot a glance at Aya, who shifted her own gaze away.

"Yes. Aya. I know my need carries no weight with you, but—"

"I'm not a fool, Djepe. He's need a guide and I'm know the way."

Dillal's lips twitched. "Don't kill him while you're at it."

Aya snorted and turned away.

"Sir . . ." Matheson started.

Dillal seemed surprised by the title. "Matheson?"

"You're . . ." He changed his mind, and raised a hand to his own cheekbone, ". . . injured."

"Ah." The inspector almost seemed stunned, yet Matheson knew he wasn't unaware of it. The smaller man merely gave one of his tilting shrugs. "Well. If we survive two more days, I'll give myself up to Dr. Andreus's mercy. And if not, it won't matter."

CHAPTER TWENTY-FIVE

Day 5: Evening

Matheson reclaimed his shoes and helped straighten up the coffee house while Aya retrieved his MDD from the loft. Then the two of them headed for Fish Market Basin, Matheson all too aware of distance that had opened between him and the woman only a foot away, and the questions that preyed on his own mind. The sun dried their clothes and left a lingering scent of canal water as Aya led the way through the riot's wrack and ruin to the Tomb.

The tunnels into the crater wall were as varied as the cliff face— some bored smooth with plasma torches, others rough, narrow, and as twisted as the society outside. For the first half hour or so, Matheson hadn't had to stoop, though there had been passages he'd been forced to slide sideways through and every place the rough stone had rubbed against him was marked with pale blue dust and the dull, irritated itching of his healing bruises. They heard eerily distorted voices, the skittering of insects, and the sounds of other people moving in the tunnels, but Matheson's Sun Spot only illuminated the flickering lizards that darted away from the light, and centipedes as long as his forearm. It made the skin at the back of his neck crawl.

Aya yanked him backward into a shadowed gap that opened into a small chamber.

He winced a little and shut off the Sun Spot as she pulled him to the ground away from the crack in the wall. A sharp edge caught the pocket on his thin shirt, tearing it open, and he barely caught the mobile before it hit the ground. He shoved into his shirt.

In a minute, a slim figure went past, soft-footed as a cat, illuminating its way with a dimly glowing chemical stick. *How did Aya hear such a quiet tread?*

Once the figure was farther down the tunnel, Aya motioned him to follow again.

"How—?" Matheson started in a whisper.

Aya put her hand over his mouth. "You're wish to come on our terms, or as prisoner, heh?"

He wondered for a moment which "our" she meant, but nodded and followed in silence.

They walked on, now ducking under low ceilings and turning through narrow entries more often. Matheson noticed his aches more the farther they went.

Eventually, a dim light came from ahead, with the soft sounds of people moving nearby. Once again, they stopped and hid in a fracture to let people pass.

She knows the way so well . . . he thought, and saw her studying him.

She tilted her head down and raised an ironically quirked eyebrow over a crooked half-smile. The expression was so much like one of Dillal's that he was surprised he'd never seen the resemblance before. "I'm raised here as much as the coffee house, and I'm honor my mother's work. No matter how ill, Mam's not give up on reform. How else's a Dreihle widow with a babe on her hip love an Ohba?" her whisper sharpened at the last and she glared at him defensively.

"Reform and love . . . So your father died when you were an infant?"

She nodded. "In th'agricamps. Same's . . . same's Djepe's. Now hush."

Matheson connected the information in his head as they waited for another group to pass. Then Aya tugged him with her out into the larger tunnel and motioned him to follow. They trotted quietly. The light brightened, flickering once in a while, as they advanced.

Around a corner the illumination was suddenly bright enough to read by as it poured from a hole high in the wall on their right. The tunnel curved slightly and branched right again, but Aya led Matheson past the gash of light and turned sharply left into a cleft that opened into a steep and narrow stair going up. She motioned him to go up the steps and wait.

He leaned close to her. "I'm going with you," he whispered.

She leveled a cold look at him and did not move until he rolled his eyes and shrugged. He was well up the steps—more a sloping ladder than a staircase—when she slipped back into the passage, leaving him to clamber into the unknown on his own.

Dillal had trusted Aya with this, but Matheson didn't know if she would betray that tenuous sibling accord because of what *he* had done. How closely did she cleave to her mother's—and by implication Dillal's father's—concept of colorblind reform? For Dillal, this case was an opening skirmish. The inspector's design was crazy and as frangible as glass, but it reached far beyond Matheson's own unfocused and damaged idealism, and guilt, or even the immediate desire to solve the case.

At the top of the stone ladder, Matheson found a wide, flat shelf that must have been carved over the passageway Aya had taken. Ahead he saw light and heard movement and soft, rolling Dreihleen voices.

Some unseen man said, "Aya," and Matheson crept forward until he could look out through a break in the wall.

Not far below lay what seemed to be a storage room carved from the rock and now converted into a field hospital. Light came from a mix of electric and chemical lamps set wherever there was room and moved as needed. Storage crates had been pushed out of the way, or stacked into makeshift beds and tables covered in stained plastic sheeting. All the beds were full and dozens of injured Dreihleen sat or lay on the ground, or leaned against the walls and crates. A few of the people murmured to each other, but most sat silent in shock. Some were bleeding, some blistered and burned from electric discharges, chemicals, or fire. The riot patrol had been brutal and indiscriminate. The insensible wounded—those whose injuries had been too severe to wait and had already been seen to—lay moaning off to the side, in too much pain to sleep. Beside them lay a few who didn't move or make any noise at all.

Among the rest, he saw a man cradling to his side a small child with an obviously broken arm, stroking the kid's hair as blood dried on their torn and filthy clothes. The child—perhaps ten years old—didn't cry, only clutched his fractured forearm and leaned against the man. Across from them, a young Dreihle woman in a blood-stained festival gown knelt in front of an elderly woman who sat on one of the crates and held up a flickering lamp. The girl was sewing up a ragged gash in the older woman's face. The light shuddered with every stitch, and Matheson couldn't tell if all the blood on the woman's face and neck was from the vicious slash or equally from the lip she'd bitten through.

The images twined with his fragmented memories of Camp Donetti. He felt ill and closed his eyes. *I caused something like this . . .* He hadn't seen it then—couldn't have—but it all knitted together, preamble to postscript, in blood and violence.

He heard Aya ask after Tchintaka and Banzet, and kept his stinging eyes closed, concentrating on the voices.

"Oso's where?" Aya asked. "I'm need speak t'him. Or Hoda."

Someone scoffed. "You're can't be trusted. You're entertain

dehkas." A male voice, Dreihleen, low and angry. "And you're help them at the canal."

Matheson could hear the chilled fury in Aya's reply. "I'm save ours. I'm let them die's make you happier, Norenin?"

Something prodded Matheson's left elbow. He opened his eyes and blinked away the dust that stuck to his wet lashes.

A Dreihle youth looked over the ledge and gave him a mean little smile, motioning Matheson forward. Had Aya turfed him? As he hesitated, the kid set a shock box on the shelf surface with a click. "You're come down. Now."

"The way I came up, or head first?" Matheson asked politely—wiser to be civil to any person pointing a weapon at your face.

The kid shrugged and teetered his unkempt, bloodstained head side to side, revealing the top of a tattoo that began on the side of his neck and vanished under the strap of his shirt to reappear on his just-visible shoulder. "Fairzee-mairzee." He was younger than Zanesh, the unaff, but looked more willing to do violence at the moment.

"I'll meet you at the bottom of the stairs," Matheson said.

He glanced down to look for Aya. She stood off to his left in an archway and stared anxiously at the ledge, no longer speaking. A man held onto her upper arm, turning an enraged glare at Matheson—it was the unusually husky Dreihle he'd seen outside the coffee house on Thursday. The kid scampered to the floor from atop a stack of crates and dodged around them, exiting the room.

"I'm coming down," Matheson called, glad most of his bruises were on his back and face as he eased toward the stone ladder on his belly.

At the bottom, the boy—no . . . girl, Matheson corrected as he got a better look—was leaning in the narrow doorway, holding out the shock box. From the careful way she held it, Matheson was sure the kid had little experience with the device. It wouldn't require much effort to take it from her, but Matheson had no desire for more trouble. He held his hands out together, palms up. "Do you want to cuff me? There're binders on my belt."

The girl shook her head, blood-stiffened tufts of her chopped-short hair bobbing with the motion. "Not want t'get so close, dehka." She looked defiantly at him, chin jutting up and her lip curled in disdain as she spoke. *How old is she? Thirteen, fourteen?* Except for the small curve of breasts, she was all bones and angles under her rough clothes.

Matheson shrugged and placed his hands on his head. He followed the girl as she backed into the wider main tunnel and motioned Matheson ahead of her.

The room down the passage was no different when seen from below. The injured and shocked Dreihleen had not vanished, but they were much closer and more than a few hateful stares turned in Matheson's direction. He dropped his gaze and raised it again only to look at Aya. This time, she met his eyes. "You're all right?" he asked.

She twitched her arm from the grip of the man beside her. "That I am." Her fierce tone wasn't for him.

The girl who'd escorted Matheson fell back and perched on the edge of a pile of crates, still holding the shock box and staying out of his reach. Slowly, Matheson dropped his hands while the man next to Aya looked him over, clearly noting the filth, bruises, and broken nose, and snorted. "You're see Dreihleen hard side now."

Matheson turned to look at the man—Norenin?—keeping his hands still at his sides, and remaining as calm as he could when what he wanted was to grab Aya and run like hell. "I have, but my own people did this to me, not yours."

The man looked cautiously intrigued. "Dehkas're beat you? Why?"

"They don't like what I'm doing or who I'm working for."

The man paused, his eyes narrowing in thought, then jerked his head toward Aya. "You're make her bring you?"

"Yes. I need to speak with Osolin Tchintaka or Hoda Banzet."

"Not here."

"Just to be clear—you won't let me speak to them here, or they aren't here to begin with?" Matheson asked.

The man looked smug. "We're not help you take Oso for this."

"For this?" Matheson glanced around the room, pointedly observing the wounded before he returned his gaze to the man in front of him. "Tchintaka's politics aren't why I'm here. Unless they turn out to be why he may have been at the Paz da Sorte with Denny Leran."

"Denny's victim, like the rest."

Matheson couldn't hold back his own bitter smile, but he kept his eyes level and his body still. "Denny was part of the crew. He killed Venn Robesh because she didn't want to be his girl. You know what he was like. Petty and mean and too quick to blame someone else for everything that went wrong in his life."

The man cut his gaze aside, staring at the dusty floor and breathing harshly to hold onto his temper.

"You think I'm wrong? You think Denny wasn't like that? That he wouldn't have killed her in a rage? That he thought she'd provoked him just by being happy without him? Furious that she was with Gil Dohan? Or wearing a pretty dress and getting the hell out of the Dreihleat? You don't think that's how mean Denny was?"

The man snapped his glare back to Matheson's face. "He's all that. How're you know Denny's kill Venn?"

"Evidence." Dillal hadn't confirmed it and he wasn't certain Starna had either—the tech's statements hadn't made sense—but Matheson was sure enough, now, of what the material had been on Leran's hands.

All his confusion, his guilt, his horror, drained to cold, still fury. "Dillal found it—Denny had Venn's blood and brains on his hands. She had his skin under her nails. She slapped him. He killed her. And it was a terrible way to die—boiled her brains like soup." He didn't look at Aya—he hadn't told her these things and he didn't want to see how she was taking it.

"Then who's killed Denny?" the man asked, narrowing his eyes.

"Whoever was in charge of the robbery shot him in the head for killing Venn."

The man didn't ask how he knew, he only looked mortified, all color draining from his face. "Robbery?"

If the man didn't know Tchintaka had been involved in the plan to rob the Paz da Sorte, he at least suspected it might be true, but he wasn't going to grass on his leader—at least not yet.

"We don't believe they meant to harm anyone," Matheson said, forcing his tone softer, covering his own growing certainty. "It just went wrong. But Denny was part of the gang and we must find the other men who were with him. I know Tchintaka and Banzet were his friends. That doesn't mean they did anything, but I need to ask them what they know. We have to find the men who betrayed your community and killed your people."

"Why you're care, dehka?" the man snarled.

"Because they are human beings who were killed just for knowing the wrong thing, for being in the way. The same way Dreihleen were hurt—and killed—today. It's unjust—the same kind of injustice that Tchintaka urges you to fight against. If he knows anything about who did this, I must speak to him. I have to find the rest of the crew or things are only going to get worse here."

"Is true," Aya murmured. "You're know today's only make the corporation more hateful."

The man looked at Aya, his expression twisted with confusion. "You're believe too that Oso's do such a thing?"

"I'm not want to. But he's know who're do't. He's friend to Denny . . . and Hoda. *Ledrew a mant*, Norenin."

"You're say . . . this's get worse?" Norenin asked, hesitating, and looking to Matheson.

"Yes," Matheson replied. "We've been urged since the beginning to simply close the case and move on. Just find the right *type* of person to blame, not to bother looking for the truth."

"Why you're not?"

He let all his own troubled conviction out. "Because that's not justice. It's not right."

Norenin cut his eyes to Aya. She met them cooly. "He's believe. And I."

Norenin grunted. "And . . . the met?"

Aya dropped her gaze to the ground, her face tight. "I'm may have . . . misjudge him."

Norenin turned narrowed eyes back to Matheson. "What you're think?"

"Of Inspector Dillal? I think he does what's important to him. He's certainly not doing anything because anyone else wants it that way. Including Pritchet."

"Pritchet? Director Pritchet?" Norenin checked.

Matheson nodded. "I think he expected something different—sure as merry hell not what he got with Dillal."

Norenin chuckled. "The snake's bite itself."

"Whatever he is, he's arguing with Pritchet right now to keep troops out of the Dreihleat and Ohbata."

Norenin scowled and tapped a knuckle against his tightly drawn mouth. The room was exceptionally quiet, except for the sounds of suffering too great to turn aside.

The back of Matheson's neck felt cold and he cast a nervous glance around the room. Every Dreihle who could raise eyes watched. The girl with the shock box had moved around, keeping all three of them in her field of fire, though she'd let the weapon drop to her side. Her expression was tense, focused now on Norenin.

Norenin humphed and Matheson's attention snapped back to him. "I'm send you t'Hoda. I'm not give up Oso." He shifted his gaze to the girl, but spoke to Matheson. "You're not convince me against him yet."

Matheson heard the girl's feet shift on the ground, but he didn't dare try to see what she was doing. Norenin shook his head, his eyes still narrowed in a warning scowl. After a moment, he seemed satisfied that the girl wasn't going to do anything untoward, and shifted his gaze to Aya. "East tunnel. Goes far as you can. Then you're find him, or you're not."

Dillal didn't go straight to Pritchet's office, but strode toward ForTech through the flux of personnel rotating through to cover for the riot patrols and take over as various teams returned. News of the downed transport had reached the offices ahead of the inspector and he received a mix of stares, mutters, and half-hearted approbation. He responded to none of it.

Beside his office, the morgue door was standing open. He stopped short.

An IO stepped through into the hall and twitched back a half-step as he saw the hard gleam of the prosthesis frame peeping from the torn spray skin on the inspector's face. Then he turned his head and called over his shoulder into the morgue, "Sir, he's here."

The IO put out his hand as if he meant to grab Dillal's arm, but turned at the last second and made it into an "after you" gesture.

"Detive Neme wants to see you. Sir." His expression wavered between distaste and nausea.

Dillal narrowed his eyes at the IO. "I haven't time to speak with her."

"You'll make time," Neme snapped, jogging up behind the IO's shoulder as he stood in the doorway.

"I'm meeting with Director Pritchet," Dillal told her, starting to turn away.

Neme pushed past the IO and stopped in front of Dillal, her lip curling. "I don't give a sollet's crap, and you can ask all you want, but Pritchet won't see you until you can explain to me why your primary med/legal tech is bleeding out on the floor in here."

Dillal was startled. "Starna?"

"That's what his ID says."

"What's happened?"

Neme stared hard at him, tilting her head slowly to the side as if she could see what Dillal knew if she just got the angle right. "Tried to kill himself."

Dillal shoved past her into the morgue.

The room was disarrayed in front of the section that had been screened away for the Paz da Sorte victims, but it appeared that latter part of the room was untouched. The air stank of blood and vomit. A red stain flowed unevenly across the floor, spreading over the cold barrier, liquid on the warm side and gelid on the other. Blood had been tracked and smeared in wide swaths and a bright spatter painted an arc up the service wall. An empty body bag lay in a crumpled heap at the edge of the largest bloodstain. Three med/legal techs in crimson-blotted coats stood against the farthest wall. Just in front of them Woskyat, covered with blood and bile, sat huddled on a gurney, averting her face and retching. A female IO stood guard over her, putting a comforting hand on her shoulder every time Woskyat heaved. The doctor shuddered away from the IO's touch. IAD Istvalk stood near the lab door, keeping a few curious techs and med/legals out, but not blocking the view much.

Dillal halted at the edge of the cold barrier, narrowing his eyes, the left clicking slightly and sending a few drops of pinkish liquid down his cheek as he studied the scene. He took a short, sharp breath, grimaced slightly, and pivoted back to face Neme, who'd stopped just behind him. "Where is he?" Dillal demanded in a low voice, glaring at her with his teeth clenched and the muscles in his neck and shoulders gone tight.

Neme raised an eyebrow very slightly. "Public Health."

"You said 'is bleeding.'"

Neme shrugged. "I lied. So send me up on charges—you've always wanted to."

"He survived?"

"So far. Thanks to Dr. Woskyat over there—who went jump-wise as soon as someone else took over." Neme coughed up a laugh. "Apparently she doesn't like blood."

Dillal let out a breath and his tension dropped suddenly away. He closed his eyes for a second, then tilted his head to meet Neme's gaze sideways. "Suicide is not a crime and as Starna is still alive, I don't see what you want of me."

Neme's voice was no louder, and no warmer, than his. "Most people don't address their suicide notes to their whip, *Dear Inspector,* and I'm not the only person who's noticed this is suicide number two for you today. You've been such a busy little man."

"Santos's death had nothing to do with me."

"So you got your pet surgeon to certify death rather than taint yourself—"

"Procedure required that I step away from a case in which I might be an interested party." Still his voice didn't rise, but it was sharp and icy.

"That's right—because you're supposed to be our shield against the shadow of evidentiary misconduct—"

"About which I certainly learned all I needed when I worked with you."

"Don't come up sanctimonious with me, you twisty little patchwork bastard." Neme closed the distance between them abruptly, forcing Dillal to tilt his head back to look up at her. Her voice snapped like the thunder of heat lightning in the room that had gone silent but for the whisk and whirr of machines and the sound of Woskyat's retching. "You're not my moral better because your hands *look* cleaner in the glare of procedure. You may have sold your soul—if you fucking well have one—to vault the ladder, and you might actually have nothing to do with Santos taking the jump, but that doesn't clear your ass of responsibility. A man doesn't put a knife in his own throat for the sake of evidentiary procedure! You're in this up to your balls and I'm going to find out how!"

The right corner of Dillal's mouth quirked and he took a step away from Neme that looked less like retreat than it looked like the gracious acknowledgment of someone else's defeat. "Then tell me exactly what happened and perhaps I can help you put my balls in a vise—if there's reason."

Neme looked askance at him as he settled his weight against the edge of a work table and watched her. His hair was matted on the right, his suit was dirty and still damp in places, and the odor of the canal clung to him, but he seemed to take no notice, any more than he acknowledged the raw patch below his mechanical eye or the fluid that gathered at the corner of the torn spray skin. A tiny shudder escaped her before she spoke again.

"Woskyat's story is that she was working in the lab and heard a sound in here. She'd assumed the room was empty, but she thought it might be you or Starna—she said you'd been looking for him—so she came in and found Starna there," Neme said, pointing over his shoulder toward the bloodstained floor at the cold barrier.

Dillal neither blinked nor turned his head. "Go on."

Neme scowled. "See for yourself." She walked to the nearest information terminal and swiped around for a minute until the monitor log for the lab came up on the display. She flicked it back to an incident hashmark and set it to playback.

On the display, Starna entered the room through the hall door, locking it behind himself. His bleached hair was slightly damp, his clothes very crisp and lightly water spotted on the shoulders as if he'd just come from a shower. He moved around the room with purpose, but little effect, moving objects, adjusting controls, checking information and tests that the monitor stream made note of in a sidebar.

Starna walked to the supply room—the monitor stream jumped to follow—and removed a flat-folded body bag from one cupboard and a sealed package of scalpels from another. The stream switched back into the morgue where he set the bag and the scalpels on a cleared work space close inside the cold barrier before going to stand in front of one of the information terminals. He started a new document and worked on it for a while, deleting and re-writing several times before he wiped out the work completely and stepped back from the terminal, frowning. He ran his hands through his hair and looked around the room until he saw what he wanted. He smiled and went to write on a pad of flimsy. This time he didn't seem to have any difficulty with what he wanted to say and wrote fluidly for several minutes, finally signing it with care. He left the pencil where it lay, but carried the pages with him as he returned once more to the terminal, checked the same list of tests and information, and logged out. His fingers lingered over the keyboard for a moment, as if he were considering logging back in, then he shook himself and turned away to walk back over the cold barrier.

He put his note down on top of the body bag and undressed, folding his clothes meticulously and placing them in a neat pile next to the scalpels. He left his shoes in strict alignment on the floor below. Then he picked up his letter, looked it over, and kissed the top page before laying the whole thing precisely in the center of his piled clothing.

He opened the packet of scalpels and set them aside again, then picked up the bag and flicked it open—it made a cracking noise in the air. Starna stepped into the bag, keeping behind the cold barrier, and raised it up to rest on his shoulders like a cloak. Then he slid his hands up the seal as far as his chest, holding the bag up with one hand as he reached for the scalpels with the other. He sat down, bringing the scalpels into the bag and struggling to close the seal over his head and shoulders.

Woskyat entered the room from the lab and paused at the door, looking around. "Starna," she shouted and ran toward him. "What are you doing?"

Startled, Starna turned his head. Woskyat was no more than two steps away. Light slid like liquid off the scalpel blade as Starna raised his left hand to his right ear.

Woskyat grabbed him, knocking his left elbow upward as Starna started to pull the blade into his skin. Blood sprayed from the cut as the scalpel flipped into the air and clattered back down, spinning across the floor. Woskyat yelled and gagged as blood spurted into her face and Starna sobbed, struggling against her.

Then he collapsed backward to the floor. Woskyat fell on top of him, eyes squeezed shut, jamming her fingers into the gushing wound in his neck even as she started screaming in hysterical, inarticulate bursts. The blood continued to leak, slower, but still thick and dark, from the wound that clung around her fingers. Then she rolled to the side, averting her eyes, her arm twisting strangely as she kept her hand in place by an extraordinary exertion of will. Starna lay limp in the slowly spreading blood.

Three techs burst in from the lab and scrambled to help. One of them snatched a can of spray seal and a pair of gloves off one of the work tables, shouting orders at the other two as he knelt down beside Woskyat and Starna. "You have to remove your hand from the wound," he said.

"No," Woskyat said, gagging. She turned her head and spit blood and bile onto the floor, clenching her eyes shut. "No . . . Spray and wrap."

"What?"

"Ohhh . . . blight and blackness . . . it's all over me . . ." She gagged again, her body convulsing as she fought her nausea and then slumping into stillness as she fainted.

The first tech snatched one of the other scalpels from the body bag and hacked a piece off one of the gloves.

The emergency alarm started wailing and lights flashed red. One of the other techs skittered up with an armload of supplies and threw himself down next to Starna's head. The last med/legal arrived as they started to work on Starna. When the first two were ready, the third pulled Woskyat's hand away. More blood squirted from the wound until the first two techs finished their seal. Then they started stanching the rest of the blood, keeping pressure on the wound in turns until Medical Intervention arrived to remove Starna.

An SO appeared on the monitor stream and Neme stopped the replay.

Dillal looked at the still frame that remained on the display. He closed his eyes a moment, then looked back at Neme. "Pathetic as it may be, this is clearly not my doing."

"Explain the fucking note."

"As I haven't read it, I can't."

"He kissed it."

Dillal tilted his head and served her a cynical look. "That a troubled young man—whatever our professional association—developed an obsession that was entirely one-sided and in no way encouraged does not place an automatic supposition of guilt upon me for his choice to take his life. I'm sorry for it, nonetheless, but guilty of inciting it? No."

"The two of you spent a lot of time together in your office—which has no monitor."

Dillal was silent and uncannily still for several seconds, then snorted and appeared on the verge of laughing at her. "He worked for me. If you study the durations of those periods when Starna and I were alone in my office, you'll see that the longest meeting we had without interruption was no more than ten minutes. Hardly time to consummate an illicit affair with a subordinate—unless you mean to insult my sexual capability as well as my judgment and professional conduct."

"I'll take what I can get."

Dillal pushed away from the counter on which he'd been leaning. "I have more pressing business than being the object of your unnecessary investigation."

He started to walk away, but Neme called out after him, "Pritchet will not see you. Not until I clear your ass."

Dillal whipped around to face her again. "Innocent people will die if I can't persuade the director to see certain things my way. I don't have time to let you indulge your spite."

She smirked at him and reached into her jacket pocket. She pulled out a small sheaf of flimsy. "Read the letter."

He snatched it from her and began reading. His right brow drew down and his lopsided expression seemed pained as he continued through to the end. He closed his eyes and handed the flimsy back to her without a word.

"What did he mean 'I can't be what you want'?" Neme asked.

"Not what you imagine."

"And the sample he mentioned?"

Dillal took a deep breath, appearing resigned to an unpleasant necessity, and looked up at her. "I need to see it again."

"See what?"

"The monitor video."

Her expression hovered between incredulity and disgust. "Why?"

"The early section. I need to see what he was doing, what he was working on, before he undressed."

"There's the sidebar list—"

"That is not enough. I need to know what he did with the information and how that's reflected in his note to me."

"And that's going to help exactly . . . how?"

"I'm not sure that it will, but it's all I can offer. As you won't allow me to leave until I've satisfied your morbid curiosity, I'll do what I can. And for the love of everything decent, let Dr. Woskyat leave. There's no reason to torment the woman."

The east tunnel wandered through the cliff for a long, dark distance, getting narrower and smaller, the air growing stale and slow-moving. It branched less and the debouchments disappeared just before it ran into a crumbling cul-de-sac. Aya turned sideways and slipped into a fissure in the rotten stone. Matheson followed.

They stumbled forward a while. The other side was a little fresher, but no brighter or larger. Matheson's mobile was uncomfortably bright when he checked it. There was no transmitter signal at all in the tunnels and it was growing late. *I hope Dillal's convinced Pritchet to hold off.* He didn't want to emerge from the cliff into a combat zone.

His night vision ruined, Matheson called a temporary halt and put his mobile in his shirt. "How far do you think this goes?" he asked.

He felt Aya sink down next to him. "I'm not know. Sit."

He settled gratefully to the ground and was silent for a while.

"Why didn't you turf me?" he whispered.

Her quiet reply was flat. "And wreck what we're go to do? Why I'm should?"

He folded his hands together in his lap, rubbing one thumb nervously over the opposite knuckle. "Because of what I did. At Camp Donetti."

"You're remember what you're did now?"

"No."

"That's why. You're come angry with me for what I'm do. Is fair. I'm all you're think I am, but I'm trust th'Eric I'm know yesterday. Today I'm see another and I'm want t'hate you for it. But how's it justice if you're not know what you're did?"

There were little scraping, clicking sounds in the dark and he wondered if there was a centipede nearby, creeping up on them. He shivered. "But you—that doesn't change my guilt . . . in your mind."

"And yours?"

"I . . . can't change it. I can only do better, *right now*."

"Then we're do. We're do as Djepe's ask."

"You trust *him* now? Even though—" Matheson struggled for the right thing.

"He's bong met? You're know it means 'the dead of mixed flesh' heh?"

That wasn't what he'd been groping for, but Matheson was almost grateful for the turn in the conversation. "What a repulsive term." The small sounds came closer. Matheson shifted and got his feet under him.

"Ohba word for a terrible thing. We're so few, and children're hard born. If not of our blood, we're dwindle away. Th'Ohba the same. So my mam's say."

He could hear her rise to her feet, felt her brush past him in the darkness. "She's love an Ohba man, but I'm never understand why. Maybe she's *want* us to dwindle—all become one thing."

"You *are* all one thing—"

Light blinded them and a heavy hand fell on Matheson's shoulder.

CHAPTER TWENTY-SIX

Day 5: Evening into Night

"There are being rats in our tunnels. Scrawny yellow rats." The voice rumbled, soft and low, like a distant earthquake.

Matheson winced under the pressure—the man's hand felt unnaturally heavy—but he pushed up from the floor as hard as he could, reaching for the wrist and shoulder of the man who'd grabbed him. He snatched for a hold that would let him drag the man over and down but in spite of his bulk, the man spun aside with ease, shoving Matheson forward and off balance. Then he felt a foot on his back, pushing him to the ground as Aya snarled nearby. He heard someone grunt followed by scrabbling noises, then the thump of fist against flesh and Aya yelped.

The man above and behind him leaned more of his weight onto Matheson's spine, sending a jolt of pain through his bruised back, and the dazzle of the light around him shifted, cast down from directly above. "Still, bitch, or this one is breaking him."

Aya said nothing, but the pressure vanished from Matheson's back, and a hard hand grabbed his upper arm and yanked him to his feet. Someone reached around him and removed Matheson's belt. Then something hard prodded his back.

"Coming nicely, or both of you are making pretty corpses."

Matheson had no choice but to stumble forward, glad he'd had to stow his mobile in his shirt where it hadn't been seen and taken from him. He brushed it with his arm, hitching it to the side where it was better hidden. He tried to catch Aya's gaze as he walked.

She did not look at him, only straight ahead with a hard expression. Matheson made a quick count of the Ohba around them: four. The one immediately behind him wasn't more than a teenager, and had all the signs of a recently broken nose. He glared at Matheson, who also fixed his eyes forward. *Can't fight these odds in such a close space.* They walked in silence for a while until they filed out of the tunnel into low light and the odor of things growing in fertile tropical rot. A pair of long, lean hounds with scarred heads and tattered ears fell in behind them.

The sun was nearly down—or an early spring storm was rolling in—judging by the gray illumination through the translucent roof. The ground underfoot was soft, sandy, and loose. Plants grew in troughs, dangled from trellises, and sprang from the ground in profusion. Matheson recognized the heavy, sweet scent of aminta, cannabis, and poppy, the sharp salt smell of salfrin, and the stink of hydroponic fertilizer. More men and a few women stepped out of the artificial jungle and accompanied the patrol. They were all Ohba of various ages, and most, Matheson noted, were armed with old guns—long-ago decommissioned military firearms for the most part, simple and gleaming with care. He recognized some of the weapons from his own experience shooting in sport and competition, but others were new to him. All looked equally lethal.

"Where are we?" Matheson asked.

The boy behind him rapped the back of his head lightly with something hard. "Not knowing where you've come? You two are making worthless spies."

"Not spies. We're—"

His escort smacked him again. "Quiet. This one is telling what you are being, sandworm."

Matheson sighed and his ribs reminded him that was still a risky activity. "Another man—or men—came this way today," he started.

This time the blow to the back of his head made him stumble and fall against one of the newcomers. They shoved him back and forth for a moment while the hounds yipped and snapped. Matheson considered running, but between the armed patrol, his aches, the dogs, and the unknown territory, he had no chance, and he wouldn't abandon Aya. He trudged on as soon as he was allowed. The occasional humid breeze picked up the smell of familiar spicy cooking—meat, onions, and hot peppers—that grew stronger as they walked on.

They wound through the weird landscape and passed a long, low building. Then the plants thinned into a wide clearing. Several rugs were strewn at one edge of the clearing and a group of Ohba sat on small stools or on the carpets, sharing food from several dishes laid before them and watching one standing man who seemed to be reciting something. Matheson thought one or two people were familiar, but in the dim light and dressed as they were in loosely flowing clothes of dull colors, details were impossible to pick out at his distance. The majority of the escort faded back into the greenery as their original captors goaded Matheson and Aya the last few meters toward the seated group, with the dogs at heel.

The gathered folk ignored them while the speaker finished what he was saying with an expansive flourish of his hands. That man stepped aside to sit with the rest of the group and revealed a large man seated on a stool that set him just a few centimeters higher than everyone around him. This man said a few low words, turned, and put out his hands to the figure on his left. They both rose to their feet. Their shoulder-clasping embrace had the look of formality to it, but there was fondness in their slight smiles.

As the couple broke apart and the big man turned to address the newcomers, Matheson recognized Christa Santos as the other half of the embrace. She gave him the same steady, impassive look she'd worn the last time he saw her, though her face seemed older now and her eyes were red-rimmed. *Stars, it's been less than twelve hours . . .*

Matheson inclined his head. "I'm very sorry for your loss," he started.

Before he could say more, the guy with the broken nose pushed down on his shoulder at the same time he delivered a sharp tap to the back of Matheson's leg. The nearest hound growled low. Matheson landed on his knees with a gasp and felt the man's hand slap the back of his head, the fingers digging into his hair.

"Still." The order was quietly given in a low, reverberant voice.

The youth released him and moved a little away. Matheson raised his eyes, then, more slowly, his head, anticipating a blow that didn't come. The women in their company had all fallen back, leaving only the men, boys, and one dog to guard them. He could just spot Aya kneeling at his side if he shifted his gaze, but knowing she was all right was enough. He watched the people in front of him.

Christa leaned in and whispered to the big man, who nodded and moved from the circle of diners, drawing closer to Matheson.

He was larger and heavier than the people with him, older, stately, and grave. If they'd both been standing, the top of the Ohba's head would have been level with Matheson's jaw. His clothes were a dark, red-brown duller than his garnet-red skin and hair, and striped in black that hid his shape in the movement of cloud shadows from above. He looked at Matheson and then to the youth beside him, giving no attention to Aya beyond the swiftest flick of a glance. "Being less quick to damage our guest, Gant. He is meaning respect to our sister, though he is speaking out of turn."

One of the other men in the main circle muttered something

Matheson didn't quite catch. Matheson turned his head to see the speaker as the old man in front of him did the same. Another familiar face: the Ohba man who'd moved in next door. *Can't be a coincidence.* Matheson kept his mouth shut and listened.

"Uncle, that is Matheson, the one the corpse is keeping."

"And the caddis fly?" the older man asked.

Matheson's neighbor frowned slightly and shook his head. "O-sum." *Nothing. Worthless. Or doesn't know . . . ?*

The big man in the center gave a speculative grunt that rolled in the air as he turned again to regard Matheson. There'd been nothing in any briefs about protocols for interacting with Ohba on their own territory. He'd broken a rule by offering his condolences directly to Christa, but he didn't know what it was. He'd talked to her before without any repercussion, but that hadn't been here. And Santos had still been alive.

He was puzzling with it when the elder man stopped half a meter from him. "Matheson. We are being titled Uncle Fahn. Tenzo and Kirita are speaking for you, so you are living a while longer. Be telling us why are you coming here."

From the corner of his eye, Matheson saw Aya stiffen a little and cringe back, her head down. Matheson raised his own head a little, but kept his eyes down, fearing a direct look would be taken as a challenge. "Uncle Fahn. I'm searching for a man, or two men, I was told came this way earlier today."

Fahn put a finger under Matheson's chin and forced his head upward—the strength of the single digit pressing into his jaw was too painful to resist. Fahn peered at him. "Two men?"

"I was told of one, but I think they were together, at least this far."

Uncle Fahn nodded slowly. "Be describing them."

"Young, Dreihleen—"

Fahn laughed, cutting him off. "It is animals you are hunting, not men."

Aya muttered under her breath and Fahn cuffed her with the back of his hand as casually as brushing off a fly. The blow looked slight, but it sent Aya falling into the man beside her. The dog made a warning snap at her, and Matheson started up, but Fahn pushed him back to his knees just as easily. "Be paying no mind to the mewling of clawless cats. You should be at telling us of the caddis flies."

Matheson shot a glance at Aya as the dog sat guard beside her. She shook her head, though she looked dazed. Fury lanced through him, but going on was his only option. He clamped his feelings down and said, "Their names are Hoda Banzet and Osolin Tchintaka. Politicals. They're involved in the murders of sixteen people—the crime that may have led to the death of Christa—of Kirita's husband."

"You were then working with Kirita's man."

He's got to know this already. Is he testing me? "Yes, sir. He was my training officer, and my friend as well."

"Be looking us in the eye, boy."

Matheson looked up, meeting Fahn's gaze, and holding onto a bland expression. The dark face in front of him seemed impossibly large, and streaked in phantom violet mud.

Fahn stared at him, the expression as piercing as any of Dillal's. His eyes were the same jade green as Christa's, but it was like looking into the eyes of a predator. Fear pricked at the back of Matheson's neck. He didn't dare close his eyes against the sudden flash of memory, but locked them on Fahn's until it passed.

Fahn gave a slow, smile and said, "You are pursuing your caddis flies for your own sake. This is not being for Kirita's dead man. Your loyalty is lying with whoever is paying best, sandworm."

"My loyalty is to the truth."

"Pretty lies are still being lies."

Focus on the case, or you're dead. "No, sir," Matheson replied. "It's best if I find these men as quickly as possible or what's been happening in the Dreihleat will happen here next. One or both of the men I'm seeking came here. You're canny. You know about them and that when the connection between the Ohbata and the Dreihleat is found—"

"There is being nothing between us and the caddis flies that Corporation House should be seeing ghosts in every corner." Threat was implicit in the deep, rolling voice.

Matheson pushed on. "Nothing? The tunnels? Ammunition traced to the Ohbata, used to kill sixteen Dreihleen—and one of your own, here in your own territory? It's all there for the Corporation to find if I don't give them something else to chew. Right now, only two people aside from those standing here know, and they won't tell."

"Who are those that we can be trusting them?"

"One is a technician who doesn't know the significance of what he's found. The other is my superior—"

"The corpse walking."

The corpse—that's Dillal! More glittering shards of information shifted into focus. "You aided their escape in hopes of obscuring that connection, even though you knew one of them was responsible for what happened at Camp Donetti." Even the name nauseated Matheson, but it made Fahn shift his gaze a moment and he knew his guess had scored. It shored up his ragged confidence. "Like you know about me, and the ammunition, and the murder of your—"

Fahn snatched Matheson into the air by the throat, shook him, and dropped him again. "Be considering your words with care, sand-worm," he said, his eyes narrowed, but his voice still calm above the warning growl of the hound.

Matheson coughed, buying time to think, as he rose back

up on his knees. He kept his head and his voice lowered as he spoke again. "A transport was brought down in the Dreihleat and the blame can be laid anywhere the corporation likes. Given any excuse, you know what Corporation House will chose to do and where it will start. The ground under you is crumbling. Killing us will only make it fall away faster. Help me, and we can stave off the corporation."

Matheson forced himself to speak slowly and ignore the menacing dog, and time fleeting by, but panic rose like smoke in his chest as Fahn's expression remained unchanged. "But it has to be now, or it won't matter who really killed whom or why or how. I need these men, their confession, or any verifiable evidence that the crime is definitively theirs. Or you and yours might as well jump without a ship." He stopped and waited, looking up at Fahn.

Fahn's mouth curled into a considering smile and he glanced over his shoulder, first at Tenzo—who closed his eyes—and then at Christa. She ducked her head. Fahn gestured and the man beside Christa put his head next to hers so she could whisper to him, then he walked forward and whispered to Uncle Fahn.

Fahn laughed loud and hard enough to shake the nearest plants and raise a chime from tiny bells hung on a dead branch nearby. The ringing reminded Matheson of the noise from his Ohba neighbor's wall—Tenzo's wall. Fahn replied quickly to the man, who darted away into the artificial jungle with the dog loping behind him. Then the big man turned and motioned Matheson to his feet.

Fahn watched with amusement as Matheson winced with his pains and stood, stepping a little closer to Aya. "We are knowing the creatures you are hunting," Fahn started. "We have already been sending one of them on, but we are knowing the place. That one was then giving us a . . . a promise never to be troubling us again. We will be giving it to you and telling you where that one will be found now, if you are agreeing to a request of ours."

Matheson dared to shake his head. "There's no time—"

"Nor o-sum. It is only taking a moment," Fahn replied with an expression far too innocent.

What kind of trap are you laying, old spider? "What do you want me to do?" Matheson asked.

"You are not promising to do this?"

"Not without knowing what I'm agreeing to, first."

Fahn gave a slight nod. "We are understanding this, but we are wishing to know where you are cleaving your loyalties. To what limit you will be now going for your . . . superior officer." Matheson didn't miss the sneer in Fahn's voice, but he didn't react to it. "For the end you are pursuing."

"As far as I have to."

"Then this is being simple, if you are speaking the truth."

The man who had run off returned alone with a sealed storage box and handed it to Fahn. Uncle Fahn patted the box. "This is being the promise the caddis fly was then leaving with us. We are giving it to you for doing the task we are setting," he said, holding the box out to Matheson.

Matheson felt the trap waiting to spring shut on him. There were rules here and he still didn't know them all, but he'd guessed a few.

"Be at opening it," Fahn demanded.

The latches were stiff. Matheson's pulse sped as they popped and the lid sprang up a little. Nothing issued from the narrow gap. Fahn gave a predator's smile at Matheson's relief and repeated his command. "Be at it."

Fahn held onto the box as Matheson flicked the lid back.

The handgun was old, fifty years . . . possibly more. Like those carried by their escort from the tunnel, it was well-kept, but smudged at the moment with dirt, or propellant residue. A sour odor of gun smoke hung in the box. "That is being the promise that they will not now betray us," Fahn said.

"This belonged to one of them—Banzet or Tchintaka?"

Fahn chuckled. "Yes. Their marks, their flesh, the filth of their deeds is being on it. You will be finding a match for your bullets—*those* were then being given by a pretty blue sandworm to that one of us who is dead. Be taking it."

Matheson was sure he was missing a subtlety in the convolution of Fahn's language, but he'd worry about it later. "Why are you so willing to give this up—to break this promise they gave you?"

"We had never been at saying *we* would not now betray *them*. Those ones are being far away, but *all of us* are being here, where danger is gathering."

Oh, he's up to something tricky, but I can't call him on it. And I want that damned gun! "And what price are you demanding from me?" Matheson asked.

Fahn turned his head a little, glancing at Aya and back at Matheson with a small smile. "You are shooting the female."

"No." Matheson had stepped in front of Aya without even thinking of it.

He felt her hands touch his sides, sliding the mobile in his shirt to the small of his back and out. "Djepe's grandfather," she murmured, bowing her head against his shoulder.

Source of damning videos and new scars. He hoped she was doing something useful with the Peerless. If there was any signal to be had, this would be the place—Dillal had said there was connection in the Ohbata only where it was too dangerous to use.

Fahn laughed. "Loyalty is lying dead at the feet of a yellow whore."

"I won't add to the tally of blood for blood between the Ohba and Dreihleen," Matheson replied.

"Nor for this?" Fahn asked, shaking the box enough to make the gun rattle against the sides.

"No."

Fahn shrugged. "You are leaving at o-sum."

"I'll find another way."

"It is nor so quick . . ."

"Time should be *your* worry. I'll let you all go to hell before I'll buy my way out with her life."

"Nor even for your superior officer?" Fahn asked with the same sneer as before. "This is being your loyalty to him?"

Matheson shook his head and glared in disgust he had no need to feign. "Name a different price."

The light shifted and dimmed with a rattle of rain on the roof high above. Fahn peered at him thoughtfully while Matheson said nothing and Aya pressed the MDD against his back.

"This thing is coming how soon?"

His confidence surged; this was a game he knew how to play. "The assault? Shift change—about five more hours. Or whenever this rain stops. If they can't beat you down in one day, they'll drop troops pulled from out system and the rest goes down just like Camp Donetti."

"This is being Ang'Das, the heart of Ariel, not the fields of Agria. Too many eyes will be seeing here."

Matheson scoffed. "Riot control came in fast and hard in the Dreihleat with no reservations about what the tourists might see. GISA sent the sweeps straight to the camps—no case reviews, no pleadings. Then a transport full of them went down in front of everyone watching. It may have looked like an accident, but it wasn't. The corporation won't need be so clever here, because no outsider comes into the Ohbata unless they're criminal or crazy. But with a view from the distance of the gates—or from the white towers on the Quay—the offensive against you will become a tourist event, like the canoe races. At best, you have a day before Corporation House finds the manpower to bring an excuse to your door.

"Give me the gun—just as it is, fingerprints, dirt and all—and tell me where I can find either man. I don't even need both, just one. Then we can derail the corporation's plans."

"You are offering what in return?"

"I've already given you information and an advantage. The Dreihleen didn't have that and your rivals—which I'm sure you've got—don't have it either. I've already paid."

"What will you be doing if we are not . . . ?"

"Walking out—"

"And you will be going straight to your masters, bringing cause against us whether we are helping you or not."

"If I'd wanted to do that, I'd have turfed you before I came. Kirita knows I keep my promises—so does Tenzo, the spy you sent to watch me. If I leave empty-handed, you'll still get a day's grace. But if you give me the gun and location now, you're buying all of their lives," Matheson added, pointing to the other Ohba who still sat or stood on the carpets behind Fahn. Matheson fixed his gaze on Christa Santos. "And a chance to find the man who killed Kirita's husband."

Christa lurched a step toward him, eyes wide—it was the most expression he'd ever seen on her face. The man closest to her snatched at her hand to hold her back but she shook him off and walked toward Fahn as if she were forcing herself through mud.

Fahn glanced over his shoulder, then turned a little farther to see her better. "Kirita. Still yourself, and we are forgetting that you are coming out of turn."

"Uncle," she rasped, staring at Matheson, shaking her head. Her voice was rough, low, and shaking. "This one's man—"

"Is nor Ohba," Fahn snapped with a stamp of his foot. "We had then given you, you are being with us again. The rest nor o-sum."

Christa fixed her glare on Fahn. "He *is* being this one's man! He is being hanged then like a thieving cat." She snatched the case from Fahn's hands. "We will be buying him—buying the *thing* that was at killing this one's man. You," she said, pointing an unsteady finger at him, "*you* protect us. Or you are not deserving to be our Uncle."

The watching Ohba stirred, some stepping out of their cover among the plants to stare hard at Uncle Fahn, some cringing aside. Tenzo, of all of them, watched with no expression. Christa stood quivering beside Fahn, clutching the box against her bosom. Her head was slightly turned and shoulders raised in fear, but she stood her ground.

Uncle Fahn took a breath and held it, glaring at her. Christa didn't look away, though she shook so hard Matheson thought she would fall. Fahn let the air back out in a disgusted huff. He bared his teeth at the woman, but she still didn't back down. Then he tossed his head and rolled his eyes. "To be giving it," he said, jerking his head toward Matheson. "You are selling us cheap, Kirita."

She didn't reply except to offer the gun in its box to Matheson. Her eyes met his for only a moment, almost accusing. As soon as he accepted the box from her, Christa lowered her head and turned aside with a jerk.

Fahn stared at Matheson but said, "Maani, to be taking that one home."

The man who'd brought her first words to Fahn stepped to Christa's side and slipped his arm through hers, leading her away.

Fahn was silent, watching Matheson until Christa had disappeared in the brush and the guards had faded back into it. Most of the Ohba turned to watch the place where the fronds swayed behind them—including Gant, who'd been so quick to rap Matheson on the back of the skull before. *What are they watching for?*

Fahn said, "Go."

Those dogs are still out there. Matheson shook his head, tired. "No."

"You are having your prize. Be leaving before we are regretting our generosity."

"We aren't done. You said you would tell me where the men are. Right now, this only ties you to the crime. It doesn't give me enough to pull Corporation House off the Ohbata."

"You are having no concern what is becoming of us."

"Maybe I don't care what becomes of *you*, Uncle Fahn, but I do care that the Ohba shouldn't be wiped off the face of Gattis. And you certainly do."

"You should be at telling me why you are concerned in our affairs."

Matheson caught himself tilting his head in a too-familiar gesture and answered slowly, "I've picked up the idea from a *superior officer* that Gattis Corporation owes all Ohba a debt. It's reprehensible to let the corporation eliminate an entire people for its own convenience. Tell me where the men are, I'll go away, and you save your people from trouble."

"There is always being a price, or the exchange is having no value." Fahn looked sly. "We should be having a wager . . ."

"I've got nothing—"

"There is still being the female."

Matheson knew the rules now, and he rolled his eyes. "Answer's still being no to that one."

Fahn shook his head and chuckled. "We are telling you where your animals are being. But if we are winning, this yellow female is staying until now you are catching your prey. If *you* are winning . . . you are both going free."

Matheson was pretty sure Fahn wouldn't kill a hostage. He was a wily bastard who would hold on to leverage no matter how distasteful he found it—which would explain his helping a Dreihle. But leaving Aya with him was not an option. "Sounds like you can't lose with this solution and you don't end up looking like you just got your principles handed to you by a woman," Matheson observed.

Fahn returned a blank stare.

Too much time had elapsed while Dillal wrestled with Neme's malice. But now rain had begun falling—seen as liquid silver running down the glass behind the executive floor's reception desk. That would delay any offensive by Corporation House against the ghettos, but only so long as the tropical downpour lasted. The lack of winds indicated that this was no early monsoon, just a storm likely to pass in mere hours.

Pritchet was not in his office. "Then where is he?" Dillal demanded of the Gattian woman guarding his door.

"Corporation House."

"What for?"

"I can't say. He was called in a few hours ago and hasn't been back."

No matter how he tried for more information, the woman gave up nothing. After fifteen minutes, Dillal moved away from her and stood within a meter of the windows. He watched the room in silence.

Just over an hour had passed when he took a sudden sharp breath, tilting his head and frowning, his gaze going still and distant.

Unnerved, the receptionist stood up and started toward him. "Inspector?"

He raised a hand to stop her, but nothing else in his stance or expression changed.

When she retreated to her desk, he dropped his hand, but continued staring into the distance, otherwise as unmoving as the Pillars of Archon that rose over the throat of the Cove of Stars. He remained distracted for twenty minutes or so, then raised his head suddenly, blinking, and looked at the receptionist.

"Tell the director we have the gun, but I can't take the man who used it unless Pritchet speaks with me immediately."

Matheson sighed. *This can't be good . . .* "What are we wagering on?" he asked.

Fahn turned and pointed just beyond the diners on the carpet to a series of posts that rose from the plantings near the dead branch hung with tiny bells.

"Tenzo is putting an orange on each of those. We and you are shooting them and winning, but if we or you are missing them . . ."

"The shooter loses. You and I both shoot from here?" Matheson asked, eyeing the distance.

Fahn shook his head with a smile and pointed to a spot near the edge of the clearing where they'd entered. "There."

It was sheltered from the rain that leaked through holes in the roof, but more than ten meters away, plus the three or four meters to the posts from where they stood. Not difficult with a rifle, under normal circumstances, but given his current aches and bruises, haunts of memory, exhaustion, lack of food . . . anything other than a lucky shot with a handgun was out of the question, as was running.

Knowing he was cornered, Matheson asked, "How many shots and with what?"

Fahn put his hand out and Gant unslung his own rifle and handed it over. Fahn held the weapon up—old and simple, with the most basic of sights, but it appeared to be in excellent condition. "Three oranges. Three shots."

"With a gun I'm unfamiliar with?" A bit of hope sparked, but Matheson knew better than to show it. He shook his head. "I don't even know that it works or if it's loaded."

Gant glared at him. Matheson put up his hands, asking. "Would you trust it if it were mine?"

Gant narrowed his eyes further, then let out a grunt and turned his gaze aside. But his swift defensiveness was almost proof enough for Matheson, who looked at Fahn. "We both use that rifle and you shoot first."

Fahn had no objection and they went through the ritual of inspecting and loading the piece and walked out to the firing distance while Tenzo set the oranges on the posts. Gant and one of his silent patrol partners escorted Aya and the storage box. The diners left the carpet and followed more slowly to assemble slightly to the left of the designated shooting position. Tenzo remained behind, keeping well off to the right and about halfway between the posts and the firing line. *Anyone half-witted enough to shoot him will be dead before they can reload.*

At the line, Matheson looked back and noted that the second orange was close to the bell-strewn branch's outstretched fan of twigs, and the third slightly behind the arch of the branch, so the shots became more difficult if taken from right to left. Fahn took a position to Matheson's right, giving himself an advantage. *No surprise.* The crowd was on Matheson's own left and unlikely to move, limiting his choice of positions and field of fire.

As Fahn raised the rifle, Matheson stuck his fingers in his ears and pressed hard. Gant and Fahn laughed at him, but Matheson ignored them. He watched Fahn as he aimed, then Matheson shifted his gaze to the easiest of the targets down range.

Fahn's first shot was slightly off to the left, but still good enough to splatter the plants behind it with pulp and juice, sending the scent of oranges and gun smoke into the resinous air of the old greenhouse.

Minimal recoil, the noise wasn't as bad as he'd feared, and there was no sudden vision of blood-soaked mud Matheson noted, but his ears would be ringing by the time the contest was over. Matheson offered Fahn a "not bad" expression, which received a sly smile in return.

Shot two was on-center and the orange vanished in a puff of pulpy chaff that rattled the nearest bells. This time, Matheson only gave a thin smile, and waited for shot number three.

Fahn reset his feet a little and lined up his last shot. From his position to Matheson's right, Fahn had a much cleaner line of fire. *And I'll probably be offered little chance to adjust* my *position.*

Shot three barely hit the orange on its right side, spinning it off the post and raising a chime from all the bells. Tenzo walked out to place new oranges on the posts. Matheson unplugged his ears and offered a congratulatory handshake to Fahn, but received the rifle instead.

"You are being at it," Fahn said.

Matheson blinked in surprise, taking the gun. He dropped the magazine, opened the breach, checked it was clear, then reloaded, taking his time, which clearly irritated both Fahn and Gant. *That's fine.*

Matheson grounded the rifle butt to free his hands and ripped away the torn pocket and its flap from his shirt front. Fahn and Gant watched him with narrowed eyes. Matheson smiled and poked the torn fabric into his ears—*better than nothing.*

Once Tenzo had returned and joined the other Ohba, Matheson shouldered the rifle and looked down the barrel—the sights were clean and easy to use, but fairly broad. *Shoots slightly left . . .*

Fahn raised one finger, drawing Matheson's attention to him.

Matheson lowered the stock from his shoulder and restrained an urge to growl his frustration. Instead, he gave an inoffensive lift of his eyebrows while pulling the fabric from his nearest ear.

"You should not be striking the bells," Fahn said.

"Why?"

"The spirit tree's bells are containing the souls of our dead."

Matheson closed his eyes and forced a smile—*of course there's a complication . . .* "And they wouldn't like to be shot." He reopened his eyes and stared Fahn down. "What's the penalty for disturbing them?"

"We are killing you."

Merry fucking hell. "Naturally." *And the dogs are out there if we make a break for it.* Matheson tucked the bit of rag back into his ear.

He dropped to one knee and lined up the first shot. The rifle was warm against his cheek and he squeezed . . .

The orange burst and threw pulp down into the bushes. Matheson's ears buzzed a little and the heat of the combustion gases fanned over his wrist as the spent case ejected. *A bit high.*

He didn't linger. He lined up the next shot, adjusting slightly down, and eased the trigger back until it snapped like glass breaking.

An expanding cloud of orange chunks was the only thing left above the post. He could smell it, but the blast and report covered any sound. The bells on the spirit tree didn't move.

Matheson grounded the rifle and dropped prone beside it. His sore back and shoulders objected to the curvature of his spine as he re-shouldered the gun. But he could see the orange clearly under the arch of the tree branch and he lined up the shot as quickly as he could. *Fahn's going to be disappointed, but he can go jump.* Matheson squeezed the trigger . . .

The spirit tree shivered as the orange vanished behind it in a fragrant spray.

The ringing in his head and pressure in his ears made Matheson a little dizzy and he got slowly to his feet. Gant was right there, reaching for his rifle, but Matheson dropped the magazine and cleared the gun before he handed them over. Gant took them with a thoughtful expression as Matheson pulled the stuffing from his ears and shook his head. The thumping of his blood vanished and took the dizziness with it, but his hearing was still muted with a high whining sound.

As Matheson turned, he could see Fahn laughing, then the shape of a word on his lips, but he couldn't hear it as more than a bass rumble. He started toward Fahn, ready to shake the location out of him, but Aya snatched his elbow and tugged him around.

Shaking her head, she began walking back down the twisted aisle of plants by which they'd entered. The Ohba stood aside and let her go. Matheson went with her. She led the way with hasty steps and handed him the gun box, revealing the mobile she'd hidden under it.

Matheson checked their backs continually for the first few minutes, then only occasionally until they were back inside the cliff tunnel, groping forward by nothing more than the illumination of the mobile's screen. No one followed them and they slipped back through the fissure to the Dreihleen side.

When they finally reached a branching in the tunnel, Aya tugged him into it and turned him to face her. She leaned into his body, pressing her mouth to his ear. "I'm have it."

She swiped the mobile screen and showed him a long log of audio stream data and voice-to-text translation. At the bottom was a single word.

The receptionist walked the inspector down the hall to Pritchet's door. She watched him go inside and the door closed again behind him. Pritchet waited on the far side of his desk.

Dillal started forward, then flinched as if he'd been hit and clapped his hands over his ears. Then he snorted as if disgusted with himself.

Pritchet stared with quickly concealed alarm. "What is it?"

"Gunshots."

"What? Where?" Pritchet demanded, stepping toward him.

Dillal waved off his concern. "In my data stream."

Pritchet looked relieved. "So it's not live."

"It is, but of no threat to anyone's health. I have—or will within an hour—a murder weapon used at the Paz da Sorte. And the location where I can find the men who used it. I need you to call off further action against the ghettos."

"Why?"

"Because Corporation House's excuse is spurious—there's no racial connection in the case. The killers are Dreihleen, just as the victims were."

"That's not what we've been told."

"Any connection between the Ohbata and the Dreihleat is not material to the case. Where did you get your information?"

"From your lab."

Dillal glared at him. "That's not possible. Someone has told you a lie."

"And yet you have a dead lab technician—"

"Mr. Starna is not dead and his unhappy circumstance has no bearing—"

"But you didn't say there's no evidence that links the two ghettos."

"It's not germane—" Dillal winced again, twice in quick succession.

Pritchet used Dillal's distraction to step close to the inspector. "The ammunition is from the Ohbata, via an arms dealer named Bomodai. And yet, despite everything I've invested in you, you didn't give me this information—if you even had it," Pritchet snapped, looming over Dillal.

The inspector grunted through gritted teeth and raised his head, fixing Pritchet with the red-and-gold reflection of light off the lens and exposed frame of his artificial eye. "Because you would have misused it, as you clearly have. You know that action against the people of Gattis is not warranted, that Corporation House is only looking for an excuse to destroy them to protect the interests of certain First Settlement families."

"It's not *my* plan—I don't want this any more than you do, Dillal, but the evidence is out."

"*Rumor* is out. If you let the corporation's plans for the Dreihleat and Ohbata go ahead, the end result will be tens of thousands of deaths. All predicated on a false assumption. The cause of the Paz da Sorte massacre is not racial strife—but if this case isn't solved, there will be strife and more death than we've already seen. Let me resolve my case and there will be no cause for violence on any side. And your faith in this project will be vindicated."

He twitched once more and Pritchet stepped away. "You actually have something. You're not blowing smoke in my face?" the director asked.

Dillal shook himself, then stood straight and still, facing Pritchet. "Yes. I'm telling you the truth. Matheson has the weapon used. It will connect the crimes to the man who used it and him to others—just men, not a conspiracy or revolution-in-waiting. An ugly, stupid crime, but not of concern to the corporation's running of the planet."

Pritchet scowled and studied Dillal. "No. No . . . you're lying to me about something, but it's more than your life is worth to fail here. So . . . if you can bring these people in, I can call off the dogs."

"You must persuade Corporation House to withdraw first, or I can't move."

"Ah. So, they're in the Dreihleat. That only makes the corporation's plans better."

"They are not in Dreihleat Ang'Das nor Ohbata Ang'Das. Moving on the ghettos at this time and for this reason will only cause exactly the uprising you and I do not want." Dillal paused and smiled very slightly, his gaze defocused for another moment before he continued, "Tell Corporation House they must hold until I bring the perpetrators in. And after that there will be no need to for the action they contemplate. No. Need."

"I won't be able to buy you much time, even with that. Maybe a day or a day and a half, given the timing. And you'd better bring back a hell of a case-closer, because I'm running out of favors to call in."

"I will."

Pritchet sighed and looked tired. "Where are these men?"

"Agria."

CHAPTER TWENTY-SEVEN

Day 6: Monday—In Transit

The lifter swayed and rattled as it rose over the planet. The sub-orbital hop from the edge of one continent to the middle of the other would take six hours to cross almost fourteen thousand kilometers.

Nothing good ever happens to cops in the middle of the night. Matheson lay on his side with his eyes clenched shut, trying not to think about the transport that had crashed into the canal. He'd never been afraid of jumps or lifters before, and he should have been asleep—he'd had little enough that his mind was slow and his body leaden as well as sore—but the thought of being trapped if this craft met a similar fate over the Sea of Pearls kept returning and knotting up in bits of memory. The SO's face in the flooding pilot pod; violet mud oozing beneath him, his knee to the ground; the weight of a rifle stock on his shoulder; shouts that became the jangle of broken bells . . . Pieces slid into his mind as he dropped toward sleep and knifed him back to the misery of the moment—traveling by continent-class freight hopper and entangled in his own wretched thoughts. Apparently "first available transport" didn't take much notice of the state of the passengers wedged in with the goods and equipment being transferred from Ariel to Agria. Two exhausted policemen were just more cargo.

It must be nice to believe in some god and leave the worry of crashing into the sea to them . . . him . . . her . . .

"Possibly."

Matheson hadn't realized he'd spoken until Dillal replied.

He rolled in his sling to see the inspector on the other side of the dimly lit passenger pod. "I'm sorry, sir. I didn't mean to disturb you."

"I'm no more able to sleep than you, Matheson. I feel I've already failed—spent too much of our time running interference in GISA's meddling on behalf of Gattis Corporation's avarice, rather than doing the job I was intended for. And left you to the fire too often. Between injuries and actions—mine included—this must have been one of the worst days you've spent here."

Matheson was glad of something to take his mind off the ceramic-and-steel eggshell that was hurtling through sub-orbital space with them inside. "Having the merry shit beaten out of me was worse. At least this time I did what I set out to do. We may have saved some people from drowning—though that's really down to you and Aya—and no one beat me bloody today, nor shot me, shocked me, or drowned me. Another thing I owe Aya, but—"

"But?"

Matheson shook his head and rubbed his hands over his face. "She hates me, but she stood with me, helped me, protected me . . ."

"Did you not do the same?"

"Yes, but, not *in spite* of who she is. When we parted at the East Gate . . ."

Aya handed him the box and stepped back, her expression stiff. "You're go to Djepe. Find Hoda—you're not find Oso I'm think."

He tucked the gun box under his arm. "You think or you hope?"

"Think. Fahn's only speak of Banzet. For Oso I'm cold. He's poison our hopes, but I'm still burn for what should be. I'm to Norenin and do what I must. For you I'm can have nothing."

She turned sharply away and left him standing as she walked back into the Dreihleat, back straight and head high.

He felt like he'd been kicked in the gut.

He dropped his hands and stared upward. "I'm guilty, but I'm not to *blame* for Donetti. 'I have nothing for you'—that's what Con Robesh told me, too, but Aya did give me . . . something. And I can't understand why you didn't tell me."

"That she's my half-sister? That I knew you were sleeping with her? Something else?" The inspector's voice seemed slower than usual.

"All of it."

"Aya and I are hardly bound together, close as rose and thorn," Dillal said. Then he sighed. "And I . . . I needed you to make your own evaluation, not to be swayed by the familial relationship."

"You told me to be wary of her."

"I would have said the same in regard to any contact you had grown too close to. But in the end, your own judgment must guide you. As hers will."

"I see."

"Your connecting the silence of the victims' families to the political cause . . . was impressive."

"Thank you." Matheson shifted in surprised discomfort, and changed the subject. "What about this business with Starna?"

Dillal shook his head. "Poor, rash Starna. Dr. Woskyat is technically more proficient, but not as driven or intuitive—and she also has problems—but she's already confirmed that the rifling on the gun you retrieved matches bullets from the scene. Positive identification of the fingerprints should be simple once the gun is fully dismantled and inspected. Now we know why they used the spray seal—to avoid leaving prints their dangerous allies could use against them."

"Can we be sure there are prints? Uncle Fahn is a twisty old bastard and while the rifling matches some of the bullets, so far it's only his word that the gun was used by Tchintaka or Banzet. And why was Fahn even involved?"

"There was a middle man—that's another link yet to be made. Everything that happens in the Green Houses territory falls into Fahn's purview, whether it's done by Ohba or outsider."

Matheson, tired and scared as he was, talked just to avoid thinking of where he was. "And how are we going to find Banzet on Agria—the continent's twice the size of Ariel and we have no idea where he is."

"Fingerprints are taken on entry to any Agrian port," Dillal replied, as if each word had grown longer. "We'll be able to discover which camp via the intake records when we arrive."

"Why didn't that come up on my search?"

"We didn't have a fingerprint, only a name that he'd be an imbecile to use." The inspector sighed again. "I feel that I am somehow culpable—at least for Starna, less so for the rest, but still stained with it. I pushed him too hard and he imagined that he could take any blame off my shoulders by casting himself as scapegoat—the deluded met who over-reaches and falls to his inescapable doom. Ironically, delusion was one thing he didn't suffer from. It all feels inevitable, from the dead at Paz to the dead in yesterday's streets, Starna, the canal—unavoidable consequences of the system gone mad."

"But not because of you," Matheson said, as much in his own defense as Dillal's.

"Why not? I'm no young idealist from out-system. I'm as much part of this culture as any of us—more, perhaps. I chose to dig myself deeper into it because I am the thing that was meant to be and never happened."

"Your sister said something about all the Gattian races dwindling down. Is that what you mean?"

Dillal peered at Matheson a moment. "I hadn't realized she'd paid any heed to those stories our mother whispered. Half of them weren't true, of course—there is no Great Breath, death bells don't contain souls, and sollets don't shed their skins to become human and dance on the islands of the Verdan Archipelago in the summer moonlight."

He turned his gaze to the ceiling, a dull red gleam smearing at the edge of the prosthesis frame. "The Three Races of Gattis, though . . . 'Once upon a time, before we were Dreihleen, there were three races of Gattis and they were called Red Team, Yellow Team, and Blue Team. They were each special, created for special work, and meant to build this beautiful planet for all to share.' It sounds like a fairy tale but it's as true as it is terrible. If you dig far enough into the charter you'll see. In the historical logs, in the records of the gene engineers and biologists . . ."

Dillal sounded exhausted, thoughts wandering, more as if he were talking in his sleep than carrying on a waking conversation and Matheson could hear the influences of Dreihleen and Ohba in his unguarded speech. "We were to be one people—red, yellow, and blue all united—but it didn't work. Low birth rates, division, marginalization . . . and then the oppression, the isolation, the tribalism . . . We tear ourselves apart, fearing for our survival, fearing the other, hating ourselves and everyone else even more.

"And the result is crimes like this. I'm willing to risk my life to change that, but I shouldn't have risked others. The Forensic Integration Project represents a chance—no more—though there are people who hoped I'd die in the process. If I fail—or even before that—they may get their wish."

"It can't be that bad . . ." Matheson objected, but Dillal didn't look well.

"The ocular functions, the mechanics, electronics, sensors, data . . . I've gained good control over the system, but this . . ." Dillal said, spreading his arms and then letting them fall back onto his chest—he looked like a corpse as he did—"this machine of flesh and bone is in distress. I've done everything Andreus told me not to do. I can feel the cracks in my skull weeping, the unhealed wounds . . ." He fell silent.

Matheson waited for the inspector to speak again, but he didn't. After a while Dillal's head lolled a bit toward him, left eye slightly open and right eye closed. Matheson's heart jolted in his chest and he sat up, catching his breath from the sharp complaints of a few still-angry bruises. He started climbing out of the passenger sling to see if Dillal was dead, but the inspector stirred slightly.

Matheson had begun to think the man didn't sleep at all and this evidence of frail humanity, surprisingly, calmed him. He lay back down and closed his own eyes.

CHAPTER TWENTY-EIGHT

Day 6: Agria—Afternoon

They'd lifted in one storm to come down in another. Even in pouring, windswept rain, Port Hyldra's chaotic bustle surpassed the first impression Matheson had gotten from Angra Dastrelas on his arrival a month before. The port was smaller, but the sense that everything must move immediately was overwhelming. The ground was a perpetual wash of thin blue mud across the hardscape of landing pads and building aprons without a wisp of plant life to be seen within the perimeter. And in spite of the downpour, it was hot. It was all under Gattis Corporation, but it almost seemed like another world.

They hitched thin storm coats over their shoulders and made their way out of the complex, passing the carcass of a local azure-and-bronze-striped razor cat hung by its heels from the top of a freight door. Scimitar claws as long as Matheson's hand scratched tracks in the ground as the door swung to the comings and goings of Gattis Corporation employees wearing Agria Corps blues, and groups in unfamiliar uniforms, bearing the hard look of experienced ground fighters. SOs with sharp-eyed dogs patrolled the fences. Matheson glanced at Dillal, who looked grim.

"Pritchet's bought us time, but not much," the inspector muttered. "And there aren't as many microtransmitters here—data connection is intermittent at best. We'll have to get to the GISA offices to retrieve whatever forensic reports Dr. Woskyat's forwarded."

The regional office in Hyldra was more like a military base than a police headquarters—an ugly, cement-printed structure only two stories tall that sprawled at the edge of the original town. Newer buildings had sprung up along each side and stretched the town north and south, but nothing penetrated into the fields on the east farther than the walls and fences of Hyldra Regional, which reached all the way out to the ring road surrounding the town.

The reception area smelled of mold and the light-blue-clad SO on desk duty was more openly shocked by the sight of Dillal than anyone in Angra Dastrelas had been. She took a step back as they stopped in front of her. "What in fuck—?"

Dillal growled impatiently as he stripped off his wet coat and laid his left wrist on the security plate beside the barrier. Matheson showed the gaping woman his own ID, not bothering to analyze his pleasure at looming over her. "Inspector Dillal—Angra Dastrelas Regional CIFO. I'm SO Matheson, his acting IAD. We're in pursuit of two fugitives. You should have access and information notices about it." He wasn't inclined to be much more friendly than Dillal—his tolerance for the staring and stupidity was at a low ebb.

The locks on the barrier clanked open without the help of the desk SO. She jumped at the sound and shot her gaze at Dillal, then back to Matheson. "Let your Regional Director know we're here," Matheson said. "We'll be in the investigation office, unless you have a private office the inspector can use."

The SO eyed Matheson warily, her eyes shifting to Dillal and back as the inspector let himself through the gate. "The senior contract intake officer is on leave," she said, pointing down the spiderweb of hallways to their left.

Dillal shook his head and Matheson mirrored the action. "We need access to the investigation database."

She darted her tongue over her lips. "Um. We only have one data trunk, here."

Matheson sighed with disgust—he didn't need to see Dillal to know his expression was the same. "That'll have to do." He took off his own dripping coat and walked through the gate before he turned back to the SO. "Which way to this office?"

"Orange slideway on hallway two to Contract Intake, then second door on the left."

Matheson nodded and turned away. Dillal was several steps ahead of him and didn't respond to the woman's hiss for attention. Matheson spun back impatiently.

"What the hell's a Sifo?" she asked.

He glared at the SO. "Look it up—you'll find it under 'nemesis.'" He turned to catch up to Dillal.

The SO's directions took them to a staff entrance, saving them the trouble of getting in through the main doors. *I should have been kinder to her.* The contract intake office was busy, muddy, noisy, and crowded with the desperate individuals willing to work in the agricamps voluntarily for pay that never seemed to get them out of whatever debt had driven them to agree to the contract in the first place. *How does anyone sink so low that they'll endure this filth and cacophony to do some of the grubbiest and least-necessary work in the known worlds?* Elsewhere, agriculture was managed by technicians and machines, not by stoop labor. But the more he overheard, the more he understood: the staple crops and livestock were not what required attention, but the exotic, engineered products— like Regausa silk—that were unique to Gattis. Matheson doubted the need, but the practice kept the prices high and gave Gattis Corporation a place to dump the destitute, derelict, and dispossessed.

The senior intake officer's lair was more like a glorified hallway than an office—long and narrow with a door at each end so the unending line of contractees could enter singly through one portal and vanish out the other. Matheson and Dillal had come in through the crowd of intakes who were trying to find the way out with their completed paperwork in hand. Only a few had been startled by Dillal's appearance—most were too dazed to notice—and none of them seemed inclined to linger or follow the rumpled ofiçes into the empty office. Matheson locked both doors while Dillal logged in.

"It's slower than the system in Angra Dastrelas," Matheson said.

"It appears it hasn't been upgraded since I was here twelve years ago. Even in the buildings the microtransmitter density is poor. We won't be able to rely on this system once we're in the field. Upload anything you'll need from here to your mobile now."

"How do they operate with a data stream that's unreachable in the field?"

"Brute force and a blind eye. But it also keeps information from leaking."

That explained the silence about Camp Donetti.

"What did Woskyat get?" Matheson asked.

Dillal barely glanced at the display. "She's forwarded Starna's reports as well—the material on Leran's wrist was, as you suggested, Robesh's tissue mixed with seal and solvent. Starna's absence is slowing all reports while Woskyat and the rest take up the slack. She pushed the sole impression down the priority queue to look for prints on the gun. She found some on interior parts. They don't match Tchintaka or anyone else, but there is DNA trace that confirms the prints as Banzet's. It won't put him at the scene, but it does put the gun in his hand, which is enough for now. And that same fingerprint was in-processed under the name 'Ebanez' three days ago—"

"Three? Fahn gave the impression he received the gun yesterday— or today—I'm not sure which day this is now."

"He allowed you to take that impression."

"Like you."

"Call it a family failing," Dillal replied.

Matheson snorted and was surprised he could be amused at anything. "So nothing on Tchintaka out here, only Banzet."

"Yes, but Norenin had little choice other than giving up one man to protect the other. Once we find Banzet, we'll know where Tchintaka is."

"You think Banzet will give him up—if he knows?"

"Banzet ran while Tchintaka stayed. Why?"

Matheson responded without thinking twice. "Fear."

"An excellent lever," Dillal said, "once we find him—the camps are large . . ." Then he frowned.

"What?"

"Zanesh—the unaff in your report—is also on Agria."

"Merry hell—I missed it!"

Dillal raised a questioning eyebrow.

Matheson heaved a sigh of self-disgust. "He was running from Jora and Halfennig and I assumed it was just petty arm-twisting, but he's the one who said Venn and Denny were connected through the Friends—like a typical Dreihle, he gave the answer I asked for, but not in a way I understood. He knows more and I—"

Dillal put up his hand to stop Matheson's self-recriminations. "You're learning but you're too impatient yet, and you still trust people too readily. You begin with the tenth question rather than asking for the nine answers you know first."

"You make this sound easy and me even less competent . . ." But Dillal wasn't listening. He had the distracted, distant stare he wore when listening to the datastream.

"It must be Ejeirie," Dillal said, "and it will be much easier to find one young criminal there than to find one contractor."

"What's Ejeirie?"

"It's the only combined agricamp—the primary penal intake, but it's a trustee unit. Well-behaved, low-risk prisoners are allowed to work there, supplementing contractees who work directly with the transports."

"Sounds like a soft berth compared to the rest of this place."

"You won't think so when you see it."

There was no rain at Ejeirie. There'd been none for years. What fell from the sky there was fire, and the ground in every direction was cinder and ash that smoldered forever. Mount Toska was more than two hundred meters farther out the peninsula—an impressive sight from upwind. The volcano had risen unexpectedly due to the cracking of Gattis' crust in the early days of the terraforming project, and now sat in picturesque splendor only a few kilometers away from Agria's northern peninsula—a peninsula that had not existed before the volcano rose and pushed magma into the seabed until the volcanic island and the continent were nearly joined by a land bridge of basalt. Theory said the eruption would subside in a few decades. In the meantime, it made a lovely tourist attraction—from a safe distance— and a perfect hell of the land below it. Nothing grew, nothing crept, and the air was too hot, dry, and dirty to breathe without filters. At Ejeirie it was tolerable and Gattis Corp's engineers, biologists, and botanists had found ways to make the ashfall pay, harnessing the heat and pressure, and breeding freakish plants and creatures that thrived in the filthy atmosphere and killing heat. The post, fields, and port were a shifting landscape of windblown ash and everything was gray with it. There were no birds, dogs, or cats to be seen around the port. Only lizards.

The silken ash and black volcanic grit got into everything.

Transports had to be moved under cover as soon as they landed and fitted with expendable filters for their initial jump out. All other vehicles were closed-system electric or heat-transfer drives because nothing else could survive the constant abrasion. Everyone wore caps and coveralls, breathing filters and eye protection, but the grime still slipped past.

The work of moving the transports and their cargo fell mostly to contractees who came and went as their shifts allowed. The trustee prisoners stayed on the enclosed side of the fence in roughly roofed staging areas, and organized cargo for transshipment. They hauled the electric pallets from the gates to the warehouses by hand. It was filthy work and Zanesh's filter barely covered his nose and mouth. Matheson almost didn't recognize the boy he'd caught outside the cliff houses.

But Zanesh recognized him. He started to bolt, but only got a few steps before he was stopped by two GISA Agria Corps Internment Control SOs. They waved their batons in the kid's face, their filthy cheeks cracking above the edges of their filters as they smiled, and the unaff turned back. Matheson waited by the electric pallet and took the boy's arm when he returned.

Zanesh lifted his chin and stared sideways at Matheson—a distinct change in attitude since they'd last met. "What you're want?" the boy asked, his mouth tight and teeth clenched even behind the filter.

In the falling ash, Matheson understood the practicality of the Dreihleen speech habit. His own mouth was already rank with cinders. "Come with me," he said, "and I'll tell you."

The boy shrugged and walked with Matheson into the dorm building's prep porch, followed by the two SOs. Matheson removed his outdoor gear, then wiped the dirt and sweat from his face, hair, and hands, but Zanesh was not given the opportunity to do more than pull his own cap, filter, and eye shields off. Matheson picked up a small pod of water and rinsed the filthy taste of the ashfall from his mouth, spat the blackened water into a wash sink, and poured out the rest. Then he led the boy down the room and into the stark gray-and-white mess hall, leaving the two SOs to return to their duties outside.

Dillal waited for them, clean and seated at a table that was set with pitchers of water and a bowl filled with fruit from more temperate camps in the south. Two new guards stood far at the back by the administration wing door, GISA's orange star-and-stripe logo bright on the light blue of their Agria Corps uniforms. Dillal shot them a glance and they stepped into the hall, locking the door behind them.

Zanesh stopped at the edge of the table and turned a cold stare on the inspector, who gave the boy no acknowledgement, and only picked up an orange from the bowl and a small knife from the table top. Matheson nudged Zanesh onto the bench across from Dillal and stood to his right, blocking the easy way out. He received a sneer for his efforts and wondered which attitude was for real—this one or the one he'd seen in Angra Dastrelas.

Zanesh watched Dillal begin peeling the skin off the orange in a long, continuous spiral, his gaze shifting from the inspector's hands to his face and back down over and over. The fruit was half unwrapped and dripping juice onto the table top when the inspector spoke. "Zanesh Farrazee. You remember my IAD beside you."

The boy made a rude noise in his throat that could have meant anything.

"In words, or I'll have your duties switched up to the admin building," Dillal said, not looking up, "and certain people will be told you've been . . . especially accommodating."

The boy glared.

"Once again. You remember SO Matheson."

"I'm know him," Zanesh grumbled.

The right corner of Dillal's mouth turned up a fraction. "And you know who I am."

Zanesh rolled his eyes. "I'm know you, too, met." Then he turned his head and gave Matheson a cocky look. "I'm fooled you, dehka."

Dillal drove his thumb into the peeled orange. The juice ran onto the table top, pattering like rain. "Ah, now that's ruined," he said and flung the fruit aside.

Zanesh watched the orange splatter on the angelstone floor. He drew in a sharp little breath, then wrenched his gaze back to the table top. "I'm tell what he's ask." He sounded defensive.

"Of course," said Dillal, picking up a round, dark purple fruit which he began to score along the meridian with his knife. One of Zanesh's eyes narrowed slightly as if the sight made him uncomfortable.

Dillal continued, "Like any Dreihle, you know the value of what you say. But you knew something much more useful that you didn't tell."

"Why I'm should? What he's offer me? Two collectors're almost take me—"

"SOs Jora and Halfennig. What did those two want with you? Shaking down unaffs is hardly worth their time, yet they were looking for you."

The thick, hard skin of the fruit split and Dillal pulled it apart without looking up. The slight smell of caramel and grass floated into the air as the bulbous white segments within were revealed. "They're would killed me!" Zanesh objected in a tight voice, his eyes flicking up to Dillal's face and back down.

"Why?"

"Go jump," the boy muttered, but his tone lacked conviction.

Dillal smashed the fruit onto the table top and swept the mess onto the floor without a change of expression or a glance at the boy.

The sweet smell of the pulp flooded upward as pale juice splashed onto the boy's coverall sleeve, leaving little clear dots in the dirt.

Zanesh shrank back a little.

"The first month is the hardest," Dillal said. "After that, you begin to forget any taste but ash, any rest without fear, or that you have ever felt clean."

The boy stared at him without speaking for nearly a minute. *What's happened to him in only four days?*

Dillal's voice remained as cool as ever. "Why?"

Zanesh lowered his gaze to the table top, swallowing and unconsciously rubbing his crusted lips together.

Dillal poured water into a clear cup, the sound unnaturally loud in the near-empty room.

Zanesh cut his eyes toward the glass and they grew wider as Dillal pushed the glass toward him. The moment Zanesh reached for it, the inspector tipped it over and the water spread across the table top, running over the edge and onto the floor, splashing over the boy's hands and turning to black mud as it washed the ash from his skin and sleeves.

The boy stifled a whimper.

Dillal tilted his head slightly, enough to catch the unaff's attention. "That will be your fate if you remain here, Zanesh. Spilled and forgotten like water in sterile ground. Answer our questions without prevarication this time and perhaps you won't have to stay here."

The boy crossed his arms over his chest. He rested one hand on his upper arm where the scarred-over mark of his old association was. His coverall was darker and stiffer there and Matheson wondered if the old wound had become a new one.

Zanesh gave Dillal a sideways look. "Agria?" he asked.

"Ejeirie." Dillal let the right corner of his mouth quirk a little. "We'll see about the rest."

Zanesh glanced down at the spilled water one more time and wiped his mouth with the back of his free hand. "I'm overheard them plan."

"Who planning what?"

"Planning robbery of Paz." Zanesh shot a look at the water pitcher.

Dillal put his hand on the pitcher handle. "Who?"

Zanesh pressed his lips together and shifted his gaze to Dillal's, wincing slightly as he was forced to look at the hard metal and raw flesh around the inspector's gleaming cybernetic eye. "Denny. And Hoda."

The inspector raised his right eyebrow, tilting his head very slightly. A trickle of bloody fluid oozed from below the prosthesis frame.

Zanesh shuddered and squeezed his eyes shut. "And Oso."

"Who do you think sent Jora and Halfennig after you?"

Zanesh kept his eyes closed. "Oso." He looked younger than his age and the name seemed to hurt him as he said it.

"You thought Osolin Tchintaka sent two bent patrol ofiçes to kill you because you knew he and Denenshe Leran and Hoda Banzet had planned to rob the customers at the Paz da Sorte and that plan had gone wrong and resulted in murder. Is that correct?"

The boy flinched and looked on the verge of throwing up or screaming. He rocked, bobbing his head until he seemed to catch a breath and swallowed hard. Then he finally looked at the inspector again, raising his head at an odd, tense angle. He forced words out. "And—and because I'm hear Oso ask Chanan Vela when's Dohan to take Venn to Paz."

"Are you saying that Osolin Tchintaka knew when Gil Dohan would be at the Paz da Sorte and that he would have Venn Robesh with him?"

The boy squirmed and rubbed at his tight mouth with the back of one filthy, skeletal hand. Then he blurted, "I'm say. I'm say that." Breath shuddered out of him as if it carried a weight away with it and Zanesh took several more deep breaths, his body loosening with relief. "When they're know I'm not tell, they're send me here."

"Who is 'they'?"

"Dehkas—Ofiçes Jora, Halfennig. They're take me up, send me here. By Oso's order."

Dillal smiled slightly and nodded to Matheson as he placed a glass of water in front of the boy. Zanesh snatched it before it could be withdrawn. He guzzled the water, letting it run over his chin and down his neck, leaving muddy tracks.

Matheson took over. "Would you recognize all three of these men on sight: Leran, Tchintaka, and Banzet?"

The unaff looked up at Matheson, frowning as if puzzled. "I'm know them all. But Denny's left—he's dead."

"I know. Do you know where the other two are?"

"I'm know and I'm not."

Dillal put a round, golden fruit on the table between the boy and himself. Zanesh stared at the thing as if afraid of it. The inspector put the point of the knife dead center on the top of the orb and pushed down. The blade plunged in and sliced until it thumped into the table top. Pink juice ran onto the table, thinned by the water and swirling across the muddy surface. It smelled of guava, but anyone would have thought it was blood from the way Zanesh recoiled.

"I shall be specific," Dillal said. "Do you know where Osolin Tchintaka is?"

"I'm not know," said the boy.

"Is he on Agria?"

"I'm not know where he's at. At all."

Dillal drew the knife out of the guava and flicked the round fruit toward the boy. Zanesh caught it, but held the fruit against the table top and shifted his wide gaze from it to the inspector.

"If I were going to kill you, it would be cleanly, not by poison—nor by abandoning you to starvation and rape in a prison camp."

Matheson felt ill. He hadn't thought the boy could be more rattled by Dillal, but he twitched and seemed relieved when the inspector turned his head away with a look of mild disgust. They both sat in silence while Zanesh picked up the fruit, cautiously inspected it, and then devoured it.

Matheson resumed the interrogation once the guava was no more than a sticky stain. "What about Banzet? Is he here, in Ejeirie?"

Zanesh scowled. "Hoda . . . he's where I'm see from the fence—in contracts' camp."

"Do you know where he is at this moment?"

Zanesh thought about it and his expression grew wary. "Where he's *should* be—I'm know that. Where he's *might* be, I'm say's more help."

Matheson looked at Dillal and turned his head slowly back to Zanesh. He said nothing for a while and watched the dust on the boy's forehead slowly streaking with muddy sweat. Dillal moved and Zanesh flinched. The inspector was only turning the water pitcher around and around but it seemed to unnerve Zanesh.

The boy looked back at Matheson, breathing though his clenched teeth. "Oso's have friends, has eyes . . ." He seemed to be willing Matheson to understand something, but he wasn't quite getting it. The boy closed his eyes and raised one hand to his shoulder again. "I'm leave today."

Puzzled, Matheson glanced at the inspector who gave a small, somber shake of the head.

Then Dillal leaned forward and spoke softly. "Tell us where to find Banzet and you'll go with us. I won't let them kill you."

It was unlikely that Banzet knew Matheson on sight, so he went with one of the local SOs to pick the man up while Dillal removed Zanesh from Camp Ejeirie.

The area outside the penal camp was large and heavily trafficked by contractees and transport crews policed by GISA Agria Corps patrols, distinguished from everyone else only by the star-and-stripe on their coverall sleeves. The ever-falling ash quickly dimmed even the vibrant orange insignia to the point of being distinguishable only at close quarters and no one noticed the presence of a tall, light-skinned stranger among them. In his coverall, breathing filter, and shields over his blue eyes, it was the first time Matheson had felt completely anonymous on Gattis. He would have liked it better if his conscience wasn't itching. It would be too easy to continue being a bastard in a place like this, where every face was swathed in filters and rags, featureless as every other in the constant pall of cinder and dust.

He ran his hand over the reissued equipment on his belt, noting the wear on the baton and the empty loop where many of the local SOs and all of the transport crews carried additional weapons—anything from black-coated blades to cased handguns. The contractees made do with rougher knives, but Matheson saw no one other than prisoners who wasn't obviously armed.

Matheson and his escort wound through the edges of Ejeirie and into a contract slum—there was no better word for it. The contractees lived in minimal stack units, concrete-printed rows of them. The streets that ran between the stacks were covered by sloped panels that dumped the falling ash and cinder into gutters with a constant, metallic patter. The narrow passages were muddy with effluvium of an origin too easily guessed by the stench, and the air was dense and stank of burned insulation. The doors at each end of the stack units stood slightly ajar in warped frames, letting ash and dust creep through to the interiors.

Each building was like the next: living units on top, shops and brothels run by Gattis Corporation and their contractors on the bottom, interrupted occasionally by narrow food stalls, drug houses, or bars growing in the gaps like neon-tinted fungi. The air was too hot and dry for OLED vines, so all the signs were painted directly onto the walls in rough scrawls on top of older scrawls in whatever color had been available. At the end of the blocks lay workshops and storage units—rented at exorbitant rates. Makeshift lean-tos and temporary constructions built of scavenged materials filled every niche. As Matheson and the SO started down the last block, people scattered from these shanties carrying their belongings in their arms, some barely dressed, hobbling from injury, or clearly too dazed to know where they were going.

Matheson frowned. "Why are they running?" His voice sounded muffled and tinny through the breathing filter.

"We have to burn them out of these places every week or so— fire hazard," the SO replied. Matheson couldn't read his expression through the eye shields and filter mask.

"So . . . you set fire to their shelters."

"Object lesson. The buildings are safe enough in a controlled burn, and the free-riders learn to play by the rules."

"Any of these people die in the fires?"

"Once in a while. No great loss." The SO shrugged and continued forward. "The 'shop we want is at the end."

Matheson was glad for the covering that hid his expression of rage—he needed the escort too badly to give in and beat the smug prick, but the desire burned like acid. He followed the SO to the end and stopped outside the sealed metal door. *Fitting that the son of a machinist should go to ground in a repair workshop.* "Is there another entrance?" he asked.

"Should be one on the side."

"Guard that one. I'll take this."

This close, Matheson could see amused doubt in the other SO's eye. "Sure you will."

Matheson gave him a cold and silent stare, and waited until the SO had walked on. He half hoped someone would shiv the bastard once he was out of sight.

Matheson used his ID override on the lock and slipped through the doorway by the smallest possible opening. With the door closed again behind him, he removed his eye shields. The room was dim, the only light coming through dirty panes under the eaves. The effect was less like the watery light in Angra Dastrelas than it was like being under a moving cloud of insects that clicked and swarmed against the windows. He unhooked his filter to kill the sound of his own breath and crouched near the door, listening for movement. The rustling of cinders across the roof almost masked the creeping of feet over the rough floor. Matheson turned his head slightly side-to-side, trying to pinpoint the direction. *Heading from the interior corner to the side door.*

Matheson eased toward the side door as well, barely breathing, his footfalls as light as possible as he edged between the bulk of a cargo lift in the center of the room and racks of tools and equipment ranged along the walls. The man in the dimness brushed something that rattled. Matheson ducked and scrambled under one of the work supports, cutting off the approach to the side door. He snatched the Sun Spot from his belt and flicked the bright beam toward the sound.

The man yelped and turned, trying to escape, and ran against the lift. Matheson ran forward as the man tried to drop and squirm under the machinery or around the corner, eyes too dazzled to see.

It was an easy catch. The young man was clumsy and scared, and he went limp as Matheson grabbed his arm and hauled him back from the bulk of the lift. The side door to the workshop banged open, startling the man, who tried to spin and face the newcomer. Matheson held on and yanked him back around as he shot a look over his own shoulder.

The SO had come through the door with his baton out and the shock box up in his other hand. "Lock the door and turn on the lights," Matheson called out. "Then stay where you are."

"I don't think—"

"Noted. Now do as I say!" Matheson shouted, returning his attention to the man in front of him. He heard the SO grumbling as he secured the door and walked to the light switches.

The lights came up. "Ebanez?" Matheson asked the man in front of him. This young Dreihle was a far cry from Zanesh. Typically tall and slim, but his skin and hair were dull, his features bland to the point of forgettable and, while he was an adult at nineteen, his demeanor was more like a frightened child's. "You're not going to give that asshole a reason to drop you, are you?"

Matheson could see momentary hope flare in the cornered man's eyes at the use of his alias. He straightened up and looked Dreihle-wise at Matheson. "I'm not."

Matheson nodded and pushed back his cap so his face was easier to read. "My name's Matheson and I'm looking for Hoda Banzet."

The Dreihle was probably the worst liar on Gattis. He blanched and said, "I'm not know him," with his eyes wide.

Matheson ducked his chin and gave Banzet a disappointed look and a shake of the head. "Don't fuck with me, Hoda."

Banzet closed his eyes and sighed, his shoulders slumped in resignation. "Fairzee-mairzee. I'm caught." He looked at Matheson again. "What you're want?"

"I need to talk to you some place safer. About some friends of yours in Angra Dastrelas." Banzet bridled and tried to step back, but Matheson caught his arm again. "You really don't want to do that."

Banzet cut his glance toward the SO lingering by the back door.

"If you run, there's nothing I can do for you," Matheson said. "You come with me willingly, and I can protect you at least that far. Anything else is up to you."

Banzet shifted side to side and looked for a way out, but there was no move that didn't put him back in Matheson's hands or face down on the floor in the best case. He began shaking his head and seemed on the verge of tears.

Matheson returned to Camp Ejeirie with Banzet, who kept close to him and shot nervous glances at the SO who walked on his other side. *How's he survived this long?*

Coveralls and other gear were left in a prep porch and the three proceeded into the administration building and down labyrinthine halls. Banzet was nearly vibrating with his anxiety the whole way.

Dillal had moved to an unused briefing room at the edge of the camp compound. The room seemed more empty for having a single table and chair than it would have without any furniture at all. The inspector dismissed the accompanying SO while Matheson closed and locked the door inside.

Zanesh huddled in the farthest corner with his forehead pressed to his knees. He was clean, dressed in a thin singlet and trousers that didn't hide his too-prominent bones, and Matheson only recognized the boy by the position of extensive, oozing scabs covering his upper arm where the remains of his old tattoos had been carved away completely. Zanesh didn't respond in any way to Banzet's arrival, and Banzet seemed not to know him, his gaze traveling over the boy without a pause. Banzet stopped in his tracks at sight of Dillal.

The inspector stood at the short end of the table—which was laden with a half-dozen drinking pods of water—and looked the young man over. Dillal tilted his head and Banzet lowered his, no longer meeting anyone's eye.

"I'm Inspector Dillal. My assistant, SO Matheson," the inspector said, making a small indicative nod. His speech sounded more Dreihleen than usual. "You're Hoda Banzet, heh?"

Banzet nodded.

"Where you're from?" Dillal sounded conversational, casual at least, if not quite friendly.

"Nort'koot." *Northcut. Hell of an accent.* "I'm come to Angra . . . eight, nine months gone."

"Good." Dillal handed the man a pod of water. "Drink this."

Banzet looked at the container with suspicion. "Will't kill me?"

"No. But we're have much to say, you and I."

Banzet toyed with the water pod a moment, then opened it and took a small sip. He rinsed his mouth and spat the water into his free hand. He looked at it and wiped the moisture onto the hem of his shirt. The smear he left behind was gritty black. "Z'like digging in mines, here. Z'dark, filthy . . ." He drank half the remaining water before he nodded and looked sideways at Matheson.

"Just answer our questions," Matheson said, "and you'll be fine."

Banzet didn't seem to believe anything was going to be fine; his face was slack in despair and he barely looked up as Dillal told him to take a seat. There was only one chair—set at the long edge of the table but turned to face Dillal at the end. Banzet didn't move the chair, but slumped into it as it was. If he turned his head he could see Zanesh in the corner, but that meant turning away from Dillal. Matheson moved to stay closer to the door, putting himself just inside Banzet's peripheral vision. There was no place Banzet could look and see them all at once without rising from the chair, which only made him jumpier.

"Where's Osolin Tchintaka?" Dillal asked.

"What? I'm not know," Banzet replied, running his fingers around the bulge of the water pod.

Dillal's lips twitched. "You're know Denenshe Leran."

Banzet frowned at Dillal's shoes and raised one shoulder in a defensive half-shrug. "I'm meet him."

"More than that. You're with him when he's left."

Banzet looked ill and closed his eyes, gagging a little, then swallowing hard. Matheson tried not to wince in sympathy while he stayed silent and out of the way.

"Why you were there?" Dillal asked.

"For money."

Dillal smiled and shook his head. "You're not need it. Your family's good business in Northcut."

"Z'not for me."

"Five nights past in Dreihleat Ang'Das, sixteen people're killed in a jasso called Paz da Sorte—the Peace of Luck—is ironic for a place's neither peace nor luck. One of these Dreihleen's a beautiful girl. Venn Robesh. Only seventeen. She's die in a terrible way. And Denny Leran's found beside her. You're tell me how this's happen."

The pod dropped from Banzet's hand and bounced on the floor, spewing water, as the young man put his face in his hands. He doubled forward, shoulders shaking convulsively, until his elbows were locked to his chest. Gritty gray tears dripped from between his fingers and ran down his wrists in dark tracks, and he pulled in a long, shuddering breath.

Dillal rested his fingers on Banzet's shoulder. The young man shivered and pushed his wet hands into his own hair. His eyes were wide with horror. "He's killed her. Denny. Her pretty face . . . And we're—and we're—He's kill me next."

"Not Denny Leran."

"Oso. Oso . . ." Banzet breathed in hysterical snorts as he twisted in the chair and pinned his gaze to the floor. "He's say we're have to—have to wait. But there's a boy. A boy's know what we're have done. And the boy. He's *left*."

In the corner, Zanesh stirred and hugged his arms tighter around his legs, but didn't look up. Matheson glanced at Dillal but the inspector shook his head in silence.

Banzet continued, "Norenin's say dehkas're come. Oso's say I'm wait—wait. But I'm run!" He raised his head at last, muddy tracks on his face and hands, and his eyes stared at nothing. "He's . . . kill me."

Dillal stepped back to the edge of the table again, unruffled, though Matheson thought he looked pale. "Why?"

"Because I'm know!"

"No one else?"

"The boy—but he's . . . left."

"Norenin's not know, or Vela?"

"Only we."

"You and Denny . . ."

"And Oso."

"No one else?"

Banzet shook his head and bared his teeth. "There's none but us!"

"But you're here and Denny Leran's dead. Who'll harm you?"

"Oso."

Dillal's silence seemed to prompt him better than speech. "Osolin Tchintaka," Banzet said.

"What happened at Paz, we believe that was a mistake," Matheson started and Banzet jumped as if he'd forgotten anyone but Dillal and himself existed, "—not something any of you intended. You think Tchintaka is capable of cold blooded murder?"

Banzet nodded, rocking. "He's would kill for this. He's do."

"And you think he'll kill you."

"Like Denny's killed the girl."

"With a gun?" Matheson asked.

Banzet shook his head, still hysterical, but not as spasmodic. "Z'plasma. Like the girl. He's got no gun now."

Matheson frowned. "But there was a gun."

"Two. We're give them back."

Dillal stepped into the young man's view. "Back to whom?"

CHAPTER TWENTY-NINE

Day 6: Late Afternoon into Evening

"Got the guns off a blue dehka. With the bullets. From old Ohba cat."

Dillal's expression darkened and his voice was sharper than before. "You're got guns from an ofiçe?"

Banzet seemed confused. "I'm say! The guns from the dehka. The bullets from the red-tar, but dehka's brought them."

"How you're know where they're come from?"

"We're see her—the tunnel. That's how I'm go. Back the tunnel. I'm give her my gun. Give her man my word, all my money t'help me go."

"Her man," Matheson asked, "what did he look like?"

Banzet scowled and bumped one fist against his head as if were knocking the memory back into place. "Big. Old. His clothes're all striped black."

"Did you hear his name?" Matheson continued.

"No. He's take the gun, sends another—a quiet one—who's show me how to go. I'm come here."

"What happened to the other gun?"

"Dehka's told us where t'leave them. But I'm not. Too scared."

"Scared of what?"

"Oso."

"You weren't afraid of the Ohba or the ofiçe?"

Banzet blinked as if it hadn't occurred to him. "Not as much as Oso." He turned to Dillal. "He's kill me. For what we're did."

"GISA will kill you for what you did," the inspector replied, dead level. His voice had lost its Dreihleen buzz and roll, become colder, more Central. "Venn and Denny. And fourteen more deliberate deaths in the commission of armed robbery. Capital murder."

"We're not make that plan! We're didn't mean t'hurt them!"

"All dead anyway. All left this world."

"Denny's fault! He's take my torch and kill the girl! And then Oso—Oso's shoot him."

"But the rest all died. Not just by bullets. By the plasma burns through their necks and temples, just like Venn."

Banzet covered his face again and Dillal wrenched his hands away, leaning over Banzet as he sat struggling to free himself. The inspector pushed and the chair lurched backward a little until it was rocked back on its rear legs, teetering as Dillal held Banzet's wrists tight, balanced for the moment, but it would be so easy to let go . . .

Banzet tensed his arms, quivering and taking sharp, fearful breaths through his nose, but holding as still as he could. Dillal leaned toward him, pushing a little harder until Banzet met his eyes, cringing.

The inspector kept the chair off kilter, but not far enough to fall, as he stared, unblinking, into Banzet's face. "You were there with him," Dillal said, cold and level. "You planned it with him. You killed with him—not just the easy way, not just at a distance with a gun, but close enough to taste their fear on the air, close enough to smell the burning of their flesh. You did not refuse. You did not come to confess. You ran and would keep on running if you could."

"He's say I'm had to! He's say I'm no choice! Say no one will know—we're safe if they're all die."

"And are you safe? Safe from him? Safe from me?"

"Didn't mean t'kill them." Banzet sounded as if he were choking on his fear and guilt.

"What you did—reloading the guns, using the pen torch—that speaks of premeditation, not panic. So what did you intend? What did you really mean to do?"

"We're only mean t'rob them—jasso full of lying vultures," Banzet cried, terrified tears starting down his face and his jaw clenched so tight Matheson could hear his teeth grind. "What's matter we're take from them?"

"Matter—? I should drop you on the floor and leave you with the vultures outside. They'll pick your bones just like this boy's."

Dillal let go with his right hand so the chair swung unsteadily toward Zanesh, who pushed himself up against the wall, standing in the corner like a vision of death. Banzet writhed and shrieked through bared teeth. Dillal opened his remaining hand. The chair crashed down, spilling Banzet onto the floor facing Zanesh.

Dillal stood over Banzet, turned toward Zanesh. "Is this what you expected to be your fate? This slow death? Starved, cut, raped, beaten . . . For knowing what you did, Tchintaka sent this boy here to die. Not a clean death with a bullet or a knife. Not what you imagined. For robbing his neighbors. For killing Denny. You would die for the things he did, as well as your own crimes."

I can't . . . Matheson took a step. Dillal shot him a stern glare and turned back to Banzet, who was still staring at Zanesh as if mesmerized. Matheson froze, fascinated and appalled.

"Tell me why," Dillal said in a low voice. "Why Tchintaka thought it acceptable to rob the Paz da Sorte's customers, why he wanted the money."

Banzet's trembling was becoming stuttering, shaking hysteria. Zanesh crouched back to the floor, frowning at him.

"Is for th'revolution," Banzet said.

Dillal's face was turned too far from Matheson, but Zanesh could see it and he pressed himself back against the wall in terror, scrambling

391

for the corner—for any extra distance from the inspector, whose hands balled into fists, every tendon tight to the quaking point. Dillal leaned forward . . . paused, arrested in motion as if time had stopped . . .

And stepped back, breathing harshly and tearing his gaze away.

Banzet cowered and looked over his shoulder at the inspector and then to Matheson, terrified.

Dillal turned on his heel, putting his back to Banzet and Zanesh. Matheson held his own ground, though—*merry fucking hell*—he wanted to back away. The inspector's face was like something torn in two: the right side a grimace of agony and rage, the left as still as death. Dillal bowed his head and clasped his hands together until the knuckles went white. He brought his knotted hands up to his forehead and pressed them against his brow.

"For the revolution," he muttered and took a long, shaking breath. He was still for a moment but for the slightest quiver in his fists and shoulders.

Then he exhaled in a gust and dropped his hands as if his anger exhausted him. The tension flowed out of his shoulders and he rolled his head a little before he raised it. Now his face was tired but calm and he wiped a runnel of gory liquid from his cheek. "Why did he choose Paz?"

No one answered.

Dillal turned and looked at Banzet and Zanesh. He repeated his question in a calm voice. "Why Paz?"

"Be—because they're profit from oppression," Banzet stammered.

Dillal sighed. "You are saying that the jasso exists and thrives because of the structure of the law, and the owners—all the business owners who go there at Spring Moon—benefit from the system that oppresses the Dreihleen. Is that correct?"

Banzet nodded slowly, watching Dillal as if he expected the man to spring at him any moment. "As you're say. They're vultures, cannibals."

"For that you chose to rob them. People like your own family."

Banzet shook his head. "Oso's idea."

"You didn't dissuade him."

"Was not supposed to be killing. I'm not—"

Dillal waved him quiet. "Yes, yes. You wouldn't have gone along with that. Leran might have. But not you."

Banzet breathed in relief and squirmed over to sit against the wall a meter from Zanesh. Dillal looked at the boy, who had sunk down to sit in his corner again with his arms loose around his shins.

Zanesh nodded. "Z'what I'm hear. They're never mean t'kill."

"I see. But I have a problem." Dillal said. "You I can save." He turned to Banzet. "But you . . ."

Banzet leaned his head against the wall. "I'm for leaving this world, do I'm want or not. Oso's kill me or someone else. How's different?"

"Help me find Tchintaka and I can make it different."

"Why . . . you're help me?"

"You killed, but you did not plan it. I want the one who did."

Air seemed to flood back into Matheson's lungs. He hadn't realized he'd stopped breathing or that he'd clenched his jaw so tightly his teeth ached until the tension left. The relief felt more personal and so much bigger than it should have been.

Dillal and Matheson rushed the paperwork to move Zanesh and Banzet back to Ariel in their custody. The port at Ejeirie was surprisingly busy and they didn't have to wait long for a short hop to Port Hyldra to connect to outbound transport back to Angra Dastrelas.

They arrived at Port Hyldra amid an unusual flurry of incoming orbital drops. Transferring Banzet and Zanesh to the next transport was complicated by the swift movement of troops from the drops to smaller, swifter craft to make room for more incoming drops.

"That's why we had no trouble getting transport," Matheson said once their two prisoners were secured in the passenger pod.

Dillal turned away in fury. "Something's gone bad," he muttered. He looked the worst Matheson had seen him since they'd met—ill, sweaty, and the prosthetic eye wasn't tracking properly. "This has the look of a coordinated build up to a push." He frowned on only the right side of his face. "Damn him—Pritchet promised me a day at the least. We've had twelve hours and this is far too much manpower for an assault on Ang'Das's ghettos."

"It might not be a push."

"What else would it be?" Dillal snapped.

Matheson grabbed the arm of a passing crewman. "Hey. We've been off grid—what's all this troop activity about?"

The man stared at him. "You didn't hear the news? There's some kind of unrest between the drecks and the humps back on Ariel—some bunch of one killed a bunch of the others and Corporation House is moving to settle it before anything gets too out of hand. They're expecting a sympathy move out here in the camps, so they're pulling in a bunch of reserve from out system."

"Merry fucking hell." Matheson's guts twisted. *No. No, no . . .*

The crewman glared at him. "Don't blame me, pretty boy. I didn't pull this lot. I just run 'em up."

"Yeah, I understand . . . Thanks."

The man hurried away to his duties.

"Stay close to our prisoners," Dillal said. "Whether this is meant to cause us, in particular, grief or not, tempers are already high. I'll see if I can get access to the vessel's information stream."

"But—" Matheson started, his personal worries getting in front of the professional ones for the moment.

Dillal peered at him with his normal eye. "Trust me. And have some faith in Aya and Minje. Now go."

He pointed Matheson toward the rear of the transport as he began forward at a slower than usual pace. Banzet and Zanesh were right where Matheson had left them and they had acquired no company. Zanesh had become quiet and withdrawn; he barely glanced up as Matheson entered, and flicked his gaze back to the deck once he recognized who it was. Banzet seemed relieved to see Matheson, but it could just have been that he wasn't Dillal.

"You're think he's can do what he's say?" Banzet asked.

"If we get you in without a problem, he will," Matheson replied in a cool voice. He was on the fence about Banzet's deal with the inspector to give evidence in exchange for a guarantee that he wouldn't be executed. *Is killing one person for the deaths of others the right thing to do?* He was equally uncomfortable with Banzet's squirming over the particulars of his guilt. *He didn't refuse to kill—he did it and admitted it—but he seems to think being panicked and revolted after the fact should exonerate him.* Dillal had quite a different view, but the details weren't for Matheson to quibble over—*how would I feel if I were certain of what I did at Camp Donetti?* They had one of their two remaining perpetrators and they had a witness, if they could protect them both long enough to bring the case to trial and keep Corporation House from razing the ghettos—or the internment camps. Matheson had more sympathy for Zanesh, who had nothing to look forward to anywhere.

Matheson made sure the two Dreihleen were secure and as comfortable as they could be in the circumstances, and withdrew to the other half of the pod. Dillal arrived less than ten minutes later and closed the barrier that separated the prisoners from the rest of the pod.

The inspector sat on the edge of one passenger sling and went through his pockets, laying several flat packets on his knees and drawing out a black, hooked instrument. "It's unclear if there's been any new violence between Dreihleen and Ohba yet, but the possibility grows. The rumor about the Dreihleat and Ohbata connection has been leaked to media," he said, his voice quiet. "A great deal is being made of the ammunition and guns. We have one weapon and Banzet's told us where we can secure the other once we reach Ang'Das, but the fear mongering is already at full boil. We need to show that the ammunition and weapons are from an outside source."

"What source? I mean . . . they're from the Ohbata . . ."

"But they were provided by this 'blue dehka' Banzet mentioned. We need to identify that individual." He leaned his head back, then pressed the hooked edges of the black tool into his left eye with a grunt of pain. Matheson cringed, but watched in horrified fascination as the inspector twisted and wrenched the mechanical eye from its socket. Dillal lifted the ocular away and laid it on one of the packets on his lap before taking one of the others and blindly tearing it open to extract a pad of material that he raised to the socket. Then he leaned forward, holding the pale wadding over the empty frame. A dark pink stain spread into the material.

"Dillal?"

The inspector gagged and coughed for a moment. "This is worse than I'd thought. Matheson, if you would, open the other packet on my knee and hand me the pad inside it?"

Queasy, Matheson did as he was asked and watched Dillal drop the used material to the floor and replace it with the fresh fabric. The stain was slower to spread this time and the inspector sat up, wiping the frame and socket with a delicate touch.

"Are you all right?" Matheson asked, fighting an irrational urge to pull away, to run, to scream. *Mud turned lavender with blood . . .*

"No, but I can go on long enough once I'm done here. And the ocular should be back online. Who do you imagine is our problem?"

Matheson frowned. "I'm not following." He also wasn't following the inspector's mercurial changes of temper. Dillal was ill and in pain, but otherwise much as he had been before they'd interrogated either Zanesh or Banzet, not the intimidating and terrifying figure he'd become in the nearly empty briefing room with the two Dreihleen.

"That person most likely to be the source of our leaks as well as the real link between the Ohbata and Dreihleat in this case. I suspect he or she is also responsible for Santos's death." He paused a moment and added, "And Bomodai's. At the moment, we still have the director's support—according to the messages I've just seen from Pritchet. But we do have to identify and take the individual as well as retrieving the other gun."

"Could we send someone to pick up the second gun before we get back? This will be a faster lift than the one we took from Angra Dastrelas, but we're still four or more hours out."

"Who could we trust? Minje or Aya won't be allowed out of the Dreihleat at this time and we have no true allies at GISA—one of them is our leak and an active enemy of our case and ourselves," Dillal replied. "Banzet can't seem to describe the individual and I'm surprised he or she hasn't already done something to injure us more directly."

"Tyreda?" Matheson suggested.

Dillal scoffed. "Wouldn't risk his hide."

"You think whoever it is would try to kill one of us or our agent?"

"Why not? He or she killed Santos."

"I still don't understand why."

"The presence of a persuasive drug in his blood makes me think that Santos didn't give you all the information he had—this other ofiçe knew that, and he or she is the last key to the problem. So, what's your instinct?" Dillal asked, switching from blotting up the gruesome fluid that had collected in the back of his eye socket to cleaning the frame with the contents of a different packet. It was a repulsively fascinating action and Matheson's mind started to wander. He had to force his thoughts aside to answer Dillal's question.

"Neme. She's been very interested in the investigation from the beginning, even though she claimed she didn't want it. Also, she's the only GISA ofiçe I'm aware of who's blue—and has the seniority to get access to the files as well as connections at Corporation House."

"I see the attraction of that solution."

"But you don't agree with it."

"Personal dislike may color our view and 'blue dehka' may refer to some other blue thing that defines this individual. The color of their clothes, or their eyes."

Dillal didn't respond to Matheson's quizzical look and concentrated on cleaning the ocular, which was still held in the tool like a gory trophy in some raptor's disembodied claw. His hands were slightly unsteady.

Matheson looked aside, but a devious idea swarmed into his head like a fever and he crouched down beside Dillal, staring hard at the deck—it was all he could stomach—until the inspector stopped working and looked up. "We need to buy back that time Pritchet promised."

"If we can."

"Then let's use this leak against . . . whoever this is."

Dillal folded his hands. "How?"

"They're using our investigation notes against us. But they haven't got this information—that we know a GISA ofiçe is involved—because none of it's been uploaded since I went into the tunnels with Aya, and I assume you're not sending anything either. So we can play this game, too—leak the information."

"GISA and Gattis Corporation will hardly care—"

"Central System will. If this is all being used as an excuse to reduce the Ohba and Dreihleen to a negligible effect on the charter before the review, then the threat of Central's early intervention under the emergency clause is the last thing the corporation wants. It wouldn't be able to execute its plans if Central is watching—not without much better provocation. They'll have to manufacture a better excuse, which will buy us enough time to finish this."

"Send to Central . . ."

"No. Send directly to Central's *media hub*. They're no more likely to let a scandal—or the promise of violence—go underexploited than Gattis's media are. I've seen them in action before. It's like watching sharks go after blood in the water. And Central's hub will ram their version back down Gattis's feed whether they like it or not. The number of transports coming down suggests that there's some kind of staging area organized on this side of the jumpway. They'll need the option to disavow it, so it'll have to have a beacon and a needlecast transmitter that's not controlled by Gattis Corp. Like the one that's coordinating the out-system troops. If we can get our story on the needlecast before this vessel lifts out of range, nothing will stop that packet from going through with the next jump. It'll hit Central and be on the media stream before we drop back to Angra Dastrelas." He felt more stable on this subject—one with no bloody memories. He shot a glance sideways at the inspector.

"You'll have to do it—I'm temporarily offline." Dillal glanced down and chuckled. The sound left Matheson uneasy. "Your family doesn't appreciate what they've lost in letting you slip the chain."

The pre-lift warning squealed and Matheson flinched. They both looked up as if they could see the sound in the air. Dillal caught Matheson's eye. "You have three minutes."

They moved to secure themselves in the passenger slings—Dillal much more slowly than Matheson, after carefully re-stowing everything in his pockets, including the ocular. Matheson snatched his mobile from the loops on his shirt and started working, copying pieces of the files and grafting them with text, hooking keywords, weighting it with his family name . . .

Initial lift was much faster and harder than the lift out of Ariel—it felt like something heavy pressed on Matheson's chest, making all the nearly healed bruises ache again. Breathing was difficult for the minutes it lasted. The mobile fell from his hands and skittered across the floor. The inspector groaned and Matheson tried to turn and look at him, but the increased pressure made it difficult. Matheson suffered through the long minutes, second-guessing himself. *Am I like the rest of my family? And what about Dillal—is he as bad, worse?*

Once initial lift was complete, Matheson struggled out of the sling, scooping up his fallen mobile as he pushed across the pod to Dillal.

The inspector seemed to have trouble catching his breath, but he managed to ask, "Did your message go?"

"Won't know till we get there."

Dillal's eye socket was gruesome, even lined as it was with metal rather than bone; drops of carmine-tinted fluid oozed along the seam of the skin and into the cavity.

Matheson recoiled for a moment, then reached to get Dillal free of the sling. "Inspector—"

"It's the pressure. She warned me . . ."

"You're bleeding."

"No. It's fine. It's not blood—not just. It will stop when the pressure eases—better to let it drain."

"What measure of 'fine' are you using here, sir? Because you look like death."

Dillal shook his head. "You confound me, Matheson. You're my best ally one minute, my reticent subordinate the next. Now I'm 'sir' again, am I?"

"Depends . . ."

"On?"

Matheson got the last of the straps clear and Dillal sank down to sit on the floor, lowering his head. The liquid in his eye socket slid down his cheek and Matheson shuddered. It wasn't the blood that bothered him, it was . . . something about the unfathomable injury itself.

"Why . . ." Matheson started, settling beside him. "I mean, I don't understand. The approach you took with Zanesh and Banzet . . . Maybe I understand Banzet, but the boy . . ."

"I'm willing to play whatever role I must. The boy needs to maintain face. His only protection here—or when we return—is the appearance of toughness, of being unbreakable. And he can survive only if we eliminate Tchintaka."

"Everyone will know the kid talked to us. Even Central's intervention won't change how that will play out."

"Certain people will know he made a deal—but so long as it appears to have been on his terms and without giving up Tchintaka himself, he will still have a chance in the community. Banzet, however . . . I admit, I let my temper get away from me—I haven't been at my best the past two days. He has no hope of survival, though he deludes himself into thinking so."

"You lied to him and said you could change that."

"Do you think he would have told us where the second gun was if I hadn't? He wasn't able to say where Tchintaka is, for certain, or who the bent dehka is. It won't be enough, come Central's intervention or not. There is no way out of a death sentence—we can't change the world at a single stroke. Were it two deaths—maybe even three— and he weren't a Dreihle, it might be argued that his cooperation was worth commuting it, but sixteen, possibly more? No." There was a note of despair in Dillal's voice—or he may have been too tired to sound anything but hopeless. "I'm trying to save as many people as I can, and a hundred thousand Dreihleen and Ohba are worth more to me than one would-be revolutionary who sees himself as a victim more than he sees the men and women he killed."

"What about Tchintaka? He's the same and when we finally catch him, will you not care about his fate?"

The chill was back in the inspector's voice when he replied, "Oh, I care a great deal what becomes of *him*. The beauty of Banzet's statement and what happened to Zanesh is that they give me hope Tchintaka won't die a martyr. The trick will be in getting him to damn himself from his own mouth without going too far and condemning the Dreihleat with him." Dillal panted and fished in his pocket.

"It was wrong-headed," Matheson started, "but Tchintaka's original robbery plan wouldn't have caused him any serious loss of status with the Dreihleen community—as I understand it—and no one else would care."

Dillal raised his head to Matheson, holding the mechanical eye in his hand. Matheson resisted shivering. "But you're assuming my original theory was correct," Dillal said, "and we know now that I was wrong. Zanesh said that Tchintaka knew when Dohan would bring Venn Robesh to Paz. He knew what could happen when Leran saw her. And if that's true, then Leran's death wasn't an accident and Banzet *would* have been next. Considering what Banzet said about the victims, there was never any intention of letting anyone leave Paz alive." He resumed cleaning the ocular.

"That's where I get confused. It's almost as if Tchintaka's been working *for* the corporation—he's given them excuses to attack the Dreihleen and Ohba without much repercussion."

"I can see that, but I know him and he abhors the corporation to the point of blindness. It's his arrogance and hate that lead him into their hands. Remember that Banzet said Tchintaka chose the people at Paz because they 'profit by oppression,' called them lying vultures and cannibals. Do those sound like the words of a young man from industrial Northcut? Or more like the rhetoric of a practiced rabble rouser who will say and do anything to reach his ends and sees no further than his own desire? You've seen it yourself. Tchintaka turned his victims into enemies with a few words, made it acceptable to rob them, then, in the heat of the moment, to kill them by reducing them to monstrous, inhuman things that devour their own kind. A neat trick to play on an impressionable young man like Banzet, but the effect didn't last—it couldn't. Once Banzet wasn't in Tchintaka's presence, his conscience and better sense returned. He began feeling guilty and threatened. He ran to the only place he thought no one would be willing to follow him."

"But you think it's no coincidence that Zanesh was sent to the same camp."

"Of course. Haven't I said so? Tchintaka eliminates two problems with a single stroke—he breaks and controls the boy without appearing to be involved, and makes him his watchdog on Banzet at the same time."

"How did you know about . . . what happened to Zanesh?" Just thinking about it left Matheson feeling sick in mind.

Dillal looked down again. "I worked in the camps for three years. I've seen every way one human being can break another. To affect so much change so quickly . . . there're only a few choices. I can smell what was done to him. I can see the result—a boy who was honestly afraid becomes one who cringes under the cover of false bravado to avoid more pain until the swagger becomes callousness and the pain becomes background noise. He has a chance to survive, but we don't know what he'll become to do so."

"We don't know what will become of us, either."

"That is always the question, isn't it?"

CHAPTER THIRTY

Day 6: Angra Dastrelas—Night

There was no sign of GISA's usual patrols or any of the out-system troops here—no one cared about Centerrun now, not even as night was falling and shady businesses emerged like poisonous flowers opening to moonlight.

The two men didn't wear any sort of uniform and carried nothing except the contents of their pockets, but no one would have mistaken them for residents. They had the manner of trouble passing on its way someplace else and no one wished to distract them as they progressed deeper into the zone. Matheson's gaze was never still, eyeing the graffiti and decay, hearing the shrieks and howls of animals in illegal fight pits, noting every shadow as Dillal stalked beside him toward an old complex of buildings that had become ramshackle and half-abandoned after the race riots nearly a generation ago.

"Is there any place on this planet that isn't some shade of perdition?" Matheson muttered.

Dillal's reply was no louder. "Where there are fewer people, it's sublimely beautiful. It's us who make it a misery."

"He's got to suspect it's a trap."

"No doubt. He's far from stupid—consider how he's manipulated both of us and this investigation—but I think he'll take this bait. If our gambit works, the blame falls fully on him and none on the Ohbata."

Matheson nodded, but didn't speak.

"I know you dislike what I'm asking you to do," Dillal murmured. "It's not the thing itself, it's what comes with it."

They entered a building and went separate ways at the base of the main staircase. Dillal started up. Matheson continued to the rear, skirting a couple having noisy, half-clothed sex against the wall while a cluster of neighbors watched, drinking and smoking and calling out crude encouragement. Their voices lowered as Matheson hesitated a moment, but he didn't intervene as the person on the bottom reached back and clutched the other's hip with one hand. Someone laughed nervously as Matheson turned his head away and walked on to the secondary stairs.

Both staircases were hazardous with wild growth watered by constant tropical moisture trickling down the walls. By separate ways, they ascended to the topmost floor where the roof had long ago collapsed at one end. Something rustled in the Gripping Snare that curled into Dillal's path and he nudged the vine runner aside with the toe of his shoe. Leafy tendrils curled closed like fingers until the tail of a small creature twitched in their curve and the plant cinched down to trap it. Dillal stepped over the squealing, thrashing animal as a second rank of barbed leaves closed over it, stinging it into silence. He walked out into the ruin of what had been a residential floor and was now a maze of tumbling walls and fallen roof beams wherever the incipient jungle hadn't penetrated.

He looked for Matheson, but the younger man hadn't arrived yet—his stairs had been overgrown to a lower level. Dillal walked surefooted through the wreckage and ruin toward an old doorway that still retained the hinges and half of its door. Cloud shadows left stripes and blotches of moonlight on the floors and walls, obscuring shapes and draining all color to gray for anyone but him. The same grasping creepers had begun to invade the corners of the room and he avoided them as he edged through the doorway and around a wall to an old drop-lid bureau. The top was bushy with moss that had been disturbed recently, leaving the dirty, angled surface partially cleared. He dug his fingers into the broken blanket of dirt and greenery and eased the desk open. The pistol lay wrapped in a scrap of cloth at the back.

Matheson eased out of the secondary staircase, watching a shadow move up from the main entry and toward the broken room Dillal had entered. Like the inspector, he took care not to touch the vines that curled along the floor bearing bundles of cinched-close leaves that writhed once in a while or pulsed grotesquely.

Dillal picked up the swaddled handgun and flipped the cloth open with care, the corner of his mouth twitching into a bitter smile. He started to turn back, pausing only slightly as another man eased into the room. He continued his turn and held up the gun, still wrapped in its shroud.

"I suppose you've come for this," Dillal said. His voice seemed loud in the dilapidated space.

Matheson slipped across the floor to the last bit of wall between him and the two men, pressing himself flat beside a ragged hole where the cheap construction had tumbled down, leaving only the bare, rotting supports in the way and a trail of creeper on the other side.

"I should have guessed you'd beat me to it, Dillal. You've always been a wily little puke. That media blast about crooked cops and the report on the gun . . . that was all meant to get me right here, right now—don't say you didn't figure it was me did Santos."

Dillal put the gun back on the desk top and looked down. "One of our witnesses identified you by your blue Agria Corps jacket—you still wear it after all this time. And the bloody footprints outside the jasso matched."

"Footprints?" The man laughed and shook his head. "Fuck

me . . . Fuck. Me. Half an impression and you pluck me out of the mess like a diamond out of trench slop and I'm not even the one did that shit at the jasso. Where's the rook?"

"Matheson? I'm not sure."

Orris sighed and stepped into a patch of light that turned his old, faded blue jacket white. He was holding up his shock box. "You're a good liar, but I'd have to be a fucking moron to believe he's not some-where up here. So I guess the real question is going to be what does he value more—your life or your case? 'Cause I bet this little spitter'll do serious mayhem to all that hardware in your skull."

Matheson dove through the gap in the wall to tackle Orris, drag-ging the creeper along as it began its slow grasp.

The older ofiçe turned aside and backhanded him. Matheson snatched Orris's right hand as he went to his knees. The vine began coiling around Orris's hand as he hit the discharge button. Matheson took the bright arc of current on his shoulder and fell the rest of the way to the floor as dead weight, wrapped in the stink of singed cloth and skin. His hand spasmed open, but momentum threw Orris side-ways and down into stronger contact with the plant's writhing tendrils.

Orris tried to swing around and put Matheson between himself and Dillal, but the inspector was much faster and slipped his arm around the taller man's throat, kicking his knees out from under him. Orris choked as he went down and tried to raise the shock box. The tangling creeper slowed him until Matheson—dizzy and weak, but struggling upward—head-butted him in the gut. Orris doubled over and Dillal came with him, slamming his free hand down on Orris's right one. Dillal crushed the shock box into the other ofiçe's palm and fingers as the creeper closed on Orris's wrist and wound its way up his forearm. Orris gave a weak yell, then gagged as he tried to catch his breath under the pressure of Dillal's forearm across his windpipe.

Shaking and twitching, Matheson shoved Orris's other hand back toward the grasping vine. Dillal finished the job, yanking the older ofiçe's wrists behind him until the vine had closed its grip. The inspector stood up, leaving the man on his knees, and retrieved the gun from the desk.

Orris squirmed and fought as the creeper's layers of stinging hairs and longer thorns began piercing his skin. "You sick little fuck!"

"Still yourself. The plant will just make your arms numb a while—so long as it's removed in a few minutes," Dillal replied. "It's no worse than what you've done to Matheson and much less than you did to Santos." Then he waited in silence while Orris made increasingly feeble attempts to shrug out of the clinging vine.

It took several minutes for Matheson to shake off the worst of the shock effect. Then he hunched into a seated position on the floor nearby and looked at Orris. "Feels like my nerves are on fire."

Orris stopped fighting the creeper and made a scoffing noise in his throat. "That's how they work, rook. Didn't anybody zap you at the academy? Or don't they demo on rich boys? But you're tougher than I thought. Most hoppers drop like a rock off the Pillars." He shook his head. "Still can't see how you caught on to me. I never gave you my shoe impressions."

"I got one off the inspector's floor when you were snooping around on Sunday. You thought everyone would be out on riot patrol. Did you prompt Tchintaka on the timing? It wouldn't surprise me, since you're in this up to your neck. You leaked intel only our missing link could have had, and you've been monitoring our reports."

Orris gave a rueful laugh. "Blame the reports on Neme. She's a twisted piece of work, that one, but she was starting to balk so I had to do my own legwork. You are so easy to push, boy."

"Yeah. I'm green as grass. I didn't figure out that it was you who set the rest of S-Office on me so you could conveniently 'save' me and sideline me at the same time. Why? I mean . . . Why in merry hell did you do any of this?"

Orris glowered up at Dillal. "Get this shit off me or I'm not saying anything."

Dillal shrugged and looked at Matheson. "He can still run."

"Go fucking jump!" Orris shouted. "Santos was gonna turf me! Me. After all I did for him and that blood-red bitch of his. He got all weepy about a bunch of drecks." He whipped his head in frustration. "Shit!"

"What? Nothing else to say?" Matheson demanded. "If you want to walk away alive, you'll keep talking."

Orris gaped at Matheson. "What in fuck . . . ? You threatening me, rook? You better have something nastier than carnivorous creeper up your sleeve, 'cause I don't think you've got the big brass ones required to whack me."

Matheson gave a bitter laugh. "I don't have to. We have evidence that ties you to a conspiracy to commit robbery and multiple murder, aggravated murder, and a double murder on your own account. I can add on insurrection, smuggling, illegal arms trading, and conspiracy to incite—just to start."

"Cat shit."

"Not a bit. You provided both guns used in the Paz da Sorte killings and coordinated with Bomodai, who provided the ammunition—which you'd sold to her in the first place."

"Specu-fucking-lation. You think that's gonna make me piss myself and roll over? You got nothing that ties me in." Beads of sweat had sprung up on his forehead and a fiery rash was beginning to blister his hands and spread up under his cuffs.

Dillal spoke up behind him. "We already have one witness who will identify you in that deal, and we know of others." Orris jerked to stare over his shoulder at the inspector, wincing as thorns stabbed deeper into his arms. "There's more, of course. You were a member of the Cafala flood team. During the clean-up, you transferred into GISA Agria Corps, and after that to GISA Ang'Das, from a military unit that was issued the particular rounds used in the Paz da Sorte murders." He held up the pistol. "This is the type of gun issued to your Cafala unit as personal sidearms and I have no doubt that the database will show that this specific piece was issued to you. You provided the one we recovered from Hoda Banzet as well. This one may not have as much DNA and forensic value, but it will have a ballistic match to bullets recovered from the bodies in the Dreihleat. And how certain are you that you never left a trace?

"You were running protection when we met and it won't be hard to confirm that you ran the bagmen who remained in the Dreihleat when you booted up—including Santos. You've already admitted he was in your debt, but ready to grass. So . . . when he suggested he might tell Matheson the truth and get off the hook of accessory to capital murder by offering you instead, you drugged him and hanged him from his own balcony. After you made sure he hadn't turfed you."

"Santos wasn't drugged—you said so." Muscles in Orris's jaw bunched and twitched and the sweat was beginning to run down his neck.

"I never did. Andreus certified death by hanging, but she also conducted a full autopsy. She found a compound in Santos's system that's used in field hospitals for pain relief in terminal patients. You've spent your share of time in those wards, sat by the beds of dying comrades, watched doctors mix their tonic . . . Could you say you don't know what 'deadman's dram' is without hiding your hands in your armpits—as you do when you're nervous? I doubt it."

"It's still just fucking circumstance and guesses."

"But this gun and the key to the Paz da Sorte aren't. Santos said he threw the key down the alley drain, but it wasn't there. It's in your pocket."

Orris flinched, setting off a chain reaction of tightening vines and torn, blistering skin that let the creeper's toxin flow, drove the thorns in deeper . . . and Dillal smiled at him. The cold, one-sided expression made Orris shudder and he wrenched his gaze back to Matheson, his eyes showing white all the way around. "He's a fucking lunatic," he panted. "You believe this shit?"

"Now you're appealing to me?" Matheson cocked an ironic eyebrow. "That's funny . . . because I think you not only drugged and murdered my training officer, but you went back to the Ohbata and shot that gun runner in the head to clean up after yourself. And I know you were at the Paz da Sorte earlier than you claimed, because you had your scene kit in your pocket."

"Why the hell shouldn't I?" Orris demanded, his voice tight.

"You were IOD—that's a desk assignment. You shouldn't have needed a kit any more than you had cause to enter the jasso before Dillal arrived. But you did both. You didn't have the rest of your equipment and there was no reason you'd have put only the scene kit in your pocket, but you had it and it was open."

"You're guessing again."

"No. You handed the inspector a solvent wipe from your own pocket while we were standing in the jasso. I saw you do it. I thought it was odd at the time, because if you were just stopping by to settle an assignment dispute, you should have had no reason to get your hands dirty. But yours were and so were your shoes. And, as IOD, you assigned Neme—because she's the most corrupt detive in the division and you thought she'd just pick a likely scapegoat and close it without a fuss, didn't you?"

"You enjoying this recitation, *Fishbait?*" Orris was shivering and fruitlessly working his arms against the tightening creeper and its spreading, gnawing rash.

"Not particularly. But the point I want to make is, you're so deep in the shit you're going to need a ladder to climb out. And while the inspector and I would both love to push you under and hold you down, there's actually something we want more. So I might have a ladder . . ."

Orris nodded, narrowing his eyes. "You want Tchintaka."

"How would you know that?"

"Because he's the big bad in this."

"Is he?"

"Stop screwing with me, rook, if you got to Banzet you know he is! And I know you got to Banzet because you have his gun," Orris snapped.

Matheson grinned. "Oh, yeah. Do keep on tying that noose around your neck. Maybe I won't have to pay for information after all."

"What?"

"I may be inexperienced, but it's a mistake to think I'm stupid, or soft. The inspector and I have enough to send you to the wall on your own account, but we'd prefer solid information that will take us to Tchintaka." Matheson watched Orris squirm at the name. "You killed Santos and Bomodai to cover yourself, but it wasn't enough. So long as there's a single witness left alive who can put the finger on you for supplying the guns and being the middle man to the ammo, you can't afford to back out. You've admitted that you spied on us for your own protection, but you're keeping Tchintaka in the loop, too—both for leverage and to make sure we didn't get to him first. You know he's a self-serving, manipulative prick, and he'll drag you down with him if he can."

Orris stared at him, shuddering as leaves and thorns burrowed into his flesh. His breathing was short and choppy through clenched teeth.

Matheson cocked his head at the older ofiçe and watched him for a minute before he said, "So, here's what I'm proposing. I remove the creeper that's trying to digest your forearms and you start talking. I want a sworn statement, proof, and physical evidence—like the key and the rest of the ammunition—that will take us to Tchintaka and nail him to that wall. Give us that, and I'm willing to make a deal with you. Me, Eric Matheson. Not Ofiçe Matheson. This will be off the books, because, really, I just want to get rid of you and your kind, and I can't be bothered to shoot you. So, you give me what I want, and you . . . get to leave."

"Leave . . . ?" Orris sounded as if he didn't recognize the sound as a word.

"Gattis. Alive."

Orris tried a laugh, but it came out shaky. "Just alive? Mother of fucking stars, rook, it's not like this fucking creeper's gonna kill me . . ."

"No, but if we leave you here, something else will. None of the residents are altruists and I hear the cats around here are bigger and meaner than the ones in the Dreihleat."

Orris began cursing under his breath, "Fuck, fuck, fuck . . . All right, kid, all right . . . just get this shit off me."

Matheson gave a cynical chuckle. "When you're done talking and *if* I'm satisfied with what you tell me—and it had better be truly damning."

"Don't ask much . . ."

"Y'know, I'd think that keeping your brains in your head instead of splattered on a certain wall would be a hell of a motivation by itself, but there is a sweetener—my family has obscene amounts of money and the power that goes with it. Once you're off this planet for good, I'll make sure some of what lines their pockets makes its way into yours, but you'll be a wanted fugitive for the rest of your life because the information *will* come out. By killing Bomodai and Santos you wiped out anyone who could have spoken up for you or taken the blame, so it'll all fall on you—their deaths, the guns, the ammo, the key to the jasso . . .

"The inspector and I will make sure you're on the next transport out of this jumpway. But if you ever put a foot back on Gattis, your former friends at GISA will snatch you up and have you against the wall before the incoming jump warning dies. So coming back here isn't going to be much of a temptation, is it? Especially with the kind of money you'll have."

Orris sat shuddering and thinking for a moment, then he raised his head to look at Dillal. "It's you."

Dillal favored him with a quirked eyebrow.

"Tchintaka's mouth is a liability. He'll start spewing his half-assed philosophy as soon as he's on the stand and then *your* old friends from the ghettos—and maybe that long-faced sister of yours that the rook here is banging—they end up on slabs to benefit the corporation. That's your angle, isn't it? See, I've had a bitch of a time figuring you out, but this makes sense. You don't want Tchintaka's revolt to happen—you want to shut him up permanently."

Dillal shrugged. "If it were that simple, I'd kill him. I need him discredited and convicted of the crimes he's committed. He needs to be a pariah among the Dreihleen. Disgraced and without hope of redemption."

Orris laughed. "Yeah, yeah. Rolled in the mud, but dead all the same. I can get into that—for the right price." He turned his attention back to Matheson. "All right, I'm in. Get this crap off me and I'll tell you where Tchintaka is. I'll give you his head. What you do with it's up to you."

Matheson shivered and rubbed his hands over his upper arms, though he certainly wasn't cold. "There isn't enough soap on Gattis to make me feel clean after dealing with him." The tingling in his fingers and arms hadn't quite left, in spite of walking and shaking his hands all the way through Centerrun and back into GISA HQ with Orris in tow. Now they were alone in Dillal's office and it still felt like there were insects crawling unseen all over him.

"If you stay here, you'll find there's never enough," Dillal said, sitting with his head down in his cupped hands as he rested his elbows on his desk. In private, he no longer hid his illness and distress, and that worried Matheson.

They'd finished their official interrogation and recording of Orris, sequestering the files within the hidden cluster the inspector had established—they were still hashed with official GISA time stamps and upload data, but inaccessible to anyone without Dillal's access. They'd left Orris locked in a conference room above the lab and the man seemed resigned to wait while Matheson and Dillal made the arrangements they'd promised. The needlecast would come back in four hours with a response from the family lawyers and then Matheson would sell his soul—if they'd still have it. His world had become a warped mirror: everything he'd reached for twisted into what he'd run from.

"Is finishing this going to make any real difference?" Matheson asked, wiping sleepless grit from his eyes.

Dillal raised his head. Distant anger burned cold in his expression, but his amber skin was bright and damp with sweat. "It will to me, but my standards aren't yours. You'll have to determine for yourself what degree of filth you're willing to endure. But it's no better other places. Policemen toil in gutters. You work for the law, even if you try to work for justice. Either way, you walk in blood and slime and hope your balance is more to the good than the bad on the day you die." His voice was bitter in his exhaustion.

Matheson wrenched his appalled gaze to the floor and swallowed hard. Dillal would not appreciate his shock or his concern. *Merry hell . . . how can he continue in such a state?*

But he voiced other thoughts. "Letting murderers go for the 'greater good,' or embracing a 'lesser evil'—aren't they the same as the evil itself?"

"No. Banzet won't go free and nothing can protect him from the choices he's made. He will suffer, and it's not your doing. No matter where they put him, no matter if he slips away, Dreihleen will find him and end him, eventually. He's too afraid of it to understand that dying's the easier way for him. And as to Orris, the corporation won't pursue him, but his crimes will. There are places for men like him to thrive, but he's no longer young and vicious. He'll eke his way across the known worlds until someone swifter and harder takes him down for the convenience of stepping over him. I told you we would hunt them to the bitter end, hound them until the earth fell from beneath their feet. We have come to land's end, stalked and driven them here, but they throw themselves into the abyss."

"Bitter end," Matheson said, remembering for a moment beautiful horses and ancient sail boats chased around the lakes at home when the world was safe and bounded in luxurious ignorance. "You know what that is? It's the loose end—the working end—of a rope."

"So it is."

The door chime sounded and one of Dillal's continual displays threw up the name "Myrine Andreus." Dillal glared at it. "Damnable woman," he muttered. But the office door opened anyway and Matheson was relieved to see the doctor, who looked as stern and cold as Dillal often did.

The inspector did not rise as Andreus marched over to him. "It's the middle of the night, Doctor—"

"Yes it is. Particularly for you."

"Meaning?"

"More patients die between 0200 and 0300 than any other time," she said, checking her old-fashioned wrist watch and putting her work kit on the table. "That's why they call overnight the Graveyard Shift. And you have one foot in it."

"You've been monitoring me."

"I thought we had an understanding." She took a small light from her kit and shined it into his natural eye. "What have you done to yourself? Jumps?"

"Sub-orbital lifts only."

"You think that makes a difference?" She put down the light and picked up a stick-like implement with a small, flattened paddle at the end. "You're such a stubborn, self-serving bundle of hormones and arrogance. You put the system under pressure when you already had breakage. You've had pain, fluid in the socket, drainage, blood . . . and you didn't call for my help." She reached for him with the stick and Dillal stood up to keep his distance, though he wasn't as quick as usual.

"Not by choice," he said. "The system was offline while we were in Agria and I removed the ocular to clean it, which shut off the stream."

Matheson watched the confrontation with a growing sense of dread.

Andreus lunged and swiped the paddle across a patch of sweat on the inspector's neck. She gave a satisfied grunt as she stabbed the instrument into the mouth of another device in the kit and stared at its display. The device issued an aggrieved whistle. "Hell!" She looked up at Dillal. "The *pressure* shut off the stream—it momentarily shut off the part of your brain that controls the system and now there's hell to pay. If you were a normal human with normal brain physiology you would have blacked out and if you didn't already have cracks and drains around the orbit, you'd have died before landfall. You're dying now because you insist on doing what I tell you not to."

Dillal rested one hand on his desk. The fingers trembled until he shifted his weight. "I must finish this investigation."

"It'll have to fucking wait!" she snapped.

"It can't wait!" he shouted back. "I have less than twenty hours left to close this and if I fail, you fail. There is no second chance. Pritchet will cut his losses, abandon me, abandon this project. You know what happens after that."

Andreus's face had gone still and her voice was much lower. "You don't have twenty hours. You shouldn't even be upright. You've already got the infection and fever, tingling and tremors in your fingers. In three hours or less you'll get dizzy, nauseated, have trouble seeing on the organic side. Two or three more hours and you'll lose fine motor control, have phantom pains in your limbs. After that come the spasms, the blackouts, vomiting, uncontrollable shivering. The system will try to save itself by taking over the rest of your brain. I don't know if you'll lose cognitive function before you pass out or after, but you will cease to be 'you' as we understand it and at that point, I can't help you. When the system starts to invade, it will shut things down that it doesn't recognize—first voluntary functions, then the involuntary, then the autonomic system. And then you die. *Then* you die. Not in twenty hours, not in sixteen. In twelve. But you'll be useless long before that. Four to five hours from now you won't be able to walk or see. You need drugs and sleep or you won't survive to sundown. Get someone else to close the case—get him to do it," she added, pointing at Matheson—he jerked back as if she'd jabbed him.

"If it is that bad, you can't hope to save me," Dillal said.

"I can. I have drugs that will stop the infection cold, but they knock you out while they do it."

"For how long?"

"Eight to ten hours."

Dillal leaned against his desk. "I don't have that to spare. The world will change in the next four and I must end this. Even if it kills me—" He stopped, looked down, and then back up to her with slow-blinking, out-of-sync eyes. "It *will* kill me, but you will be vindicated, and the corporation won't have the opportunity to wipe out thousands of innocents. It's not enough, but it's all I can reach."

Andreus shook her head and ran her hand over the kit, picking at objects as if she weren't sure what they were anymore. "No, it's not enough." She picked up a thick, square pad no bigger than her palm and worried it between her fingers. "You have to survive, because you're the only one who ever has."

But we've come too far to quit now—not after what we've done! Matheson leaned forward, but the doctor shot him a warning glance. "Don't help him kill himself." He stepped back, his heart hammering with anxiety. *Death or failure, what choice is that?*

"I'm sorry, doctor, but it isn't up to you," Dillal said. "I must be alive and awake long enough to close or everything we've done will go to ruin. Don't tell me you have no tricks to delay death, no way around the details of drugs and complications and short-term gains with lethal results."

"Not ethically."

Dillal put more of his weight on the counter and crossed his arms over his chest to stop the trembling of his hands. "As if that's bothered you in the past. Drugs may be too slow, but virals—"

"Won't work on you. Your chimeric immune system will smother them the way you'd step on an insect. It's half of the reason you function and the others all died."

"There has to be something. I only need twenty-four hours."

"There *is* something, but you must have it now and it will drop you in your tracks for eight to ten hours."

"I haven't that much time."

"You'll take it anyhow," she said. She stepped in front of Matheson and slapped the odd little pad against the inspector's neck even as he raised a too-slow hand to stop her.

"What—what have you done?" Dillal asked, his gaze unfocused and his frown lopsided as he tried to pull the patch off his skin.

Andreus blocked Matheson's instinctive move toward Dillal as she replied, "Remember when I said the surgeon doesn't get to choose who lives and who dies? Well, this time I do. Good night, Inspector."

Dillal might have done something, but as he started to lean away from the work table, the last of the color drained from his face and he collapsed as if the sinews of his joints had all been cut at once.

Matheson stared. The inspector had fallen face down. The hand he'd raised to his neck was bent at an awkward angle and the spill of his too-large suit over his limp form made him look small and vulnerable. The sense of fragility disturbed Matheson, yet relief loosened his muscles and he took his first normal breath in minutes. *So, we go from here.* He turned to the doctor.

Andreus gave him a wary stare. "I'm sorry about your case, but I won't let him destroy himself."

Matheson gave a small, tired laugh. "I'm no threat to that plan."

"I can tell—you look pretty rough, too."

"Not enough sleep."

"Do I have to put you out, as well?"

Matheson shook his head. "I'd just dream things I'd rather not. And someone has to look out for him, don't they?"

She cast a shrewd, seeking glance over him. "For now." Then she grabbed an injector from her kit and crouched down beside Dillal. It took two injectors and some swearing on her part to manage her plan. The inspector lay dead still the whole time.

"I hate to tell you," Matheson said, watching, "but you're going to have to find some way to get him back on his feet in five or six hours or this whole thing will fall apart. If he's not the one to close the case, it won't matter that he lived through it because Pritchet won't consider that a win for your project."

"Pritchet can jump for all I care," she said, getting back to her feet.

"But you do care or you wouldn't be trying to save Dillal."

"He's an arrogant pain in my ass."

"Yeah, I had guessed you're not best friends. But he's functional and he's all you've got. You need him alive to keep the project going, but to prove the project is viable, *he* has to be the one to solve this case—for which there's a very narrow time window before it's all moot. Ergo, you have to get him back on his feet and able to close this investigation—or at least appear to—in five hours."

Andreus glared at him. "You may be too smart for your own good, Eric Matheson."

"I've heard that before. What can you do?"

"He's got the drugs in his system, now. I can't change them—and I wouldn't. They'll do the job, but they run the body's systems down pretty hard in the initial uptake phase. He should be in a hospital bed with an IV and a monitor, but I don't think you're going to let me do that . . . are you?"

"Me? I've got nothing to do with it. This game of Flinch is between you two and Director Pritchet."

"What utter crap. You have as much to lose in your way as we do. So long as Dillal's in control and you're his second, your star is rising. Soon as he's down, so are you."

Matheson took Dillal's stool and sat, feeling so worn down he thought he'd fall. He glanced at the man on the floor and blew out a long breath. "That's not entirely true, but I want to see this right." He looked at her. "So what can we do?"

She frowned and put her hip against the edge of the desk as she faced him. Night glow and sign light sparked colors in her pale hair and coursed down her face like psychedelic rain. "We? Suddenly you're in this."

"I've been in it since I checked him out of the hospital six days ago. He's impossible—you're right—demanding, arrogant, all that. But he's what we have, and I—I actually kind of like the crazy bastard. I want to nail the lying, murdering piece of shit who caused this, and keep on trying . . ."

Andreus rolled her eyes. "You really are two of a kind. Okay." She looked around as if making mental note of all physical assets—which weren't many in Dillal's' office. "There's got to be a cot or a gurney somewhere in ForTech. Go find it and bring it in here."

Matheson darted off to scavenge, and found a serviceable folding cot in the back of ForTech's dressing room. He dragged it to the inspector's office and helped Andreus lift Dillal onto it.

"He's heavier than he looks," he muttered.

"They all are."

"All of who?"

"Ohba and Dreihleen—super-dense muscle tissue and some interesting structural changes with it. The Ohba also have increased motor nerve density and blood supply so they can use the big muscle mass efficiently. In this one's case, he's built like a Dreihle with the Ohba nervous system so he's quick as a damned snake," she said, dropping Dillal onto the cot face up, "but he's got less stamina."

"So I could run him into the ground in a distance race, but he'll always beat me in a sprint."

"Probably."

They both looked down at Dillal. The shifting, colored light through the office window cast strange shadows and shapes over him. Unconscious, the inspector took slow breaths that each seemed to go on far longer than they should have. Matheson found himself watching . . .

"Almost mesmerizing, isn't it?" Andreus said, passing her hand over Dillal's forehead. "Drugs are kicking in," she muttered, more to herself than Matheson.

"You think they're going to work?"

"They should." She went to the desk and took her mobile from her kit. "That chimeric system's been a bitch to figure out, but it's the reason he's functional. Let's just hope it functions as I think."

Matheson tumbled the word around. "Chimeric . . . chimera . . . That's some kind of hybrid organism, isn't it?"

Andreus frowned at him. "Not really, but most people don't even guess that close." She peered at him through the colored gloom and started to pick up one of her instruments. "You have blue eyes . . ."

He caught her wrist. "Yes, I know they're rare. My family's been improving on nature for a few generations, so I've heard a little about genetics. But I'm not interested in me. Tell me about him." He let her go and she drew back.

"He's a patient—I've already told you too much."

"I'm helping you save his life. It would be useful to know why he's so special."

The doctor thought about it a while and gave a bad-tempered

sigh. "All right," she said, settling herself solidly against the desk. "Broadly speaking, a chimera is a single organism with two or more discrete DNA profiles—in his case it's three—so, genetically speaking, he is his own siblings. The chimeric immunological tolerance, coupled with the way the genes differentiated, got around the lethal incompatibilities of certain gene combinations in Gattian races. It also did a few . . . unusual things to his brain physiology that enable him to run the system without being swamped by it or rejecting it. But even beyond that, he's adapted and improved on my design—*from the inside*. That's one reason among many that I can't afford to lose him—he's solving the system's problems every minute he's alive and he's the only one there is. If he fails, the protocol demands deintegration."

"Deintegration?"

Andreus nodded, looking frustrated. "Remove all the non-organic modules—salvage them for another try. There is no safe way to remove them right now—not in his state or anything like it. But that's the protocol I had to agree to."

Mother of stars . . . "You'd have to kill him. To retrieve your machines." Matheson felt sick.

"That's how it would go." She glanced down at the inspector again. She looked as if she'd swallowed water poppy seeds. "I had five others before him. They all died on their own. As bad as he is right now, he's still not going to go easily, and there won't be another like him unless I just get lucky again."

"Lucky?" Matheson recoiled.

"Yes," she snapped. "I didn't realize what I needed—it was pure luck that he volunteered. I could find a geneticist to do the work of creating others *like* him, but there's no guarantee they'd have the brain physiology that allows him to dedicate continuous unconscious processes to controlling and using the system while the rest of his mind performs all the normal functions—along with those inscrutable mental gymnastics of his. In all the other cases, either the system failed to integrate, or it became invasive and took over. It killed them—every one. Not him. I need to study him." Andreus said.

Her gaze darted from point to point as she seemed to be talking to herself and Matheson drew farther from her as she went on. "That brain physiology . . . and the mechanism of organ rejection's drastically different in chimeras. But the side effect of *his* adaptation is an otherwise super-aggressive immune system—that's something to do with how he works in the system. And that's why virals won't work. The tailored drugs do, but they're slow and they beat the crap out of that immune system, so he sleeps—" She raised her eyes to the ceiling and began tapping her fingers against the work table in a rapid tattoo for most of a minute. "Wait . . . I do have something I can try, but I'll have to go back to the hospital for it."

She glared at Matheson. "Watch him." Then she scooped up her kit and rushed away, leaving Matheson alone with Dillal, who didn't stir except to breathe his long, slow breaths.

CHAPTER THIRTY-ONE

Day 7: Tuesday—Dawn

The reception area outside Pritchet's office teemed with sleekly groomed media sharks even this early. Matheson almost backed away at the thought of being recognized, but he couldn't. He'd washed up, managed to get a clean uniform—which seemed to fit looser than it should—from supplies, and hoped the regional director had really meant "right now" in his reply to Matheson's request, and not "when I can be bothered."

The receptionist was male, Gattian, and unrealistically perfect. He turned up a lazy, knowing smile on the group encroaching on his desk, and caught Matheson's eye, making the tiniest of gestures to send him down the hall without pause or diversion. Matheson took the opening and darted for the goldwood doors before the crowd could turn and catch him. The door gave way before him and he slipped into the office.

Pritchet was taller but Matheson didn't give him the opportunity to loom. He managed a decent salute—he hadn't bothered with one in nearly a week—and closed the distance to the desk as the director was still rising to his feet. With the rain-drenched dawn light behind him, Pritchet looked like a thing of stone and shadow.

"Sir—" Matheson began.

"What in the Blackness are you two doing? Where's Dillal?"

Matheson banished his comfortable self, and reached for the things he'd tried to throw away—the privileged, unflappable certitude of being a Matheson. *Not just Eric. Eric* Matheson. His voice came low and calm, almost lazy. "He's unconscious, sir."

Pritchet appeared ready to spit. "This is hardly the time to take a nap!"

"He's not asleep. Dr. Andreus put him under for medical reasons."

"What? Why? That woman—"

"He hasn't slept in at least forty-eight hours and I suspect more. If you'd prefer him dead or insane before the end of the day, then, by all means, tell her to wake him up."

Have I just cut my throat . . . ? I need you on my side, Pritchet. Right now.

The director drew his head back slowly and looked down his nose, studying Matheson from his greater height—he was about fifteen centimeters taller and he used it to his advantage. Or would have with anyone else. Matheson was unimpressed and knew it showed.

Pritchet lowered his head a bit and narrowed his eyes. "You're . . . Matheson, right? Any relation to Park—"

"He's my father," Matheson answered. "But that's not relevant here."

"Everything is relevant. You and Dillal have put me in a hell of a spot. I assume that media leak about the situation came from you."

Now they were back where Matheson wanted to be and he made a dismissive shrug. "I don't know what you're talking about, sir."

Pritchet laughed—it wasn't a reassuring sound. "I'll allow for deniability. But I'm displeased with the attention Central System is turning on us right now."

"It's better than the alternative. And it will go away as soon as this case is closed and everything looks normal to Central's investigators. From my experience, they aren't particularly tenacious." A bigger lie he didn't think he'd ever told—Central's oversight investigators were the continual bane of Callista's machinations. He had no personal experience, but he didn't mind implying that he'd been in the thick of the family business since he'd picked up his first mobile, and he would wield that connection to his advantage. "We can close this today, if you let us. We have one of the two surviving perpetrators in custody and have identified the remaining subject at large. When we receive confirmation, we'll know exactly where he is, and Dillal and I can take him. I need a few hours, and then it's over."

"*You* need a few hours? You and your whip—you seem to think I can change the course of time."

"No. But I know you can push Corporation House to hold off on any ill-advised moves—"

"Not as well as you think," Pritchet snapped. "There are troops inbound. I can't stop them."

Cold fear squeezed on Matheson's heart, but he just raised inquiring eyebrows.

"Corporation House and the GISA board are less afraid of the media than they are of this situation getting out of hand. Dreihleen murders, Ohba violence . . ."

"There hasn't been any violence in the Ohbata."

"But there's a connection to your case—one I've already discussed with Dillal. And now this corruption rumor just gives the corporation cause to bring the heavy artillery into play and claim it's for the sake of neutrality—cutting GISA out of the action. You tied my damned hands!"

Is this distant, chilly terror and determination what Dillal feels all the time? Matheson found it exhausting, but pushed on with his facade in place. "I came to untie them. We've determined that there were only three perpetrators. We have one dead, one in custody, and one at large. We'll take that final subject down in a few hours. There's no connection to the Ohbata—the guns and ammunition came through another source, regardless of any spurious rumors. We have physical and forensic evidence, statements, witnesses, and we have a perpetrator willing to cooperate in exchange for lenience. We have a complete case."

"But you don't have the final perp! And I can't push back on the corporation with words made of smoke. Who do you have? Who are you after? Where is he or she? What's to stop them leaving the planet on the next jump-bound transport? Give me that and I'll give you the day—I can't guarantee more—maybe not even that much. The damage may be too great already."

"The perpetrators were all Dreihleen, as were all the victims. Simply a crime of opportunity gone wrong."

"That's too vague. You have two prisoners in holding."

"Yes, but they're at risk if they're moved."

"They won't be. Tell me why they're important—the names mean nothing to me."

Matheson breathed slowly through his anxiety, giving Pritchet a thoughtful look as if he were evaluating the director's ability to use the information reasonably. Pritchet scowled back and Matheson smiled a little before he said, "There's a Dreihle boy named Zanesh Farrazee—he was a witness to the planning meetings and he was illegally detained at Camp Ejeirie to keep him from talking to us."

"But that means there is an ofiçe in the mix."

Matheson rendered an insouciant shrug. "Yes, but corruption is not the core of the case and it's not whetting the corporation's appetite—it's holding them back. As much as we don't like it, the source here needs to be protected until the case is officially handed off to prosecution. That crooked ofiçe is your shield and scapegoat until then."

Pritchet stared at Matheson. "You sound just like your whip. Who's your bent copper?"

"I won't say at this time."

Pritchet's eyes narrowed and Matheson might have been intimidated a week ago, but today he wasn't. "Won't say . . ."

Matheson restrained his urge to rush—it would only make him seem desperate and he couldn't risk it. "It's part of the confirmation I'm waiting on, but it doesn't affect the arrest of the remaining subject. We have statements and evidence from that source that make the case stronger, but you'll understand that the CIFO doesn't want to bring them into the light until we're certain. So I can't tell you anything on that topic. Yet."

Pritchet breathed heavily through his nose, frowning at Matheson, then glancing toward his windows and back again. "All right. That I can use. That and the witness in custody. What about your other prisoner?"

"He's the other surviving perpetrator. Another Dreihle. He was identified by the witness in custody and corroborated the witness's evidence. He's willing to cooperate with the prosecution—if the death penalty is off the table. We've guaranteed that it will be."

"We? You and Dillal. High-handed in a case of capital murder."

Matheson nodded. "It was the deal we had to make."

Pritchet closed his eyes. "Your perp's a fool."

"Quite probably. But that's what he asked for."

"What's his name?"

"Hoda Banzet."

"Never heard of him—lucky for you. Who's the subject at large?"

"His name's Osolin Tchintaka."

"Tchintaka . . . Dreihle. Well, he won't be leaving the planet, that's for certain. Name's familiar . . . local streeter?"

Matheson hesitated, but nodded. "Yes."

"So this *is* political."

Matheson gave a dismissive snort. "He would like it to be, but in fact, it's just money and stupidity. Tchintaka's a small-time criminal with delusions of grandeur. But if the media casts him as a dissident being silenced by the powers-that-be, that will put you in the same bad odor as the rest of the board when the charter review comes up. Now, I know that pushing the Forensic Integration Project was not motivated by your concern for better policing—it's a maneuver to retain power after the review. Frankly, I don't care, but it works for me now, and I like being at the front of the line. Dillal and I can close the investigation and shut the rest of the situation down with no fuss if Tchintaka can be taken as quickly—and quietly—as possible."

Pritchet gave him an appreciative grin, but he said, "I wish you good fucking luck with that. The media is going to nip at your heels like dogs whether I can hold the troops or not."

"Find a way. Sir. You want the FIP to be a success and that means the CIFO has to close this case. You gave him a week. That ends tonight. I'll have him back on his feet in a few hours and then we'll finish this up. All you have to do is convince the board to hold those troops until midnight at the latest."

"GISA is no longer in charge of the security of Gattis, as I told you."

"But we are in control of the investigation and the SOs can back the troops already on the ground—which puts them in position to foul any precipitous action. We just need to keep anyone else from closing this prematurely by putting a bullet in Tchintaka—as tempting as that may be."

"That would be a mess, but manageable."

"You don't want that to happen in front of the media observers. Or before your project is vindicated. Dillal and I need the day—only what we were promised originally. That's all I'm asking for. And I've given you everything—"

Pritchet scoffed. "In a cat's eye you have. Whatever you're holding for 'confirmation' is something you can't risk getting out—something that can take this investigation or this division down hard and fast—at least as long as Central is watching. With the way this investigation has leaked like a dried-out canoe, I appreciate that caution. I *don't* appreciate being played—not by the Mathesons, not by Dillal, or that twist of a doctor—but I see the point."

Pritchet looked out his window at the sun-streaked edges of dawn beyond the retreating storm clouds. He stared a while, then exhaled a snort of annoyance and turned back to Matheson. His eyes held a spark of calculating enthusiasm and he rubbed his fingertips together as if he could feel the threads of influence in his hands. "I'll do what I can, but chances are good it's not going to be what you want. And you, Matheson, are going to owe me, because we wouldn't be in this situation if you hadn't brought Central's eye to bear on us. If you protest it's nothing to do with you, I will transfer you to Camp Ejeirie myself."

Matheson returned the sort of blank smile he'd learned from his sister long ago, while agreeing to nothing. "Thank you, sir."

Pritchet's veiled gloating faltered and he narrowed his eyes a little, saying, "Just close this today and close it quietly—Spring Moon ends in two nights and I don't want this to be the thing everyone remembers."

Oh, but you do. Matheson knew the timing wasn't just convenient. The bigger the mess Pritchet could claim to have saved Gattis and the corporation from, the happier the Regional Director would be.

CHAPTER THIRTY-TWO

Day 7: Early Morning

Dillal woke with a violent start that knocked Matheson to the floor. Andreus snorted in amusement. "I told you he'd come up like an emergency jump." She stood a half-meter away from the cot, holding onto an antiquated intravenous unit. "He'll be up for six to ten hours, depending on the circumstances. The drug will keep him from falling asleep, but it doesn't do a damn thing for the mental fatigue or physical exhaustion."

Dillal sat up, blinking, as the doctor sat down on the edge of the cot next to him and removed the cannula from the back of his hand. He shied away from her, then gave her a hard stare. The re-polished ocular made a quiet whirring sound as the iris and filters shifted without a hitch.

"Dr. Andreus," he said.

"The system's working and you recognize me—that's good. Do you know who that is?" she asked, jerking her head at Matheson, who'd picked himself up and edged to the foot of the cot.

Dillal scowled at her, the left side of his face responding very little, but better than it had before. He didn't turn his head. "Eric Matheson, who else should it be?"

She ignored his pique and applied a patch of spray skin to the tiny IV wound. "How do you know him?"

"He's my acting assistant." He glanced around the room, his lopsided expression clearing past relief to calm. "My office . . . morning . . ." His attention snapped to Matheson. "How long did I sleep?"

"Six hours—she wouldn't let me talk her into less. But I think we're still—"

"Don't think, Matheson."

The younger man sighed, but he smiled as he did. "Right. Don't think—know. So here's what I know. It's 0834. The needlecast and negotiations went fine. I'm now back on the family hook—but it's done. Then I walked Or—our friend down to the port and sent him on his way personally."

"And you're certain he stayed aboard all the way to the jumpway?"

Matheson hesitated a moment before replying. "I didn't go up to the jumpway in person, but I tagged him, so unless he cut off a piece of his foot and stuck it in someone's baggage, I'm pretty sure he jumped through about forty minutes ago. And he had thousands of reasons to want to."

Andreus stood up and started collecting her effects. "As fascinating as police work isn't, I'm done here, so you two can stop watching every word you say. I'm not going to grass on you, because I'd have to turf myself in the process."

She caught Matheson's attention with a tilt of her head and a commanding glare. "Keep an eye him. As the drug decays he may get a little psychotic—or in his case I should say *more* psychotic. Risk evaluation won't mean a hell of a lot and especially not if he's putting someone *else* at risk. He's not going to be too worried about the impact of his actions on others after the first five or six hours and at eight, if he's still awake, he's going to be actively dangerous to anyone in his way. Luckily, the action of the drug should be overwhelmed by cumulative exhaustion and the residual effect of the antibiotics and boosters

I gave him earlier, so he'll need to go to sleep again, and might just pass out. Timing's approximate, so call me in as soon as you're done or the clock runs out on this risky little cocktail. We don't want any other doctor taking a look at him before I do."

Dillal raised an eyebrow—the slow left-side response made it look sinister. "Doctor, you may consider me to be out of my mind, but I can still hear."

Andreus looked down at him. "You're not out of your mind yet, but you will be. I've given you a substance we use for treating narcolepsy. It's not a stimulant—because that would screw you up more than I can describe. This stuff just blocks the sleep center for a while so you *can't* fall asleep. But it comes with all the complications of insomnia. You had six hours of sleep, but the drugs I gave you to heal the damage burned up most of that advantage, so you're not very far ahead in terms of rest and mental state than you were when I knocked you out. But you're not currently dying. Try to keep it that way."

She started to walk out and turned back. "And eat. You've pushed yourself so close to the edge you have no reserves." She looked at Matheson. "Food is as necessary as sleep and water, so get some—both of you."

Dillal watched her go without a word while Matheson glanced at the floor.

Once the office door had latched behind her, Dillal turned to Matheson. "What did Orris tell you about Tchintaka's whereabouts?"

"He gave me the location and now I know why we weren't able to find him."

"He wasn't in the Tomb."

Matheson appeared bemused. "How long have you known that?"

"It's a leap of faith. If no one found him in the Dreihleat or the tunnels, it's because he wasn't there to be found. So where is he and how has he managed to avoid being taken up for being outside the ghetto?"

"He's on the quay. GISA assumed all Dreihleen outside the Dreihleat during the riot would either head for home or run like hell so they watched the streets and the port, but they didn't count on any Dreihle outside the ghetto staying put—especially not on Cove Quay. I don't know for certain but I guess—may I?"

"So long as you're inferring from fact, yes."

"I'm working backward from what Orris told me. Tchintaka went to the quay because he had a service uniform from one of his followers. It was most likely hidden somewhere near Aya's café and he slipped out before the gates were shut, while I was busy running for my life. He thought we were too close and the riot was just a diversion to let him escape—overplayed as usual. I haven't looked at the security feed footage—I'm afraid I fell asleep for a while—but I could probably pick him out now that I know what to look for. According to Orris, Tchintaka's been using this service uniform dodge for a while. He gave me three locations, but I eliminated one on the way back from the port."

Dillal stood up, looking around and brushing himself off as if he'd slept under something dusty. "How? What did you eliminate?"

"Corporation House."

Dillal gave a sharp laugh. "Bold of him."

"He has—or had—a page's ID that allowed him access to the general messenger pool. Not much use in this instance, since the ID of all Dreihleen and Ohba working at Corp House has been invalidated, but that blue-and-gold jacket usually makes its wearer into a piece of the landscape on the Quay. If he kept a change of clothes at one of the other locations, he'd be able to come and go without any notice."

"Go on." The inspector seemed satisfied that he'd dusted himself off adequately and assumed his usual still and watchful stance.

"The other locations Orris gave are Casino Archon and the White Hotel—which currently has two new towers under construction above the original floors, though the crew is on hiatus until the end of Spring Moon. I'm thinking the hotel's more likely, but also a bigger problem for us since it's booked full and he can cause a lot of grief by choosing to make this a stand-off."

"Then we'll have to make sure it doesn't become one."

"So you assume—"

"That he'll choose the hotel. Because, as you point out, it can cause the most grief, and that is Tchintaka's fondest wish."

Dillal started out of the room, but Matheson caught up to him in two strides and grabbed his arm to turn the inspector back. He got a furious glare for his trouble.

He let go of the inspector's arm. "Dillal—Sir. There's something else."

Dillal tilted his head a little, waiting.

"I had to go to the director."

"So Pritchet knows."

"I didn't have a choice—we were going to anyway and I couldn't wait for you to wake up. I had to take him some cause—those troops we saw on Agria are moving and some are already here. The best I could do was lock them in place for a few hours by telling Pritchet the tale so far as we agreed on it. So he knows who we're going after and he's holding the intervention troops back as best he can. But he had to take it to Corporation House and the fact that Tchintaka had a pass to the building caused an uproar. I tried to keep that information out of their hands, but if I can run a verification search, so can any staffer who works for a board member. And someone did. The news broke an hour ago—"

"And you let me sleep!"

Matheson twitched. "I didn't. I got Andreus here as quickly as I could, but getting you to wake up was a fight. Corporation house has agreed to let you run this until your original deadline, but that's only twelve hours away. GISA is no longer in charge of security so those troops are going to be wherever we go once we walk out that door. I know as well as you that Tchintaka is more interested in his revolution than in his life or anyone else's, and if he sees those troops on our tail he won't come quietly. We need to nab him before he knows we're in the building. If Andreus is right about the drugs, you have about four hours to nail Tchintaka, or it's your coffin that'll be nailed shut."

"Andreus told you."

"About the deintegration. Yes. And some other things we don't have time to discuss. We can't be wrong about the hotel."

"We aren't, but we need a schematic of the building."

"What do you have in mind?"

"We want—we need Tchintaka to air his brilliance as he sees it. So . . . we'll give him the opportunity."

New clouds had rolled in, but no new rain. Steam rose off the ground from the morning downpour, heated by the sun in hiding. Cove Quay was sparkling white, even under the stormy sky, and the tourists were largely oblivious to the presence of troops, since most were still in bed. The few who were up and about seemed irritated by the intrusion, but not enough to raise a fuss. Casino Archon stood in the sharp curve of the quay where a long jetty thrust out into the water for the moorage of pleasure boats—which happened to screen the lower edge of the cove from sight with their masts and white hulls. The White Hotel sprawled a half kilometer farther up the quay, leaning out over the vibrant, blue water as if admiring its own reflection as its new towers reached into the sky with skeletal fingers. From the top of the casino the view toward the hotel was partially obstructed by the next few buildings, but only at the near end. The curving frontage turned the view inward, always back to the quay and the unstained white expanse of luxury—never out toward the working waterfronts on either side.

Dillal and Matheson entered the casino through a service entrance on the landward side. It meant walking down a ramp that vanished below street level. The world below the street was a lofty warren built of printed concrete or angelstone with extruded trusses to bear the weight of the cantilevered buildings that hung over the water. The resulting tunnel was encircled by thick metallic ribs at uneven intervals.

Matheson looked around. "So, this is where the service personnel disappear to."

"Some of them, yes," Dillal replied. "The service corridors here run from end to end of the quay and out into the city on each side. Storage, maintenance, workshops . . . they're stacked in the next level down. The crater floor is flooded to a depth of twelve meters at high tide and this would all be awash if not for the seawall."

"Why aren't the troops covering this area? It's a natural escape path—"

"It's a death trap." Dillal pointed to the wide metal flanges in the floors and walls. "Fast sealing air tight doors at the end of each construction block—in case of flooding, in theory, but equally useful for trapping anyone fleeing through the area. All accesses seal so water—or air—can be evacuated within minutes. The flow can also be reversed. And all monitored through GISA's system."

Matheson's expression darkened and he said no more as he followed Dillal down the tunnel, looking for monitors and signs of Tchintaka's passage.

The service tunnel was ventilated with cool dry air to keep mold and mildew out of the machinery and supplies. Even at a mild jog, they reached the base of the hotel service stairs without breaking a sweat. Dillal used his access to pass them through the security door and they made their way up into the White Hotel through the service corridors and lifts to the locations they'd thought most likely for Tchintaka to choose for his hideaway.

Matheson checked his mobile. "This stair is a bit of a dead zone. Signal's weak except near the doors."

"I noticed," Dillal replied. "We'll check the service apartment on the next floor. If he's not there, he must be in the construction floors."

Every floor had a small suite where personal service workers were housed. It reduced the cost slightly for the wealthy guests who brought their own cook or secretary and put to use awkward corners created by the architecture. There was one currently vacant and it seemed a likely place for Tchintaka to utilize, but it proved to be as empty as it was supposed to be.

"Shielded," Dillal muttered as they moved toward the lifts after their check on the room.

"What?"

"The guest rooms in this hotel are constructed to resist sensor scans. I can get response in some of the spectra, but not all. It's difficult to tell if anyone is inside."

"The powerful are paranoid about their private spaces and this hotel caters to them. I should have thought about the sensor problem, though," Matheson said, annoyed with himself.

"No. That should have fallen on me, as it affects me and not you. But the shielding may not be an issue on the floors under construction."

They took the lift up as far as it would go and then returned to the stairs to access the unfinished towers.

The lock override was unnecessary.

"Not too secure," Matheson noted.

"But exactly why Tchintaka chose it. It looks intimidating and gave him a hiding place with access to everything he could want. You notice there aren't as many monitors in this hotel either."

Matheson nodded. He'd never considered going unobserved a luxury—much less an irritation—before.

Only two of the new stories had been enclosed yet—the rest were still raw limbs carefully dressed in temporary surfacing to make the view more attractive for those whose windows looked toward the White.

Matheson and the inspector exited the stairs to the lower of the two enclosed floors. The space was shuttered and dark, though a few errant beams of gray light passed the edges of windows. Dillal preceded Matheson, stepping to the right as he cleared the door. Matheson came through looking the other way, shock box in his hand, and they continued deeper into the unfinished story.

It wasn't like the old stack where they'd caught Orris—there was nothing growing down the dense walls and the ambient sound was caused by the constant wind brushing and tapping at the exterior, sending echoes and whispers through the hollows of unfinished rooms. Their own steps seemed loud.

Matheson heard the door lock behind them and shot a glance at Dillal, who shook his head and tapped his chest. *Well . . . if he can do it with his own office, what's to stop him manipulating any lock connected to the GISA security system?* But it left Matheson a little unsettled.

They walked on, checking rooms as quietly as possible until the inspector drew to a halt and stood still, listening intently. Then he closed his eyes and took a breath, frowning in thought. He opened his eyes and looked around the corridor they were standing in until his gaze settled on a pair of doorways side-by-side. He studied them, tilting his head, and motioned Matheson toward the empty one on the left. Matheson advanced with careful steps as Dillal moved to the doorway on the right, in which a door had already been hung.

They went through their doorways at the same time, Dillal's door making a click and a bang as it hit the wall.

The room ahead of Matheson was bare but for a pile of security crates and construction materials, the raw subfloor stretching to the floor-to-ceiling glass that wrapped that section of the building. The clouds outside barely illuminated the room at that end. He turned back, noticing how much darker the entry seemed now by comparison, and saw a connecting door in the wall between the two rooms.

From the room beyond, he heard a rustle, a scuffle and a crunch, and an aborted word.

Matheson went through the connecting door low and fast, with the shock box close in front of him. The door slammed shut behind him.

Dillal stood straight and still a meter or so into the room with his head tilted slightly back and his compact shock box smashed on the floor at his feet. Matheson stopped and frowned into the darkness around the inspector.

"Be still, heh?"

It wasn't Dillal who'd spoken but someone in the shadows. Someone who had one arm across the inspector's windpipe from behind. The man couldn't see the faint smile that crooked the inspector's mouth. This wasn't quite as planned—or not the plan Dillal had discussed with Matheson—but the situation was salvageable if neither of them got killed.

"You're lay it down," the shadowed figure ordered. Dreihleen inflection ran the words together into "late'down." Dillal stumbled a step out of the darkened entry so the weak light fell on the long, narrow chamber of a pen torch pressed to the inspector's temple. The man behind him was a head taller than Dillal and still hard to see in the gloom, but Matheson recognized Tchintaka nonetheless.

"You won't kill him, because then there wouldn't be anything in between you and me," Matheson said, "and you know I'm fast."

"You're assume I'm want to leave. But I'm where I like." His language was as carefully articulated as his speech in the Dreihleat had been. "This trick with the door lock—you're do that?" he asked, casting his gaze down at Dillal and jerking his arm against the inspector's throat.

Dillal gagged a little but didn't answer.

The wind rattled the glass outside.

"I'm not need to kill you, Cousin," Tchintaka said, and twisted the pen torch toward Matheson, touching the igniter only long enough for a white-hot dot to flash at the tool's mouth. Dillal yelled and jerked his head aside as the intense heat burned the red hair and tawny skin high above his right ear. The stink turned Matheson's stomach. Tchintaka glanced at him. "Lay it down, or it's get worse for him."

Matheson let his shock box fall to the floor.

Tchintaka smirked and turned his attention back to Dillal. "So you're tell me about the doors." He tapped the end of the pen torch against the inspector's singed skin.

Dillal winced. "It's an extension of GISA's lock override—if the doors are linked to the system, I can control them—even the emergency bars on the inside."

"You're can do that here?"

Dillal considered his answer a moment, then said, "Yes."

"You're control who comes, who goes."

"Up to a point."

"That'll be enough." Tchintaka raised his head to regard Matheson for a moment. "You're leave. I'm keep Djepe a little longer. You're tell

Director Pritchet I've everyone here and I'm wish to speak to all people of Gattis so they're know what the corporation does to them. You're only the one may come and go. They're try to trick me, lie to me, one of these people're die here. And on and on until there're none left." He glanced at Dillal. "Including him, though I'm hate to kill my cousin who'd once believe as I do."

"Your beliefs are offensive," Dillal said, "and dishonor the courtesy of 'Cousin.'"

"Hush." Tchintaka turned his attention back to Matheson. "You're bind him and leave the box. We're use his mobile to talk."

Matheson drew back. "*Bind* him?"

Tchintaka raised his eyebrows in amusement. "You're have binders—use them. Or I'm kill you both."

"It's best if you don't," Dillal said without heat. "If you want out of this, you need a bargaining chip and I'm all you have. Dead hostages are worth nothing."

"You're think I've no plan? I'm not unprepared. There's gas here and there—not fool enough to tell you where—and weapons more than this."

"You have no allies left. Banzet has turned against you, Zanesh is safe, and Orris jumped out system hours ago. Everyone else who helped you is dead. There is nowhere on this planet you can run and no way off it—not for you."

"There's still Norenin, still Dreihleen. The people won't betray me." He spun Dillal to face him and pushed the pen torch to his right eye. "'Twould be a pity to blind your Dreihleen eye as well, more so to kill you. You're not wise to force me, Djepe." He glanced over Dillal's head to Matheson. "You're fix his hands behind him. I've fair idea what he can do, left free."

The message indicator on Matheson's mobile lit as he closed the distance.

Tchintaka looked intrigued and plucked the Peerless out of Matheson's shirt as the SO reached for the inspector's wrists.

"I'm sorry, sir," Matheson murmured, frustrated, and uncomfortable about restraining his whip.

"It hardly matters. At least I don't have to swim this time," Dillal replied.

Swim? Fear lurched in Matheson's chest. *It's barely been two hours—he can't be losing himself already . . .*

"Tighter," Tchintaka said, glancing away from the mobile.

Matheson cinched the cuffs as tight as was safe and glared at Tchintaka, who held out the mobile.

"You're show me the message."

Matheson swiped past the lock screen and the message—red flagged and blinking—appeared. Tchintaka read it to himself. "Director Pritchet's raging." He chuckled, caught Matheson's eye, and smiled—the confident, intimate smile he'd offered to each person in the crowd that then became a mob. It only chilled Matheson. "You're best go, tell him what goes here. Heh?" Tchintaka handed the mobile back and moved deeper into the room, dragging the inspector along and keeping him between himself and Matheson. "Go!"

Matheson glanced at Dillal, who gave a minuscule nod. Then he stepped back and crushed the shock box under his foot.

Tchintaka swore, but Matheson bolted and slammed the door as he left and no one pursued him.

CHAPTER THIRTY-THREE

Day 7: Cove Quay—Morning

Matheson sent a message to Pritchet as he made his way out of the building, hearing the doors lock behind him every step of the way. He exited by the hotel's front door and the sound of the locks was like a gunshot in his ears. The quay didn't seem much different as he walked away from the building, but rounding a corner brought him face-to-face with two SOs and a handful of out-system troops. *Merry hell . . .*

"Matheson?" the SO closest to the front asked. Matheson didn't recognize him—but he didn't know every ofiçe in S-Office.

Matheson nodded and reached for his ID, but the SO waved it off. "I believe you. Director Pritchet wants to speak to you and Inspector Dillal immediately."

"How did you get here? I mean, why are you in this particular place?"

"White Hotel security system sent an alert. Pritchet thought it was probably to do with you and your whip—where is he?"

"Captive. The whole hotel is locked down and unsafe to approach."

"Then you need to come with us."

Matheson didn't argue. This wasn't the outcome he'd expected, though he thought Dillal might have. His mobile pipped as the SOs walked him to a skimmer.

He glanced down. The mobile indicated a message from Dillal. *How . . . ?* Matheson frowned and opened it.

The text was hastily formatted and a bit jumbled, but he was able to read it: "Voice ping @ 1110. Will hear not respond. Monitor my outgoing voice stream. Record discreetly."

Like when he was diving to the transport—Dillal could hear if someone called, but he wouldn't be able to talk back. Matheson wasn't sure how the inspector's trick of sending directly to the datastream worked without the mobile or a microphone, but the voice ping should open a channel. As long as Dillal intercepted it and not Tchintaka, it might work. Matheson had to assume the inspector had a plan for that, too, and hoped the stream wouldn't be loud enough for Pritchet to hear if Matheson was still with him when it came up. He set up the ping on auto.

Pritchet was displeased, but kept Matheson away from the few media-heads who still lingered in the office—most had rushed to the quay to investigate rumors of the hotel's security flag.

Matheson had no time to wait for Pritchet to wind down, so he utilized Callista's first line of attack and talked over him. "The White Hotel is locked down—let all the personnel and the media in the area know it's unsafe to approach or attempt to enter the building through any door or window. Inspector Dillal is in Tchintaka's company—"

"Company? A hostage, you mean," Pritchet snapped.

"As are all the guests in the hotel. Tchintaka claims to have gas and weapons at his disposal and I think it's wise to assume he's telling the truth, considering he's had two days or more to prepare. He wants planetary broadcast access. He seems to have something he wants to say before he'll let anyone go. And he says he'll kill people—including Dillal—if he doesn't get what he wants, or is interfered with."

"This should have been an easy arrest, but now it's a blighted stand-off. You and Dillal—"

"Had nothing to do with that. This isn't what we wanted, but in the changing scenario, it plays to our need. Tchintaka will want everyone to know what he's done for his cause. I think he knows he can't walk free, but he'll let people live so long as he's getting what he wants. Tchintaka doesn't realize how Dillal's already manipulated him, and as long as the inspector's alive, the doors remain locked and everyone's safe. When Tchintaka's done, Dillal will bring him out."

"You have no guarantee of that."

"No, but the alternative is to storm the hotel and hope Tchintaka's less prepared than he says. You know the White is jointly owned by the corporation and out-system investors with a lot of political pull in Central Senate. The guests are pretty much the same mix. You don't want to get them killed with the media from half the known worlds watching." *And we need them watching, so long as it plays out in our favor.*

Pritchet glowered at him. "You are a Matheson through and through. Blast you."

"I'm trying to help you. Arrange for the broadcast stream he wants."

"And you will be the deliveryman to keep him distracted while backup moves in."

"Backup?" Matheson asked with a cynical laugh. "You mean those ground troops."

"I don't have a choice. If the cooperation you advise is unsuccessful, the hotel still needs to be evacuated somehow. Dillal's override is executive level, which means there aren't many of us who can take it down and none of them are as expendable as he is. So there will be a breach team. There will be a perimeter, snipers—whatever it takes to make sure the area is under *our* control and we can go in when necessary, without letting this get any further out of hand."

"*If* necessary. Not before. I can guarantee that precipitous action will kill the inspector and as many civilians as Tchintaka can reach."

"It's a last resort, but it has to be in place."

"Do you have no faith in the man?"

"Faith is for fools," Pritchet spat. "If this plan doesn't work, there will be nothing else I can do. I have to let the media at it if that stream is going out and I have to protect the rest of Angra Dastrelas at the same time. This could ruin me, so I have to be in position to salvage what I can."

"Salvage. Like the bits and pieces in Dillal's head?"

Pritchet lifted his lip in a condescending sneer. "Those won't matter if this falls apart, so you, Eric, had better pray to any god you can think of that Dillal pulls this off, and soon."

Pritchet's not as confident as he pretends, but neither am I. "Get me the equipment for the broadcast, and he will." *I hope.*

Pritchet narrowed his eyes. "Central Media will bring it to you back at the scene. And you had best be right."

The mobile in Matheson's shirt pipped as the voice ping went out and he wondered how quickly the situation—and the inspector—would unravel.

Even with blackening clouds overhead, the view back toward Casino Archon was breathtaking from the new levels of the hotel's south tower. The sweep of the quay like pale arms embraced azure water that deepened to sapphire as the light changed and the wind ruffled the surface into rills and foam-capped peaks. Tchintaka stared toward the scurrying people below—ground troops, media observers, tourists, and locals surging together like the waves in the cove—with an amused expression.

"Like insects," he said, "when hive's disturbed. I'm cat that's eat the children, am I not?"

"I expect they don't know what to make of you at all," Dillal replied from his place sitting against the wall beside the window. His hands were still behind him, clasped to his forearms to protect the ID array on his wrist. Above his head a small bump in the ceiling covered the room's secure communications node that hung separated from the shielded walls.

"Why's that? You're think monsters can't recognize doom?"

"Is that how you see yourself? The doom of the system?"

"Is what I'm make of myself, Cousin. How're you see it?"

Dillal scoffed. "As if my opinion of you matters."

Tchintaka squatted down in front of Dillal and squinted at him. "It does. Or did, once." He patted one hand against his chest. "Your pursuit's hurt my heart."

Dillal glanced through the glass at the troops on the roof of Emporia and, farther away, a handful of them mixing with the media observers on the roof of the casino. "Move away from the window, Oso, or someone may shoot you."

Tchintaka shuffled to Dillal's far side and smiled. "You're care if I'm die."

"No. I don't care if you die—you will one way or another—but I care that others have died and more may because of you. I *did* believe as you did, years ago when we met in Agria, but I've learned more, read the charter, the history, the books, tempered my anger to a more humane resolve. I didn't track you down because of your political belief, but because you murdered sixteen people, and sent two more to die in the camps. If there is a monster in this, it's you."

Tchintaka looked bemused. "Was given no choice. Denny's killed Venn." He shrugged. "What's justice for that? We're all should hang for him?"

Dillal shook his head and turned his gaze away from Tchintaka. "None of it was necessary. You could have walked away from the Paz da Sorte with only Leran dead and no one would have turfed you for it. You could have opened the jasso door to that young ofiçe you just met—he was on patrol that night—and Robesh would have said you protected her from Leran and the rest would have said nothing if you returned the money. You knew this. You knew how Leran felt about Robesh. You knew she would be there, and you knew what could happen. None of the events of that night was beyond your control."

"You're think I could be so cold, Cousin?" Tchintaka asked, looking saddened and hurt.

Dillal brought the weight of his unnatural stare to bear on Tchintaka's face. "I know you are. The shot that killed Leran was too good. You've never been one for direct action—you influence others to do your violence as you did at Camp Donetti a year ago and at home on Sunday. But when you shot Leran and the rest, that wasn't the work of a man unfamiliar with a gun and shivering with adrenaline. That was coldly done, calculated, and without passion."

Tchintaka's expression flickered and his lip curled slightly before he regained control and made a face of injured surprise.

Dillal went on in a voice as bland as angelstone. "You wanted it to happen—it gave you an excuse to take everything and leave no one behind to threaten you. You've always had a knack for turning the dispossessed and miserable to your own purpose—you charm them, tell them what they want to hear, instill your own desires in their desperate minds—"

"I?" Tchintaka gave a harsh laugh. "Is you who's care nothing for people. Nothing for Dreihleen, nor your red-tar family. You're betray your birth, embrace the corporation, worship the system that's devour us. I'm reject it, cry for justice—"

Dillal snorted. "You cry for supremacy and destruction. Nothing in your philosophy speaks of peace, law, or a future any different than the present but for the color of the overlord's skin. You have no plan beyond waste and retribution. You led Leran and Banzet to their deaths—or would have if Banzet hadn't run—because you knew they were weak, that you could manipulate them to your will and pretend what happened at Paz was an accident."

"'Twas!"

"Never. You planned every minute of it. You knew Leran would hurt Robesh, maybe kill her—you hoped for it so you could kill him yourself, justify the murder of your accomplices, justify the pillaging of your own community for your self-serving 'revolution' without the troublesome weight of guilt or responsibility, or the testimony of anyone who might reveal you for what you are. You saw the Dreihleen at Paz as cannibals who eat the flesh of the innocent and cleave to the corporation—just as you see me."

Tchintaka shook his head, his mask of pity imperfect with underlying rage. "You're an abomination. Lapdog of the corporation, who's believe the lie—"

"I believe in the rule of law and I pursue you because you don't!" Dillal shouted, his voice running faster as he went on. "You believe in nothing but your own hate, your greed for power! You pose as a man of the people—a compassionate humanist above bigotry and avarice— while you take what you want and leave death in your wake. What sort of humanist uses slurs like 'red-tar' and labels his victims vultures and cannibals, sends innocent boys into the hands of the same sort of men who once beat him for their own amusement? You're a liar, a thief, and a murderer! Even your voice is a lie—made agreeable for whichever audience is watching. You're a con man no better than Denny Leran, and a killer no less than the corporation that works prisoners to death in camps that you—"

Tchintaka snatched at Dillal's throat and rammed the inspector's head against the glass, his expression twisting into a snarl of fury. "Stop your mouth, Cousin," he hissed, his voice chill venom. "Stop your mouth, or I'm kill you as I did Denny—is true I did," he added, nodding and glaring into Dillal's eyes as if searching for a spark of fear that never lit. "Should do you like he's killed Venn—with the torch so I'm hear you scream, let your sanctimony pour out your head like steam. See what's run you now your brain's corporation machinery."

He closed his hands tighter around Dillal's neck and slammed him against the glass until the surface began to crack.

The sun had torn a small hole in the cloud cover and the air was thick with humidity as the light brightened overhead and the temperature rose. The woman from Central Media met Matheson at the foot of the jetty, cut off from most of the cove's breeze, but also hidden from the White Hotel. The crowd was slightly thinner since Casino Archon blocked the view from the ground, and the operations base had been set up at the Emporia building—which was closer to the hotel.

Even without the ID tag on her sleeve, the observer rig she wore—with the tiny retina-projected monitor pointed inward and the camera outward over her eyes—picked the woman out as media. The ultra-thin support, data, and transmission wires fully encircled her head and ran in curling loops down around her ears. As she removed the headpiece, Matheson could see her features were so even and symmetrical that they had to have been sculpted that way. The warm brown tones of her skin and hair seemed engineered for unchallenging beauty. She reminded him a little of Dillal in that she was ambitious enough to remake herself for the job she wanted, but unlike the inspector, she was not quite enough of something to have gotten any further up the ladder than this. Matheson was tempted to laugh at his thoughts, except his sense of humor had gone to cower in a corner of his mind behind cynicism and anger and he feared that what might come out of his mouth would be too caustic for safety.

The woman smiled with perfectly white teeth and offered her hand. "Petr Kettenberg. You must be Eric Matheson. It is a pleasure to meet you." Even her voice was Central and prettily bland. She did not flirt.

Matheson kept the handshake as perfunctory as possible. "I'm Security Ofiçe Matheson, yes. You have some equipment for me?"

Kettenberg blinked. "Uh . . . I do." She waved at a box on the ground by her feet. "It's about as simple as they come and pretty lightweight, though I don't suppose you'll have any trouble carrying it," she added, reaching up to pat Matheson's shoulder.

I don't need solicitous media-heads trying to befriend me. Matheson flicked the woman's hand away and reached for the handle on the box. "Instructions?"

Kettenberg frowned a little, ruining the smoothness of her brow. "In the case. The frequency of the broadcast booster is already set."

"This doesn't feed straight to the broadcast stream?" Matheson asked.

"No. Units that small don't have the power to stream very far for very long, so it's preprogrammed to a specific signal booster back at the temporary base that feeds direct to the broadcast stream. The head rigs work the same way," she added, holding up the observer headpiece she'd had on. "The case unit just has a bit more power in the antenna, battery, and capacitor, and it's easier for a user who needs to be in the shot."

The mobile in Matheson's pocket muttered "*. . . don't know what to make of you at all.*"

Matheson mentally cursed the need to keep the stream open and lowered the volume as Kettenberg looked curious. "What's that?" the observer asked.

"Communications monitoring."

"Between whom?"

Matheson gave her a blank stare. Kettenberg pursed her lips, then shrugged as if she couldn't care less—though of course she did care quite a bit.

Matheson looked back to the case. "Tell me how it works."

"You set the A/V unit on the stand and push the power button," Kettenberg said. "Once it's green, you can flip the broadcast switch any time and the rest is automatic for up to twenty minutes. The rig needs a power source if it's going to send longer, and it has no recording capability—that's managed at the base."

"Can this signal be interrupted?"

"Oh sure—any signal can be blocked if you know what you're doing. And the booster can be shut down or switched to a different feed or incoming stream, but that's all done at the base. The White Hotel has secure nodes in every room, so that unit should have no problems reaching the base unit at Emporia without being disrupted by the usual privacy shielding, as long as the node's operating."

"How can I tell if the node's operating?"

Matheson's mobile whispered, *"As if my opinion of you matters."*

Kettenberg raised curious eyebrows before she replied, "You can ping it if you know the node's ID, or you could just call any phone in the room. If it connects, the node's up. And if it's already streaming, well. . . ." She flicked a significant glance at his pocket.

Matheson nodded. "Thank you." He started to turn away with the case in his hand.

Kettenberg caught his free arm. "Hey. I'd really like to talk to you some more."

". . . May shoot you," came from the mobile.

Matheson shook her hand off and gave the media observer a poisonous glare. "I'd really not."

Tchintaka's nearly muted voice said, *"You're care if I die."*

Kettenberg smiled. "I'll be on the casino roof when you change your mind, Ofiçe."

"Casino? Not Emporia?"

"View's better. I'm all about the view."

Matheson turned away.

"No. I don't care if you die—you will one way or another . . ."

The trip back into the hotel and up to the tower twisted Matheson's stomach into knots. He could hear the conversation between Tchintaka and Dillal growing more tense as he went up in the lift.

"You're an abomination. Lapdog of the corporation who's believe the lie—"

"I believe in the rule of law and I pursue you because you don't!"

He lost the stream in the staircase and hoped the recording was still running properly as he raced up the steps to the unfinished tower. At the top he forced his way past the lock, then snatched up the case again, and pushed through the door. He switched the stream from the speaker to the earpiece and hoped it was still live.

" . . . you like he's killed Venn—with the torch so I'm hear you scream, let your sanctimony pour out your head like steam. See what's run you now your brain's corporation machinery."

Someone choked and struggled for breath, then came a crashing sound on top of another directly ahead of him.

The stream died.

Matheson snatched the mobile into his free hand and forced a voice call through to Dillal's mobile. Panic burned his lungs and jabbed needles into his heart.

The incoming voice notification echoed in the rough hollow of the unfinished space.

The crashing ended.

Matheson stopped, holding his breath.

"Who's this?" Tchintaka asked in his ear.

"It's Matheson. I'm here. I have the broadcast equipment you wanted." He was breathless and hoped Tchintaka put it down to his having run up the stairs. "I'm in the hall outside the room," he added. "May I come in?"

"You're leave everything but what I'm need. Your jacket, mobile, shoes—all but you and the broadcast."

"Everything?"

Tchintaka laughed and it sounded like a hungry ghost roamed the place. "You're keep your clothes—I'm not want to see it. But the rest's stay there."

Matheson stripped off his sweat-damp jacket and dropped his equipment, belt, shoes . . . emptied his pockets and put the mobile carefully on top of the pile. Then he picked up the case and crossed the distance to the suite door barefooted, grateful the surface wasn't too rough or covered in building materials.

The floor felt cold and he was sweating as he stood there.

Then the door opened and Tchintaka looked him over with an amused smile. "Good man." *Not a right man, no, definitely not.*

Matheson walked through the doorway, casting his gaze around without turning his head. His gut clenched when he spotted Dillal leaning in the corner against the window. A bloody circle marked the spiderwebbed glass behind him, but the inspector was breathing and he opened his eyes to gaze at Matheson. Matheson tried not to let his relief show and turned his exhale into a sigh of annoyance.

He looked back to Tchintaka. "Where do you want this?"

Tchintaka pointed to the center of the room and Matheson put the case down there.

"How'st work?"

Gotta sell it. Matheson explained most of what Kettenberg had told him. "Total run time is twenty minutes—I assume that will be enough."

"Goes planet-wide?"

"Yes, direct to everything. There are media observers out there from Central and other places, so your audience is . . . very large. Everyone will see you."

"Is good."

Matheson started toward Dillal, but Tchintaka stopped him. "You're leave him."

"You have what you want. Let me take him."

"He's stay."

"For pity's sake, man—he's injured."

"Is no matter. He's stay."

The cold in Matheson's belly turned to ice. "Then . . . then let me take someone else. A show of good faith. I gave you what you asked. Give me something in return."

Tchintaka seemed to think about it, but Matheson was sure it was merely a show. "Take who you're like from downstairs. Eight minutes, then he's lock the doors on everyone."

That was barely enough time to get back down to the lobby. Matheson glanced at Dillal, but the inspector didn't seem to be focused on him now.

"Best run," said Tchintaka.

Matheson bolted for the door.

He scooped up his gear and clattered down the stairs to the lift, jerking on his shoes and equipment as the lift descended. It couldn't move fast enough to ease the pounding in his chest and head or the churning in his guts.

As he hit the lobby, he started yelling, "Out! Everyone out the doors as fast as you can! Out!"

He got out with ten others before the doors wrenched closed and the locks slammed back into place. Those trapped inside pounded on the doors, but it made no difference.

The escaped hostages ran behind him to the edge of the cordon, where they were absorbed into the breathless crowd or escorted toward the operations base by SOs and ground troops holding the perimeter. The sound of the locks snapping closed had reassured Matheson that Dillal was still alive, but he didn't know how much longer that would be the case.

He ran for the casino, fumbling for his mobile to send another voice ping.

"You're have your hostages," Tchintaka answered.

"Let me talk to Dillal."

"I'm not inclined to it."

"Now that the doors are locked, I have no assurance you'll leave him alive. Let me talk to him, or I'll tell the director to block your transmission and to merry hell with you. Dead hostages are worth nothing."

Tchintaka laughed at him, but Matheson heard him moving away and in a moment Dillal's voice sounded low in his ear. "I'm well, Matheson."

"No, you're not."

"Well enough. If you have the files, do as you've been told. The rest is nothing."

The call broke off into silence and Matheson kept running.

"Do you expect to survive this?" Dillal asked, still leaning in the corner near the bloodstained glass.

"I've my way out," Tchintaka replied as he set the A/V unit on the unfolded stand.

Dillal nodded. "Of course. But it's best you stay away from the window, just in case."

"Thought you're have no concern for my life, Cousin—so you're say."

"I don't. But I suspect that seeing your brains spattered across the view will ruin it for me in future. If you move closer to me, the men on the Emporia roof will have no shot."

"But there's you, Cousin . . ."

"I'll move to the other corner if you think I'm so dangerous with my hands locked behind my back."

Tchintaka turned around and studied the room and the view beyond it. "What's chance for the casino roof?"

"It's a half a kilometer away and the only people up there are media observers."

Tchintaka gave him a curious look. "How you're know?"

"How do you imagine?" Dillal asked, turning his head away from the view so the light sparked a moment off his gold-rimmed eye. "My vision's not calibrated for the distance, but I can tell a soldier in body armor from a civilian in street clothes. And they're all standing. Snipers don't stand."

"How do you know your inspector's still alive?" Kettenberg asked. "I only see one man up there."

The observer and her assistant had moved next to Matheson and a bit away from the other media members and the handful of SOs and troops who'd been assigned to protect—or muzzle—them. The soldiers were all lethally armed, which Matheson found less intimidating than the media-heads did.

"He was alive when I left the building and Dillal's darker and shorter than Tchintaka." Matheson crouched to look through the observer's monitor on the signal booster. "He's the man leaning against the window in the corner."

"That's a man?" Kettenberg adjusted something on her head rig and stared at the window of the unfinished tower. "Huh. He's so still I didn't realize that was a person."

"You didn't see what happened earlier, when I went in with the equipment?"

"Not all of it. We had to get back up here from the street and these bas—uh . . . security-conscious members of the Anti-Incursion Support Group caused us some delay. Did I miss something I'll get reamed for?"

"Depends on how much your whip values getting the complete story."

"That depends on who it favors. Shit . . . is that blood? On the window by your guy's head?"

"Yes. He's injured and that may be why he's not moving much."

"Well, he is now."

Matheson started to crouch again, but Kettenberg's assistant raised the monitor for him instead. He watched the image captured by Kettenberg's head rig: Dillal got slowly to his feet and crossed the window to the other side. Sparks of gold and red reflected in the window as the sun shone on the inspector's prosthesis. He stood straight, but lurched a little as he went, his hands still behind his back and his head brushing the glass, leaving a broken, bloody line across it. Then he sank into the new corner and leaned into it, turning his head away as if he were watching Tchintaka. Matheson looked at the line on the window. Then he turned to Kettenberg.

"Maybe you should listen to this," he said, and held out his mobile.

Kettenberg took it and listened to the recorded conversation, a sickened grin spreading over her face. "This . . . is this . . . ?"

"That's what you missed."

Matheson could barely hear orders being issued through the mobile links and he paid them no attention for his own sake, but watched everyone else on the roof. Some of the armed personnel began disposing themselves at more strategic locations rather than just holding position near the access points. One lay down with his rifle supported on the parapet, muzzle pointed toward the White Hotel's south tower.

Tchintaka had already been talking to the stream for three minutes, not in tones of demand or self-righteousness, but of heartache and sorrow that was beyond tears. And with his Dreihleen diction and accent deliberately softened. Dillal remained still and silent in the background, out of the camera's sight. It turned and tracked Tchintaka automatically as he paced and gestured, but the Dreihle remained away from the north end of the room. "Whatever you've been told about me's probably a lie," Tchintaka said to the A/V unit. "Gattis Corporation profits on lies. Truth can only paint it as the monster it is. This planet's beauty's maintained by slavery and death, and corporate profits're bolstered by oppression of the native races. We who're yellow or red were born here just as those who are blue and our blood and our sweat waters the fields and fills the seas, yet we enjoy no part of the bounty. When we rise to protest, to ask for what's ours by right, we're struck down like predator cats of Agria, murdered by troops like the ones standing on Cove Quay this minute. What justice is that? That foreigners and mercenaries crush us at the pleasure of Gattis Corporation? That we're denied educaion, opportunity, equality because of the color of our skin? We've no seats at Corporation House. We're forced into ghettos where our livelihood—our lives—come at pleasure of Gattis Corporation. They color us parasites and criminals—

but is they who're eaters of human flesh and thieves of dignity and right, they who rape our posterity, who rob and murder and lie."

His voice soothed and sang as he looked into the A/V unit's eye, persuading, swaying, seducing his invisible audience. He seemed oblivious to his surroundings—to Dillal and even the A/V unit itself—as if he stood face to face with each individual who watched him, and poured out his compassion and despair into sympathetic ears.

"They're the tyrant and is't not right and proper that good people should cry out for relief, rise against tyrants to demand redress, and if they're denied, should they not revolt? Should they beg the tyrant for bread, beg for common decency, for their lives, when so much blood's already been spilled? Is this right? No! No, good people must rise up, they must demand their proper rights, and if the tyrant will not make way, they must take what should always have been theirs. It is the proper way of an oppressed people to water the roots of liberty with the blood of tyrants! And if we've risen against the tyrant in the Dreihleat and the Ohbata and in the filthy penal camps of Agria, then it is because we have no other recourse. We don't run riot for petty gain, and I don't speak, now, from this embattled place, for my own glory. I'm but a man who cries out for justice, for relief, for redress, for change—I'm no terrorist, nor are any of those who cry out as I do. They are the innocent who bleed and die for justice."

From the corner came Dillal's voice, calm and tired, but strong enough to be heard clearly on the stream. "You're no innocent. The innocent were the sixteen people you murdered at the Paz da Sorte and the two more you sent to Agria to die."

On the casino roof, Kettenberg stiffened, clutching Matheson's mobile to her chest as she stared toward the White Hotel. Even the armed men leaned toward the nearest monitor. She pointed at her assistant. "Keep that channel open—whatever it takes." Then she turned to Matheson. "Is he out of his mind? Tchintaka will kill him—he's already tried once."

Matheson cast a glance up and then down to the tiny shadows that lay like dense pools under everything. "What time is it? Noon?"

"Eleven fifty," Kettenberg's assistant said.

Matheson nodded. "It's a little early for insanity, yet."

"What are you talking about?" Kettenberg demanded.

"Nothing, except I'd be surprised if provoking Tchintaka's temper isn't exactly what Dillal's up to."

"But—"

"Could you splice that audio into the live feed if you had to?"

Kettenberg turned her head back to the view across the cove. "I could . . ."

On the monitor, Tchintaka's eye twitched and he stiffened just a little. Then he closed his eyes as if in pain. *"This man belongs to the corporation and he believes I'm responsible for this hideous thing—"*

"I don't believe something that is not true. I am the investigating ofiçe who came to arrest you with proof of these charges and am now your prisoner along with everyone in this building."

The camera juddered, swinging toward Dillal and then dipping in a wild, bouncing fall. The image blurred and filled with static for a moment.

"Keep it up!" Kettenberg yelled, concentrating on the window across the quay, never turning her head away.

"He's turned it off," the assistant shouted back.

"Force it as long as the cap will stand! Hold onto the audio." She backed up, holding out Matheson's mobile. "We'll go from my feed on one and prepare to splice this audio in when I give you the hack."

Her assistant snatched the mobile and Kettenberg moved forward almost to the edge of the parapet. She knelt to gain stability as she kept her head rig pointed at the bloodied window where Dillal slumped.

"Three, two . . . one," Kettenberg shouted.

The monitor flashed a colored indicator in the upper right corner as the image changed to the view from Kettenberg's rig. Text scrolled across the bottom of the display: Live—Petr Kettenberg, Casino Archon roof, Angra Dastrelas. The colors were a little pixelated from the extreme zoom, but with the cloud-striped sunlight directly above, the image was as clear as if the viewer stood in the air less than four meters from the windows.

Matheson couldn't see the downed camera, but he saw Tchintaka turn toward Dillal. Even in the lowered resolution, Tchintaka's posture radiated rage and his voice through the link was icy and clear.

"You're think you're make people doubt me, now? They're see you're the corporation's dog," Tchintaka spat.

"The doubt is your own doing. Your lieutenants know you planned the robbery of the Paz da Sorte and they suspect that what happened was not an accident, though they want to believe in you. You're persuasive, spellbinding, but I have a witness who knows the truth and he will speak."

"A boy's got no clan? A fool who's dream of glory? Criminals, both of them."

"So are you. Even before you chose to rob and murder your neighbors, you did unforgivable things and called them justice. You roused a riot that killed one-hundred twenty people at Camp Donetti a year ago, and another here on Sunday, but it was never you who was hurt, as you won't be hurt this time either. You'll run now that your chance to lie your way out is ruined."

"Will I?" Tchintaka asked, stepping closer, menacing Dillal, who was still slumped in his corner.

"Yes. Down the tunnels and out through a watertight lock door into the cove. It's the obvious path, but the water's so clear here that the troops the corporation's brought in will see you in a heartbeat from their positions on the rooftops."

"They're not see me when they're distracted."

"What distraction could keep them from looking into the water? Ah . . . but they can look all they want, can't they? You won't be the only man in the water. So there really is gas secreted around the hotel, but it's not toxic—it's flammable. The hotel burns, people dive for the water . . . I'll have to be alive to unlock the emergency bars for that to work."

Tchintaka crouched down over Dillal, glaring at him. "I'm never intend to kill you, Djepe."

Dillal gave a harsh laugh. "But now you do. You can't afford to let me live. What will you do? Leave me chained here, knowing I'll open the doors to save as many people as I can while you vanish in the crowd as you always do? Will it please you to think of me burning to death? The stench of it, the sound of my screams of agony and terror as I hope for someone to find me, to rescue me before it's too late . . . But of course it will be too late. Another regrettable accident like Paz, like Donetti, like Zanesh and Banzet . . ."

Tchintaka lunged and grabbed Dillal's shoulders, hauling him to his feet and throwing him against the wall. "You're open the doors! Now!"

"And let your birds fly before you're safe? Or are you surrendering to me?"

"Never to you, Cousin. But you're not let people below die," he added, sneering. "You'll open doors when you're smell the smoke, hear the screaming."

Dillal slumped in Tchintaka's hands. "I will open the doors."

The locks on the room doors slammed closed.

"All but these."

Tchintaka shrieked and flung Dillal against the window. The inspector's head rebounded off the glass and he stumbled forward into Tchintaka, who grabbed him by the throat.

Matheson tore his gaze away from the monitor, looking up at the troops around him. He grabbed the nearest man in uniform and shouted at him, "Check the doors—tell them to rush the doors! They should be unlocked, now!"

Over his shoulder he heard Kettenberg clap her hands and shout "Splice!" Then his earlier audio recording began to play back.

" . . . *Think monsters can't recognize doom?*"

"*Is that how you see yourself? The doom of the system?*"

"*Is what I'm make of myself, Cousin. How're you see it?*"

"*As if my opinion of you matters.*"

"*It does. Or did, once. Your pursuit's hurt my heart.*"

"*Move away from the window, Oso, or someone may shoot you.*"

"*You're care if I die.*"

"*No. I don't care if you die—you will one way or another—but I care that others have died and more may because of you. I did believe as you did, years ago when we met in Agria, but I've learned more, read the charter and the books, tempered my anger to a more humane resolve. I didn't track you down because of your political belief, but because you murdered sixteen people, and sent two more to die in the camps. If there is a monster in this, it's you.*"

"*Was given no choice. Denny's killed Venn. What's justice for that? We're all should hang for him . . . ?*"

The soldier in front of him didn't move. "What's the matter with you?" Matheson yelled. "Tell Pritchet the doors are unlocked. Get those people out!"

The man shook himself from his shocked stupor and spoke rapidly into his mobile.

Matheson glanced again at the media monitor, but the situation only grew worse as explanatory text rolled along the bottom of the display. Tchintaka had flung Dillal against the window again. Tchintaka's face—visible above a bloody smear on the glass where Dillal's head had struck it—was twisted in unreasoning rage. The inspector's bound hands jerked upward and scrabbled at the glass behind him as Tchintaka grabbed him by the throat.

Matheson heard the order to rush the doors.

"Cut off the video," Matheson said. The assistant shook his head and Matheson screamed at Kettenberg. "Cut the video!"

"No," Kettenberg shouted back.

"You're going to watch a man murdered in front of your eyes and do nothing?"

"Mother of stars, Matheson, there's nothing I can do from here! My job says I stay put—I watch, I don't get involved. You want it done, you do it! Blackness take it," she added in a mutter, "do something . . ." And shifted her view down to the street.

Now the monitor showed the troops and SOs rushing for the hotel doors as they swung open under the press of frantic people inside. The hostages flooded out, running for the cordon, into the arms of soldiers and ofiçes. Matheson was relieved and ill at once—they were out and nothing was burning, but even as fast as he was, he couldn't make it up to the tower before Dillal would be dead. He saw the sniper still lying at the edge of the roof and ran to him.

"Do you have a shot?" he demanded.

"I do."

"Then take it."

"I have no order, SO. You are not my commander."

"Then stand down—if you're not going to take the shot, you're no use here. Stand down."

"I can't."

Matheson glanced over his shoulder at the remaining people on the roof—only two additional media observers besides Kettenberg and her assistant, and a single SO to secure the door. He slipped the baton from his belt. "Then I'll stand you down," he said, kneeling, and struck the rifleman sharply behind his right ear.

The sniper collapsed face down. Matheson hoped he wasn't dead, but he didn't bother to check as he threw himself down and took over the other man's gun and position. The shot was already fairly lined up, the scope sighted in, and he ignored everything but the height line Dillal had made—the bloody smear on the glass half a kilometer away.

Tchintaka's face was so close to the window as he leaned his weight into choking the life from Dillal's body that his breath made a cloud on the glass. *It should take longer to strangle a Dreihle, shouldn't it? Just above the breath . . . just above the blood . . .*

He breathed in . . . and out . . .

And squeezed the trigger.

CHAPTER THIRTY-FOUR

Day 7: Afternoon

Blood sprayed into the room, but he didn't know if he'd killed Tchintaka alone or both of them. He dropped the rifle and started to his feet, but only got as far as his knees before his stomach knotted and he vomited with such force that he had to catch himself on his hands. Everything seemed darker . . . was he going to faint as well?

Another shadow fell over him and he turned his head.

Kettenberg and both the other media observers were crowding over him, babbling, as the SO from the doorway tried to push past and grab him.

"Nice shot, Ofiçe Matheson," Kettenberg said. Matheson could barely hear her for the ringing in his ears.

He stared at the ground and sank back on his heels, then slumped away from the mess he'd made. He didn't want to know how elegantly he'd taken a life, only if it had been the right one. He sat down harder than he'd meant to. He was shaking now, sweating hot and cold, not sure if he was going to heave again and hoping he was done. He didn't raise his face, just wiped his hand across it and stared at the roof tiles.

"Quite impressive," Kettenberg continued. "You were a pentathlete in college, weren't you?"

Who gives a merry fuck about that? Matheson shook his head as much to clear the buzzing as to ignore the query. He didn't want to ask, but he had to know, "Did I—that is . . . who was hit?"

"Only who you were aiming at." Her voice sounded distant and chopped by static, but he could still pick out her words, if he concentrated. She turned away and he lost her for a moment, then she turned back and said, "It looks from here like Inspector Dillal is alive—he was moving. There's no sign of Tchintaka from this vantage point, but we did see the shot. I can show it to you if you like."

"Merry hell, no." He shuddered and glanced up. "You still streaming?"

"Not now. I just dropped feed control to an associate at ground level—that's where the hot action is, at the moment. I can pick it back up . . ."

"No!" He coughed and spat, wiped his mouth again, unable to rid himself of the taste. "May I have my mobile back?" His voice sounded hollow in his own ears.

"Oh. Certainly," she said. She motioned behind her back and then produced the Peerless, but her movement made room for the SO to shoulder through the tight group around him.

Matheson swiped through to re-secure the file, and called Andreus.

The SO pushed forward, but had to stay a bit to the side to avoid standing in puke. "Matheson . . ." He cleared his throat and started again in a loud voice. "Eric Matheson. Put your hands where I can see them."

"Can't you see them now?" Matheson replied, holding the mobile on his bent knees.

The SO hesitated and said, "I think I'm supposed to detain you."

"Oh. Just this call, please. Then, whatever you want."

"What?" Andreus snapped—she sounded tinny and mechanical through the mobile's speaker, but he didn't want to put the MDD up to his ringing ear.

"Doctor, I think your patient needs you."

"I already figured that out, thanks to the media. I'm almost at the quay. Meet me at the hotel and show me the way."

"I'm afraid I can't—I think I'm being arrested."

He cut the connection and put the mobile in his shirt. Then his stomach heaved again, but he didn't throw up this time.

The sky growled and flashed, and rain poured down as if the lightning had gutted the clouds. He huddled on the tiles while the media observers scattered to drier ground. The SO stood over him until the sniper beside him groaned and sat up.

The man looked dizzier than Matheson felt, but he still punched like a falling skimmer. Matheson sprawled backward onto the puddled tiles and chose to lie still until others came to carry him away.

The sniper hadn't broken anything with his fist and that was a pleasant surprise. Matheson stumbled along with the two SOs who'd arrived to move him, and Neme right behind them. She'd given him a sour look as they walked him down and confiscated his equipment and ID. He'd balked at the loss of the mobile, but in the end he couldn't object—it was his own but he'd used it on the job and that made the content and access GISA's property for now. He knew he should keep his head up—act as if he had confidence in his decision—but he couldn't. He didn't feel confident about much, but at least his hands had been cuffed in front and not behind—which he figured meant Neme was just following procedure and didn't think he was a real danger. He appreciated that, though he didn't know why he should.

Neme pushed him into a chair in the casino's small employee conference room that she'd commandeered.

She leaned over him, bracing her hands on the chair arms. "You understand what's happening here?" she asked.

"Not really." Water ran from his hair and down his face—not that it mattered. His head and hearing were almost clear, but his thoughts were a jumbled mess, and he felt that he watched the whole thing from a distance.

She rested her hip on the table. "All right. So, Eric Matheson, you may be royally fucked. You're being detained—they call it 'supervised, indefinite suspension'—pending review of the shooting that you were just involved in."

"Do I get a rep?"

Neme chuckled ironically. "Not around here, baby blackbird. No union, no union rep. I'm familiar with these reviews, so I volunteered to explain it to you—call it my good deed for the decade. Because you were on active duty at the time and ass-deep in this whole fucking fiasco from start to finish, the usual position would be that you acted to save a fellow ofiçe and the hostages who were under immediate, deadly threat. But this one's uglier than usual. When we're done here, you'll be transferred to a detention cell and held until the board decides your fate."

"What board? Gattis Corp or—"

"Review board. GISA is a private firm on a corporate planet, so this doesn't run like it does in Central System. It's similar to a Grand Jury, but it's all *in camera*. Pritchet and the GISA execs make up the board, and you might get to speak on your own behalf, or you might not. Normally your whip or someone he chooses would speak for you, but at the moment, you seem to be in no man's land—Dillal's not available and neither Feresintavi nor Belcourso will own you. A hell of a lot depends on who your friends are. Either way, you're going to be waiting a while."

Matheson let his head sink a little lower "Well . . . I guess I am merry fucked."

"Maybe. If it goes against you, you'll be charged with murder with special circumstances, remanded for trial—which'll take about five minutes—and it's pretty much a straight, short walk to the wall after that."

"It's a capital offense?" he asked, glancing up from beneath his dripping brows.

"If they call it aggravated murder, you bet your narrow ass it is." She straightened, crossing her arms over her chest, and drummed her fingers on her upper arms. *Probably wants a smoke.* "Things got sticky when you hit that out-system asshole and used his rifle in front of all those tourists and avid viewers to shoot a guy who was trying to kill your whip—who had just embarrassed a bunch of heavies by letting some of their dirty deeds out into the light. They'll be arguing if you were really acting within your scope as a GISA Ofiçe, or if you were working some other angle—your own, or your whip's, or whatever sollet-brained excuse they need to charge you with Osolin Tchintaka's murder. Usually these aren't so . . . showy, but Central was watching when it happened, so there will be repercussions. GISA and Gattis Corp can't take it out on Dillal, so they'll take it out on you. There. That's the speech. You want the formal version or is that good enough?"

"That'll do. Are you taking over the Paz files?"

She reached down and flicked her own mobile off. "Yeah. That a problem?"

"No. But you'll have to get them from Dillal—I don't have access to most of it—or I didn't. He was a little nervous about leaks . . ."

She coughed—or laughed, he couldn't tell. "He's always been paranoid. Some things haven't changed."

Matheson raised his head. "Did you have anything to do with the leaks? Orris said you did and I—"

"You thought so, too. All right, yeah, I dogged you guys. I got screwed by him too. But I want this case closed right, so I'm taking it."

"Right? What does that mean? Right for whom?"

She bent closer, her expression narrow and hard. "Straight out, Matheson—and treasure this because you'll never hear it again— Dillal was right and I was wrong. And beyond that, you're going to have to swallow whatever I bring in."

"Won't your solution determine whether the GISA review finds me justified or not?"

"Yes."

"Oh." He closed his eyes and sighed. *All for naught and I'm so tired . . .*

Nothing broke the silence for a while. Finally, Neme took a hold of his arm and made him get up and out.

He didn't notice if there was anyone outside, if he was escorted past mobs or just across an empty street and into a skimmer. Nothing registered at all except a chill.

CHAPTER THIRTY-FIVE

Day 8 and beyond

The bruises on Dillal's neck looked like dark gray paint. He lay on his left side, which partially obscured the empty, metal-lined eye socket, but left the damage at the back of his skull and the burn on his right temple exposed. Dr. Andreus gave Neme a hard, appraising look that the senior detive returned full force.

Andreus snorted. "Ten minutes. No more," she said and marched out of the room, shutting the door behind her.

Neme closed the distance to the bed and leaned her hip against the side. "Bit of a hardass, isn't she?"

"You should know," Dillal replied. His voice was very low and slow. "You're here why?"

"Need access to your case files. The rook said you sequestered them."

"You're closing."

"Since I opened the case, yes, I am."

"I can't grant access remotely. Not at this time."

Neme peered at him, inspecting his injuries. "That bashing knocked your miracle offline, did it? Well, you can struggle along like the rest of us, now, can't you?"

"Dr. Andreus has shut the system down until my body recovers."

"Not worried about your brain much, is she?" Neme asked as she handed him her mobile.

Dillal had difficulty holding the mobile where he could see it and still swipe through the permissions and hashes. "Speak with her if you like, but let us stay on topic."

Neme took the mobile and held it for him with an impatient snort. She waited with ill grace as Dillal unlocked his files and updated the access, then swiped through the numerous releases with decreasing speed and strength. He didn't waste his breath to curse. When it was done, he closed his eye and breathed heavily for a minute or more.

Neme watched him. "Tires you out, being broken."

"Yes."

"Tell me what you've got that isn't in the files."

He opened his eye again, but it was hard to tell where he was looking—it didn't seem to be at Neme. "Very little. Two material witnesses in secure holding will tell you most of it."

"Zanesh Farrazee and Hoda Banzet—I talked to them last night. It was heavy going. Their tale is that Tchintaka planned the Paz da Sorte incident as a straight robbery, but things went wrong and everyone died, including Leran, who was one of the gang. The version I got out of the Tchintaka recordings is it went pretty much the way he intended—except that those two in holding didn't die in time. So it really wasn't a racial thing and it really was aggravated murder from minute one. Sound right?"

"Yes."

"Things get a little confusing when I start looking at the Santos information, though. Orris's notes are useless—when they aren't total cat shit lies."

"Dr. Andreus conducted the autopsy."

"If it's relevant, I'll talk to her."

"It is. How Santos died revealed Orris's connivance in the Paz da Sorte case." Dillal paused to close his eye and breathe slowly after every sentence. "Orris killed him after he was sure Santos hadn't talked. You can extract the details from his statement and our report."

"How did you get on to him in the first place?"

One corner of Dillal's mouth twitched. "Footprints at both crime scenes."

"You and those damned impressions."

"Details . . . Matheson also noted Orris was IOD, but was using his kit at the Paz da Sorte scene. Orris retrieved the jasso key from the drain and cleaned the spray seal off Leran's hands."

She made a disgusted face. "One of your witnesses kept talking about someone, or more than one person, in the Ohbata . . ."

"A middleman. Orris also killed her, but . . ."

"Yeah—it's the Ohbata. Things just . . . melt into the ground. But Orris jumped out on the sneak. Was that with *your* connivance?"

"You'll hang me for it?"

"Me?" She chuckled. "That would be ironic, wouldn't it?"

Dillal didn't reply.

Neme looked at him for a while before she said, "No."

Dillal nodded a little. "Orris knew where Tchintaka was. The information had to be bought."

"I see." She went quiet again, tapping her fingers on her biceps as she frowned in thought. "Was there anyone else in this that you're not telling me about?"

"No."

She stared hard at him for a while. "I'll pretend that's a real 'no' since I don't give a razor cat's left testicle about your family connections or who you're protecting, so long as it doesn't undermine the case."

"It won't."

"Fine. And I should be able to confirm that once I've had a look into your files?"

"You will."

"You know your witnesses didn't want to tell me much, though they were a little more comfortable once I told them Tchintaka was dead."

"Is he?"

"You were there."

"I was . . . distracted. Who shot him?"

"Your boy, Matheson. I've seen the video—it was a hell of a shot. Did you know he was a competitor? Did you rely on that?"

"I didn't."

"So you figured to sacrifice yourself to close this case. Fucking noble of you."

"No. I miscalculated."

"You got lucky, and your blue-eyed blackbird's still in the box for it."

"And GISA awaits your closure to pass judgment on his action."

"Not entirely."

"Then what else?"

"State of mind."

"Unknown to me."

Neme gave a cynical snort. "Was it your order?"

"No. He was aware of factors you aren't."

"About the case or about you?"

Dillal's eyelid flickered and he fought sleep. "Did you wonder where the troops came from? So quickly? Why the corporation called on them and then cut GISA out? Or what happened at Camp Donetti?"

Neme grunted and stepped away from the bed. "I'll bear your legends and mess-hall tales in mind."

"What if they're true?"

Andreus pushed through the door and interposed herself between Dillal and Neme. "You're done," she said.

Neme didn't move. "I want to talk to you about the Santos autopsy."

"I have a *live* patient to manage."

"And I have an open case that could make him a dead patient."

The two women glared at each other until Neme stepped back. "I'll wait."

"You'll do it out of my way. It's like a fraggin' parade ground in here."

Matheson wasn't sure how long he'd been in custody. Time without sunlight bent and moved in strange ways and he hadn't really noticed how much he relied on his mobile until he didn't have it anymore. His only timekeeping was by the block guard's hourly passage. He hadn't seen anyone else in a while—not even Neme. His thoughts chased their own tails and the silence was going to drive him nuts long before anyone put a bullet in him.

He'd already exercised and slept as much as he could stand to—which wasn't much considering the nightmares about mud and death and brain matter splattered red and gray on white walls . . .

Stop it! This isn't Camp Ejeirie . . . or Camp Donetti.

He would never know what he had done there, so he would live—and die—with that. But shooting Tchintaka? No; the killing sickened him, but he didn't regret doing what had to be done to save lives. *Did Dillal survive? Or was I too slow? Surely this would be over by now if he's died . . .* Matheson hadn't remembered to ask Neme and there wasn't anyone in shouting distance.

But now he was certain he'd done the right thing, even if some of the connections were still confusing. He bent his thoughts to the case, thinking about the past and how disparate pieces tipped one into another, from the fault line of First Settlement all the way to Dillal's arrival at the Paz da Sorte. Maybe, as he'd said, a crime of this sort was inevitable, but the inspector's influence had thrown all expectations out the air lock. Neme had implied that there would be political fallout, but he hadn't heard anything about the review, and there was no indication that anything had changed since he'd been detained. He closed his eyes and built his mental landscape of the crime again, looking for the negative space that might be a picture of its own.

He fell asleep without waking in a sweat or screaming for the first time in days.

An odd sound disturbed him: the click of high heels on angelstone that sent a familiar cold shiver up his spine as he woke. The block guard opened the door, locked the visitor in, and stood outside. Matheson peered at his unexpected guest, but no matter how smug her expression, he wasn't going to attack his own sister. He stayed on the bunk.

"Eric," she said.

He sat up slowly. "Hello, Callista." Not much had changed in two and a half years. She was still perfect and cold in the shades of a charcoal sketch. "Is this some ritual I'm unfamiliar with—sort of familial last rites?"

He hoped she'd just get on with it.

"No," she said. "I'm here to offer you a proposition on the family's behalf."

"I don't think I'm in any position to accept or refuse a proposition," he said. "In case you're unclear on the circumstances, I'm here for killing a man and embarrassing a lot of Very Important People in the process. The only debate seems to be whether I'll die in a work camp in a few months or die here in a few days."

She gave a sigh and shook her head. "Don't be so dramatic. It can go that way if you like, but I think you'll prefer the alternative."

He could wait her out, but why bother? "What alternative?"

Callista took a deep breath through her nose and glanced toward the ceiling as if she needed permission from some god before she spoke. Maybe she did—maybe she communicated with their father the way Dillal interfaced with the GISA database.

Matheson frowned at the memory, and something hard twisted in his chest. "What happened to Dillal?" he blurted. *Shit. Shit, shit, shouldn't have asked.*

Callista cast him a bemused frown. "Your whip? Gruesomely injured, but quite the hero of the moment. And you might be, also, if you take what I'm offering."

The hard sensation in his chest became a bubble that almost felt like panic. "What is it?"

"You live, go back to your job, and do as we say."

The bubble broke, crushing like thin glass. "No."

"No?" She seemed honestly surprised. "Why? Isn't this what you wanted? I admit I wasn't at all pleased with your choice of career, but it turned out to be so much more useful than we'd imagined. It might have been better if we'd been able to place you here two years earlier, move you up the ladders sooner, arrange things in a manner more . . . tasteful. But as it is, you've given us a very nice bit of legend to build from. It will take a while, but this route may prove by far the best—however unusual for a Matheson. But that's where the beauty lies. The ethnic natives will be much more supportive of an outsider who's risked everything to save them and their grotesque tourist-trap of a planet, than a rich boy who was simply planted here by the family."

Matheson gaped at her. "Useful? *Planted* here . . . ?"

Callista laughed—that also hadn't changed—still as falsely musical as ever. "You didn't think this was an accident? Oh no, the family had to salvage something out of your ridiculous ambition.

We'd have come to Gattis soon in any event and the chance to have a Matheson already on the ground was too good. You were sent here because we wanted you here. You've done very well. It was risky, but by attaching yourself to this . . . unusual inspector," she made Dillal sound dubious, "you've leapt ahead and secured a very nice position from which to build."

The thought forming in his head was appalling. "Build to what?" he asked.

Callista narrowed her eyes at him. "The family doesn't compete for second place."

Matheson started to speak, but had to stop and swallow back the bile that rose into the back of his mouth. "Pretend I'm stupid. Tell me what you're expecting me to do."

She shrugged. "Become planetary governor. Eventually. It's years off, but that's the only goal worth pursuing on a corporate planet. It will take quite a while, but you've already started on the hearts-and-minds campaign with your selfless-policeman act. Though parts of it *were* stunningly stupid."

"The Julian Company's presence wasn't a coincidence." He stared at her and gripped the bunk rail to keep from jumping up, grabbing, and shaking her in fury. "Did you cause this somehow? Pay Leran to kill Venn? Have me assigned to the case?"

Callista drew back with a scowl. "Of course not! How could you think such a thing? I liked the girl. She was really very . . . sweet. It's a blow to lose her—and she was *so* young. But it's a loss we can weather. It might even help."

Matheson forced his gaze from her. "You disgust me."

Callista scoffed and rolled her eyes in annoyance. "Be practical, Eric! It's a tragedy, but we'll get nowhere crying over it. Pick up your injured sensibilities and get back to business! I'm not going to let your childish emotionalism stop this from working. If I have to leave you here and cut the family's losses, I'll do that, but after all the investment in time, money, preparation . . . I won't abandon Gattis. This project is worth a very great deal to the family and we're going to get it done with or without you."

She paused and took a breath, settling her mask of reasonable big sister back into place. Matheson edged deeper into the bunk until his back was pressed to the wall. "Besides," she added, "you've already 'sold out' to us. Did you think the bankers wouldn't tell me? I know about your deal with Mr. Orris. I have no objections, but if you're going to go that far, why not all the way? You're already *dirty*."

Callista watched him with clear, ice-cold eyes and the tiniest of smiles. When he'd been silent a while, she said, "So, here is the deal. At our pleasure—and for a great deal of money—the review will rule this shooting completely justified. You'll be released to return to your job as a hero who saved his superior officer at great personal risk, exposed a monster for what he was, thereby saving the ethnic natives of Gattis as well. One could go so far as to say you saved the whole planet—but that might be better held for later. You'll even get a promotion out of this so you can continue to work in this very successful partnership you've formed. It's an excellent strategic position, since the CIFO's office is still developing and its career track can be molded as we need it. With the right words in the right ears, we can make sure you have the best opportunities to advance in the corporate structure both before and after the charter review, while building a legend for yourself that will make you an irresistible choice for planetary governor, when the time comes. And we'll make sure it does.

"You and your whip have brought Central System to Gattis eight years early. That's given the family an invaluable advantage. We're going to be working very hard to ensure the Gattis planetary charter remains a corporate one, and that the changes made will favor us. And there will be a Matheson at the top of the heap. One or another, one *way* or another. It might as well be you, since you seem to have fallen so much in love with the place." Her last words were tinged with derision, but he made no issue of it.

"What's the other option?"

"Your situation remains as it is and we cut our losses with you. Whatever the review's result, we'll offer no objection. If they let you go, so be it, and you go back to—what's the phrase—pounding a patch in the ghetto. You'll make your own way with no help from us. Of course some little . . . things may come to light, because, as you know, we don't take well to being thwarted."

Mother of stars! What has she already done? Fresnel, Donetti, here . . . What can't she touch?

Callista continued with a sad lift of her dark, delicate brows. "If the review doesn't rule in your favor, we'll send flowers—unless you'd prefer a donation to some charity or another."

At least they weren't going to make *sure* he died. *I want nothing from you—I never have.*

Callista smiled as if she could read his thoughts. "It took quite a bit of ingenuity to find a way to salvage you, little brother, but I think it will be well worth it. It even turns out that your frivolous pastimes are useful—I hear the shot you took was superb and that you dove down into a filthy canal to save people from a crashed transport. You really are the archetype of romantic hero. Women will flock around you—it is still women you favor, isn't it? Because your relationship with the inspector has its risky side."

Sleep with the boss? Matheson drew further away. "Merry hell, Callista, you have a nasty little mind."

She looked smug again and gave an arch shrug. "I like to make sure the spin is in the right direction." She dropped the affectation. "I personally find romantic heroes trite, but it appears that a white knight is what this foul little planet needs. So . . . will it be you? Or do I have to go trolling for someone more reasonable?"

We saved people, and Central is finally looking, but will it matter with the family here to twist any good thing I do into more Matheson family influence? And Camp Donetti . . . ? Merry hell, don't let that be the defining moment of my life.

Matheson forced open the fists he'd unconsciously made. "So, the family will run my life after all."

Callista studied him for a minute with a cool smile. "Don't act the martyr," she said. "We won't run it and we won't interfere in your work except where we have an interest you haven't recognized. We want you to look as pure and unbiased as possible. We're not simpletons. This planetary corporation can't stay—it's too corrupt. We're in favor of change—so long as the final charter eventually favors a *revised corporate* structure."

"With the Matheson interests in front of everyone else's," he added.

"Naturally." She paused a moment and shook her head in exasperation. "We aren't monsters, Eric. We want the disenfranchisement and oppression of the Dreihleen and the Ohba to end as much as you do—that situation isn't good for business. You won't find working for the family as disagreeable as you've always imagined. You'll be able to do a great deal of good—which I know just warms your altruistic little heart."

She finally shut up, raised interrogative eyebrows, and waited.

How much good *could* he do? He'd always found ways around Callista; there was hope . . . *Hah! There's that bitter little pill. But Aya said sometimes it's all you've got. Aya . . .* He had no real choice, but he wasn't going to roll over for it. "If I agree to this," he reiterated, "you don't interfere with my ordinary work or personal life."

"Of course."

"It's never 'of course' with you, Callista. Your option isn't really an option. So, I'll agree to the *goal* you have, but not to having my every move dictated by the family."

"You don't get—"

"No, no. *You* need to get *this*: Gattis and its people aren't going to fall in line with the usual Matheson way of doing things. I'm the one on the ground with the intel, so if you expect your shadow campaign to succeed, you'll have to trust me in the particulars. You can navigate, but I get to steer."

Callista narrowed her eyes in thought. "So long as we're all sailing for the same port, I think we can allow that."

"Not allow. Support. You want me to play politics and that's an expensive, filthy game. I'll get where you need me, and you'll give what I ask and do what's necessary, or I stop playing."

Callista's smile sent a chill over him. "As you say, but our game, our goals, our timetable."

Matheson cast his gaze down and nodded. "Then we have a deal."

The monsoon season had come on while Matheson was detained and the rain was loud enough to hear through the windows and roofs of the holding facility as the guard and Neme walked him out. She waited while he changed out of the prisoner's coverall he'd been issued and collected his effects.

The uniform he'd been arrested in had been new and it had been recently cleaned, but it didn't fit quite right and wearing it felt odd. He brushed it compulsively until he noticed Neme watching him. She'd lit a smoke while she waited, and she gave him a cynical smile as she exhaled.

"Feels wrong, doesn't it?"

"Yeah."

"You're missing something," she said, holding out the cigarette.

He frowned at her. "I don't—"

She scoffed. "Just hold it a second, tip-tits." She reached into her own jacket to draw out his mobile and a slim card case. She flapped the case open and offered it to him. "Try this."

She snatched back her smoke and drew on it like an addict as Matheson took the items she held out. He slipped the mobile into his jacket pocket and looked at the small case. A new GISA ID card snuggled in one side. The other was still empty, waiting for a badge. Matheson peered at the ID. Investigation: Assistant Detive Eric Matheson.

He frowned and glanced up. Was Neme screwing with him? But she only raised an eyebrow and curled her lip. "Read the whole damned thing," she suggested.

"CIFO Liaison. What does that mean?" This was Callista's hand in play and it made him as nervous as if he were about to step out onto a very narrow wire.

"Fuck if I know, but it seems to make a lot of people sweat and scurry. You jumped a whole rank and a half. I think they'd have booted you all the way to Detive if they thought no one would scream about it."

"I'm not really trained for this . . ."

She smirked. "As much as any IAD. Paz was a fucking minefield of a case. One of the toughest I-Office has fielded since I came on, and I've seen some real shitstorms. So take the bump and shut the fuck up—it's better than dragging your feet as an SO or IO for another two to four years."

It left a taste like the ash at Ejeirie. "Yeah, great work. I shot the primary subject, and spent a week in jail."

"Sixteen days. You missed Spring Moon Night, but no loss there. And as to the other . . . I'd say shooting that prick was pretty good for a lot of people."

"It's not closure; it's just punctuation."

Neme smoked, shivered, and looked amused. "Technically, Dillal and I closed—"

"Dillal's all right?"

"That would be a matter of opinion, but, yeah, he's still sucking in air. What did you think—they were going to strip him down for spare parts? There's plenty of people who don't like that he hung the corporation's dirty laundry out, but he's untouchable at the moment. That didn't hurt you any at the review. You've made your bones and he's made some enemies, but I think he collects them like brats collect festival rings."

She finished her smoke and ground it out against the intake desk. The ofiçe behind the property cage yelled at her, but she only sneered and dropped the lip end in her pocket. "Back your jets, Hollister." Then she started to walk away and paused to look over her shoulder at Matheson. "I wish you the best fucking luck, Matheson—you're going to need it with a boss like that. Invest in good body armor—Regausa if you can afford it," she added and went out the door that led back to GISA by a long, subterranean slideway.

Matheson had come in by the slideway sixteen days earlier. There was a second door that led to the civilian waiting room on the other side. He shifted his glance between them. His knees were loose and his guts twisted nervously. Here was that high wire again. *Straight to it, or out to cleaner air?*

The ofiçe in the property cage—Hollister—glared impatiently. "Not gonna get easier the longer you stand around like the Pillars. Pick a damned door, or I'll have someone toss you."

Matheson folded the ID open—his ID—and tucked it into the appropriate place face out. Then he walked through the waiting room door.

Callista rose to her feet from a chair nearby and her dry storm coat flowed like smoke. She looked at his ID and gave him a small, smug smile. He returned a blank stare. She raised an eyebrow, then turned with milkweed grace and walked to the exit without a further word or gesture.

He turned his attention to Dillal, who'd sat against the exterior wall without moving since Matheson entered. The inspector's hair had all been clipped short and the burns and scars showed through the bright red stubble; his prosthetic eye had healed in more and the frame was no longer exposed, but the ocular itself looked different. Perhaps Andreus had changed it, or maybe the improved mobility of Dillal's face reduced its strangeness. Either way, he looked like a young bear that had just emerged from hibernation—weakened and scruffy, but still dangerous.

Dillal stood and offered Matheson his fleeting smile. "You're well?"

"Well enough."

The inspector tilted his head. "Something worries you. Is it this?" he asked pointing to Matheson's new ID.

Matheson hesitated. "Not really, but this isn't the place for that discussion."

They took storm coats from a rack beside the door and went out into the sideways-slashing rain. They walked toward one of the public gardens with their collars pulled up to their cheeks.

"How . . . is Aya?" Matheson asked.

"She can't see you."

"Because of Donetti."

The inspector shook his head. "Because of Tchintaka."

Matheson hadn't thought he could feel any more off balance.

Along the park's path, an Ohba man in coveralls squatted to tie one of a row of saplings to protective stakes and mound the small trees' roots with mulch and gravel, and secure it all with screen. Then the gardener moved crabwise to the next, soaked, but making no complaint.

"She's become Norenin's right hand," Dillal said.

Matheson gaped at him.

Dillal looked blandly back. "Do you see?"

Matheson shook his head, dazed. "I can't see anything," he muttered. "I killed a man—possibly others—and you almost died, and nothing changed except the weather."

Dillal stopped in the lee of a crooked cement sculpture. "No. The weather is the only thing that remained the same. We saved future lives—not just the Ohba and Dreihleen in the ghettos and camps that day, not just the people in the hotel. And what happened at Donetti has been exposed; it will never happen again. We threw ourselves against a wall and, though it still stands, we've knocked out the first stubborn brick. Each void we make weakens it further, allows more light through the cracks, and it will come down if beaten hard enough and long enough."

"How? We're not officers of the law, not really. We're ofiçes, employees of a corporation that makes promises it doesn't keep and treats people like parts."

"*We*," Dillal mused. "If you wish to affect change, you first change yourself. Don't imagine that is accomplished without mistakes, pain, or loss. If you won't willingly risk your own security and comfort, then you can't change the system because you *are* the system. But you have changed, and I have changed."

"You climbed inside the beast, but how can you be sure you won't just become it?"

"Because I am no longer alone."

Dillal's level stare cut to his guilt, fear, and anger. Matheson took an unsteady step back, out of the calm and into the storm. The rain cut through small rents in his coat and worked down past his collar, soaking him as a million mental shards shifted and the negative space between the scattered objects began to have a shape.

ACKNOWLEDGMENTS

There's always a list here. The longer it takes to get a book onto shelves, the longer the list gets. At the top is my agent, Sally Harding, who read the first experimental chapters years ago and said "Where's the rest?" Brian Thornton read the manuscript twice—I'll be paying for his therapy. The Ladies of the Write (Raven, Bridget, Janine, and Teagan) read it in chunks and beat it mercilessly. Jim Richardson and Elizabeth Rose read it, gave advice and technical corrections, and haven't yet exiled me from the family. I am indebted to the following people for diverse support and assistance (and in no order): Stephen Blackmoore, Kari Blackmoore, Randy Henderson, Richard Shealy, Rob Durand, Rachel Sasseen, David B. Coe, Cherie Priest, Laura Anne Gilman, James Ziskin, Stephanie Burgis, John Hartness, Janna Silverstein, Monica Valentinelli, Patrick Swenson, Gail Martin, Barb Ferrer, Trevor Carroll, Marci Dehm, Jacque Knight, Dave Morrison, Nisi Shawl, Mary Robinette Kowal, John Scalzi, Dana Cameron, Charlaine Harris, Jeremy Lynch, Steve Mancino, Jon Jordan, Ruth Jordan, Jennifer Jordan, the R.A.M.s, Stina Leicht, Diana Francis, Kevin J. Anderson, Warren Ellis, Christopher Golden, John Hemry, James Moore, Charlie Stross, K. B. Wagers, Yasmine Galenorn, P. J. Manney, Maria Alexander, Richard Morgan, Sandra Carpenter, Marc MacYoung, Mario Acevedo, Warren Hammond, and "the Lads."

Special thanks to Fran, J. B., and the rest of the crew at the Seattle Mystery Bookshop (now closed), and the team at Pyr.

ABOUT THE AUTHOR

K. R. Richardson is a bestselling Washington-based writer and editor of science fiction, crime, mystery, and fantasy. A former journalist with publications on topics from technology, software, and security, to history, health, and precious metals, Richardson is also a lifelong fan of crime and mystery fiction, and noir films. When not writing or researching, the author may be found loafing about with dogs, riding motorcycles, shooting, or dabbling with paper automata. Learn more at gattisfiles.com.